Vlad

a Novel

By

Melodie Romeo

ISBN: 0-7596-9437-0 (Electronic)
ISBN: 0-7596-9438-9 (Softcover)

This book is printed on acid free paper.

1stBooks - rev. 05/16/02

Acknowledgments

I would first like to thank Betsy Selby for proofreading and adding her grammatical expertise to this effort. I also wish to thank my family for their support and patience with the many hours I put into writing this book. I could not have done it without their cooperation and encouragement. Michele, thank you for taking care of yourself while I was at the keyboard. Peter, thank you for your inspirational input, for hours of listening to me read passages, and for your sustaining belief in my success. Johanna, for all of your hours of in-depth research, critical proofreading, lightning-fast typing, helpful suggestions, and vital emotional support, I dedicate this, my first published work, to you. May I be able to in some way help you realize your dreams the way you have and continue to do for me. Finally, I wish to acknowledge and further dedicate this book to all people of the world who are forced to live under oppressive, terror-driven, totalitarian regimes. May the light of freedom not burn out before shining full bright upon you as it has on us.

Introduction

Thanks to the fiction writing of Bram Stoker, almost everyone is familiar with the name of Dracula. The blood-curdling sound of that name conjures to mind an evil, immortal creature who feeds on the blood of the innocent, who cannot go into the sunlight, and has special powers to hypnotize and shape-shift. Although science and history pay no credence to the existence of vampires, Stoker did base his character on an actual person, Vlad Tepes, Prince Dracula of Walachia, who lived in the 15th century. In this case, fact proves to be more horrifying than fiction, for the vampire count appears as harmless as a puppy compared to the real Vlad Dracula of history. Some call him a Romanian hero, others the villainous impaler, but some facts are clear, and those are presented in this tale along with the fictional characters who set about to secure his destruction. Some of the facts are: Vlad III, son of Vlad Dracul, began his reign by purging Walachia of its noble class and appointing a new nobility; Vlad Tepes killed or murdered an estimated 100,000 people, many of them his own citizens, during his longest reign of six years (at a time when the estimated population of his principality was only around 500,000 citizens); detesting crime, Vlad enforced the death penalty for any and all offenses; Vlad Tepes defeated the Ottoman Turks, preventing an invasion of Europe, and was considered by some a hero of Christendom; Vlad Tepes was assassinated in December 1476 by an unknown assailant, believed by most to have been one of his boyars or a Turkish spy. It has been recorded that he enjoyed torturing his victims, even taking his meals as he watched them die. Now come and enter the realm of the real Prince Dracula, if you dare.

Chapter 1

The Easter Party

"Here begins a very cruel, frightening story about a wild blood thirsty man, Prince Dracula."

From the front piece of a pamphlet printed by Ambrosius Huber in Nuremberg, 1499.

Tirgoviste, Walachia, 1457

"Care to dance, my Dear?" Lord Nicolae extended his hand to his elegantly attired wife with a debonair smile while the musicians played a lively tune on the fiddles, lutes, and reeds. The lord of Cozia wore his finest hip-length szur[1], ornately embroidered by Italian artisans.

"I would love to," the dark-haired Lady Olivia replied as she took his hand with hers, covered with a black lace glove. She felt like the queen of the affair in her formal black fota[2] interwoven with silver and gold threads and her matching cojoc[3] with an even finer embroidered pattern. The white blouse she wore had a high collar and was elegantly trimmed in red, and her marama[4] was the most exquisite at the feast.

The Easter banquet in Tirgoviste promised to be the most memorable event of the season. Little did the Walachian boyars know, it would prove to be one of the most memorable events in their country's history. Prince Vlad Tepes, in the first year of his reign, had invited the Boyars of Walachia, together with their families and chief household staff, to a grand celebration at his palace. This was seen as an encouraging move by the

---

[1] szur - Hungarian style full length coat for men, decorative with full sleeves, stylish in the 15th century Romanian states.
[2] fota - one piece wrap around wool skirt with decorative pattern worn over the shirt-tail and held in place by a cummerbund or belt.
[3] cojoc - an embroidered open bolero jacket, often fur lined; sleeveless for men, with sleeves for women.
[4] marama - a rectangular gauze veil which can be worn in many ways; a long, decorative, sheer scarf.

boyars. They had not been on the most excellent of terms with Vlad III since he seized the principality from Vladislav II, who had made Walachia a vassal state to the Ottoman Turks. But Vlad, the intrepid diplomat, had aligned the country with Hungary, acting the fox, cleverly playing one power off the other. This young prince's plan was to strengthen his land into a kingdom in which he need bow to no one higher than himself.

Nicolae's fifteen year old son, Nicolae Anton, sat on a courtyard bench with his black boots set a yard apart watching the outdoor dance. Not comfortable wearing fine attire, he had already dirtied his sheepskin trousers. He wore his black velvet bolero casually over his white embroidered shirt which had become far too loose from his crooked cummerbund. Young Nicolae was bored with the affair and didn't seem to care who noticed. He snatched the black clabatul[5] from his sandy brown hair just to have something in his hands to fidget with. Then as he glanced up at the dancers, the boy's midnight-blue eyes caught sight of his lovely sister, Eveline.

At least she is enjoying herself, he thought. Eveline's long red hair was artistically veiled with her marama which was accented with a fresh spring flower. It was her first eligible season, and as she was seventeen, her parents hoped to find a husband for her at this gala event. Anyone who was anyone had been invited.

At the end of the dance, a formally dressed valet rang a bell and announced that all were invited into the banquet hall for the feast. One by one they filed in with aristocratic fashion and took seats on the many benches set up in the huge hall. Together, they were well over six hundred.

"It is quite an honor for the prince to prepare such an extravagant dinner, don't you agree?" Olivia commented to her husband as she noticed how many were filling the hall.

"Quite so," he concurred. "I can't help but wonder though, why the change of heart?"

"What do you mean, Tata?" Eveline asked in curiosity.

"Just that this is the first occasion upon which Prince Vlad has seemed to take notice of his boyars. We have not been invited to his court before."

---

[5] clabatul - a sheepskin cap that is gray, black, or white

"About time," Nicolae Anton announced as he straightened up. "They are bringing out the food." The athletic lad had always been much more interested in horseback riding and hunting than in attending a ball, but now the aroma of lamb stew, goulash, and roast pork with pudding made the wait worthwhile.

Eveline constantly scanned the hall as she excitedly sized up her prospects. Soon her caramel eyes spied their host sitting in the royal chair at the end of the head table. He had black silky hair that draped down his back and parted in front of his shoulders with sausage curls. His ebony mustache flowed fluidly below the corners of his mouth but turned out above his aristocratic chin. Dark, piercing, jade green eyes gleamed from under his thin, arched brows while his chiseled Roman nose plunged to rest on his wide mustache. He wore the crimson suit with jet-black cape of the Order of the Dragon to which he belonged.

"Mama." Eveline motioned. "Isn't that Prince Vlad?" Her mother, having just taken a bite of the black bread, nodded. "He seems quite handsome."

Olivia swallowed and smiled at her daughter. "I suppose young ladies might think so, but I have found no man in all the land as handsome as your father."

Nicolae Anton gave the prince a passing glance then turned his attention back to the more important matter of his meal. "When will we be going home?" he asked between bites.

His mother answered, "In a few days or perhaps a week." Then she smiled at her daughter. "This is Eveline's best chance for a good match, and we must take time for her to be noticed." He grunted and took another bite of roast pork, washing it down with a goblet of table wine.

The boyars and their families had just finished eating and drinking to their satisfaction when they heard the ringing of a knife being gently tapped on crystal. All eyes turned toward their Prince who stood at his table. "I am delighted that you all have enjoyed the sumptuous repast I have laid before you, my loyal boyars. Now I have but one question which I would like to put before you - how many princes have ruled in your lifetimes?" He awaited their answer with a twisted knowing grin on his lips.

The noblemen looked to one another and shrugged as they tried to count. One of the oldest answered comically, "My lord, there have been so many I cannot number them." After a little chuckle from the crowd he mused, "Possibly fifty or so I would guess."

"I could name twenty and five," a man answered while another recalled thirty.

Nicolae of Cozia ventured to guess. "I recollect twenty different princes." Some of the younger boyars only remembered the most recent five or six.

When all who were willing had answered the question, Vlad very matter-of-factly stated, "I wish my boyars to have served only under my reign."

"But my lord," the eldest replied. "How can we erase the past? You are a young man, and many princes have ruled before your time. There is nothing we can do about that."

"Perhaps not," the prince agreed as he set down his chalice. "But there is something I can do about *you.*"

A fearful hush fell over the hall. Nicolae glanced about anxiously and noticed the guards posted at all the exits. He locked eyes with his son who had also felt the silent, apprehensive wave that stunned them all.

Vlad leaned forward and smashed his fist onto the table, causing the plates and goblets to jump. As he raised his chin, his face took on a condemning visage. His voice boomed out, permeating the hall with its commanding resonance. "It is because of your scheming and treachery that so many princes have fallen from their rule, while *you,*" he accused pointing his finger across their ranks, "have continued to grow rich and fat, comfortable in your security. You think that because I was a captive of the Turks as a youth that I did not know what went on here!" He paced before them, setting his jaw with purpose. "I discovered your little plot - yes, I know. You wish me to believe that it was only the Hungarian, Janas Hunyadi, who murdered my father and brother, Mircea, but I know better. You were all in on the conspiracy, you murderous traitors!" he thundered.

A sickening feeling began to rise in Nicolae's throat. He knew full well at that moment that their lives were at an end. He took his wife's hand and squeezed it tightly to assure her that he would not leave her side.

"But Prince Vlad, my lord, we never -" began one of the frightened boyars, but Vlad cut him short with a vengeful glare.

"None of your lies! You assassinated Dracul and then tortured his heir, my brother, finally burying him alive. This I know, my *loyal*

4

vassals," he sneered spitefully as he whirled about, his black cape swirling against his thighs. "I opened his grave; I saw for myself. I have heard the names you have called me." The prince paused dramatically as he slowly paced back to the center. He gave them a moment to reflect. "Blood-thirsty butcher, sadistic, black hearted, even 'Mad Vlad.' Lying, self-righteous hypocrites all of you! Now." His icy green eyes scanned the banquet hall, deliberately passing over each breathless form. "Now, you will know yourselves the judgment you passed upon my father and brother."

A collective shudder swept through the boyars as some of them began to panic, fearing for their lives. But there was no escape.

"Surely he is mistaken, Father," Eveline pleaded. "Tell him you are innocent!"

"There, my dear," Nicolae tried to calm his daughter. "Your mother and I had no part in the affair, but there is some truth to what he says."

"Then tell him, Tata," young Nicolae implored as he realized the gravity of their situation. "Tell him we live across the mountains and had no part in their murders."

"I can try, son, but he will say, 'Why then did you not come to their defense?' His mind is set, but I will attempt to make him see reason."

Cries and murmurs could be heard throughout the hall as husbands tried to give solace to their wives and children. Anxious voices rose until they became a deafening roar. "Silence!" Vlad commanded. Immediately all was still, every eye trained upon the prince. "All of you who are the age of twenty and five and younger, stand to your feet."

Nicolae Anton looked to his father who gave him a slight nod, and he hesitantly rose to his feet clasping his sister's hand and pulling her up with him. Sensing that she was about to cry, he drew her closer and whispered, "Hush, don't make a sound."

"You will be marched from this hall to Poenari where you shall build my new castle. Guards, you have your instructions," Vlad added darkly.

"No!" Eveline cried out as she reached back toward her mother.

Olivia touched her hand with tears in her eyes. "Go with them," she said gently.

"Nicolae," his father instructed earnestly. "Take care of your sister and stay alive." There was a tremble in his voice as he set his jaw with bold defiance toward the impending disaster. "You survive, my son.

Whatever it takes - you must survive." It was meant as a direct command, not to be broken, and Nicolae Anton had every intention of carrying it out.

The boy caught his sister's upper arms and held them firmly, protectively. "I will, Father. But what about you?" His dark blue eyes were wide with fear and uncertainty. He wondered if he would ever see his parents again.

By that time a guard was prodding the youths away to join the others. "Don't worry about us, Nic. Remember your upbringing and make me proud."

"Mama!" Eveline cried out, but at the soldier's rough prompting, her brother dragged her out with the scores of other youths and young adults.

"God help them," Lady Olivia sobbed as she grasped her husband's hand and arm. "And us." A somber expression drained all life from his face, and the Lord of Cozia contemplated the fate that awaited them.

"Let the women go, too," Nicolae then spoke up above the clamor. "They had no part in any political dealings."

"No," Vlad returned philosophically. "Marriage makes a man and woman one flesh. His sins become hers also."

"But Nicolae and I were across the mountains in Cozia," Olivia dared speak out. "My lord, he had no part in any plot. My husband has always been loyal to your family."

Vlad did not acknowledge her with a response but indicated to the remaining soldiers that it was time for the old boyars to be removed from the hall.

"Let our servants go," pleaded one of the nobles. "Let them serve you now."

Vlad sneered at him then emitted a wicked laugh. "I must clean all of the dirt from my principality before installing my new, true boyars. Now I shall take my leave of you, and I wish you all the pain, suffering, and misery you so richly deserve." The Prince turned and began to leave them, but spun back with a theatrical flair. "Ah, yes - one more thing. None of your children will survive, even the little ones you left at home. Your seed shall be completely wiped off the earth, and it shall be as if you never existed." With a satisfied smile, Vlad left their presence.

That was the most horrific, final blow for these nobles, for continuing their family line had always been paramount in importance to them. Nicolae held Olivia in his arms. She sobbed into his shoulder as a slow bitter tear ran down his cheek. "Survive, Nicolae Anton," he whispered as if in prayer, his eyes closing. "You must."

Outside the palace, the young boyars, the youths, and older children had been lined up in ranks to begin the arduous march to Poenari. It was a winding dirt road that meandered up, down, and around the lower Carpathian mountains. Though not that far from Tirgoviste as the crow flies, it would be a fifty mile trek by road. Several of the soldiers were mounted on horseback while others, armed with pikes, stood behind the ranks. The stunned and disillusioned young people looked ridiculously out of place dressed in their Easter Sunday finery.

Then the captain of the guard called out to them. "There will be no stops for rest or food until we reach Poenari. Anyone who cannot keep up will be killed and his body left behind for the wild animals. Do you understand?"

No one said a word; they only looked at each other with dumbfounded, dazed expressions. He couldn't be serious. Who could do that? "When we arrive, you may rest before we begin construction. Food and water will be rationed to you, and as long as you do good work, you will be allowed to live. Now, move out." He clicked to his horse, and the pikemen began to advance on the rear of the group. Some of the girls and children screamed and began to run ahead. Young Nicolae firmly took his sister's hand and started to walk, leading her down the road.

"Fifty miles, Nicolae; I cannot do it!" A veil of panic covered features that only an hour before had been so gay.

"Yes, you can, Eveline - you must. Now pull yourself together and think positively. It is what Tata wanted," he told her resolutely.

"What will happen to them?" He could feel her cold hand quiver in his.

"Don't think about that now," Nicolae insisted with a sudden surge of authority that she found unfamiliar in her younger brother. "Father said he would tell the prince he was innocent; perhaps Vlad will believe him."

"Quiet in the ranks!" a guard called out in a harsh voice. "Keep it moving."

Eveline lowered her voice to a whisper and leaned her head toward her brother. "Nic, I'm afraid."

"We all are, Evie," he breathed in a hushed tone. "But all we have to do now is get there. It's not that hard. Just keep putting one foot in front of the other. That's all you have to do."

After several hours on the march, the reality of the day's events began to sink in. No one tried to talk anymore. Their mouths were dry and their feet sore from treading the rough road in fancy dress shoes. Nicolae was glad he had been defiant and worn his boots despite the protests his mother had made. Then that realization set him thinking. *Have I been too defiant and rebellious? Have I been a good son? Did I make my mother sad too often? Was my father proud of me? No.* He shook himself. *I cannot think about that now.* Resolutely he focused once more on his marching.

A few more hours had passed and darkness now loomed around them. On either side of the road stretched vast expanses of dark forests with the eerie sounds of night insects radiating from the verdant foliage. "I'm hungry." Nicolae heard one of the children say. "Are we almost there?" A wave of pity ran through him as he realized the child might not survive the journey. Then his own stomach churned with hunger as the darkness of the forest closed in around them.

"Nicolae, I'm getting tired," Eveline pleaded pitifully. "Walk slower."

"Keep going," he insisted. "I don't want to be in the back where those pikemen are."

Suddenly a scream rang out behind them as a young woman covered her face in horror. One of the soldiers had just driven the point of his spear through the body of a child who fell to the road. Nicolae glanced over his shoulder briefly and then gave Eveline a gentle tug as she tried to look back. "Keep going."

"You don't understand," her brown eyes pleaded with him. "I'm not as strong as you are, and…I'm bleeding."

Chapter 2

The Long Road

"All those who were old he had impaled around the city, while those who were young, together with their wives and children, all dressed up for Easter, he had taken to Poenari where they worked to build the fortress there until their clothes fell off and they remained naked. For this reason he was called the Impaler [Tepes]."

From Istoria Tarii Romanesti, 1290 - 1690

"Bleeding?" A surprised look crossed Nicolae's face.

"Shhhh," she warned as she looked around to make certain he had not called too much attention to them. "My courses have started," she whispered.

"Oh." Nicolae knew that women often had restricted activities on their 'sick' days. His mother would lie around on couches making excuses to him before he was old enough to know of such things. Even the servant girls would be given siesta times on those days. His mind raced as he thought of what to say to her. "Come, lean on me." He motioned, opening his right arm for her to step closer. "I'll bear part of your weight."

Her eyes smiled at him, reawakened by his unfailing determination. "Thank you." Eveline reached her arms around her brother's neck while he braced her back with his right arm. It was not comfortable since she was barely shorter than he, but he was at least helping to support her tired body, and that made a big difference.

As twilight closed in, the two noticed that a few of the younger children were falling by the side of the road. "What will happen to them?" Eveline asked in a hushed whisper.

"I don't know," Nicolae answered shortly. "Let's keep going." Even as he said the words, the youth's legs ached, and his feet had already become numb. His parched tongue longed for a cool draught of water.

9

"Keep up the pace!" a guard snapped abruptly. The entire party had slowed quite considerably since the march began and even the foot soldiers were tiring. However, they did have water, salted pork, and biscuits to pass about and sustain themselves with - the young boyars did not.

It was well past dark and the moonlight was partially blocked by the tree tops when Nicolae and Eveline tripped over a body in the road. "Look out," Eveline called to those behind them, and the exhausted marchers parted around their fallen comrade. Nicolae helped his sister to her feet and glanced down at the young man in the road. He felt pity for him, but he had his own hands full with Eveline. He turned her to move once more. The brief moment of rest felt good to his limbs, but they must press on. "How much farther?" Her eyes searched her brother's face. "I don't want to be left on the road."

"I won't leave you behind," Nicolae promised. With that assurance, Eveline leaned on her brother once more for support. It seemed to Nicolae that this time he was bearing even more weight than before, but he kept his legs moving as his mind drifted farther away.

By the wee morning hours before dawn, the line had slowed to a virtual crawl. With his head drooping, Nicolae kept his feet pressing methodically forward. He could hear soft cries of a young woman and then a short scream; another one would not be building the prince's castle. Then all at once Eveline's arms went loose, and she began to fall at his side. Immediately he was aware of her, and his eyes opened wide as he stopped to catch her.

"Eveline wake up," he said frantically. "It's almost morning; we're going to make it." But he could not revive his sister, who had passed out from utter exhaustion. Her body could not do what had been required of it and had shut down. "Evie!" Nicolae stared at her in disbelief. Others began to walk around them, and the boy from Cozia was suddenly wide awake with terror. *"Take care of your sister."* His father's words seared his conscience.

"Here, I'll carry you," he spoke to her as if she could hear him. Taking hold of her arms, he draped them over his shoulders and grabbed her thighs, hoisting her onto his back. Once he had her legs situated above his hips, the youth stepped out again, now very close to the end of the line. "I can do this; I can do this," he kept telling himself, but Eveline was

10

almost as large as he was. Nicolae's legs felt like lead and each step sent a double shock through his tingling body; nevertheless, he pressed forward, forcing himself to do the impossible.

Within the hour it had become light enough to see, and one of the soldiers noticed them. "What are you doing boy?" he called gruffly. At first Nicolae's ears did not interpret the sounds, and he continued to march. "You, boy," the soldier repeated, stepping through the ranks to get his attention. "What do you think you are doing?"

Nicolae raised his eyes to the tall, broad, dark skinned soldier holding a steel pointed pike. "My sister just needs a little rest, and she'll be fine," he answered without breaking stride. He was afraid that if he stopped, he would not be able to get his legs going again.

"You won't make it, boy. Put her down."

"I am strong; I can do this," Nicolae insisted. It felt rough inside his mouth to speak, his dry tongue scratching like sandpaper. "My sister is strong and will be a good worker on the castle when we get there. She is just enduring her sick time right now. In a few days she will be the fittest worker you'll have. She is too valuable to leave behind. I can do this." He continued the never-ending task of placing one foot before the other.

"The hell you can," the soldier swore shaking his head. "But it is your life; you may try." Then the tall soldier made his way back to the side of the road and pointed them out to one of his fellow guards. "Look, Dagmar, what a little tiger that one is," he said with an admiring grin. "Carrying a sister as big as he is."

"Ha!" the smaller soldier laughed. "Much the same strain as you'd put on a donkey, Ivan. Determined little bastard, and strong, too. Now give me a crew like that, and we'd have that fortress finished in no time."

"I hope he makes it," Ivan said wistfully.

"Now don't go getting sentimental on me," his fellow warned. "You know our orders, and you know what happens to those who disobey them. Prince Dracula richly rewards those who faithfully serve him, but woe to the man who crosses him. Besides, look what he is doing for us - getting rid of the land-hoarding, money-grubbing, high and mighty boyars. And," he added with a laugh, "the irony! Our prince of the people does not conscript peasants to do the heavy labor, but employs these fine aristocrats!"

"Yes, you are right, of course," Ivan agreed. "Still, he is a more admirable lad than that boyar a few hours ago who left his pregnant wife behind without a second thought."

"Quite so," Dagmar replied. "A drink?" he offered, holding out his canteen.

"Da," Ivan replied and took a long draw. "Thanks."

"Ah, what have we here?" questioned Dagmar with a twisted grin as he spotted a youthful lad lying unconscious by the side of the road. Ivan gritted his teeth but said nothing as his fellow raised his spear and plunged it into the boyar's chest. With an automatic reflex, the youth writhed into a fetal position, drawing up his knees and tucking his head as a mournful cry escaped his chapped lips. His beardless face was twisted, mouth agape as Dagmar yanked the spear from his body. A red fountain issued forth spontaneously to soak his elegant white blouse and the brown earthen highway.

Ivan turned his head deliberately and stepped around the boy's body. "Why do you do that as if you enjoy it?" he asked his comrade in a tone void of expression.

"If you are asking why I killed him, the answer is, it is my duty; these are our orders, or have you forgotten? They are our enemies - the enemies of our prince, and we are his army. Do not forget that these murdering bastards killed Vlad's father and brother." Dagmar's boots stomped hard upon the road, a scowl dominating his features.

I doubt that boy had much to do with it, Ivan thought to himself as his aching limbs trod beside his fellow soldier. As disgusted as he was to be assigned to this duty rather than combat, Ivan knew when it was time to let go of an issue. "I suppose you are right," he answered and silently moved ahead.

During the next few hours, the sun rose as did the incline of the road. As the weary group trudged up and around the mountain, Nicolae began to fear he was exceeding the reaches of his endurance. He knew if they did not arrive soon he was finished. With each step he drew a heavy breath, and it took every essence of his being just to take the next. Carrying Eveline, he had been passed by all of those still upright. The soldiers had became very tired and irritable from having been awake all night and into the next day.

It's bound to be around this next bend, the boy told himself. *I can make it that far*. But to his great dismay, when they rounded the turn he saw only the road, the great forests, and more mountains. Suddenly Nicolae could see nothing but white, and his knees gave way. He was met by the hard ground. Immediately he began struggling to rise although his head was light and spinning. The sounds around him were a blur in his ears. He could feel a weight lifted from him and a jerk on his arm as he was thrust back into the weary ranks.

"No, wait!" he cried feebly as he whirled around and tried to focus his eyes.

"March!" a stern voice ordered.

"I cannot leave my sister!" With dazed eyes staring blankly toward where she lay, Nicolae lunged back, reaching out his right hand toward her.

"It's over for her," the voice declared.

"No," he protested pitifully, his desolate heart shattering into even more pieces. "She will be a good worker. Just give her a little water and she'll wake up. Don't leave her here," he said with a twisted face and a dry sob. "For Christ's sake, don't just leave her here!"

He was met by the cold point of a metal pike pressing against his chest. "You tried, boy," Ivan said as he stood over Eveline's inert body. "You did what you could, and no one will fault you for it. But we have our orders."

Filled with hopeless rage, young Nicolae defied the soldier. "Damn your orders!" he retorted and pushed the pike away with an uncoordinated effort. But a club to the side of his head sent him tumbling backward to the ground.

"Get in line and march, you little bastard," Dagmar said harshly. "You are a strong, determined lad. You will make it there, build the fortress, and be on your way - or I can run you through right here. Which will it be?"

Nicolae panted as he lay shaking in the dirt. As he wiped his face he recalled his father's last words to him: *Survive; you survive.*

"I'll tell you what, boy," Ivan spoke up. "I'll wait with your sister and try to wake her up. If she revives, we'll be right behind you, and if not...well it's worth a try." The tall, dark-haired soldier winked to his comrade who held the spear on Nicolae. The soldier nodded back to him and pulled the boy to his feet.

"Now march," he said giving him a little shove. At that moment Nicolae felt very alone and defeated. Then it was as though his mind and spirit became separated from his body. He continued to trod blindly up the steep incline, but he no longer felt the stabbing pain in his lactic-acid soaked muscles. His pale face was expressionless, and he was unaware of the outer layer of dry skin flaking off his dehydrated body. He was somewhere far away - praying, pondering, *Why? Why is this happening? What have I done - what has my family done to deserve this? Where are you, God? You are supposed to be here, where are you? If I could, I would trade places with her. Oh, Christ have mercy! We fought sometimes, but she is all I have left. Oh, Mary, Holy Mother of God, protect her! Please God, if you must have a life, take mine, but don't let her die...*

It was mid-afternoon when the bedraggled weary group finally arrived at their destination. The moment the captain called for them to halt, they fell to the ground in exhaustion. Ivan called for aides to pass canteens of water around. Glancing over the group, he did a quick head count. Only two-thirds of the captives had survived the fifty mile trek to Poenari. The captain of the guard rode up to Ivan and gave him his orders. "Let them rest three hours and then put them to work."

"But captain," a wide-eyed, exhausted Ivan protested. "They - we - have been marching for two straight days without rest."

"Precisely," the commander confirmed raising his smooth chin. "And we do not want to hold up progress. These ruins are waiting to be rebuilt, and the stones will not put themselves together. Prince Dracula wants the job completed with all haste."

"Yes, sir, I agree," said Ivan, who even towered above his commander. "But he does want the job finished, and to do so, we must have workers - live workers who are strong enough for the task. If you let us all rest the whole day and begin tomorrow, I believe you will see much more accomplished."

The silver-haired captain of the guard snorted, placing his fists on his hips. His silver breast plate heaved up and down with his deep breath. "Very well, sergeant, but I will expect a full day of fast-paced work on the morrow. And I am placing Dagmar as overseer; I do not believe you have the stomach for this type of work." His piercing blue eyes looked in disdain upon his subordinate.

"Captain, I am a soldier, a warrior, and no better one will you find. The fortress will be completed as scheduled," Ivan replied with an equal amount of contempt.

The following morning the ragged prisoners were awakened and given bread and water to break their fast. The moment their meal was completed, they were given their instructions on rebuilding the ruined fortress of Poenari on the high bluff overlooking the Arges River. Anyone who appeared to be slacking was whipped. Those whose footing was not sure would fall to instant death on the rocks far below the precipice. When the boyars' fine clothes became torn, worn out rags, they were not replaced and they were obliged to keep working with or without clothes. Nicolae's thin embroidered linen shirt did not last long, but his sheepskin trousers, boots, and cojoc were sturdy enough attire for the task at hand. However, the state of his clothing did not matter much to the boy. It was as though the very life was sucked out of him when Eveline did not return with the soldier. He never saw her again. A small glimmer of hope sparked once in a while that perhaps his father had convinced the prince of his innocence and would return to free him. After all, he must have something to hope for.

A few months had passed, and the castle was almost complete when one night a heavy, dense fog rolled up the gorge. An opaque sheet of gloom settled over the camp, the mist so thick one could barely see his own hand before his eyes. The enslaved boyars huddled together, fearful of falling into the ravine below. Even the soldiers were worried, and their horses neighed nervously.

"I need one of you to guard the bridge to the road," the captain requested of his men. "It is the only way one might escape this night."

Ivan volunteered for the duty. Wearing his Spanish-cut helm, silver breast plate and light-weight yellow-gold cape, he positioned himself in front of the bridge, prepared to let no one pass.

Young Nicolae, however, was a resourceful lad. He had studied the cliffs and steep embankments ever since they had arrived at the fortress. Indeed, there was no apparent way up or down. It was an ideal spot for a castle. But he had observed one possible route on the south side of the cliffs close to where the secret escape tunnel had been built. He could not get inside the lower chambers to use the tunnel, but if he could negotiate about forty feet of sheer rock, he would come out at the steps and path leading down to the river.

Slowly crawling on his hands and knees through the impossible darkness, Nicolae felt the ground for the ledge and the stump that would identify the exact spot. Thanks to the most fortunate cover of fog, no one noticed that he was missing. His heart was pounding with fear and excitement when he found the stump. He felt it several times to make certain it was the right one. Then he quietly eased himself over the edge and painstakingly made his way down, careful to feel his way. He was glad that he had spent the past two summers at home rock climbing with his father; the experience would certainly be put to good use now. Slowly he reached out finding a strong root here, a secure rock there, wherever he could find a hold.

A surge of renewed hope and energy shot through him when his foot finally came to rest on the solid flat stones of the narrow steps that had been chiseled into the face of the escarpment. Suddenly a frightening thought shot through him. What would happen when the guards found him missing? They would certainly put out a search party. No one was allowed to escape Poenari. Like a streak of lightening an idea came to him. Looking around he found a large stone - that would do! Cupping his hands to his mouth Nicolae let out a helpless cry and then threw the stone as far as he could, creating the illusion that he had fallen to his death in the river below. Hurriedly, he carefully hugged the wall and crept down the ravine to the river and swam away from the place of his captivity. At last he felt free…but not completely. He had to return to Tirgoviste to discover what had become of his parents.

By morning the fog had lifted, and the camp was one worker short. A recount was made. "There is one conscript missing, sergeant," the captain announced. "Who is it?"

The enslaved boyar youths had not engaged in much socializing, but a few of them had learned his name. One of them, afraid of punishment, spoke out, "Milord, I do not see young Nicolae of Cozia. Perhaps it is he."

"Nicolae of Cozia, come forth," the captain commanded. They all looked around at each other but no one moved. "Ivan!"

"Captain, sir." Ivan removed his helmet to address the officer. "He did not escape on my watch. I swear it! Not a soul crossed that bridge last night. He must have fallen off the precipice during the blackness of that cursed, unearthly fog that so wickedly engulfed us last evening. His body may have been washed away by the river."

One of the near-naked boyars timidly spoke out, "I heard a noise last night. A scream like some-one fell from the cliffs." A few others corroborated his story testifying that they had heard it too.

The captain knew that Ivan was a competent soldier and would have kept a good watch. He also knew Vlad's orders to kill all of the young boyars once the castle was completed. He didn't want anyone alive who might tell of the secret tunnel. The captain further knew that if anyone did escape under his command his life would be forfeit. "It shall be so recorded," he announced. "Nicolae of Cozia fell from a cliff to his death in the heavy fog. Now, all of you, back to work. We should be finished by the end of the week."

Ivan breathed a sigh of relief as his commander walked over to him. "Are you sure he fell?"

"Sir, I swear by all that is holy that he did not pass this bridge. He must have fallen - he certainly didn't grow wings and fly away."

"Very well," the captain consented and placed a hand on young Ivan's broad shoulder. "Get some rest now."

"Yes, sir," he replied and was dismissed. But in the back of Ivan's mind, he silently wondered if the boy just might have found a way.

Vapor rose from the black water as Nicolae Anton floated down the Arges River toward the Danube. He came ashore when he thought he was far enough south and headed east through some farming country. Spying a darkened barn, he crept in and wrapped himself in a horse's blanket to dry. Afraid of being caught there, Nicolae grabbed a handful of the dry oats which looked mighty good to him by then, crammed them into his pocket, and was on his way. After crossing the Dimbovita River, he found the road to Tirgoviste and followed its path from a safe distance amid the trees and bushes. By mid-afternoon when he could see the buildings of the city ahead, the exhausted youth took refuge in an old abandoned corn crib and slept.

In the very early morning, before anyone was out, Nicolae nervously traipsed up the road leading to the city. He had been this way several times before when traveling to and from Cozia, but this time something seemed different. A meadow was supposed to lie on that hill to his left, yet tall, dark figures pointed skyward, trailing their tree-like black shadows. Nicolae's stomach tightened as he left the road and walked toward the new growth of forest. Then, as the morning fog rose and shifted, terror seized the young man's heart, and he stopped dead still in his tracks. They were not trees at all, but the corpses of the boyars hanging on high impaling spikes. A new ray of light hit the mist as it softly drifted up through the skeletal remains, creating a grisly, ghostly aura.

Nicolae felt his hands and knees begin to shake as he took in the entire scene. Men, women, servants…perhaps four hundred in all…a forest of the impaled…the death of the entire boyar class of Walachia. He wondered about those back at Poenari; was this their fate as well? He gazed on the spectacle before him as though it were an unreal thing, like a nightmare or ghoulish vision. But reality hit when a crow landed on the body nearest him and began to peck at the carrion. "No!" he shouted in horrific despair and disgust. "This did not happen!"

Nicolae's heart rate accelerated, his stomach knotted tighter, and his head began to spin. He was forced to drop to the ground and lower his head between his knees lest he pass out. Breathing erratic, shaky breaths, he tried to calm himself, but he felt as if all the boyar specters were staring at him, expecting him to free them.

The youth held his head in his hands until the spinning sensation began to dissipate. Then a burning, driving need overtook his being - he must find his parents. He must know if they were here among the impaled. With a relentless determination, his searing cobalt eyes set out to find his mother and father. He rose to step lightly, then trot, then run through the ranks of ghastly victims. The sight was repulsive and the odor sickening, but Nicolae staunchly removed himself from the horrible surroundings, consumed with singleness of purpose.

It was not an easy task. The eyes had all been pecked out and much of the facial flesh eaten or weathered away. Hair remained a sign on most heads and the distinctiveness of their dress. Nicolae arrested his memory and demanded that it recall what his parents had been wearing. He closed his eyes and saw them dancing together once again. *Yes, of course*, he thought as he frantically scanned the scores of bodies. For most, the pikes were entered through the buttocks and exited through the back, chest, or mouth - a slow and tortuous death that could last hours or days. Others were spiked through the gut or upside down. One pike had even entered through the victim's mouth. But Nicolae had to shut out these nightmarish horrors to accomplish the task at hand.

Identifying clothing would not be easy either. Blacks had become sun bleached and whites turned brownish-gray. The once-bright colors had faded, and strips had been torn from the cloth by wind, rain, and wild animals. The most identifying items would be his mother's exquisite marama, his father's light reddish-blond hair, and their jewelry. Most Walachians were Romanian - olive skinned from Mediterranean stock - but his father's family contained Saxon blood. Nicolae had gotten the light sandy-brown hair color and his sister the red.

As the sun began to rise higher, Nicolae's search became more frantic, for he knew he would have to hide soon. As he passed row after row of corpses, he began to have hope that they were not among the dead. All at once he halted in front of a stake. He swallowed hard as his eyes became transfixed with abhorrence, and his ashen face became a mask of desperation. His knees quaked as his heart palpitations thundered within his chest. "Mama," he moaned pitifully.

Nicolae dared to move his eyes to the figure beside her. "Tata," he uttered in broken hearted despair. Tears streamed from his eyes as he felt his body becoming violently ill. The horror-stricken youth fell to his knees and bent toward the ground emitting dry heaves, for there was no food or drink in his stomach to come up. Their bodies were wasted, picked apart by scavengers, but he knew it was they. Bones protruded through in some places, pale, swollen tissue in others. Ants and flies crawled without and within their rotting forms. It was more than the young man could bare to look upon.

"Oh, God!" he wailed, his face buried in his hands. "Why?" The orphaned youth began to sob uncontrollably, speaking whenever he could form the words. "Didn't you tell him? You didn't do it!" Then he felt like his father was right there, staring down at him in a convicting manner. "I tried to save her, Father...I tried," he moaned between gut-wrenching sobs. "I carried her as long as I could, but I wasn't strong enough. Oh,

God, I tried, but I couldn't do it. I wasn't strong enough!" Then the boy broke down completely and fell upon the ground, recoiling in pain, consumed by agony.

Eventually, his sobs began to subside, and Nicolae wiped his face. He felt life return to him in the form of a newness of purpose. He remembered his father's last words to him and raised his head to reply. "I survived, Father; I did what you said, and I survived. It is for a reason - I know that - and I will continue to survive. I must leave now, Father, but one day I will return. Then Dracula, that son of the devil, will know that the plan he devised has failed. He will know that Lord Nicolae of Cozia escaped his purge and I will punish him for what he has done here." Displaying wrought-iron courage, young Nicolae stood on tip-toe and reached up to pull the signet ring from his father's bony finger. No grave robbers had visited this haunted forest; they knew that the penalty for any crime under Vlad's reign, even robbing the dead, was punishable by burning, boiling, disemboweling, or impalement. Any tortuous death would do for the cruel, sadistic despot who found amusement in watching his helpless victims die.

Nicolae tried the ring on, but it was much too large for his emaciated finger. The workers had been fed enough to live, but no more, and the already lanky youth had grown even thinner. So he thrust the ring deep into his pocket and let out a long sigh.

Suddenly Nicolae heard a rustling in the grass behind him. He spun around wide-eyed, clenching his hands into fists. There, among the stakes, he spotted two dogs tugging on either end of a human leg bone. It was a disgusting sight that turned his stomach and filled the youth with an even stronger loathing of Prince Vlad Dracula, the Impaler. He swallowed hard and with nerves on end uttered through clenched teeth these last words. "If he enjoys death so much, then I will give it to him!" The mist was quickly dissipating under the warmth of the morning sun when Nicolae Anton turned abruptly and fled the forest of the impaled.

Chapter 3

Justice

"People remember about Dracula that he was a man of unheard of cruelty and justice."

from the Chronicle of Antonius Bontinius, <u>Rerum Ungaricum Decades, vol. III, 1936.</u>

Castle Poenari, November 1476; nineteen years later

"See what has happened while I was away?" Prince Vlad complained to his personal valet, Petru, who lengthened his stride to keep pace with his impatient master. "Crime is running rampant once again. That stupid brother of mine; Radu the Handsome - bah!" Vlad stopped abruptly in front of a hanging mirror to adjust his long, silky curls which lay upon the shoulder of his royal blue silk embroidered wool jacket. His black hair showed only a marginal amount of gray, and he had kept his mustache black with an ink-based dye. "Handsome indeed!" he retorted, demeaning his younger brother's acquired nick name.

"It is true that he did not rule with the measure of authority you did, my lord," Petru interjected, sensing that a compliment was called for.

"And then that traitor, Basarab the Old! I should have had him executed. I should have sent troops after him to kill him, but in my haste to recapture my throne, I let him slip away. When all is back in order, remind me to hire some assassins."

"Yes, milord," Petru dutifully replied. Petru was an older man, in his forties, with short, graying hair, a round face, and a charcoal mustache and goatee. He had been in the service of the royal family of Hungary for many years and had been sent to accompany Vlad back to Walachia after his time of captivity and exile there. When Prince Dracula had been deposed by his younger brother, Radu, he had fled to Hungary seeking refuge. Instead, King Matthias Corvinus had him imprisoned. With great diplomatic prowess and charm, the young Vlad soon ingratiated himself with the royal family and was let out of his cell in house arrest. Matthias found it advantageous to have Vlad at his side when negotiating with the Ottoman Turks. Just the mere sight of the Impaler sent shivers down their spines. Sultan Mehmed II remembered well that fateful day in 1462 that turned the tide in their war. The Turks had outnumbered Vlad's army three to one, but Prince Dracula had devised a devilishly effective plan. As the Muslim Turks advanced on the capital of Tirgoviste, Vlad impaled thousands of Turkish prisoners around the city, some with severed limbs and exposed nakedness. When the massive Turkish army bore down on the city and was met by the ghastly forest of their impaled countrymen, they became demoralized. Some even began to panic, declaring they were waging war on Satan himself. Mehmed saw the effect on his army. They refused to advance another step; therefore, he was forced to retreat across the border when victory was within his grasp.

After that, Prince Dracula was hailed as a hero for halting the advance of the Muslim Turks, saving Walachia, and preventing an Ottoman invasion of Europe proper. The Turks, however, gave him the name of "Tepes," the Impaler.

Petru remembered how Vlad had caught the eye of King Matthias's sister, Princess Ilona. She saw him as a handsome, enigmatic man who exhibited power even while under arrest. Nothing could have pleased Vlad more. He took full advantage of his chance for a marital alignment with the king and becoming, in essence, part of the Hungarian royal family, so he asked Matthias for her hand. The two were married and spent a lot of time at Visegrad Palace overlooking the beautiful Danube, but the Hungarian king kept Dracula on a leash.

Petru served the royal couple there at Visegrad where Ilona bore Vlad two sons. The proper valet had often noticed strange things around the palace, but he had kept quiet because he feared his new master. Sometimes he would find pathetic little birds hopping along the ground with all of their feathers plucked out or mice impaled on tiny little stakes in the garden. Petru found this trait in the Romanian prince most unsettling and unnatural. Rulers often execute enemies and criminals, but he had never heard of one torturing creatures simply for pleasure.

Now that Prince Dracula was in control of his own country once more, Petru was beginning to understand the full measure of cruelty his employer possessed. Princess Ilona had been left in Hungary with

Dracula's sons until the prince was certain that it was safe enough to send for them. Petru thought that Ilona's presence had a tempering effect on Vlad, but in her absence he was back to his old self again. His conversion from Orthodoxy to Catholicism had meant nothing but a mass to Dracula who needed Catholic Hungarian support to win back his throne. Petru thought to himself, *If King Matthias knew that Vlad was up to his old tricks, he would depose him personally,* but the valet said nothing. He did not live so long in the service of nobility by criticizing them or informing on their actions. He planned to live on long after someone else had disposed of the prince.

Satisfied with his appearance, Vlad turned away from the mirror and continued down the hallway with Petru, papers in hand, right behind him. "Crime, dishonesty, and immorality cannot be tolerated," Vlad explained. "There is no letting them off with a warning - they pay no heed. To curb the behavior of men and bring them under control, justice must be swift and final - no second chances. When others know the fate that awaits them, they will most readily obey. My father taught me that as a ruler it is better to be feared than to be loved. I wholeheartedly agree."

By then they had reached the courtroom where Vlad would hear the cases of the day. The accused had no attorney, and the charges all appeared on the papers Petru carried. The prince would hear them, judge them, and pass sentence on them. There were no appeals.

Vlad was announced as he entered the side door with Petru following. "Most high viovode[6] and prince of Walachia, His Majesty, Vlad Dracula." He took his seat in the red velvet stuffed chair on a raised platform at the front of the sparsely occupied hall. A fit, muscular man stood at the rear door of the chamber with his bare arms folded across the sheep chamois tunic that covered his chest. The chief executioner's dark hair was cut close to his head, and his pock-marked face bore a prominent scar. Sergei was a leading member of Vlad's elite armasi, unscrupulous men who carried out his gruesome bidding for pay. "Sergei, show the first one in," the prince commanded.

Sergei nodded, winking one brown eye at his lord as he pulled open the heavy oak door. Another guard pushed the first defendant through. "Costi." Vlad's voice echoed around the chamber. "So you are a Transylvanian merchant."

---

[6] viovode - the Slavic word of prince; Vlad often used it as part of his title.

"Yes, milord," he trembled, hat in hand, as he slowly inched forward.

"Come here to cheat my people," the prince stated as though it were fact.

"No, milord!" Costi swore as his round eyes widened.

"You've grown fat off Walachian profits I see," Vlad mused at the round bellied merchant dressed in fine embroidered attire.

"No, my lord; I am an honest merchant and never charge unfair prices."

"Your prices do not interest me so much as the quality of your merchandise, or rather the lack of it. This report says you sold a chair to a Walachian citizen which broke when he sat in it for the first time. He injured his hip in the fall and missed two days of work. Costi, it seems you are interfering with productivity in my country," Dracula stated.

"Your Majesty," Costi pleaded. "I did not know the chair was defective. I do not make the merchandise; I simply sell it."

"Then you should have been more careful."

"I will gladly replace the chair and pay the unfortunate customer for his missed time at work," the merchant offered as he reached into his pocket and took out a sum of gold and silver coins. He approached Petru - afraid to go near Dracula - and handed them to the valet.

"That is most considerate of you, merchant of Transylvania, but a measure I deem too little, too late. I must send a clear message to the Transylvanians and all other foreign merchants. Cheating my people will not be tolerated." He then turned to Petru to record the verdict. "Impalement," he said casually.

The merchant suddenly paled and gasped in terror. "No! Prince Dracula, 'twas only a broken chair!" Costi was bewildered and mortified. "I can make the transaction right. I have goods and money to offer you," he pleaded.

Prince Dracula leaned forward and peered at him intently. "Do you think your wealth is not already mine?" Then he straightened up and waved his hand to the armas. "Take him away."

Sergei grabbed the trembling man and ushered him to the back door. "Next," Vlad called while inspecting his manicure. A young woman was brought before the prince, and he glanced at her paper. "Ah, yes, the adulterous wife."

"Milord, it was not that way at all," the woman tried to explain. Fear had gripped her the moment she entered his presence. His cold green eyes studied her condemningly.

"My report indicates that you were caught in the act of dalliance. You were unclothed in the presence of a man not your husband when the witness walked in on you, and yet you deny it?"

"Wine was spilled on my dress and I had to wash it immediately, or the stain would set. My dealings with the gentleman in question were purely innocent, I assure you, milord. Have you spoken with my husband? He is well pleased with me."

"Doamna[7], your husband has nothing to do with this trial. There is a law against adultery, and you have broken it, regardless of his opinion on the matter. Furthermore..." Vlad darkened as if in a rage. "I find your deceitful, lying tongue to be an abomination in my presence."

"My lord, forgive me!" She fell on her hands and knees in tears. "I only wished to protect the gentleman in question."

"I have already spoken with your lover," Vlad sneered in disgust. "He was completely honest and forthright with me. You are married - he is not. You have committed two unpardonable crimes - adultery and lying to me. He was flogged and released for having consumed my valuable time. You, however, shall be impaled. Show her out."

The thick arms of the executioner dragged the hysterical woman roughly from the chamber as she wailed pitifully over her fate.

Vlad sighed, as though he were bored already. "Who is next?"

Petru handed him the next defendant's form. "Oh, Jan the thief. This shouldn't take long. Show him in."

The door opened again, and a thin, olive-skinned boy of twelve wearing dirty, tattered clothes, entered.

"Why, he is only a boy," Petru said softly in amazement.

"Old enough to have broken the law, it seems," Vlad replied in an amused tone. "Stand up straight, boy, and straighten your shirt tail. Do you not know you are in Prince Dracula's court?"

Jan was a common boy and did not know how to conduct himself before the prince. He was also frightened nearly to death after seeing the responses of the last two criminals. He promptly smoothed his long shirt

---

[7] Doamna - Romanian for Madame

tail over his trousers and adjusted his sash as he tried to make himself more presentable. "Yes, sir, milord," he stammered.

"It says in my report that you stole a loaf of bread from the bakery and gave my policemen quite a chase before you were caught," he read then looked down at the poor lad.

"That is true," Jan replied as he stood up straight. "My most high prince, I cannot lie to you; I stole the bread, but only because without it I would surely starve to death. I am an orphan with no home. I do odd jobs when I can, but times have been very hard lately under Prince Basarab, you know. If given a chance with the improved conditions you will no doubt bring about, I am sure I can become an honest worker."

Vlad smiled at him. "Possibly. But stealing is a serious offense punishable by impalement or burning."

"That is true, my lord, but not much of an option when one is already dying of hunger. Most mighty prince, I know that you detest crime, but more so lying. I may have been caught as a thief, but at least I am an honest one," Jan pleaded his case with humility.

"Quite so," Vlad mused. "There shall be no tortuous death for one as honest and forthright as yourself. But the law is the law. Therefore the sentence is a quick and simple beheading - no pain. Unfortunately for you, there is no place for thieves or beggars in my principality."

Young Jan was stunned. He didn't know whether to be happy or sad. His young life ended for a loaf of bread, Jan could only be consoled by knowing it would be over without suffering. He slowly turned, his numb legs carrying him from the chamber.

Petru held his tongue, but had Vlad chanced to look at him he would have read the displeasure in the Hungarian's eyes. *What a waste,* he thought to himself. *Couldn't the boy at least be made a slave? Does he intend to execute his entire population?*

Petru's thoughts were interrupted when a messenger brought him a note. "My lord, the merchant, Cristian, who had the coins stolen from him is here to see you."

"Ah," Prince Dracula's eyes lit up with interest. "Show him in."

The middle-aged Cristian strode in with a flare and bowed respectfully before the prince, careful to remove his hat. "I wish to thank you for the recovery of my money which was stolen - and you accomplished it so quickly!"

"Efficiency in criminal matters is one of my strengths," Vlad beamed with self-satisfaction. "It was quite simple. I threatened the whole town with annihilation, and they turned over the thief right away. He has already been sentenced."

"Marvelously good, milord," the fancily clad merchant praised. Then his head tilted curiously. "But most gracious prince, one thing puzzles me. I had exactly 160 ducats stolen, but when I counted them, there are now 161. However could that have happened?"

Vlad rose from his chair with a consummate grin as he approached the merchant. "To test your honesty, Cristian, which has indeed saved your life. I had a stake reserved for your impaling had you not mentioned the extra coin."

Cristian's eyes widened with fearful surprise as his palms began to perspire nervously. "But certainly, my prince. I would never accept a ducat more than that which is rightfully mine." He fumbled in the silk pouch that hung from his embroidered baldric[8] and pulled out one of the coins. "I believe this belongs to you."

Vlad laughed and patted the merchant on the back. "You may keep it, and rest assured that you are welcome in my cities and towns anytime."

The merchant smiled in return. "Thank you, most honorable Prince Dracula," he replied and made as speedy an exit as he could without drawing undue attention.

Vlad, then standing beside Petru, reached to take the stack of accusation letters. "There are so many," he sighed shaking his head. "I am taking the noontime meal with Stephen Bathory and will not keep him waiting." Then Vlad began glancing through the pages issuing sentences and Petru's pen raced to keep up as he made the notations. "Impale, impale, impale," Vlad said as he handed one after the other back to his valet. "Ah - this one," he mused thoughtfully. "Burn alive, and this one should be boiled in oil," he said with a hateful glare. Then he looked through the next several sheets. "Emasculate then impale, impale, disembowel, burn, and this one," he proclaimed reaching the last page. "Fillet the bastard - alive of course - then have his flesh cooked and served to the other prisoners before their executions. There," he said satisfactorily. "All finished."

---

[8] baldric - broad sash made of leather that was worn diagonally shoulder to hip for a sword or pouch

Vlad then removed a folded piece of paper from his szur pocket, unfolded it, and handed it to his valet. "Sergei, come here." The executioner quickly complied with buoyant steps. "See this design I created?" he asked excitedly, showing it also to the armas. "I want the poles arranged in this pattern. These in the middle are where the burning stakes are to be set. Can you envision the effect when the fire is lit?" Petru studied the geometrical design the prince had drawn and gave a little nod. "Oh, and Sergei, remember how the sexual offenders are to be impaled."

"Yes, milord; I will see to it right away." Sergei took the paper with the drawing, beaming with pride at his prince and exited at once to make the arrangements.

"The executions should be set for tomorrow morning," Vlad added to confirm the date. "Tell the cook to have her staff set my table at the site."

"But Prince Dracula," Petru said. "Tomorrow is Sunday."

"What of it?" Vlad asked with a raised brow. "As good a day as any for an impaling I'd say. Now, I must prepare to meet my guest. Steven Bathory is most important to us, you know."

"Yes, milord. His assistance has proved invaluable. I will take care of this matter right away." Then Petru and the prince parted.

Maria trudged down the dirt streets of Curtea de Arges beside her friend Nadia that morning. The palisade-walled town was only a few miles from Dracula's castle of Poenari and fell in the feared prince's shadow. It was an old town, and people still perpetuated the legend that when Vlad's great-grandfather, Neagoe Basarab, built the Monastery of Arges there, his wife was built into the walls in order for them to stand. Villagers in this mountainous region south of Transylvania were both staunchly religious and extremely superstitious. Here, fortune-telling Gypsies and Hungarian priests held equal influence with the people. Despite the presence of some Catholics, most Walachians were of the Orthodox faith. While the two churches put aside their differences to join in crusades against the Turks, during times of relative peace they competed for converts, each accusing the other of heresy.

Curtea de Arges was a fair sized-town serving the needs of the Poenari garrison as well as being a stop-over point for travelers and merchants between the lands to the north and the Walachian capital of Tirgoviste to the south. It was a town of craftsmen, merchants, weavers, sheepherders, timber cutters, and small farmers, for the uneven, rocky ground of the highlands did not lend itself to large fields of grain. Deep, dark, thick forests, inhabited by hordes of wild beasts, surrounded the town which lay near the origin of the Arges River. When the temperature changed, murky fogs would rise up from the river and weave through the trees, feeding the imaginations of the superstitious peasants.

The land near the town had been granted to the Dobrin brothers by Prince Dracula for aiding in his escape from his brother Radu's forces back in 1462. It must be said that while the prince persecuted his enemies, he also rewarded his friends. The Dobrin family - who had essentially been elevated from peasant to boyar in one fateful night - still owned the land and was most pleased to see their generous prince return. The same could not be said about Maria.

"Maria, it has been weeks," her exasperated friend, Nadia, implored. "Lift your chin; smile. Come pick out a new kerchief, and I'll buy it for you."

"It's no use," Maria sighed. Her long, straight, black hair was tied back with the same faded red kerchief she had worn for years. She had a few others, but this one matched the valnic[9], apron, and peasant blouse she had worn that day. Her dark brown eyes did not look up from the road where her melancholy feet trod. A sudden cold wind swept down the street behind them, catching the women's skirts. Maria pulled her woolen shawl up around her dusky shoulders. "I just can't believe he's gone."

"Maria, darling, these things happen. My sister lost her little girl last winter to consumption," Nadia explained compassionately. Like Maria, Nadia had dark coloring, but she was younger and more petite. Her gatya[10] was made of coarse, homespun linen, and was rich in earth tones. Nadia's work at the pottery shop did not require her to dress as formally as Maria's position waiting tables at Dimitry's tavern and inn. A wicker basket on Nadia's back carried her own baby safe and sound.

"That was different," Maria replied emphatically. As they passed in front of the bakery, she inhaled the aroma of fresh tarts coming out of the oven. Nadia stopped beside her and watched as a tear streamed from her friend's eye. "My Georgi - he was all I had."

---

[9] valnic - pleated skirt often worn instead of the fota; could be covered by an apron.
[10] gatya - a peasant dress of course linen, usually homespun.

"You are a beautiful woman, Maria, and still young. You can marry again and have other children."

Maria turned her hopeless gaze to the young mother beside her. "I am already twenty-eight years old and work at a tavern. I have no family and no inheritance. Who would want me when there are younger, more fortunate virgin brides to choose from? An old man with one foot already in the grave? I had that the first time around! It was a blessed miracle that I was able to get Georgi from him. Miracle," she sighed shaking her head. "Curse. Never was a child more loved or more needed. Now I am alone, so very alone…and with no reason to go on living."

"Now listen to me," Nadia said sternly as she took her friend's hands in hers. "You have been a good friend to me. You gave Jean and me a place to stay when our house was lost to a fire, and you were there when both my children were born. Now I am here for you, Maria. You will get through this, and life will go on."

Maria sighed and looked up into Nadia's greenish-brown eyes. "I do care for you, sweet Nadia, and I thank you. But it is hatred for that bloody bastard that drives me out of my bed in the mornings," she said deliberately, her eyes darkening.

Nadia's hands began to tremble and grew instantly cold. "Who do you mean?" But the fear in her eyes already knew.

"Dracula, that nosferatu[11], who else?"

"Shhh." Nadia turned her friend and began to walk her down the street. "You mustn't say things like that; someone will hear you."

"I know I should be afraid, but I am not. When one has nothing to lose, then she has no reason to fear. But Nadia," Maria turned her eyes to her friend, lowering her voice to a soft, chilling, determined tone, "I will kill him. God in Heaven help me, but I will find a way." Nadia gave a little gasp and opened her eyes wide toward her friend, her heart nearly skipping a beat.

All at once, a strong hand clamped down on Maria's shoulder.

---

[11] nosferatu - a demonic creature said to prowl the land which could take on different shapes and forms.

Chapter 4

The Art of Impaling

"Early in the morning he gave orders that men and women, young and old alike, should be impaled...at the foot of the mountain. He then sat down at a table in their midst and ate his breakfast with great pleasure."

From the German pamphlet "About a mischievous Tyrant called Dracula voda," 1460's

Maria stood stock still. The lump that gathered in her throat and the weakness in her knees awakened her to the reality that she could indeed feel fear. As deep as was the depression into which she had sunk, the instinct for self-preservation was ultimately stronger.

Nadia turned to look at the man while a voice in Maria's head told her to break away and run. But the lovely, olive skinned widow could not have moved even if she wanted to, for in that moment she was paralyzed by the sudden dread that gripped her heart. She knew if one of the prince's policemen had heard her threat, her life would be forfeit. A moment ago her life did not seem to matter, but now with the strong grip of a broad hand on her shoulder...

"Dimitry," Nadia greeted him with a smile. "It feels like winter is blowing in today, doesn't it?"

Maria's tension eased as she breathed a sigh of relief. "It certainly does," the tavern keeper replied with a broad, toothy grin peeping from between his bushy salt and pepper beard and mustache. "And where do you think you are off to, strolling right past your place of employ?" A gray felt hat covered Dimitry's balding head, and his decorative fur-lined cojoc could not close around his barrel chest. His bright hazel eyes smiled at the women standing outside the tavern door.

"Dimitry, you nearly scared me to death!" Maria exclaimed with relief in her voice. "Don't sneak up on me so."

"Who's sneaking? I am your employer, it is nearly mealtime, and I have to pluck you from the street it seems," he explained jovially.

"I apologize," Maria replied. "Nadia and I were so busy discussing which new kerchief I should buy that I had not noticed we passed the door. But I assure you, I was straight on my way to work."

Dimitry placed his hands on his hips and raised one brow at her. "My best waitress, and she can't even find the door." He shook his head at her. "Are you sure that is all, my dear? You haven't taken much time off since _"

"I am fine, Domn[12] Dimitry," she quickly answered.

"Listen, Maria," Nadia said as she started to step away. "Come see me on your break. I'll be across at the pottery shop helping Jean get those bowls painted for that customer who wants everything done yesterday."

Maria smiled back at her in warm, knowing appreciation. "And if you get hungry, I'll be here serving customers who want tomorrow's menu today." Carrying her baby on her back, Nadia crossed the dirt street toward the pottery shop which shared walls with shops to its left and right, all covered with clay tiled roofs. Maria's countenance betrayed the pain she tried to hide as her brown eyes trailed Nadia walking away. Quickly she regained the cheery facade she kept ready and walked into the tavern with Dimitry.

Prince Dracula, dressed in his finest blue linen trousers, white silk shirt, and elaborately embroidered felt cojoc, sat at the table in the bright hall with his distinguished guest, Stephen Bathory, the prince of Moldavia. Stephen the Great, as some called him, was a bit shorter in stature than Vlad but possessed an equally regal air. His rusty red hair encircled his head with loose curls that were cut shorter than his cousin Vlad's. His hazel eyes were bright and a cordial smile peeked between his burnished goatee and mustache as he greeted his fellow prince.

An immaculately attired servant poured a swallow of wine into Vlad's goblet for his inspection. The prince shot him a commanding gaze and the servant took a sip from the chalice. As he suffered no ill effects, he set the wine before Vlad. Having sampled the vintage, he nodded in satisfaction, and their cups were filled. "I would like to thank you once again for the marvelous support you have given me, especially for your recommending

---

[12] Domn - Romanian for mister

me to King Matthias. Without your vote of confidence it would be doubtful that I would have ever regained my throne. To the Prince of Moldavia," Dracula said, raising his goblet to salute his guest.

"Thank you for your kind words, Vlad, but it is I who owe you a debt of gratitude.

Most assuredly you saved both my person and my army when you went out of your way to assist me at the Oituz Pass against the Turks," Stephen declared as he raised his own chalice to his host. "To Prince Dracula. May his name be long remembered in the land." Both princes sipped their costly, imported Italian wine.

"You are most gracious, dear Stephen, but you know me - any excuse will do to kill Turks," he smiled darkly. "Nevertheless, I remain grateful and loyal to my cousin, the prince of Moldavia."

"Then we are even," Stephen concluded with a courtly smile.

"One thing concerns me, however," Vlad said with grave sincerity after swallowing a portion of his roast mutton.

"Pray tell what that may be," Stephen responded with a burdened expression.

"King Matthias has recalled the troops he gave me to command against the Turks and to chase out Basarab. I am now left with a mere 2,000 Romanian soldiers to defend the border. I know Sultan Mehemmed - his hunting escort is larger than that! The western powers are so ignorant and thoughtless when it comes to the Ottoman hordes. They round up their band of crusaders and send them east to kill Turks. They sack a city or two and then return to the safety and comfort of their homes while we are left to endure the retaliatory wrath of the infidels. Why, the western crusaders do more harm than good! They are like a child throwing rocks at a hornets' nest. And who gets stung?"

"We do," his ally answered. "I agree totally with you, Vlad. Holding the line of Islam has fallen to us, whether we like it or not. Whatever was King Matthias thinking to recall his troops like that?"

"Oh, something about needing them on the border with Albania. But my friend, this leaves me very short handed at a crucial time with winter moving in."

Stephen set down his cup and stroked his slender beard thoughtfully. "I'll tell you what I can do. I am traveling with my personal guard of two hundred loyal and well-trained soldiers. I can lend them to you to guard your person should the Turks advance against you. In the meantime, I suggest you begin conscripting some new recruits. I know winter is a bad time to have to feed an army, but it is almost certain the Turks will make a move in the spring."

"I believe you are right. It seems they cannot rest for want of new territory to conquer. I just hope Matthias changes his mind. He must realize that if Walachia falls, Hungary will not be far behind." Then Vlad's eyes brightened at his ally. "Thank you so much, Stephen, for the use of your guards; hopefully they will not be needed, but again you have done me an invaluable service."

"Not at all. Protecting Walachia also protects Moldavia."

After the meal, Prince Dracula offered Stephen an invitation. His jade eyes took on a surreal quality not present earlier in the conversation. "Tomorrow morning I have planned an execution that should be a welcome diversion from these more serious matters of state. Impaling can be quite entertaining, you know - how the little beggars dance on their stakes!"

"I am sorry, Vlad, but I fear I must decline your offer. I have been away too long already and must leave for Sibiu this afternoon before the snows begin. I cannot neglect my new governorship in Transylvania. Perhaps on another occasion," Stephen declined graciously. Prince Bathory considered Dracula to be a competent ruler and an extraordinary military leader. The alliance he had formed was in the best interest of his own principality's security, for there was no man alive better to pit against the Turks than Vlad the Impaler. Whatever bizarre personal idiosyncrasies he possessed would have to be overlooked for the greater good of Moldavia, but Stephen himself had no wish to witness one of Dracula's detestable impalements.

"Then let us make an eternal pledge of allegiance between the two of us. Friends, kinsmen, and allies, may we never fail to come to one another's aid in time of need," Vlad proposed as he rose from the table.

Stephen Bathory stood to his feet and took a step to clasp arms with his cousin, Vlad. "Let it be so," he agreed with a nod.

On Sunday morning Vlad set out to descend the 1,400 steps to the road at the base of his foreboding fortress. The stables, coach house, and blacksmith's were situated there alongside a small grassy area that had been cleared originally for the horses to graze on. That day it served as the canvas on which Dracula had painted his morbid art. Petru was obligated to follow the prince and to serve him at table while he took his morning meal. But the ever-ready valet had taken precautions for the morning's event. He had prepared a lard-based ointment with crushed mint leaves which he rubbed into his mustache and on his nose to hide the smell. Knowing that he would be posted to the prince's right, he melted wax into his right ear to block out the pitiful cries and screams of the victims while leaving his left one open to hear Vlad's instructions. Then he counted on his poor eye-sight to preserve him from the grotesque visual details of the impalings.

In keeping with the tradition of the Order of the Dragon, the Catholic military order that his father, Vlad Dracul, had first joined, Dracula wore his crimson suit and high-collared black cape on this, the first day of the week. The hems of his trousers were tucked into his polished black boots, and he wore his favorite matching headpiece. The red velvet cap which came to a soft point had a wide black band around its base that was studded with rows of silver beads. In front, looking most impressive as it pointed between his brows, was an eight-point star of gold with a large, square ruby in its center. Eight white pearls surrounded the sparkling ruby, and the ornate golden star held a unique grayish-white plume in place. Its rounded pentacle stood just higher than the rest of his hat.[13] His long, black sausage curls trailed out from under the crimson cap and bounced down his back as they descended the steps.

"I feel winter coming on," Vlad commented to Petru as he observed the dark sky and felt a chilling wind.

"Yes, milord," Petru agreed as he carefully placed his footsteps on the narrow walkway. "The castle forecaster has predicted an imminent snow storm."

"Ah," he said with a sigh. "If only 'twould start this morning! What a lovely touch to my creation to have the white of falling snow lighting upon the writhing bodies. And it would so bring out the red of their blood."

Petru felt himself chilled to the bone at his master's words. Had he known back in Hungary what a sick and depraved mind possessed the

---

[13] The famous portrait of Dracula wearing this outfit now hangs in the Monster Gallery at Castle Ambras in Tyrol.

prince, he would have refused King Matthias's request that he accompany Dracula. But being a prudent man who preferred life to tortuous destruction, and fully intending to return to the court at Buda one day, Petru said nothing to Vlad about the matter.

The table was prepared when they arrived at the clearing, and two of the cook's attendants stood guard over the food. Dense forests of bare, lifeless trees stood against the rock face of the cliffs in the Carpathian Mountains that provided the back drop to Poenari. To look up at the fortress from this location gave the impression that the gray stones and round towers had erupted forth from the bowels of the earth and now pierced the clouds like one of Dracula's impaling spikes.

Once the prince was seated, one of the servants lifted the silver lid from his plate, displaying a scrumptious assortment of delicacies. After taking his first bite, Vlad looked up at those slowly dying before his eyes. The ones he had spoken with - Costi, the merchant and the adulterous woman - were impaled nearest his table and the boy, Jan, stood nearby, his hands tied behind his back, with the armas beside him. Moans of pain and desperate, agonizing cries arose from his victims frequently. Some begged for mercy, but none dared curse their antagonist, lest their deaths be made to drag on for weeks.

"Sergei," Vlad raised a silver chalice, and his chief executioner made haste to his master's table. As Vlad's long, slender fingers placed the cup into Sergei's rough hand, he spoke with a gleam in his eyes. "Fill this for us, and we will sop bread together from it."

The trusted servant gladly took the cup, brimming with pride that he was invited to share such intimacy with his prince. Then he walked over to the pitiful, writhing bodies of the criminals, slowly pacing before them, eyeing each as a prospective buyer would eye a leg of mutton. His boots stopped at the foot of Costi's pole and he slowly raised his dark eyes to the Transylvanian. Deliberately, he drew out a long silver blade, reached up to the man's thigh, and inflicted a deep cut to his artery. Costi cried out in pain, flailing his limbs about as his face paled, but Sergei raised the ornate chalice and filled it with the flow of the merchant's blood. When it was nearly full, he removed the cup and brought it back to his master, leaving a river of crimson gushing down the dying man's leg. His eyes met Vlad's as he set the vessel on the table.

"What are you doing?" cried Costi weakly.

Dracula broke a small loaf of bread and handed half to Sergei. They dipped their bread into the blood, soaking the loaf scarlet, and then partook of it together. For Dracula, this ritual was like his own dark Eucharist. Petru turned his attention away and chewed a bit of chickle to settle the bile he felt rising from the pit of his stomach.

As he often liked to do, Dracula spoke to his victims to see what reactions he could draw from them. "I trust you all enjoyed your last meal," he smiled in amusement. "I'm sure the poor fellow you ate wasn't too pleased, however." He smirked with wicked delight as he watched the sickening expressions spread over their faces. One of the women even began to gag and vomit at his statement. But when she moved to lean forward, the pike was driven farther into her body, piercing internal parts and creating trapped pools of blood. She cried out in agony, her face paling, pleading for death to come quickly.

"Yes," he continued to mentally torment them. "I wanted you all to know that you were cannibals before you died. Take that thought with you to meet God. Tell Him how you greedily devoured the flesh of another human being."

"The devil take you, Dracula!" one of the disgusted men cried out from his stake, his arms fluttered helplessly having nothing to grab hold of. "You deceived us - you gave us the meat to eat." His mouth twisted in torment as he spoke.

"Yes," he smiled darkly. "But I did not force you to partake of it. Could you not discern that it did not taste of mutton or pork? Did you not wonder what it was?"

Petru summoned all of his internal fortitude to keep himself from becoming physically ill on the spot. He had taken all necessary precautions, but the episode was proving to be more hideous and repulsive than he had ever imagined.

"My lord, what of this one?" the armas asked, nodding toward the boy.

"Ah, yes, the honest little thief. Bring him forward. I promised him a swift and painless death," Vlad said pleasantly and took another bite from his meal.

Jan trembled as he walked. He was afraid of dying and afraid of the big man with the ax. What if his aim was off? What if the first blow did not kill him? Would the prince change his mind and spare his life?

"On your knees," Sergei commanded once Jan stood in front of Vlad's table. With shaky, shallow breaths, and eyes wide with fright, he dropped to his knees and quivered.

"Boy," Vlad addressed him. "Do you think you will go to Heaven?"

"Only God knows, my prince, but I do hope to," he answered in a wavering, high pitched voice. He swallowed the lump from his throat while goose-bumps from both the cold and his fear ran up and down his arms and legs.

"If you do, would you mention to God how I had mercy on you today?"

"Y-yes," he answered through chattering teeth.

Prince Dracula smiled at him. "Very good." Then he gave the armas a nod. The big man pushed Jan's head down into place and told him not to move. Petru closed his eyes as the ax came down with a powerful, accurate blow. But Vlad watched, transfixed by some perverted fascination as the boy's head rolled away and a river of blood spurted forth from the stump. Then the limp body fell over on its side and continued to drain its crimson lifeblood onto the cold, amber ground.

Even as a very small boy in Transylvania, Vlad would climb up to a certain window in the palace so that he could look out and see the criminals hang. The thought of snuffing out the life of a person had always fascinated him. As an adult, he had found it to be a pathway to power. He fed on that power - the power over life and death, the power to terrorize both the helpless and the mighty. Whenever he killed someone, whether he did it himself or ordered it, Dracula experienced a surge of chemical energy through his body, creating a euphoric high that most normal men felt when engaged in a totally different activity. Perhaps he believed that the energy and power of his victim's life-force was transferred to him. Nevertheless, Dracula was able to rationalize all his executions. After all, these were criminals, and crime must be punished to its fullest extent. And others? Enemies both of the crown and of the state. They must die, as well as foreigners, beggars, the homeless, crippled, and sickly. They were parasites on the land, only taking while contributing nothing. They, too, deserved to die, so Vlad rationalized.

One of the men tied to a stake on a stack of wood in the midst of the geometric design of poles suddenly cried out in anger and bitterness. "Only a monster would kill a child!"

The prince looked up from his meal somberly to see who had spoken. "The wind is chilly," he said dryly. "I think it is time to light our fires." Then Sergei took the torch from its holder and walked to the stake in the center of the moaning, whimpering assembly.

"I may burn now, but you will burn forever!" the frantic, enraged man shouted as he instinctively tugged at his bindings.

Vlad's emerald eyes darkened at the man as he commanded through clenched teeth, "Light it." An icy wind blew across the meadow catching the tiny flame to send it racing through the dry kindling.

"You will burn in hell forever, you bloody bastard, you devil you!" Sergei stepped back and watched as the condemned man was consumed in a swirl of flame, smoke, and screams.

Chapter 5

The Dandar

"Remember well who started having people impaled."

from a document dating from the reign of Basarab cel Tanar, 1477-1481

The shutters were closed tight against the winter snowstorm while an inviting fire blazed in the hearth at Dimitry's tavern that night. Wooden tables and chairs, each centered with its own lamp, were arranged in the great room. Guests of the inn and people from the town had huddled inside the safety of the warm hall to eat a meal or have a drink. The patrons consisted of a wiry man with gray tufted hair and beard seated beside a plump woman with wrinkled face and a wool cap, several young men telling stories over their ale, a traveling family seated near the hearth feeding their children dinner, a spindly old woman with a plain marama drawn over her head, and a few craftsmen from town who had met to drink and play cards. Teo, the middle-aged helper, swept the floor.

A garland of garlic hung over the inside of the tavern door to ward off evil spirits that might wish to enter, and several crosses and crucifixes adorned the walls. It was generally accepted that people did not go out after dark - especially on a night like this. The mysterious forests were said to be filled with ravenous wolves and the werewolves who passed among them. Tales were told of the strigoi[14] who drifted among the barren trees with the mist. Likewise, village folklore conjured up the pale, living dead creature who stalked the earth in search of blood - the vampire. Most feared was the evil being, nosferatu, who could take on many forms and always brought death. The more sophisticated minds knew these stories stemmed from the dread and incomprehension of the Black Death. For the common peasants of the village, it was better to be prepared.

Maria was waiting tables that night. Before Georgi died, Dimitry only employed her on the day shift so that she could spend the evenings with

---

[14] strigoi - Romanian for ghost or phantom

her son, but recently she had preferred to work nights. The little cottage that once served as a home for three seemed very empty when she was there alone. Maria had even considered selling the cottage to rent a permanent room at the inn, but Nadia had talked her out of it. "You cannot sell the cottage, Maria; it is all you have," she had argued. "With it at least you can offer a man a private home when he is ready to move out of the crowded house of his parents. But without it, you are without any property at all to attract a marriage."

However Maria was of no mind to attract another marriage. She was not desperate nor destitute. She had good employment and could make her own way without a man. She had done what was expected of her and still had no husband or son to keep her company at night. She had determined long ago that if she ever married again, it would not be to meet a social obligation, for convenience or comfort, and not even for mere companionship. Maria determined that if ever she would marry again, it would be for love.

"One more round before we head home," called one of the young men at their table.

Dimitry nodded. "Maria," he called.

"Right away," she replied and began to fill their mugs with ale from the tap.

Dimitry smiled at her as she worked. "There is a room upstairs for you tonight," he said matter-of- factly. "I do not want you walking home in this viscol.[15]"

"Thank you most kindly, Domn Dimitry," she replied pleasantly as she started across the room to deliver the ale to the young patrons.

Then the gray-haired, bearded man spoke. "Tis a very wicked night out there. Only a fool would go out in this storm." Just then the wind whistled eerily through a crack in the closed shutter.

"A mere palisade will not keep out the ravenous wolves," added the plump woman beside him.

Then wide eyed, the old woman wrapped in her marama gave her warning. "Not to mention the strigoi, vampires, and spirits of the dead who are driven from their hiding places on windy, snowy nights such as this. In my lifetime many who ventured out on such a night were never heard from again."

---

[15] viscol - a snowstorm or blizzard

"Tales to frighten the superstitious," Dimitry dismissed her words. "There are no ghosts or vampires. If people disappeared in a snowstorm, they no doubt fell from their horses, were covered over by snow, and froze to death. Then the hungry wolves would drag them away. It is all logical and scientific." Dimitry prided himself on being a man of the world, a knowledgeable, feet-on-the-ground, there's-a-reason-for-everything, Romanian Renaissance man. After all, he could read and cipher well enough to keep his own ledgers and run the inn, but even he would not lay claim to being a well-read man. Nonetheless, with the exception of the doctors, bankers, and merchants, he was the most educated, scientific gentleman in Curtea de Arges.

The old woman raised a brow at him and pursed her lips. "I suppose that is why you hang garlic over your door."

"Oh, that," Dimitry said casually with a wave of his hand. "It is for ambiance and to please the patrons. In addition, the strong aroma is good for covering smelly travelers' sweat or the scent of wet wool."

As Dimitry stood behind his bar wiping it down in preparation for closing time, the tavern door opened and a frigid, snowy blast swept through the room. In the doorway stood a very distinguished looking dandar.[16] From the look of his dress he was Hungarian. His cream-colored gatyak[17] trousers had very wide legs that hung in pleats below his knees and past the top of his wet, black boots. His matching wide-sleeved shirt had an elaborately embroidered collar, cuffs, and front piece. The distinctively Hungarian szur overcoat with wide lapels was fastened across his chest by a leather strap and buckle. The traveler did not wear his arms inside the wide sleeves, but rather draped the coat around his shoulders like a cape. A gluga[18] of swirling gray, black, and white fur - probably that of a wolf - protected his head from the cold.

Although his suit was distinctively Hungarian, the thirty-something year old man's appearance was more Saxon. His ivory skin contrasted with rosy cheeks reddened by the cold. His lower lips showed some chapping where they met his light brown mustache and chin beard variegated with sundry hairs of blonde, brown, and rust. Sandy-colored

---

[16] dandar - Romanian for a foreign man

[17] gatyak - very wide legged trousers with a wide decorative belt worn in 15th century Hungary

[18] gluga - warm fur hat worn in bad weather

hair covered his ears and neck from beneath the fur gluga but did not reach his shoulders. His dark blue eyes and aristocratic poise made the stranger even more distinguished looking.

He spoke very good Romanian, tinged with a Hungarian accent, and a lofty yet gentile and polite tone. "I say, but what a blustery night we are having, gentlemen. Is the fine owner of this establishment present?" He raised his brows as his blue eyes scanned the room curiously.

"Here I am. Dimitry's the name. Do you think you might close the door?"

"But certainly," the stranger answered cordially and took a step in pushing the door closed behind him. "I wonder if you might have a room available and a stable for my horse."

"I surely do," Dimitry replied. "Not many people out on a night like this. Teo," he called. "See to the gentleman's horse."

Teo set the broom aside and quietly walked toward the door. "She is the murg[19] - a fine Sckweiken. Big girl, comes from the finest breeders in Szeged."

Teo glanced at the traveler as he passed him. They were about the same height, but the foreigner seemed to have broader shoulders, unless it was an illusion created by the great coat. Teo pulled up the collar of his coat before exiting the door into the snowstorm.

"Allow me to introduce myself," the traveler said with a grand gesture. "I am Stefan Kubana of Szeged, and I would like a room for several nights, a hot meal, and a warm brandy if you please."

Stefan strode in and surveyed the tavern. It took him only a moment to notice Maria. Dimitry answered with a grin, "The room and the lamb pie I can do for you, but brandy? My man, this is a tavern, not a bloody palace! We have wine and ale."

"Oh, yes," he answered stoutly. "I see. Very well, then. I shall have a chalice of Burgundy, '45," he said with a flare.

Disgruntled, Dimitry eyed the wealthy traveler. "We have Romanian table wine and plain ale, my good fellow. Take your pick."

"I do beg your pardon, Domn Innkeeper," Stefan replied as he began to pull off his tan calfskin gloves. "I am not knowledgeable as to the beverage selections at village taverns. Table wine will do nicely, I am sure."

---

[19] murg - a dark bay horse

Dimitry poured the new red wine into a plain chalice with an amused shaking of his head. "And what in Heaven's name, Domn Stefan, brings you to our town in the midst of this dreadful snowstorm?"

Maria carried the cup of wine to an empty table and motioned questioningly at the fair traveler. He smiled, nodded to her politely, and took a seat at the table. "I have business with the prince," he answered cheerfully, and then he sampled his wine.

Maria immediately scowled at him with displeasure. People around the tavern began to mumble and whisper among themselves. "Dracula," Stefan heard one say in a hushed tone.

Dimitry spoke as casually as possible. "That will be five ducats - in advance if you please."

"But of course," Stefan answered with reservation as he placed the coins on the table.

"The Impaler," whispered another. Stefan looked around to see fearful looks on the other patron's faces as they shook their heads.

"The son of the devil," he heard the old woman say with spooky wide eyes.

Stefan's chin bunched up and his brows came down. "What is all of this murmuring and speaking of the devil. I said I have business with Prince Vlad."

"Dracula means 'son of the devil,'" the gray bearded man explained. "Even his name is evil."

"Or 'son of the dragon,'" one of the younger men added. "His father was called Dracul, the dragon."

"Beware of him," the old woman warned solemnly.

"You people see a demon behind every bush." Dimitry discounted their fears as unfounded. "Prince Dracula is a hero; he saved us from the Turks."

Then Maria spoke up in a most serious tone. "And who will save us from him?"

"*Maria.*" Dimitry looked at her in warning to keep quiet.

"I will see to your dinner now, domnule[20]," she said in an obligatory fashion and then proceeded toward the kitchen door. Stefan's eyes did not leave the tavern server as she crossed the room. He was drawn to the way her full, hour-glass figure was molded into her skirt and blouse. He

---

[20] domnule - Romanian for sir

44

noticed the ease with which she gracefully glided across the wood planked floor. The corners of his mouth turned up slightly beneath his mustache as he studied her smooth featured face, dark eyes, and long, black hair.

"Do you need to be saved from your prince?" he asked almost absently as his eyes trailed Maria.

"He tortures and kills men, women, and children for pleasure," the old woman in the shawl accused.

"Dracula is hard on criminals," Dimitry explained, "but no law-abiding citizen need fear him."

"Have you ever met the prince before?" asked the plump woman in curiosity.

"Only once," Stefan replied in his stately voice. "Briefly, and it was long ago." He raised his cup of wine to his lips and sipped gingerly.

"Then there are certain matters of protocol that you should know," she said with concern.

"Protocol, do you say?" Stefan repeated with interest as he set down the goblet.

The family who had been eating by the hearth began to stir. The father decided that if people were going to start telling Dracula stories, he had better take his wife and children upstairs so they would not become unduly frightened. "Dimitry, all was more than satisfactory," he said placing a few coins on the table. "It is late and we shall retire for the evening. If the weather breaks, we will depart on the morrow."

"Very well," Dimitry smiled as he ambled over to collect Stefan's money and theirs. "Sleep well." The father led the way while his wife herded the children toward the staircase, carrying the smallest, sleepy one.

The men who had been playing cards quit their game, apparently finding Vlad stories better entertainment. The oldest craftsman in the group spoke first. "Be sure to remove your hat in the prince's presence, lest he nail it to your head."

"Good Heavens!" Stefan laughed as though it were a joke.

"Tis no laughing matter," the lean, gray bearded man scolded him. "It has happened on several occasions to Turkish ambassadors and to visiting diplomats from Italy as well."

Stefan's face began to sober and he quietly took another sip from his chalice. About that time Maria returned with his dish of lamb pie. "Your dinner, domnule," she said indifferently as she set the plate before him.

She eyed the stranger warily. He was handsome enough, she supposed, and polite, clean, and well groomed. *Too much of a dandy*, she thought. *Business with the prince - I have business with that butcher!*

"Thank you very kindly," he said with great vocal inflections. "And this is for your services," he added handing her several silver coins.

Maria's eyes became as round as saucers when she saw how much he had tipped her. "I beg your pardon, domnule, but I do not provide *that* kind of service!" she exclaimed incredulously.

"Whatever do you mean?" Stefan replied quite innocently as he broke open the crust of his lamb pie. "You brought my wine and this fine meal. Do you not accept gratuities in this establishment?"

"Yes," she answered, still a bit uncertain of him. "But they are generally not this much. You are obviously a wealthy man, and a generous one. I do thank you."

"Think nothing of it," he said casually, and he took a dainty forkful of meat and potato and carefully placed it in his mouth. "Ummm," he sighed, closing his eyes in bliss. "What a delectable pie. Just the right amount of pepper, and the gravy, which many cooks get wrong, is indeed divine. Maria, won't you have a seat and join me at the table? These fine people are advising me on protocol."

Dimitry nodded at her. "Take a break. We are almost ready to close." Maria hesitantly took a chair at the table, but out of Stefan's reach. "I noticed that you travel without a woman," Dimitry addressed Stefan. "Are you married?"

"Indeed not!" Stefan exclaimed with a little chuckle as if it were the last thing he would want. "I am a bachelor."

"Then be careful not to be looking too closely at our women," another of the craftsmen warned. "Prince Vlad is very strict in the area of sexual morality. Even fornication is punishable -"

"No, let me guess," Stefan interrupted with a light, amused expression. "By impalement, no doubt?" He daintily blotted the corners of his mouth with a monogrammed handkerchief and wiped moist drops from his mustache.

"It is no laughing matter," Dimitry loudly warned with an almost angry tone. He stopped polishing the glasses and loudly slapped the rag down on the bar. He placed both fists on his hips and raised his voice to the Hungarian. "I have seen the way you have been looking at Maria ever since you walked in here, and I will not have her hanging in the public square because of you."

Suddenly it was as though a wet blanket had been thrown over Stefan. "My God, you are serious!" he exclaimed as he gave the inn keeper a long, searching look.

"Any excuse will do for Dracula to enjoy his favorite past time," Maria uttered sourly, her eyes fixed on a blank spot on the table.

Stefan swallowed a lump in his throat. His voice squeaked as he asked, "Now, what is this protocol I should be most careful about?"

"The hats, of course," answered the oldest craftsman. "And you should not be too presumptuous."

"Flattery and being most agreeable will help," the plump woman added.

"But you must always be sincere," urged the tawny old man. "Above all, Dracula detests lying and liars. Poor Teo, there, had his tongue cut out for lying." He motioned toward the tavern worker who had slipped back in from the kitchen after stabling Stefan's bay mare. It was easy to overlook the quiet, unassuming man, for whom silence was not a choice but a fact of life. A gray cap covered his lank, brown hair, and his homespun wool clothing blended in everywhere. He was neither tall nor short, heavy nor thin. His features were average in every way, and he never made any noise. Because he could not speak, people overlooked the fact that he could still hear and that his bright eyes caught everything that happened around him.

"Dracula must have been in a good mood that day," the old woman in the back declared. "Usually it is the impaling stake for lying. Unless he burns you or boils you alive," she mused thinking back over the years.

"Burning?" questioned Stefan as he held a bite of pie on his fork. "Boiling alive?" His eyes widened and his face took on a greenish hue as he plead, "I would so much like to be able to finish this fine meal if you don't mind."

"You want to know what to expect don't you?" asked one of the young men who had just drained the last of his ale. "Thanks, Dimitry, but we should be heading on before my mother becomes too worried."

"Good evening, boys." He waved to them as the quartet headed out the door.

"Brrr!" The plump woman who sat near the entry shivered as the cold wind whipped over her. "Are you an ambassador?"

"No," replied Stefan as he tried to resume eating his meal.

"That is good," she sighed. "I remember back in '56, wasn't it Andei?" she peered at the gray bearded man across from her. He shrugged and she went on, "Fifty or more ambassadors from all over - Hungary, Saxony, Transylvania and the like, were all arrested. The prince suspected them of treachery and when he had frightened them enough, he had them all impaled."

"Good Heavens, doamna! Impaled for suspicion?"

"Now you know those foreigners were up to something," Dimitry replied. "Very few of our citizens have ever been harmed by the prince."

"Unless they were poor or Gypsies or Saxon or under suspicion or in the wrong place at the wrong time or of the wrong religion or -"

Maria was interrupted by Dimitry's stern voice and warning glare. "Maria, that will be enough!"

Stefan's eyes glanced over at her where she sat with her eyes cast on her folded hands. His gaze was soft and compassionate as if he could sense very deep wounds beneath the beauty he beheld.

Then the leather craftsman spoke out catching Stefan's attention once more. "It is said that he likes to play games of words with his guests. If they answer correctly, all is well. If not, they may be tortured and killed."

"Oh," Andei added as he remembered something else. Stefan turned his head to the gray bearded man. "If he does invite you to an impaling - which he may - never, never voice a complaint about the sights or smell. Once a nobleman who visited the prince accompanied him to an impaling. When he complained of the stench, Dracula obliged him by having a very high stake brought out so that he may be impaled above the bad odors below."

"We've all heard the story," said the carpenter. "But no one is sure if that is how it really happened."

"These things have indeed happened in our own country," said the wrinkled old woman in the marama. "Priests and peasants, women and children, boyar and commoner, foreigner and friend have all been pierced with a bloody spear, tortured, burned, chopped into pieces, mutilated and deprived of their sex organs, boiled alive, buried alive, skinned, filleted, and even more unspeakable horrors have been done to them while the great devil watches, licking his blood thirsty lips in delight. He is inhuman, the nosferatu. For if he is human, then the rest of us most certainly are not."

A hush fell over the hall at the conviction of her words. Even Dimitry did not dispute her. Stefan patted his mouth with his handkerchief once more and turned his face back toward Maria. "Maria," he addressed her. "I have not yet heard your opinion or advice."

She eyed the dandar suspiciously and replied, "I believe Dimitry would prefer I not voice an opinion in front of the present company."

Stefan puzzled for a moment, then his eyes lit up, and an amused smile crossed his face. "Do you think I am a spy? Sent to you by Vlad?" She did not respond, only lowered her gaze. "Saints be strong! You think that since the prince has just returned from many years in Hungary and I am Hungarian and on my way to see him that I am to spy out which of his subjects are loyal and which are not?" Stefan leaned back his head and let out a hearty belly laugh.

All eyes were on him as they waited for him to answer his own question. "My goodness, no! Please, Maria, kind gentlemen, let me put your minds at ease. I am a merchant from the city of Szeged, and I represent a guild of merchants who specialize in Far Eastern merchandise. I have come to secure a new trade agreement with Prince Dracula - that is all," he said innocently. "Being a gentleman of commerce, I am not capable of harming a single hair on your heads. Nor does it matter one bit to me whether you loathe or love your prince."

A few of the patrons began whispering among themselves while Dimitry, who had resumed polishing the glasses, began to sing a little doina.[21] "Fare-thee-well, my friend, fare-thee-well."

An ironic smile started to cross Maria's face as she raised her eyes to Stefan. The laughter faded from his face as he observed the people's reaction. "What is the matter now?" He took one more bite of his dinner while awaiting an answer.

Maria replied, "Only that the last time a group of Hungarian merchants came to trade in Walachia, Vlad confiscated their money and goods and had them all impaled."

All at once Stefan spewed the food back into his dish and pounded his chest a few times with his fist while coughing particles from his throat and

---

[21] doina - Romanian word for "popular song"

49

lungs. His face had paled, and his eyes were round as full moons. With one hand he pulled out his handkerchief and with the other raised the wine to take a sip. After properly patting his mouth, Stefan questioned horrifically, "Impaled for what? Being merchants?"

No one laughed, though under other circumstances the episode may have been funny. "No," answered the oldest craftsman. "For being *foreign* merchants."

A visible shudder ran through Stefan as he deliberately set down his empty cup. He let out a long breath of air and stared blankly ahead. Dimitry felt he must say something to calm the delicate gentleman before he fainted. "But Stefan, that was long ago," he explained. "I am sure that you are in no danger."

At that very moment the tavern door flew open with a loud bang and everyone inside jumped in surprise. A frigid blast blew snow onto the wooden floor, and all eyes turned to the entryway. Then a large, dark figure wrapped in a black cape stepped in. "I have come for Stefan Kubana, Merchant of Szeged. Prince Dracula demands your presence at Poenari Castle *now*."

Chapter 6

Captain of the Guard

"And then the merchants and their entourage went with their goods from Tara Barsei to Braila on the Danube; there were 600 of them. Dracula captured and impaled all of them on stakes, and took their goods by force."

From the German Pamphlet, "About a mischievous Tyrant called Dracul voda," 1460's

For a moment no one stirred or made a sound. After the conversation that had just taken place, the men and women in the hall were all stricken with a chilling possibility - their new acquaintance was doomed.

Stefan looked up at the big man in the doorway as the color drained from his face. He was a soldier clad in a steel breastplate and wrapped about by a black cape. His indigo trousers were tucked into his wet, black boots, and a sheathed sword hung from his belt. A military hat with gold insignia was perched atop his trimmed hair of black and gray with white along his sideburns and over his ears. He was tall and broad shouldered, obviously older than Stefan, and apparently of an important position. A stern look was etched into his stone face, and his eyes focused on the Hungarian.

Stefan swallowed hard and blinked his eyes. "I am he," he eked out.

"Come," the soldier commanded in a deep voice. "You have an appointment to keep."

Stefan innocently explained. "I am terribly sorry for any inconvenience, but the weather slowed my travel and because of the lateness of the hour, I stopped in here. I thought to ride on to Poenari in the morning at first light."

The soldier growled at him as if he addressed an inferior being. "Dracula is not concerned about a little snow or darkness. You needn't fear the night; I will escort you. Do you have a horse?" But it was not the night Stefan feared at that moment.

"Y-yes." The genteel merchant turned his eyes questioningly toward Dimitry who wore an expression of grave concern.

"The stables are around back. You'll have no trouble finding your horse," he said.

Stefan gave him a nod of acknowledgment then turned his eyes to Maria. She was sorry she had laughed about the murdered merchants. It just seemed so improbable that it would happen again and that very night. Her face was haunted by the images that ran rampant through her mind. He was a stranger, a man she did not even particularly like. But the thought that he might suffer some horrible fate at the hands of the tyrant she despised drew her heart to him with a kindred bond. A few minutes ago she could have cared less if she ever saw him again, and now she was afraid she would not. But in the instant that their eyes locked she saw something different in him. His gaze seemed to sear straight through her as if he was an omnipotent being. Strength and confidence permeated his deep blue eyes which radiated at her with a power that took Maria completely by surprise. That surprise registered on her face and she was not sure whether she should be more alarmed or relieved by what she saw in him.

In the time required to take in and let out a breath, Stefan moved his eyes from Maria to the waiting soldier. As if a mask had been removed or replaced, Stefan returned to his usual fanciful demeanor. "Very well, then," he responded, his voice now trembling as all of that momentary strength disintegrated. He stood to his feet and began to pull on his gloves. Glancing back to Dimitry, he made his farewells. "Dimitry, the dinner was quite enjoyable, but it appears I will not be requiring that room tonight after all. However, I request that you reserve it for me in case I might be needing it tomorrow."

"The room has been paid for - it will be there," Dimitry assured him hopefully.

"Thank you most kindly." Stefan took a few tentative steps toward the door then looked back over his shoulder. "Gentlemen, ladies, Maria." He motioned with a nod and a slight bow. "I bid you all a good evening."

Maria felt her stomach in her throat. She wanted to say something to him, but no words could be found. She puzzled about the look he had given her and how uncharacteristic it was of the polite merchant. Perhaps he really was a spy, and that is why he was not really afraid. But maybe the wealthy bachelor truly was attracted to her and wanted to somehow make his feelings known before meeting his demise. While she silently pondered these things, Stefan, followed by the big soldier, exited the tavern, the door slamming shut behind them in finality.

Once they had started on their way, horses trotting along the snow covered road, Stefan tried to strike up a conversation. "Domnule, I'm afraid we have not been properly introduced," he said cheerfully. Peering through the darkness he could barely make out the figure riding at his side. The snow was still falling but the wind had died down a bit. After a moment with no response, Stefan tried again. "In whose company do I have the pleasure of riding this evening?"

The big soldier was not in a mood to be sociable, but he realized the merchant would not simply give up. "I am Ivan, Captain of the garrison at Poenari Fortress," he finally answered gruffly.

"Captain of the garrison?" Stefan puzzled. "An awfully important man to be sent after such an insignificant fellow as myself."

"Not at all. Prince Dracula is most concerned with the matter of foreign trade."

"I am glad to hear that," Stefan replied with optimism. "How far is it to the castle? I am not complaining, Ivan, but a gentleman such as myself is not accustomed to being out in the elements like this."

"Not far," Ivan said brusquely then turned narrowed brows toward his charge. "You talk too much."

"My apologies, Captain," Stefan said in a defensive tone. "I was only trying to be polite, but I shall bother you no further." He raised his chin, eyes set straight ahead with the look of one who had been offended.

Ivan snorted and scowled at Stefan. Then his callousness softened toward his companion. "Take no offense, merchant. The hour is late, and I enjoy riding in the snow storm no more than you. Let us make the best of the journey. Stay close to me; I would not want to arrive at Poenari without you."

"Of that I am quite sure," Stefan agreed. They continued on through the bleak night in silence.

An hour later, Stefan noticed some cottages and a few small buildings lining the road. "Are we there?" he asked, teeth chattering from the cold.

"Yes," Ivan answered, sounding much more pleasant than before. "This catun[22] helps support the castle and its garrison. You can't see them in the dark, but there is a blacksmith's, some clothiers, a stable, a butcher's shop, and the like." He pulled his steed to a halt and then said to Stefan, "We walk from here."

"Walk?" Stefan asked curiously.

"The horses cannot climb stairs," Ivan chuckled. "Off you go, Domn Dandy," and the captain dismounted his horse. Stefan followed the captain's instructions, and Ivan took his reins. "Wait here while I have the horses stabled."

By that time the snow had stopped falling, the clouds were beginning to break up, and the light of the moon illuminated the fortress on the high bluff. Stefan stared up at the brick and stone castle where it loomed over all the earth below it. He absently took a few steps out into the road to get a better view. The glow of the moonlight through the crack in the clouds on the snow-covered walls and towers gave Poenari a surreal appearance, more like a vision, a mirage, or a dream than an earthly structure. Stefan's heart rate and breathing accelerated as his deep blue eyes fixed on the castle in the sky, and he nervously swallowed the lump that rose in his throat. A shiver ran the length of his spine, and this time it was not from the cold.

"Why, Domn Stefan, you look like you've just seen a ghost!" Ivan exclaimed in surprise when he returned.

"Oh." Stefan cleared his throat. "It just looks like such a long climb."

"Fourteen hundred steps, to be precise." Ivan smiled at him in amusement. "But you will make it." Then the captain turned his eyes up to the castle. "Magnificent, isn't it?" He sighed with pride. "It is especially breathtaking the way the moonlight hits the snow. Prince Dracula knows how to pick his location, all right. This fortress is impenetrable. I remember when the ruins were rebuilt. I was a new recruit in those days - a mere plebeian foot-soldier. But I have been fortunate enough, and a skilled enough warrior, to have survived this long in my profession and risen to my present rank. It is quite an honor to hold command over the key fortress in my country."

"It must be indeed," Stefan responded ponderously. Then he turned his face toward the captain and regained his usual manner of speech. "I

---

[22] catun - a small village

have heard a story that Prince Dracula enslaved the young boyars of Walachia and forced them to build this castle. What a devilishly clever idea."

Immediately the admiring smile faded from Ivan's face as he recalled the event. "Yes," he said in a business-like fashion. "The peasants were well pleased and amused by Prince Dracula's choice of a labor force, and he gained much support within their ranks by the move."

"It would be quite an arduous march to get here," the capricious merchant noted. "I'd wager precious few of their kind would have made it here at all."

Ivan's face grew more pallid as he narrowed his dark brows and exhaled a puff of steam into the cold air. "I am told some did not survive the march." The entire incident was not one of which he was proud, but it had been his duty. Those days were long gone and he wished them to be forgotten.

"I heard the stragglers were stuck through the belly like fat pigs," Stefan said in an almost accusing manner. Ivan's eyes flashed at him angrily as he clenched his big fists tightly by his sides. "And whatever became of those young boyars when the castle was completed?"

The tension hung in the air more sharply than the cold and more pervasively than the black of the night. "How should I know?" he snapped. "I am a soldier. I have fought in many great battles and killed many pagan Turks who would invade our land. I have spent my life protecting wealthy dandies like you who wouldn't know a sword from a longbow. Because of me and others like me, you have known the privilege of being able to travel about trading your goods and collecting your money; otherwise, even Hungary would have fallen to our enemies. Today I command this garrison, but those many years ago I was only a peon who followed orders. Whatever did or did not happen here then was not my responsibility," he concluded defensively.

"My goodness, Captain! One might have thought I had accused you of wrong-doing," Stefan exclaimed with his characteristic flare. "I was merely inquiring as to how this impressive structure came into being. I did not intend to cause you any distress."

Ivan snorted. He could have sworn the merchant was accusing him of something. Or was it really his own conscience? In either case, he was now embarrassed by his outburst of emotion. "Come," he ordered taking

Stefan's arm. "We are keeping the prince waiting." As they began to climb, Ivan let Stefan go first so that he could catch him if he slipped. "Be careful of ice," he warned.

Stefan took careful steps, snow crunching beneath each one. About halfway up he stopped and pulled out his handkerchief to blot his face. He panted as if he had never climbed stairs in his life. "Why have you stopped?" Ivan scowled at him.

"Captain, I must catch my breath. My legs are aching as if they would fall off," he explained.

"A brief rest I suppose," the big soldier consented with a sigh. Stefan braced his hands above his knees as he bent forward panting heavily. After a few moments he straightened up a bit and leaned against the rock wall. A cold wind caught the side of the mountain, and Ivan pulled his cloak around his chest. "Let's move along, merchant. It's warm in the castle."

"Very well," he breathed. "As long as we can climb slowly."

Ivan shook his head at Stefan's frailty and set his left foot on the next step. As he pulled his weight up, the captain's foot suddenly slipped out from under him on an icy patch beneath the snow and his large frame tumbled to the left over a sheer drop. "Help!" he cried frantically as his fingertips caught the edge of the stone stairway.

Immediately Stefan turned, wide-eyed to see what the matter was. "My Heavens!" he exclaimed in dismay. "Where are you?"

"Down here!" Ivan strained. The big man raised his right leg and tried to find a foothold for his boot, but between the dark and the slick surface of the rock, none could be quickly found. Then he tried to look down and find a crack or crevice for his left foot.

"Hold on, Ivan, and quit flailing about," Stefan cautioned as he carefully knelt on the steps beside where the captain dangled. His frozen fingers did not have much to grip. The carved stone step slanted naturally toward the ravine, and years of being trod upon had smoothed any rough edges he might grasp. A frosty wind blasted against the bleak mountain, sending Ivan's black cloak into a swirl. Suddenly images of everything he had ever done whirled through his mind like the cape that flapped in the wind. Ivan raised a desperate gaze to Stefan, and when their eyes met, they both realized it was a life or death moment.

Ivan knew the Hungarian had been afraid of him ever since his arrival at the tavern. Perhaps he feared that he was being escorted to his execution. *Will he let me fall?* he thought. But beyond that, Ivan feared that such a weakling could not help him even if he tried. In fact, they might both plummet to their deaths on the rocks below.

Stefan's eyes seared through Ivan's in that moment the same way they had Maria's in the tavern. He discerned that Ivan was an honest and decent man, one who would not let him fall if the situation were reversed. He reached down with his left hand while bracing his right on the step and grabbed the captain's arm. "Hold on there, man. Take my arm."

"I'm too heavy for you," he bravely protested. "I shan't pull you off with me." Then he instantly realized the strength of the grip that held him. It was not at all what he expected, but he was glad to feel it. While still holding the step with one hand, he grabbed Stefan's arm with the other.

"I'm steady. Pull yourself up." Amazed and very much relieved, Ivan pulled up on Stefan's arm and re-gripped the step. Then he swung his right knee up onto the path below Stefan and scrambled onto the stone stairway. His heart pounded as he lifted his curious and grateful gaze to the merchant.

Stefan was plastered against the rock wall behind him as far from the ledge as he could get. He had already withdrawn his handkerchief and was fanning himself as if he would faint at any moment. "Captain, you frightened me half to death - I do not think I can take another step up this mountain!"

Ivan plopped down beside him with a dazed and dumbfounded expression. Stefan leaned out a bit and peered over the edge into the chasm below. "It looks like a long drop, my fine fellow. You could have been seriously injured had you fallen."

"Injured, my ass! I would have been dead!" Wide-eyed, the big soldier stared incredulously at the foppish merchant. "You saved my life. You are really quite strong - did you know that?"

"Oh, fiddlesticks," he replied waving his kerchief at Ivan before returning it to his pocket. "All I did was put my arm down. You pulled yourself up. Why, you must have the strength of an ox!"

"But, but -" Ivan stammered, still shaky from his near-death experience.

"It is simple science, my man. Don't you know about balance and counter weight? Momentum and mass? And there is the mathematics of the situation as well, not to mention the up draft that gave you a boost."

Ivan was more puzzled than ever. It was as if Stefan was suddenly speaking a foreign language. "Oh, I see…I think. Anyway, I'd like to thank you, Stefan, for saving my life; I will not forget it."

"Tut, tut. I am sure that a capable military man such as yourself was at no moment in need of being saved, but I am glad I could be of some assistance. I am a gentle fellow by nature and could not bear to see another human being harmed," Stefan explained modestly.

"Thanks just the same. You proved to have a cool head under pressure. Domn Kubana, I realize that this incident has frightened you, but we cannot spend the whole night out here on the face of this bluff. It is quite warm and safe in the castle if you would be so kind as to try and continue up the walkway."

Stefan sighed and looked up toward the mighty fortress. He could see candlelight from one of the tower windows. "Very well," he consented. "But you must promise not to fall over the side again. Anymore such excitement, and I am sure my heart will cease to beat."

Ivan let forth an amused smile. "I assure you, I will do my best," he promised and rose to his feet. He held out his hand to Stefan and helped him up.

The two proceeded cautiously until they reached the top. There stood a long draw bridge which crossed a deep ravine to the castle. "Hold onto the railings," Ivan advised, "and don't look down." He followed closely behind Stefan who could not resist the temptation to peer over the side.

"Good Lord!" he gasped and gripped the railing tighter. "Does it plunge to the very center of the earth?"

"No," Ivan chuckled. "Not that far. Best to keep moving with your eyes on the door." For some reason Ivan's memory flashed images from long ago onto his consciousness, remembrances of the young boyar slaves who plummeted to their deaths from those very cliffs so long ago. Sometimes their mangled, broken bodies had been found; other times they had been washed away by the river. He remembered Dracula's wife who had leapt to her death from the battlements when Radu's victory seemed imminent. Then as they neared the great door, he was drawn back into the present. "Open the door for your captain," he called. The sentry looked out from his window and upon spying Ivan, hurried to open the door.

"I was about to give up on you, Sir; didn't think you'd make it back tonight," commented the sentry as Ivan and his charge entered the castle gates.

"No reason to worry," Ivan assured his man. "All is well."

"The prince is in the main hall," the guard informed them.

"Thanks, soldier. Now close up that door and pull up the drawbridge for the night; then get some sleep."

"Right away; thank you, Captain!" he replied enthusiastically.

"This way," Ivan said as he escorted Stefan toward the fortress's living quarters. Ivan caught sight of Petru standing outside of Vlad's hall, which was a frame and stone two-story structure with a thatched roof that lay adjacent to the back wall of the castle. They could see light radiating from the windows and smoke rising from the chimney. "Ah, Petru," Ivan greeted, "we are here at last."

"About bloody time - I'm freezing out here," he replied impertinently. "I'll announce you at once." Petru opened the door for Stefan and Ivan and ushered them in. Immediately they both removed their hats. "My lord, Captain Ivan and the merchant Stefan Kubana have arrived."

The warm hall reflected the amber glow of the common brass hanging chandelier and the dying red embers in the fireplace. The yellow-tan plastered walls were adorned with several tapestries, a coat of arms bearing the image of a dragon, and portraits of Vlad and his father, Dracul. The room of about twenty by thirty feet had several sets of wooden tables and chairs where the prince and his guests could dine. But the presence that overpowered the hall that night was that of Dracula himself.

The enigmatic prince half sat, half leaned on the edge of a table trapping his black cloak under his crimson trousers. One black boot rested on the seat of a chair, and the other was planted firmly on the floor. Vlad held a golden jeweled Saracen dagger which he was polishing with a soft cloth. He studied the luster he had put upon the blade and the sparkle of the emerald, ruby, and sapphire that adorned it. At first he did not bother to turn his face towards Ivan and Stefan; he was aware of their presence. He spoke out loud as if it did not matter to whom he spoke.

"Beautiful, isn't it?" Dracula held up the blade. "Beautiful and deadly. It was a gift to me by Sultan Murad during my imprisonment in

Adrianople. I plan to use it to cut out the heart of his son Mehmed, the reigning sultan. Fitting, don't you think?"

At that moment, Prince Dracula turned his head toward the door slowly, casting his penetrating green eyes upon Stefan. Suddenly there was a stiffening chill in the air of the warm hall as it was overrun by tension. Vlad was studying Stefan - studying him the way a tiger might study his prey before deciding whether or not to pounce. "Thank you, Captain, for delivering the merchant. You are dismissed."

Ivan hesitated for a brief moment. This man had just saved his life; he could not simply leave him alone with the crazed despot. But neither was he prepared to commit treason and be himself impaled. He looked at Vlad and then at Stefan. *Perhaps all will be well,* he told himself. *Stefan hasn't done anything yet.*

"Yes, my prince," he bowed clicking his boot heels together. Ivan exited the hall into the snow-covered castle yard. After the momentary warmth of the room, the night felt colder than ever. Concern weighed heavy on the big man as he trudged back to his quarters, a small, private cell along the wall near the tower barracks. He genuinely hoped the merchant would be safe. *At times like this I despise myself,* he thought reflectively, *but there is nothing I can do.*

"Petru, you may leave us also," Vlad said as his eyes once again were drawn to the shine of his jeweled knife.

"Yes, my lord," he dutifully responded with a bow. "Will you be requiring my services anymore this evening?"

"No," he mused slowly, drawing the word like an arrow on a bow. "You may attend me in the morning."

"Very well. Good evening, Prince Dracula, Domn Kubana." Petru turned and exited through an interior hall door that led to his chamber.

Stefan was fully aware that he had been left alone in the room with the very same brutal impaler who had been the subject of all the stories told at the tavern earlier that evening. Was the prince simply a stern but fair ruler who did good as well as punish like Dimitry had said, or was he the non-redeemable evil being the others believed him to be? The Hungarian was about to find out first hand.

"Merchant," Vlad addressed him in a superior tone. He once again turned to face his guest with piercing eyes and a taunting voice. "If you are here to cheat and rob the good citizens of Walachia, you will find your visit to be a very short one, if you get my point," he added with a twisted smile and a flick of his dagger.

Chapter 7

A Treatise on Trade

"With faith in our Lord Jesus Christ, I Vlad voievod, by the grace of God Prince of all Walachia...My Majesty orders that from now on...every man will be free and able to trade, to buy, and to sell."

Vlad Dracula, in the "Decree of Vlad III Dracula in Brasnov, 7 Oct., 1476."

Maria sat quietly on the side of her bed in her sleeping clothes, brushing her long ebony strands by the light of a single candle. The room Dimitry had chosen for her was directly above the kitchen making it the warmest room in the inn. She smiled as she thought of how kind he was to her, but she was also intensely aware of how utterly alone she was. Dimitry had gone home to his jolly plump wife and string of stair-step children. They would all gather around and give him hugs and kisses; then the couple would take the smallest children with them into their great bed where they would be warm and cozy.

A family, she thought reflectively. Maria had never really had a family in the terms that she defined it. Her husband, Serbul, had not been unkind to her, but he was more than twice her age. His children from his first marriage were grown, and when the common carpenter's wife died, he was lonely. Most girls Maria's age were already married, and her nanny was getting along in years. When Serbul made an offer she couldn't refuse, she agreed to give Maria to him. At first she had protested. "Nanny, he's so old," she had said.

"Child, look at you! A grown woman with no husband and no employment. I am old and cannot support you forever. You have no dowry, no inheritance to attract a husband. Serbul's late wife was my friend, and she said he treated her well and was a good provider. I know he is not a young man, but he is the best we can do," her nanny had explained.

At least he was company, she thought sadly. And he did show an interest in her...at least several times a month. Five minutes of heated excitement, with or without any results, and he would roll over, asleep. *Yes*, she thought with a humorous grin, *it was a miracle Georgi was born.*

The brush suddenly went still in her hands, and she lowered them to her lap. In the midst of her reflection Maria had realized for the first time that her little boy, Georgi, was the only person she had ever really loved who had unconditionally loved her in return. True, her nanny had taken care of her, but she was always so formal that their relationship was not like she imaged having a mother would have been. And Serbul, God rest his soul, looked at her more like a maid or simple companion than how she thought a husband should. She was sorry when she heard that he had been killed in a fall while constructing a new building in town, but certainly not heart-broken, not like losing her child. It did, however, mean that she would have to find work. As it happened, the previous waitress at the tavern had just gotten married and left the position. She was very glad to have a fair employer like Dimitry. Nadia was a good friend to her, but she was very busy with her own husband and children. *Yes*, Maria brooded. *I am all alone in the world, and but for one brief moment of sunshine, I always have been.*

The devoted Orthodox girl slid off to the side of her bed and knelt for her night-time prayers. After making the sign of the cross, she began to recite the Lord's prayer. "Our Father, which art in Heaven, hallowed be Thy name. Thy Kingdom come, Thy will be done on earth as it is in Heaven. Give us this day our daily bread and forgive us our trespasses as we forgive those who trespass against us. Lead us not into temptation, but deliver us from evil." She paused for a moment then added. "And protect the merchant, Stefan, from evil this night. He seems like a nice man; he gave me such a large tip, and he was very polite," she recalled. However, Maria did not include how handsome she found him to be in her prayer. "Protect him from the evil son of the devil, Dracula. Post your angels around him as you did Daniel so that the ravenous lion will not be able to devour him. And God, give me strength - give me a sign. I would so willingly become your agent of destruction and smite the murdering blasphemer from the earth. But if I am not the one, I pray Thee, God, send another deliverer to free us from Satan's clutches. I know that the face of the Lord is against those who shed innocent blood. Strike him down, oh

Mighty God, and save us all." Then Maria crawled into bed under her blankets and blew out the candle.

As she lay in bed thinking over these things, she considered the handsome Hungarian she had met. He was nice enough, rich enough, fair of face enough, but the man of her dreams would be no such fanciful dandy. She had dreams of a real man's man - a take-charge, daring man of action - someone strong enough to protect her from any danger. She sighed to herself thinking how silly she was to ponder these things…and yet…there had been that one moment when their eyes met, and she had seen something different in him. Was that good or bad? Would he prove to be villain or hero, or just the well-dressed, sophisticated Hungarian merchant he appeared to be?

Stefan cleared his throat and swallowed with a calm, unassuming expression. "I assure you, Prince Dracula, that I come to Walachia with only the most honorable intentions. Neither I nor my guild wish to cheat anyone," he vowed while clutching to the leather saddlebag that hung over his shoulder.

Vlad studied the Hungarian's response. Then a little smile crossed his lips. "For my sake, I hope you are right. You see, it is to my advantage to remain on a friendly footing with Hungary at this time. After King Matthias helped restore me to my throne, it would appear ungrateful of me to immediately begin killing off his merchants. But mark my words, Kubana, if you step one toe across the line of the law, I will cut it off."

"Then neither of us has any cause to worry," Stefan replied cheerfully. "My particular guild deals in Far Eastern merchandise - pepper, spices, silks, exotic things that will in no way encroach upon your local artisans' businesses. We would also be interested in organizing a fair in Tirgoviste in the spring."

"Oh, really?" Vlad rose from the table and walked over toward his guest. "We shall discuss business tomorrow. Come, I will show you to your room."

"How very kind of you, my lord," Stefan said with a smile as he took a step to walk just behind Dracula. "You have a fabulous fortress here - absolutely invincible!"

"Thank you," he returned with satisfied pride. "I am quite pleased with it." The prince opened an interior door from the hall into a corridor.

"I have a guest room on this hall. I believe you will find it quite satisfactory."

"I am sure I will, my lord. Your hospitality is most generous."

Vlad paused thoughtfully at the door of the guest room to pose a question. "Tell me, Stefan - may I call you Stefan?"

"Most certainly, my lord."

"What is your opinion on the philosophy of the Divine Right of Rulers?" Vlad asked inquisitively. "Now that I am back in power again, I have been giving the matter much thought."

"Most honorable prince, I am but a mere merchant," Stefan proceeded modestly placing his left hand upon his chest in gesture. "I do not know about such lofty matters as philosophies and Divine Rights. Those are matters that noblemen contemplate. I am well acquainted with investment prices, shipping costs, supply and demand, and the like, but I fear that I am completely unqualified to offer an opinion on a matter I do not understand."

Vlad smiled to himself, his eyes sparkling. "I find you quite refreshing, Stefan. Most men I speak with have an opinion on everything and generally believe their opinion to be the correct one. But you are prudent enough to realize your limitations." Dracula slapped his hand down on Stefan's shoulder in camaraderie. "I perceive you to be an honest man who knows his place in the scheme of things."

Stefan blushed a bit, his deep blue eyes shining with a knowing light. "My lord, you are quite correct in saying so, and most gracious as well. Perhaps if you were to explain this philosophy to me, then I could become enlightened to its significance."

The dark prince was more pleased than ever with the admiring way Stefan spoke to him. He raised his chin a little higher and opened the door to the guest room. "I would be most pleased to. Do you find your quarters suitable?"

Stefan strode into the small but comfortable bedroom which already had a fire blazing in the hearth. The bed curtains were of crimson wool, and the spread and pillows were white linen. A beautifully woven blanket of many colors was folded at the foot. "I am not deserving of such attention, my lord!" Stefan declared as his eyes widened.

"On the contrary," Vlad corrected as he followed the merchant into the room. "Equitable trade and commerce are of great concern to me. Now, you asked about the philosophy." Stefan turned his interested gaze from the details of the room onto the prince. "According to the Divine Right of Rulers, when one is anointed - whether as emperor, king, or prince - it is a sign that God has chosen him and placed him in the position of power by divine will. Therefore, the ruler is not responsible to any human authority, court, or parliament, but to God alone."

"Let me see." Stefan considered his words thoughtfully. "So the ruler is, by virtue of Divine selection, above the law."

"Precisely," Vlad concluded pleasantly. "But I hold another angle on the philosophy as well. To me it logically follows that because the king or prince has been appointed by God to govern, he therefore is also directed by God in his administration of affairs such that he cannot do wrong."

"Humm." Stefan's brows furrowed as he stroked his fingers along the lines of his mustache and bearded chin. "I had never thought of that - as I mentioned, such things are far above my meager abilities. But it seems a logical course. Surely, if God is omnipotent, one could not become ruler without His express consent and approval. Then, if in the course of events, the ruler strayed from God's will and purpose in his rule, an all-powerful God could easily have him eliminated and raise up another in his place."

"Precisely!" Vlad announced triumphantly. "I believe I have been reinstated specifically because I was a superior administrator of the principality than Radu and Basarab. My services are once again needed to abolish crime and immorality. I am in fact the Divine instrument of cleansing in our land. I shall smite the infidel Turks with a vengeance, as well as the thief, cheat, beggar, and harlot. And, as I consider it, the church should award me a sainthood for my most diligent efforts."

Stefan was not sure how to reply to Vlad's last comment. He nodded in deference to the prince then agreed, saying, "You are indeed diligent, my lord, and the Turks fear even the mention of your name."

Vlad grinned from ear to ear. He relished the thought of Turks trembling at his name. Then he recalled an incident to share. "Of course, not all educated people agree with me. I remember an incident during my former reign when I was visited by two Catholic monks. I was Orthodox at the time, but it makes no matter. I asked them the question, 'Do you think I will be admitted into Heaven?' The first monk gave a prudent answer by saying, 'Sire, certainly you can obtain salvation because of the depth of God's mercy. It is possible for anyone to be saved.' But the other monk blasted me with hellfire and brimstone. He accused me of every evil deed and proclaimed that not only would I never see the gates of Heaven, but I was so wicked and detestable that Satan himself would not even grant me entrance into hell!" Dracula's green eyes blazed as he recalled the words.

"Oh, my Heavens! How rude!" Stefan stepped back in disapproval.

"Yes, well, I thought it to be quite presumptuous and proceeded to strangle that heretic with my bare hands and impaled him through the skull in that very spot. Monks should learn to keep their tongues civil," he explained with regal indignation. "But the hour is late, and I should leave you to your rest. We shall discuss the trade agreement in the morning."

"Yes, Prince Dracula," Stefan responded with a polite bow. "I look forward to it."

Stefan's entire demeanor changed once Dracula had left the room. He loosened his tie and collar and pulled off his great szur coat, tossing it carelessly into a chair. He let out a long, loud sigh and flung himself onto the bed. His breathing and heart rate accelerated as he stared up at the ceiling with a blank, dazed look. His last thoughts as he tried to sleep were horrific ones - a holy monk being strangled and pierced through the top of his head with a steel pike. Whether he opened or closed his eyelids, the image of bulging eyes and blood trickling from the monk's mouth refused to leave his mind. He puzzled as to whether or not Vlad wanted to give him nightmares as a kind of psychological ploy, or if the prince was himself so devoid of conscience that such a scene was pleasant in his imagination. Eventually, Stefan concluded that both were true.

An older maid wearing an apron and her gray hair in a bun called on Stefan the next morning, bringing him a tray holding a light breakfast. "The prince will send Petru for you when he is ready," she told him and then left. Stefan ate his meal while setting all thoughts straight in his mind in preparation for the meeting with Vlad. Then he changed into a fresh shirt from his saddlebag and splashed on a bit of cologne. Before long the valet arrived to escort him to see the prince.

Dracula stood in the top of a tower overlooking the Arges, wearing a black fox suba[23] fastened around his shoulders. His full sleeved royal blue silk shirt had silver embroidered cuffs, collar, and front panel, and his silver studded cojoc was lined with fox fur matching his cape. A decorative cummerbund of black silk encircled his waist and held his thick, black trousers in place. They were wrapped to just below the knee in matching royal blue carbatine laces which extended from his leather shoes. His wide brimmed black palsa[24] sported a large blue and white plume.

"Sire," Petru addressed him, rousting the prince from the thoughts which had consumed him for the moment. "Domn Kubana is here as you requested."

"Very good, Petru," replied Dracula without moving his gaze from the mountains. "Stefan, would you like a tour?"

"That would be fabulous, my lord," he answered enthusiastically.

"Come then." In flamboyant grace and style, Vlad led the way from the tower out onto the battlement walkway. "The castle was first constructed generations ago and had been nearly destroyed through battle, vandalism, and neglect. But I restored it to its former majesty, and it has been my favorite fortress - not as luxurious as my palace in Tirgoviste, but I can feel its power and invincibility when I am on these walls." The wild expression blazing on the prince's face proved the truth of the words he spoke.

Suddenly, Dracula stopped, seized Stefan by the back of his neck, and thrust the upper half of his body over the stone railing of the battlement. Stefan's white knuckled fingers dug tightly into the weathered rocks to prevent him from falling. "Look down there," Dracula's voice boomed. "See how long, how far, how steep the drop?" Stefan swallowed hard, but was unable to speak. All color had left his face, and he was afraid of losing his breakfast as well. Petru froze, not even venturing to guess what his master might do next. "See those sharp rocks below and the river that rages by?" A madly wicked grin crossed Vlad's face as he felt the power over life and death once more in his hand. Then, slowly, he released his

---

[23] suba - an informal warm weather covering made of sheepskin or fur; could be a coat, cloak, or sleeveless cape.

[24] palsa - black felt hat with a stiff, round brim, popular in Mediterranean and Balkan countries.

grip from the merchant and chuckled humorously as Stefan tried to catch his breath.

"It - it is quite a drop," he managed to eke out.

"This is the spot where my first wife leapt to her death. Pity. She panicked, I'm afraid, when Radu's forces arrived in great number. She feared what the Turks would do to her and took her own life - a damnable offense and totally unnecessary. I could have led her to safety." He sighed. "All for the best, though. I am much more pleased with my new wife, a Hungarian princess. Now, tell me, Stefan," Dracula asked with a morbid sense of humor and a playful gleam in his green eyes. "Were you afraid I would drop my wife's countryman off this wall for no reason?"

"Certainly not, milord," Stefan replied as he regained his composure. "You are a fair and just ruler. However, I must admit that I do suffer from a slight fear of high places."

Vlad laughed out loud and slapped a friendly hand onto Stefan's shoulder. "I should have guessed as much. Come, walk with me." Vlad walked regally with his hands clasped behind his back, and Stefan obediently followed. "Tell me, Stefan, are you married?"

"Me?" he questioned in good humor now that he felt his life was safe for the moment. "Goodness no, my lord! I am a confirmed bachelor. I made a conscious decision years ago to put aside some of man's more carnal needs and desires in order to focus my energy and thoughts on loftier matters."

"Ah, a spiritual man then." Vlad stopped at the doorway to the corner tower and turned his eyes intuitively to Stefan's. "You do not fool me, Stefan Kubana," he said in an omniscient tone. Stefan's heart skipped a beat, and he froze breathlessly as the dark prince's cold green eyes stared into his own. "You may appear to be a fop and a weakling, but I know better. Any man who can resist the wiles of the feminine devils, keeping himself pure in spirit, mind, and body, is indeed a very powerful man." He then opened the oak door and ushered Stefan inside.

The merchant breathed a sigh of relief as his cheeks flushed red. "I would not go so far as to say powerful, Prince Dracula. You yourself are far more powerful than I, and yet you have a wife."

"True," Dracula mused as he followed Stefan into the round, stone room, Petru trailing dutifully along. "But with her exception, I find all women to be deceitful, dangerous, and utterly detestable." His eyes and voice darkened as Vlad continued to spit out his words venomously. "How they tease, beckon, and flaunt themselves just to torment a man, then withhold from him their pleasures. They plot to capture a man's soul and then manipulate him to do their bidding. Damnable whores, the lot of them, leading men into sin and then claiming innocence." Vlad paused for a moment, his eyes fixed on an open window. He rested against a crude cannon that was mounted in the tower aiming out toward the road in front of the fortress. "Few women deserve to draw breath, Stefan, and to find one that does is a rare thing indeed. Ilona is a king's sister and has thus been properly trained. She has borne me an heir and a spare and keeps her place gracefully. My mother was decent also, I suppose. I do not remember her well..." Dracula's thoughts began to drift.

Stefan felt it was his turn to speak. "I am afraid that once again you have me at a disadvantage, my lord, for I am not experienced nor knowledgeable where women are concerned," he confessed.

"That is to your credit, my man," Vlad smiled, bringing his thoughts back to the present. "Petru, let us show our guest to the court room and draw up the terms of this trade agreement, shall we?"

"Certainly, Sire," Petru acknowledged and led the way down the spiral staircase.

"Have you read what the German pamphlets have to say about me, Stefan?" Vlad asked with a suspicious measure of curiosity as they descended the stairs.

"I must confess that I have seen such pamphlets in the bookstores of Szeged but have never actually taken the time to read one. Oh, my," he chuckled nervously. "I do apologize, milord; I am sure they must praise the admirable way you dispatched of the Turkish threat to our realm."

"On the contrary," Vlad's voice stiffened. "They call me a fiend and a bloodthirsty monster."

"Good Heavens!" Stefan exclaimed. "Do they now?"

"They call me Vlad Tepes, the Impaler, and purposely misinterpret my surname of Dracula. But there is much they do not tell." The trio had reached the bottom of the staircase and set off down a corridor lit by mounted oil lamps toward Vlad's courtroom. The lamps filled the narrow hallway with a particular aroma and a thin haze of smoke.

"Please enlighten me as to the real story," Stefan requested with interest.

Dracula was pleased and continued. "You cannot possibly know what it is like to be separated from your father, mother, and older brother as a mere youth never again to see them alive," he explained solemnly.

Stefan's eyes darkened to a cold cobalt. "I can only imagine," he replied sympathetically.

"My younger brother and I were taken as security against my father's pledge to pay tribute to the Turks. Sultan Murad held us hostage at Adrianople, and while we were there, Dracul's own 'loyal' boyars plotted and assassinated both him and my brother, Mircea."

"I do vaguely recall these events," Stefan replied. "It must have been horrible for you. Were you kept in a dungeon?"

Vlad laughed, and his dark mood was lifted for a moment. "Hardly. That is not how things are done with royalty. Radu and I were 'house guests' of the sultan. We were educated and trained alongside his sons. But Mehmed - whose heart I will one day cut out - never let me forget that I was both a foreigner and a captive. Sometimes he would spill the ink and blame me. I would be the one who had to scrub the floor. But never did precious Radu get in trouble," he said with a scowl.

Petru opened the door to the spacious courtroom, and they proceeded inside the wheaten hall.

"Radu was everyone's favorite; he could do no wrong." Dracula's face tensed, and his eyes narrowed as he recalled. "My younger brother, and even the harem preferred him! Radu the Charming, Radu the Beautiful," he mocked. "He had all the privileges while Vlad got all the restrictions. They praised him but laughed at me in scorn. Well, who's had the last laugh now?" Dracula turned his waiting gaze to his guest.

"If I am not mistaken, milord, your younger brother is dead while you sit on the throne of Walachia," he pronounced.

"Precisely," Vlad concurred with a pleased smile. "But I did learn some important things from my years in Adrianople. Impaling I learned from the Turks - a most slow and painful death. In time I gave it back to them in abundance. Murad reinforced the lessons of my father about ruling through fear and terror. A man may obey his prince out of love, or he may be negligent, relying on his mercy. But a man will do anything required of him if he knows he will die a hideous death otherwise. Now," Vlad said pleasantly as he motioned to a table, "let us sit and discuss our agreement."

71

"Very good, milord," Stefan replied eagerly as he took a seat at the table. Vlad and Petru joined him, and the valet took out paper, a quill, and ink.

"Do you know why I have had so much trouble with foreign merchants in the past?" Dracula asked as he removed his hat.

"No, milord, but pray tell me so that I can assure you that no such trouble shall be found with my guild."

"During my former reign, Hungary and Transylvania wanted to give their merchants free rein to traverse the Walachian cities and countryside, freely selling their merchandise while greatly restricting the activities of our merchants. Walachian merchants were required to stop at the borders and sell their goods at trading warehouses. Then the Hungarians and Transylvanians would sell our products adding on a commission for themselves. This made our products more expensive and less attractive to foreign buyers. Yet they insisted their merchants move freely in my country."

"What did you do about it?" Stefan asked innocently.

"I impaled them all," Vlad answered matter-of-factly. "And I attacked and burned the border cities containing those abominable trading houses. How dare they try to cheat Vlad Dracula out of honest trade!"

"Most high prince, King Matthias has assured us that he wants to open the borders for free trade for both sides," Stefan answered openly and honestly.

"Yes, I know," Vlad affirmed setting Stefan's fears aside. "Why else would I have agreed to meet with you? Now, how does this sound? There shall exist, as of this day, a free trade policy between the merchants of Hungary and those of Walachia such that each may freely pass the other's borders without duty or tax nor be prohibited from selling their wares in any town. Furthermore, if any merchant of Hungary or Walachia be found guilty of tipping the scales or otherwise cheating their customers, they shall be dealt with according to the laws of that land."

"That sounds most excellent, Prince Dracula," Stefan beamed triumphantly as Petru rushed to write it all down. "This is exactly what my guild had hoped for. However, my lord, being a mere merchant and having no knowledge of a king's tendency to change his mind regarding policy matters, I wonder if we might attach one more provision."

"Oh? And what might that be?"

"Milord, only that if either party were to in any way violate the terms of this agreement, all foreign merchants operating within either country's borders may have at least forty-eight hours in which to depart that country before any retaliatory actions are taken?" he asked in a timid but very earnest voice.

Dracula peered at him incredulously for a moment and then broke into laughter. "Kubana, for your sake I would do this. I find you too interesting and amusing alive to have you wasted on a pike if the fault is your king's and not your own. Petru, write in the provision." Stefan relaxed and his countenance brightened. "You spoke of a fair?"

"Yes, Sire, in the spring, with exotic animals, troubadours, performers of all kinds, and items to purchase from all around the world. It will be the event of the year!" Stefan became highly animated as he exuberantly explained the fair. "It should last at least a month so that citizens from all over could travel to the capital city for the event. Your own merchants could set up booths next to ours, Italians, Castillians, and Germans. Your fair will be the envy of Europe." His bright blue eyes sparkled.

The prince was both pleased and entertained by the enthusiasm the Hungarian displayed. A smile lit upon his lips as he pictured himself riding in the opening parade, leading the procession in a golden colored coach with elephants and tigers in cages trailing him. His eyes gleamed even brighter as he envisioned the power and majesty of the regal beasts. He fancied the idea of involving the tigers and lions in any executions held at that time, and Dracula almost aroused himself with the mental images of the savage animals tearing screaming men and women to pieces. "I think a fair is a wonderful idea, Stefan. You may begin making plans. Now, as much as I have enjoyed your company, there are many demands on my time. Petru, do you have the proposal ready?"

"Yes, my prince," he confirmed and handed Dracula the paper for inspection. Vlad looked it over and then signed his name.

"Return this to me with the proper signatures of your guild and government and all will be in order," Vlad said as he handed the document to Stefan.

"Prince Dracula, I am most indebted to you for your confidence and support. I believe that free trade will benefit both of us. I should be back in about ten days with the proper seals and signatures. This has indeed been an enjoyable and enlightening visit for me," Stefan concluded satisfactorily.

"Come, Domn Kubana, I will see you to the castle gate," Vlad offered with a grand gesture as he rose to his feet. Stefan graciously accepted and walked with the prince out of the chamber and across the castle yard. There were soldiers and civilians walking about, busying themselves with various tasks. Each had left a trail through the morning's snow-covered ground such that there wasn't a single spot left undisturbed.

Vlad's blood already flowed hot in his veins after his lustful imaginings of crimson flesh dripping from a great cat's jaws when he spied the new garden girl across the way. The young, fair-haired Saxon girl knelt gracefully in the cook's small herb garden to gather the leeks and garlic whose green sprouts protruded through the snow. She could continue to gather these cold-hardy vegetables along with onions and potatoes as long as the ground was not frozen. She wore a colorful kerchief over her head and her hair pulled back with a tie. She did not seem to notice the prince at first with so many people walking about. But when the young woman felt that intuitive tugging that told her she was being watched, she looked up. She smiled a polite and respectful smile at Dracula, just to stay on his good side, but he took her look to have a different meaning.

"God's speed and safety on your journey, Stefan Kubana," Vlad wished his guest. "I look forward to your return."

"As do I, milord. Your hospitality has been outstanding." Stefan bowed in deference to the prince and then proceeded through the open fortress door and across the drawbridge that spanned the chasm below. But Vlad spun on his heel and paced straightway to the little kitchen garden and the pretty, shapely girl who worked there.

Chapter 8

Passions

"In order that no form of cruelty be missing, he struck stakes into both breasts of mothers and thrust their babies into them; he killed others in other ferocious ways, torturing them with varied instruments such as the atrocious cruelties of the most frightful tyrants could devise."

From Papal Legate Modrussa's report to Pope Pius II, 1462

Black boots disturbed the snow beside a stand of leeks. "You are new," observed a deep voice above the girl.

The pretty, young garden girl was startled. She had neither seen nor heard the prince approach; it was rather as if he suddenly appeared beside her, materializing out of thin air. "Oh, sire, it is you!" she exclaimed with a hand to her chest when she turned her head up to see him. "Yes, my lord. I have been here only a week. Doamna Stella hired me to her kitchen staff, and caring for this garden is one of my duties although if the snow continues, it will soon go to sleep until spring." Flori's amber brown eyes were alive with hope and promise. Peasant girls often dreamed of acquiring employment in the household of a boyar as a ticket out of poverty, and there she was, assistant cook for the prince. Flori had been the envy of all the young unmarried women of Curt de Arges. She hoped to meet a handsome young soldier or perhaps a coachman or courtier who might wish to marry her. But for now, the golden-haired girl wished to please both Stella and the prince to keep her coveted position at Poenari.

"I can think of other duties you could fulfill during these cold winter months." Vlad cast his ravenous eyes down on Flori who suddenly felt a cold wind of fear blow across her face. Her eyes were almost level with his crotch, and it was more than obvious that he had purposely opened his trouser flap to expose himself to her.

Flori quickly stood to her feet, diverting her eyes from his aroused manhood. She shuddered, not knowing what to do and giggled nervously like a child. "Sire," she replied blushing. "Someone may see you."

But Dracula's expression hardened at her response. "It appears someone already has." For each heavy footstep he took in her direction, Flori took one backward until in a few steps, he had trapped her against a half wall which surrounded the garden area.

"My lord, you flatter me," she said wide-eyed, her heart leaping into her throat. "Perhaps inside -"

"How dare you laugh at me!" he demanded quietly through clenched teeth. His eyes shot flaming arrows into hers, and the girl began to feel panicked.

"No, Sire, I was not laughing at you!" Flori pleaded earnestly. The avarice consuming Vlad's face mortified the girl, and she trembled uncontrollably.

The back of his hand smacked hard and fast against her face, sending her head into a dizzy swirl. "You goddamned bitch, how dare you laugh at me," he hissed like a mighty serpent.

"Sire, I did not laugh at you," she insisted. "I was - I am afraid. It was a nervous laugh, for I did not know what to say. Please, my prince, I'll do anything -"

"I'm sure a whore like you would do anything," he retorted, his hot breath puffing steam onto her face. "First you lure me over here with the flaunting of your body and flirtatious smile, and then when I almost fall prey to your wickedness, tempting me to commit adultery, you laugh in my face as if it were a joke."

Was he insane? The puzzlement and bewilderment on her face indicated that Flori thought so. "My lord, I was only pulling up onions," she declared innocently.

Vlad ignored Flori's statement entirely. His every muscle was tense and hard as he pressed against her, grabbing a handful of her hair in his left hand. "You are no different than the pagan harem girls. They laughed at me, too, did you know that? It was their purpose to please me, and yet they ridiculed me as though I were inadequate. Me, can you imagine?" Then his eyes darkened menacingly at her. "That is what you think, is it not?"

"N-no, milord," she stuttered, tears stinging her eyes and making icy paths down her cheeks. "I can please you. I know I can."

"Perhaps you will," Dracula replied with a twisted grin. "But it is obvious that I cannot please you." Then his tone and expression changed again. "What is this talk? Look what you are doing - trying to tempt me into sin again, into your adulterous lair. You are evil, like all women, worming your way into a man's mind and turning him to sinful thoughts. You must pay for your crime."

"Oh, God, help me!" she cried out pitifully. "No, please no, Great Prince! I was obviously wrong, but I'll do anything."

But the enraged dark prince was not listening. Instead his mind was creatively contemplating what he would do to her. Then his eyes sparked, as though a light went on, and he looked on her with amusement. "So you think I am mic - too small, do you?" She shivered wide-eyed and tried helplessly to catch her breath. Vlad plucked his golden Saracen dagger from its sheath tucked in his cummerbund and held it in front of her face as a dark veil covered his own. "Maybe this will be more to your liking," he spat maliciously.

Taking Flori by her hair, he flung her a few yards across the way against a hard, fortress wall and approached with deliberate steps, the dagger gripped tightly in his hand. "No," she pleaded beneath her sobs, but he proceeded to press her against the stones and grabbed the hem of her skirt. At that moment Flori let out one desperate, blood-curdling scream which Vlad quickly silenced by covering her mouth with his own, and he thrust the blade beneath her skirt.

Stefan had nearly reached the bottom of the long and arduous stairway. His thoughts were on the raven-haired waitress from Dimitry's tavern the evening before. He smiled as he thought of Maria, the way she looked, the way she moved, the concern he detected in her eyes when Ivan had arrived. The fact that she clearly hated Prince Dracula made her even more attractive to him. He wondered if she had thought of him at all and wistfully hoped that she had. Whether she had or not, Stefan was on his way to see her again. *Will she be pleased to see me?* he thought. Then he frowned, reflecting on his own personality, speech, and mannerisms. *What if she doesn't like me the way I am?* he wondered. *Even worse, what if she does?*

But Stefan's thoughts were shockingly interrupted as he heard what sounded like a woman's scream echoing around the mountain. His face paled as his imagination took flight. Whatever was happening up in the castle, there was nothing he could do about it. *Maybe it's not that; women are prone to scream. It could have been a bobcat or anything*, he tried to convince himself. But a sick feeling that grew in the pit of his stomach told him instinctively that another virgin had been sacrificed on the altar of Dracula's bloodlust.

His last few steps were slow and ponderous. They were guilt ridden, condemning steps. Was there anything he could have done to save the unfortunate woman? Perhaps if he had stayed longer or left sooner. *No, no,* he shook his head despairingly. *Don't torture yourself.*

Stefan walked through the melting slush on the road and up to the stable door.

"Ah, that fine bay Sckweiken mare - couldn't forget her," the stableman recalled. "You must have paid a pretty price for that one."

"I have found that a good mount is a well-placed investment," Stefan spoke pleasantly as if he were not torn up inside.

"There she is." The bony peasant pointed to the big mare grazing on the stubble she had pawed through the snow to find. But Stefan stood stock still, all color drained from his face and his body tingling all over.

At first he could not say a word. There were a few other horses milling about the snowy pasture but he did not see them at all. His midnight-blue eyes were morbidly fixed upon the bodies hanging from their pikes. Suddenly the merchant's mind took flight to a time and place far, far away.

"Domnule?" The stable keeper noticed the blank gaze and hollowed expression Stefan wore. "Have you never seen impaled bodies before?" Stefan did not reply. "There was an execution Sunday morning - criminals. Sometimes the prince uses the pasture. There is not much flat ground near the castle. Now, there, Hungarian, all is well," he comforted his customer, fearing he might faint. Then he turned Stefan's shoulders toward the barn. "You wait inside, and I will bring your horse. I am so sorry to have disturbed you. I didn't think." The stableman was very apologetic, and Stefan did as he was instructed.

78

It was not a long ride back to Curt de Arges, but it seemed like one to Stefan who was consumed by heaviness. He brooded about the woman's scream and the cadavers on the poles and sank deeper and deeper into melancholia. As he neared the town, Stefan arrested his thoughts and forced them back onto things at hand, such as seeing Maria again and traveling back to Hungary to complete the trade agreement. He had almost put himself in a pleasant temperament when something in the town square caused him to pull his horse to a halt. Dimitry's tavern was just down the next street to his right, so he had to have passed this way last night. Obviously it had been too dark and snowing too heavily for him to see, but now in the daylight, the grotesque display was an all-consuming thing for him.

Bile rose in Stefan's throat, and he quivered in his saddle. In the town square near the public well where everyone would pass by was erected a large wooden gallows. The naked, disfigured body of a woman hung from a meat hook; her breasts had been cut off and a ragged slit extended from her groin up past her belly so that her entrails had spilled out. Ruthlessly jabbed onto another hook beside her was a crusty fetus, perfectly formed but about half the size of a newborn babe.

Searing hatred and wild outrage ran rampant through Stefan's soul as he clenched his fists and his teeth. *When I think I have seen all the horrors that monster can conceive,* he thought in silent rage, *he always comes up with one more.*

Maria went through the motions of clearing empty plates and cups from the tables as the mid-day customers were finishing their meal. One day seemed to blend into the next for her with no real meaning. Each step she took seemed more arduous, each dish she lifted heavier than the one before. Despair loomed over her like a cloud, and hopelessness enwrapped her like a shroud. She did her job, ate enough to sustain her, slept whenever sleep would claim her, and otherwise existed. When the tavern door flew open she did not even bother to raise her eyes in curiosity. No one interested her - not until she heard a foreign accent in a familiar voice.

"Maria, if I do not receive a glass of water immediately, I think I shall faint!" She looked up, her arms piled with dishes, to spot the Hungarian merchant alive after all. His face was as wan as his ivory coat, and he barely managed to stumble into the nearest chair. Once collapsing there, he rested his head in his left hand and drew out his handkerchief with his right.

Maria hastily set down the stack of plates, dutifully rushing to fill his water glass. His arrival, sickly as it was, shot a jolt of life back into her and gave her a momentary purpose. Her emotions at the sight of him were like a kaleidoscope, shaking, shifting, and merging within her. Her prayer for his safety had been answered, but something bad had obviously happened to him. This flurry of feelings that stirred in her hollow chest surprised Maria.

"My goodness, Domn Stefan!" exclaimed Dimitry who stopped what he was doing and looked on his guest with concern. "Are you ill?"

"I do believe so," he replied weakly. "I just witnessed the most atrocious, horrifying spectacle in the town square." Stefan daintily fanned himself with the linen cloth.

Dimitry relaxed, relief showing on his face. "Ah," he nodded. "The woman was found to be with child but not married. 'Tis a pity, but Prince Dracula's laws are quite strict on the matter."

"My God," Stefan gasped as he reached out to take the water glass from Maria's hands. He swallowed a small sip and then set the glass down slowly. Carefully, the fastidious gentleman dampened his handkerchief in the water and blotted his cheeks, lips, and forehead with the wet cloth.

Maria's face was etched with concern as she lingered just a moment at his table. "But it seems so barbaric," Stefan commented as he placed the cloth to his throat. "The odor has made me nauseous and remembrances of such a gruesome sight will give me nightmares."

The tenderness that Maria was feeling for him at that moment all but evaporated as she took in the subject of his words. She sighed to herself, thinking that his only concern in the matter was for himself. Sadly she turned away from him and resumed clearing the empty plates from the tables.

"Prince Dracula feels that such public displays act as deterrents," Dimitry explained, "to give a warning to others. That is why his executions are both deplorable and public."

"It will certainly deter me from breaking any laws," Stefan breathed weakly, but his eyes followed Maria as she worked.

"Dimitry, you know she was raped," Maria scowled as she passed him, speaking in a low tone but one Stefan could hear. He raised his head a bit to listen for the debate that was sure to ensue.

But Dimitry, who noticed Stefan had heard, shrugged and casually told the story. "A group of out-of-town rabble-rousers were here for about a week during the summer - it was before Prince Vlad's return. They'd had a bit too much to drink and got playful with a few local girls, that one included. But you know how it is, Stefan," Dimitry shrugged knowingly.

"They raped her," Maria stated blatantly. "And not a thing happened to them, but she and that innocent baby were strung up. Dimitry, don't you see?" she implored.

"I agree the child was an innocent," Dimitry concurred, lowering his head in shame as if his own mother had just scolded him. "But no one knows for sure if that is really how she became pregnant. There could have been other men."

"Then why don't they ever get punished?"

"I don't know, Maria," Dimitry whirled at her in irritation. "Maybe they aren't as obvious to spot as a woman with her belly out to here!" he motioned with one hand.

Maria let it go. She knew the innkeeper was tired of the subject, tired of having to defend the prince at every turn, and tired of being berated by his waitress for wrongs he himself had not committed.

"I am sorry, Domn Dimitry," she said contritely, bowing her head toward him. "I will be quiet." He snorted, and shot her a speculative look, then went back to his work.

Stefan took another sip from his glass and wiped his forehead once more. "My friends, I fear I could not eat a bite at this moment and would do best to retire to my room for a siesta."

Dimitry nodded. "Room number six upstairs has been reserved for you just as we agreed last evening."

"Thank you so kindly." Stefan started to rise, but appeared dizzy and held onto the table to steady himself. "My, my," he said in embarrassment. "I must have stood too quickly."

"Maria." Dimitry motioned. "The dishes can wait. Please see Domn Stefan up to his room so that he does not fall and break something on the stairway. And Teo, see to the man's bags." Teo, who had been in and out of the room throughout the conversation, nodded to his employer and headed out back to the stable to collect Stefan's bag.

Maria huffed a bit in annoyance, but agreed. She took Stefan's arm to steady him and walked with him toward the stairs. His muscles seemed firm enough, and his shoulders were quite broad. She wondered at her paradoxical charge, how he could appear so strong yet act so weak.

"I would like to thank you very much," he said cordially in a diplomatic tone of voice. "I fear I am not used to such sights."

"Soon you will be in your home country and your home town and will not have to endure such atrocities," Maria replied almost in envy of him for being able to escape.

On the staircase and out of hearing range of the others in the dinning hall, Stefan's voice slowly began to take on a warmer, deeper quality. "Does he do that often?"

"He's only been back in power a couple of months," she answered as she thought back over the many brutalities in that short amount of time. "But, yes, it has happened far too often, and many people are living in fear. But you needn't be afraid. Obviously you got along quite well with Prince Dracula," she uttered his name with disdain.

"I was successful in securing the trade agreement, if that is what you mean," he said casually. But then all formality faded from his tone. "Maria." He stopped at the top of the stairs to catch her attention. "I think it is unforgivable what he did to that woman and child, and to so many others." As he spoke these words, the timbre of his voice transformed itself into that of an entirely different man.

But Maria was not paying close attention to him, for her heart was remembering the loss of her own child. As she stepped forward, leading him to his room, she solemnly thought of how tomorrow the handsome dandy would be leaving, and she would be trapped in Vlad Dracula's domain. "It was quite horrible," she agreed. "But there isn't much any of us can do about it."

"Well," Stefan speculated as his voice lofted once again into that of a fanciful, Hungarian merchant. "I suppose nothing lasts forever. Sooner or later someone else will rise up and take the principality away from him the same way he took it from Basarab."

"I can only hope and pray that he does, and quickly," Maria said with biting desire in her voice.

"Thank you again," he said gallantly as they reached door number six. "I am feeling much better now." He covered his hand over hers and gave it a gentle pat. His dark blue eyes smiled at her, and she looked up to spy a genuine expression of affection on his face. Perhaps he did have an eye for her, but she dismissed the idea because it would not matter anyway.

"You are quite welcome," she replied matter-of-factly. "It is my job to see to our guests here at the inn."

"Will you be serving dinner this evening?" he asked with interest, not letting go of her hand.

A dry laugh, devoid of any humor, passed her lips. "I haven't much else to do."

"I will look forward to seeing you then." The gleam in his eyes betrayed his thoughts shamelessly.

A slight blush arose in Maria's cheeks, and she turned back down the hallway without uttering another word. This man puzzled her. He was at once formally aloof and tenderly affectionate. He was tall and brawny enough, quite handsome of face, and yet so weak and effeminate in his mannerisms. Maria tried to shake the man from her mind. *What difference does it make?* she asked herself as she descended the stairs. *Tomorrow he will be gone, and then there will be no interesting stranger to entertain my thoughts.*

Stefan stepped into his room with a smile, closing the door behind him. Immediately he loosened his tie and collar, threw off his coat, and kicked his boots halfway across the floor like a schoolboy. He took a few gleeful steps and hopped onto the bed which bounced beneath his weight. He lay back, his hands clasped behind his head, a broad grin across his face, and he sighed, closing his eyes. He was very tired, for he had not slept well in Vlad's castle the night before. But he did dream, and the woman he dreamt of had flowing black hair and deep brown eyes.

A couple of hours passed, and the dining hall had cleared of all patrons. Teo went about sweeping the floor, clearing mud from the boots which had trod through the melting snow. He swept up a few dead leaves that had blown in, crumbs, crusts, chicken bones, and the old, soggy straw. When he was done sweeping, he would scatter new straw on the floor to absorb the new wet things the dinner customers were sure to track in. Although Teo worked silently, his ears were always open, attuned, listening to what might be going on around him. Maybe some bit of gossip, some interesting news, anything his attention could latch onto. That afternoon it was a plump, boisterous cook from Poenari Castle who came trouncing in. Her gray hair was pinned in a neat bun, and flaming hot eyes burned from above her hooked nose. She was in a terrible fit of dismay.

"Dimitry, I need a drink," she demanded, "and I don't mean tea."

"Good Heavens, Stella," he replied as his eyes widened to her.

She scowled, her cheeks red from both the cold and her mental state. "I swear, I don't know what I will do. I cannot keep a staff! How am I to run the kitchen?" she complained.

"There, there, Stella," he tried to calm her, handing her a small glass of vodka that he kept hidden under the counter and did not sell to regular customers.

She put the potent clear liquid to her lips and swallowed nearly all of it in one gulp. Then she slammed the glass down. "I have lost another assistant, a gardening girl. That is the third one since he returned," she explained.

"Stella," Maria quivered. She had known the girl, though not well. She had been in and out of the tavern. "You mean Flori?"

"Yes, Flori," she sighed. "I'd like another please." Then her countenance dropped from anger to despair.

Maria came around and sat beside her on a stool at the bar. "What happened this time?" she asked with great concern.

Chapter 9

Old Wives' Tales

"There was in Walachia a Christian prince of the Greek faith by the name of Dracula in the Romanian language, while in ours the Devil, so evil was he. As was his name so was his life."

The opening line of an old Slavic story about Dracula

"I really shouldn't be telling you this," Stella admitted as she glanced around the room. "But since there is only your company here..." Stella wrapped her hands around her drink glass and raised her eyes to Maria's. "There was an incident this morning. Prince Vlad approached the girl - I don't know all that happened." Stella sighed in despair. "But she ended up quite dead, I am afraid."

"I know what your problem is, Stella," Dimitry said in a serious voice of authority. "You must stop hiring pretty, young girls to assist you." He gestured toward her with his cleaning rag still in his right hand. "I mean, if you had any sense, you would find the homeliest old hag and hire her! Dracula would never bother your helpers then."

"I suppose you are right," Stella agreed looking up at the stout tavern keeper. "But I need someone young who can bend easily to tend the garden. It may not be that vital over the winter, for soon the ground will freeze. Oh, Dimitry!" She raised her hands from her glass as if trying to draw a solution from thin air. "It is all so tragic, so sad, and I don't know what to do about it."

Maria smoothed a hand across Stella's shoulders as a silent tear began rolling down the older woman's face. "Flori was so young and pretty and eager to please. She tried extra hard to do everything right. Whatever could she have done that would have infuriated him so?" Her dark eyes moved from one face to the other with her question.

"You don't even know why he killed her?" Maria asked.

Stella took a sip from her drink, set it down, and wiped her hands on her white apron. "Like I said, I wasn't there - I didn't see it happen. He usually treats the staff so well," she explained. "I just don't understand what Flori could have possibly done."

There was so much Maria wanted to say, but she held her peace. Teo, quietly scattering new straw, heard every word but was unable to join in the conversation.

"No use tearing yourself up over it," Dimitry advised. "It was not your fault." He leaned over the bar, his arms folded on the smooth wooden countertop.

"I know...but still, I did hire her, and I knew he had killed the last girl. You are right, Dimitry. This time I will find someone very ordinary that he wouldn't notice - one who is too fat, whose nose is too long, or who is too old to draw his attention. That is exactly what I will do," Stella determined bringing her hands down on the bar for emphasis.

Maria was too numb to even be angry. Thoughts poured through her mind like wine. *Will he not stop until he's killed us all? Then who will he rule over? Who will work for him?*

As evening approached, townspeople began to trickle in to the warm comfort of Dimitry's tavern. Stella had gone in search of a new gardening girl, her presence being replaced by drinkers and eaters of varying ages. Maria was once again busy bringing the patrons their meals and drinks.

Stefan was exquisitely attired in his clean, pressed shirt, Hungarian trousers, and woolen plum dinner jacket as he descended the stairs. His hair was combed and cheeks shaven, accenting his eloquently groomed light-brown mustache and chin beard. The scent of masculine cologne followed him into the dining area.

Dimitry spotted him at once. "Ah, welcome, Domn Stefan, and how was your siesta? Are you feeling better now?"

"Oh, yes, much!" he replied with a broad smile. "Dimitry, I do declare that you have given me the best room in your inn - soft bed, crisp linens, and not a thing to make me itch."

Dimitry chuckled. "I am glad you found the room satisfactory, domnule."

Stefan espied an empty table near the bar, strode across the room toward it, and then sat down ceremoniously in the oak frame chair, waiting for Maria to come. Seeing that she was currently busy with other customers, he crossed his legs, clasped his hands around his knee, and watched her. She moved with eloquent grace, he thought. Her rounded hips swayed to just the right degree. If he strained his neck and his eyes just a bit, he could catch a glimpse of cleavage when she bent over a table. That evening she wore a green kerchief which accented the green embroidery of her apron. He thought the color suited her well.

Maria noticed that he had taken a seat but determined that she would be in no hurry to wait on him. It was almost as if she could feel his eyes following her around the room, and if he was going to behave in such a brazen fashion, then she felt it was her duty to keep him waiting. So when everyone else had been attended to, she approached Stefan's table.

He did not try to hide the delight in his eyes when she neared him. "You look lovely this evening, Maria," he commented.

Maria overlooked the compliment and moved on with business. "What will you have tonight, Domn Kubana?"

"Oh, so we are calling me by my father's name now, are we?" he asked smiling playfully. "Do you have goulash?"

"Yes, that happens to be on our menu this evening."

"Marvelous! I'll take a healthy portion," Stefan said, adding, "I didn't have lunch today, you know. And I'll have a glass of table wine, some water, and whatever pie the cook has prepared for desert."

"It will be a few minutes," Maria answered in a business-like tone, and then she walked toward the kitchen.

Stefan's spirit fell as he wondered what he might have done to offend the lady, and why, after he had made a slight breakthrough, she now seemed to be ignoring him. *I am leaving tomorrow,* he thought. *Maybe she is being distant because she thinks I will not return.*

The proper Hungarian merchant sat back in his chair and tried to pick up bits and pieces of conversation around the dining hall. One table of patrons speculated on the weather, while another was involved in some sort of religious debate centered around the growing Catholic influence in an Orthodox land. "Their monasteries loom large in our principality," the gray-haired man declared, raising his hand to model. "And Prince Vlad himself has converted to Catholicism."

The clean-cut younger man with him shook his head. "What a pity for him to give up his place in Heaven just to gain political power."

Stefan snorted, a cross look on his face. *As if!* he thought. Stefan had become disillusioned with both religions for their continual bickering and excommunicating. He then turned his attention to the table behind him where a man only slightly younger than himself sat listening to two of his friends offer advice concerning his soon-to-arrive wedding night.

"Now, Anton, the first thing you must do is offer her some wine to loosen her up a bit, for she will be nervous," the thinner, clean-shaven friend explained. "Her mother has probably told her horror stories, and she may be in no mood to accept you."

The young man listened intently as he nodded, awaiting his next instruction.

"Say a few sweet words to her," the married man continued with his counsel. "Women like that sort of thing."

Anton counted on his fingers as he repeated his instructions. "Wine, sweet talk - I've got it so far, Bela."

"Forget that ridiculous advice," a raucous, bearded lad at the next table announced with a knowing laugh. He then raised his glass to swallow a gulp of ale. "Cut straight to the chase."

"I should chase her?" the groom asked in bewilderment.

"No, no," Bela answered, shooting a look of disapproval toward the barrel-chested, black-bearded young man who had spoken. "Do not listen to that fool. But once you do get her in the bed, use your fingers first. Check to be sure she is a virgin before you embarrass yourself. If not, take her back to her parents."

"But, I don't want to take her back," Anton explained. "I want to keep her."

"Not if she has been someone else's," Bela warned gravely, holding up a hand. "What if she were to have a child - how would you know it was yours? Or if her former lover were to return and kill you as you slept?"

"Oh." Anton lowered his gaze, slumping over the table. "There is that. But she is very pretty and a good cook. I know because I was invited to dinner." He lifted his eyes hopefully to his friend.

But another voice answered. "Ha! Did you watch her prepare the meal?" asked the boisterous, bearded man. Anton shook his head. "Then how do you know her mother didn't cook the food? Parents will stoop to all kinds of deceptions to marry off an undesirable daughter."

This was all very amusing to Stefan, and he grinned as he listened. The poor, befuddled groom sighed. "Suppose I have checked, and she is a virgin - then what do I do?"

The man with the black beard laughed out loud and smacked his empty ale glass down onto the table. "My poor fellow, do you need every detail explained, or can't you let nature take its course?"

But the older Bela had had enough interruptions. He rose to his feet deliberately and glared at the loud man. "There is a fine art to love-making, you ruffian! The man who learns it well may have as many children as he wants and his wife as often as he desires her."

"A real man knows how to take what he wants from a woman," his antagonist gruffly retorted, folding his arms across his broad chest.

"Would you two quiet down!" scolded one of the men who had been having the religious conversation. He scowled at them from beneath narrowed brows. "You should not be voicing - much less entertaining - such lustful, sinful thoughts. And you should beware of what dangers lie ahead with an unknown woman."

"Dangers?" Anton looked up in alarm at the clean-cut man in the black suit.

"Yes, dangers," he reiterated, turning his chair in toward the little group. "If you know so little about these matters, perhaps you should not even consider marriage until you have all the facts."

"And what facts would those be?" questioned Bela in an irritated tone.

The man in the black suit looked intently at the young groom. "There are diseases a woman can give a man that he cannot rid himself of for all his life, not to mention the spell some women cast over a man. Once he has entered her, she possesses his soul, and he becomes consumed by his desire for her. No rational man would live at the beck and call of a woman; it is a spell, I tell you."

"A spell - as in witchcraft?" Bela questioned with a disbelieving half-smile. "There are no witches among our women."

"How can you be so sure?" asked a scruffy old man missing a front tooth who had been drawn into the discussion. He ambled over from across the room to take a seat nearer. "No man in my family is ever the first to take his wife on her wedding night."

"What?" Now Anton was more confused than ever. "But Bela says she must be a virgin, so how -"

"Mark my warning." He shook a bony finger at the groom. "You never know what dangers lurk between those thighs. I have heard stories," he continued, catching everyone's attention, "of women who have stolen their husband's manhood, sliced it right off. And there are some women who appear to be as innocent as doves, yet once under the covers, evil snakes come slithering from their womb to bite with fatal poison the man who would dare enter there."

Stefan could not help but laugh at the ignorance of these superstitious, country people. "You must be joking!" he exclaimed. "We are no longer living in the Dark Ages. Do you have no knowledge of science at all? Do any of you read?" The entire group of men peered at him incredulously as if to say, *Read? What is that?* Then he sighed and shook his head. "There are no witches or spells or serpents, and women do not have devices to slice off one's manhood. These outlandish stories are preposterous although I must concur with this gentleman here that there are diseases. But a man can give them to a woman as easily as she can give them to him. And that, my young friend," he said to Anton, "is where virginity does play an important role. For if she has never been with a man, she could not contract such a malady. It is well known in the scientific community how they are passed from one to another."

"Well, thank you, Domn Hungarian," Bela announced, crossing his arms and smiling with satisfaction that the superstitions had been laid to rest. "I was afraid these fools would talk my friend right out of his marriage."

"And this revelation coming from a confirmed bachelor," Dimitry noted with a grin. As Stefan looked around, he noticed that all in the hall had stopped to listen to him, and his cheeks began to redden. He glanced over at Maria, but she refused to look at him. About that time a voice called from the kitchen; his meal was ready.

Maria dutifully placed the dish before Stefan, but her eyes avoided him. "Ah, thank you, my sweet," he praised as he turned toward his own table and planted both feet on the floor. "Won't you sit for a moment and join me?" he asked, casting up a hopeful smile.

"I am working," she whispered. "I cannot sit with you."

Stefan nodded in understanding and finally caught her eyes with his. "Maybe later I could walk you home, then."

"Thank you," she replied politely, "but I am a grown woman and do not require an escort."

"We shall see," he answered nonchalantly and took his fork to his steaming meal. "Ah, it smells delicious." Then he began to sample one dainty bite after the other.

By the time Stefan finished his meal, many of the other diners had left, including the young groom and his friends. However, a few new men had stopped by for drinks before heading home and off to bed. By the time they had drunk two or three rounds, the young men's topic of conversation had turned to Prince Vlad.

"He is a bloodthirsty menace, a despicable despot who would have us all hanging on poles," emphatically declared one of them wearing a clabatul cap.

A younger Romanian with a long black mustache and wearing an astrakhan-lined hip length coat disagreed. "One must rule with power, and I think he has done it quite well. Look how he has turned back the Turks and defended our land." He motioned as he looked from one face to the other. "Yes, he executes people - criminals, those who deserve it. But he richly rewards his friends, and his army is growing every day. I am even considering joining it; then I will have a chance to get into some real battles with the infidels."

"I wouldn't be so quick to join Vlad's army," a bald man in the group warned him. "A soldier's life is generally short and uncertain."

"I agree with Remie," a pale young man with a scar on his cheek said with a nod which jostled his fur gluga. "Look at us - we are all prospering just fine under Vlad's reign, as did my parents many years ago when he ruled the land. It is only wrong-doers that need fear anything from the prince. Dracula is really no different from any other monarch. They are all the same," he explained matter-of-factly and then took another sip of his ale.

Maria could take no more. "Are you all mad?" she asked incredulously. "You call mere children criminals? Do you call the old, the destitute, the lame wrong doers, just because they cannot productively serve 'his royal majesty'?"

"What do you mean?" The mustached young Remie turned toward her.

"He murders people, children even," she accused bitterly, "those who are helpless."

"Murder is such a strong word," his friend in the gluga replied lightly.

Then Stefan joined in the conversation with a thoughtful observation. "It is a prudent move, and often a common practice," he said coolly, "for a military leader to kill the offspring of his enemies. For if one was allowed to remain alive, he would certainly grow up to avenge the death of his parents. So, in that way it can be said that Vlad is only looking out for his own security."

Maria threw her hands to her hips and shot a hateful glare at Stefan. "My son did nothing wrong, and his parents were not Dracula's enemies, but that did not stop the monster!"

Suddenly Stefan froze, gazing into her mordant and deeply wounded face. He felt his stomach catch in his throat; his mouth dropped, but no words were able to come forth. Within his powerful frame, he felt a tremble that he could not control, and it was as if an arrow had been shot through his own heart.

Chapter 10

Bless the Child

"In addition, he invited all of the beggars, the sick, and
the poor to a great feast but after they had their fill of food
and wine, he had them burned to death."

From the Chronicle of Antonius Bontinius[*]

Maria's eyes scanned the room as she swallowed and raised her chin.
"My husband died years ago, and I was left with only my son, Georgi. I
had to go to work to support us, and I couldn't be with him all the time."
Anger slowly drained from her voice, being replaced by sullen sorrow. "A
few weeks ago Georgi was out, skipping up and down the street, when the
baker put a tray of fresh tarts out on the sill to cool. He must have been
very hungry waiting for me to get off work. He smelled how good they
were and asked the baker if he could have one. When he asked Georgi if
he had any money, he answered, 'no, but my mother does and she will pay
you when she gets off work if I could just have one to eat now.' They
must have looked so good to him, and the baker would probably have
complied - he knew I would pay the money." A tear streamed down
Maria's face, and she sniffed a bit but continued the story. "It was then
that Prince Dracula came walking by," she said with bitter hatred in her
tone at the mention of his name. "Seeing a young boy alone, begging for a
tart, he must have assumed he was an orphan or a vagrant or a Gypsy or
beggar's child. He didn't even bother to ask or find out. He simply put
his hand on my son's shoulder and said, 'Come, my boy. Why, at the end
of the street I am giving a feast. I am inviting all that are hungry to come,
eat their fill, and have as much as they want; Prince Dracula wishes for
none to go hungry in his principality.' Later the baker told me of these
events, how he led my son down the street."

At that point Maria stopped and had to sit in a chair, for she felt weak
in her knees. The nearest seat was across from Stefan at his table. She

---

[*] This story appears in all three major accounts of Vlad III's activities

had lost her anger toward him as grief consumed her being. All eyes in the tavern were on her as she took a deep breath and continued. "There was a large hall at the end of the street, and the prince had indeed called for all of the lame, the beggars, the homeless, and the sickly to come where he had promised them a great banquet. Once he had gathered them inside, servants began passing out bowls of hot soup." Her voice began to crack, so she swallowed hard and continued with her hands folded in her lap. "That encouraged more to enter until every seat was filled. There must have been a hundred people."

Maria wiped the moisture from her face. Stefan's heart ached within him. He longed to reach out and touch her, but he dared not. "He said, 'I have arranged that none of you will ever go hungry again.' Oh, they were so full of hope and excitement - the young, the old, the helpless. Then Vlad and the servants all left the building and bolted the doors from the outside." It was so quiet in the tavern at that moment that each man and woman could hear the beating of his own heart. Maria looked down into her lap; when her face rose, hatred flashed in her eyes.

"Even from inside the tavern, we could hear the screams. I ran out into the street and saw smoke billowing from the burning building. They were all trapped inside. I ran out and began to frantically call for Georgi because I didn't see him anywhere." Her voice cracked again, and she was on the verge of completely breaking down into sobs. "That's when the baker told me that Vlad had walked him down to the end of the street," she cried.

The two young men at the bar who had spoken well of the prince hung their heads. This was an event they had not heard about. It left a bitter taste in the back of their throats. Dimitry remained silent. He knew that Maria's story was true. He had been there, seen the burning building, and heard the screams himself. But he did not speak of it, and he always cautioned Maria to keep her tongue quiet. He was truly afraid that one of Dracula's secret police would hear her and take her away to be punished for disloyalty to the prince. But he knew the poor woman's heart would burst if she did not tell her story to someone, and that the anguish would never work its way out of her soul if she was not allowed to release it. He would protect her if he could; she was his employee.

"Well," she sighed in conclusion. "They were never hungry again, now were they? Was their poverty a crime deserving of death? He was all I had in the world," she began to sob, "and that bastard took him from me with never a thought."

Stefan was filled with grief, almost more than he could bear. Maria's story had touched him in a very deep and secret place in his heart. He took out his handkerchief and stretched it across the table to her. "I am so deeply sorry, Maria," he said, his words echoing true into her soul. "I didn't know."

"You, his business partner, who condones the killing of children, wants to offer me your handkerchief?"

"You can accuse me and display your disdain for me later, doamna, but now I suggest that you blow your nose." The soft calm in his voice and the practicality of his words made the situation almost humorous to her for an instant. She took the cloth and wiped her eyes and nose. All the while something was happening inside the big Hungarian. His heart, long locked shut, was opened and flooded with a myriad of emotions. He spoke tenderly and compassionately to her. "But Maria, you are still young and very beautiful. You will marry again and have another child."

"That is unlikely," she scoffed. "I myself am an orphan with no property, no dowry, nothing to bring to a marriage, and am far beyond the age of most eligible young women. No, domnule, there will be no husband for me, no child, no future."

The tugging at Stefan's heart said otherwise. At that moment she looked up into his eyes and saw something there she had not seen before in this man. All barriers, all pretenses were gone, and she saw in him a totally different person from the one who had presented himself for the past two days. In that sea of blue, she saw the reflection of her own pain, as if the man himself had been deeply and mortally wounded. It seemed to them that there was no one else in the room; they were in a world of their own, eyes locked, peering to see inside each other's souls. The only thing she could be certain of was that there was more to Stefan Kubana than he was letting anyone else see. In that moment she lowered her own walls of protection as well. "I thank you for your concern, Domn Stefan, and for the use of your handkerchief." She began to hand him back the wet cloth, but he stopped her with a motion of his hand.

"Why don't you keep it," he suggested. "It appears to me that you may be needing it again. Besides, I have another."

Maria forced a small smile and then placed the handkerchief in her apron pocket.

For the first time, someone else in the room stood to speak, awakening them to the fact they were not alone. "Time for me to be getting home," the customer said, laying a few coins on the table.

"I had better be getting back to work, too," Maria admitted with practicality. She was suddenly embarrassed about telling her story to a room filled with strangers, but Stefan was glad that she had. Even though it had made his eyes betray him and opened a floodgate of heretofore captured emotions churning within him like the billows of a great sea, complicating his life to no end, he was still very, very glad she had told him what happened to her son.

As Maria arose from the table, Stefan was suddenly aware that he had let down all of his guard, and he at once sat back in his chair, took a sip from his wine glass, and resumed his air of superiority. But being able to think of nothing appropriate to say, he remained quiet for a while.

Within a few minutes, the tavern was back to its usual level of noise and activity. One by one the patrons began to leave as the evening wore on and darkness covered the town. But a dirty, stubble-faced peasant did enter in a bit of a foul mood and ask for a drink. As she handed the customer his third cup of ale, Maria wondered why Stefan remained at his table when he had already sat for hours. He tried not to stare too obviously at her as he nursed his glass of wine while making small talk with Dimitry.

When Maria brought the scruffy peasant at the bar his fourth cup of ale, he reached out, catching hold of her wrist, his wide grin displaying a missing tooth and a fair amount of decay. He looked at her lustily with wide eyes. "Hey, pretty maid," he said slyly. "Come and sit with me and be sweet."

"I am sorry, domnule," she said trying to pull her hand free. "But I am on duty and have work to do."

"You will be closing down soon," he sang out boastfully, "and I will be ready to entertain you."

Stefan glared at the ruffian who had had too much to drink. "Please," Maria insisted, finally wrenching her hand loose.

But the scruffy, drunkard caught the hem of her skirt and held on tightly, halting her retreat. He slid from his stool and grasped her forearms. "Give me a little kiss now, wench. One won't hurt," he sputtered, his heavy body swaying a bit as he kept his grip tight.

Dimitry started to move in that direction with a disapproving glower. He had already opened his mouth to speak when he noticed Stefan bolting up from his chair and prancing ceremoniously towards the two. He thought this might be an interesting exchange, so he waited and watched.

"Unhand the lady, you ruffian!" Stefan pronounced in a haughty, high-pitched voice, placing his hands on his hips. "I have been informed that the lady does not perform that kind of service."

Maria remembered her words from the night before and chuckled inwardly. *So he is defending my honor, is he?*

The drunken man leaned to one side, shifting from one foot to the other, and raised his eyes to survey the Hungarian merchant. Then he laughed aloud. "What are you going to do to stop me?" he demanded impertinently. "Bludgeon me with your handkerchief?"

Stefan scowled like a wounded pup and then gathered himself to form some new words. "If you do not unhand the lady immediately, I will be forced to report you to my friend, Prince Dracula. I recall from our conversation earlier today that Vlad has a most unhealthy dislike for adulterers and fornicators. I do not know which you plan to be, but I do know what fate Dracula has in store for such as you."

The man froze, sobering up instantly, his eyes fixed on Stefan, his face pale as a linen sheet. He slowly removed his hands from Maria and took a step backward. Then he forced a half-smile. "I was only joking. I have n-no plans to, to do anything with this woman. Th-there is nothing to tell the prince," he stuttered nervously. "I think I'll be on my way now." The peasant did not bother to finish his mug at the bar but threw down a few coins and made a hasty retreat.

Stefan smiled and crossed his arms over his chest in quiet satisfaction at his victory. He was expecting to be showered with Maria's praise and wrapped warmly in her thanks, but he was rudely awakened when she spun around on her heel, glaring at him as if he had been the perpetrator. He responded with an alarmed expression, his hands falling to his sides.

"Friend of Prince Dracula." Her words were spoken as a poisonous accusation in a seething tone while her lips pursed with suppressed fury.

Stefan quickly collected his thoughts. "I assure you, Maria, I use the term loosely, and for the ruffian's benefit - not your own."

"Nevertheless," she spat out hatefully toward him. "I do not now, nor will I ever, need help from a friend of his. Why don't you just mind your own business!"

Dimitry shook his head. Didn't she realize what he had done for her? "As you wish, doamna," Stefan replied and took a step towards his chair. Formality hid the hurt in his voice, but his deep blue eyes were haunted with disappointment. Turning over his shoulder, the gentleman added, "But I feel that it is my duty to escort you home this evening."

"What!" she exclaimed. "I do not need an escort home. I would feel safer with a snake than with you."

But Stefan held up his hand and raised his chin. "I'll not hear another word. The rake could still be out there; he could have gathered his friends. They could be waiting for you. No. An attack has been made on your virtue, and it is my duty as a gentleman to see you safely home." Having concluded his speech, Stefan turned his back to her and walked to his chair.

"Dimitry, will you tell him -" Maria began.

"Actually, I must agree with Stefan. I think it is wise to have someone walk you home. It is late, and dark, and cold, and…you have had a very disturbing evening," he added softly. "There's hardly anyone still here. Teo and I can see to locking up. Now, let the gentleman see you home."

She pouted, stamping her foot lightly and crossing her arms. She glanced at Stefan scornfully. He beamed in satisfaction and finished the last swallow from his wine glass. Maria had not budged one inch when he looked over to her. "Shouldn't you be getting your coat now?" She grumbled something that was inaudible to him then shuffled over through the door to the kitchen.

When she returned, she was wearing her warm, woolen wrap. She spied Stefan standing by the door to prevent her leaving without him. He and Dimitry exchanged smiles and nods which aggravated Maria even more. The two men had sided against her. *Whatever could they be plotting?* she thought.

The frigid wind bit the couple as they stepped out into the night air. "I hate you!" Maria announced as they forged their way down the snow-covered street.

"No," Stefan said calmly. "You hate Vlad Tepes."

"I hate you both," she replied and pulled her wrap closer, folding her arms so he had no way to take hold of her.

Stefan carefully hid the wound she had dealt his heart as his boot crunched into a patch of ice. "Ah, I am not such a bad fellow once you get to know me," he said cheerfully.

"Likely that happening, seeing that you are leaving tomorrow," she answered without looking up at him.

Stefan lowered his chin, a slight grin tugging at the corners of his mouth. "I will return in less than a fortnight."

At that Maria did jerk her head up and peer into his face with surprise. "Coming back?" she asked as she continued to walk toward her cottage. "Whatever for?"

"Well, I have several good reasons for returning," he said slyly, indicating with a raised eyebrow that she indeed might be one of them. "One is to bring back the signed agreement binding our trade treaty."

"Oh," Maria replied bluntly then turned away, her eyes back on the road. "Coming back to see 'your friend' the prince," she mocked.

"It is business, Maria," he said gravely and earnestly, imploring her to listen to him.

"Business," she repeated disdainfully. "Would you sell your soul to the devil himself for a few pieces of silver?"

Stefan stiffened, his features harsh. "Doamna, free trade benefits both our countries. It happens that I am required to deal with the head of state in this particular instance, to secure the safety of my own merchants. I hardly want to see them all dangling from pikes."

"I suppose not." Maria walked a few steps in silence when her thoughts suddenly stumbled across something. She spun around to him in horrific shock, regarding the foreigner with cold speculation. "You were there this morning," she accused in a dark tone. "You were there when he killed that girl. Did you participate or merely watch?"

Stefan was stunned, and he stopped still, his blue eyes wide at her and his mouth agape. "She's dead?" he questioned.

"As if you didn't know." Maria turned a cold shoulder to him and quickened her pace down the road toward her house.

"No, I didn't." He stepped behind with long strides, easily catching up. "I - I had already left the castle. I heard what could have been a scream, but-"

"But I know - there was nothing you could have done."

"Maria!" This time he did grab her arm and pull her around to face him. "There are 1,400 steps to that castle, and I was at the bottom. If you think I condone what he does-"

"Why would you do business with a man and visit him so frequently if you do not?" she inquired.

"It is not he I do business with - it is your whole country. Can't you understand that?"

For the first time, Maria perceived heated anger rising from the self-controlled merchant - possibly even a real display of emotion. Maybe her words had struck a chord in him, she thought slyly to herself. "You needn't trouble yourself anymore, domnule. That is my dwelling across the street there." She pointed to one of the numerous small villas that were squeezed tightly together. It was a mixture of stucco and frame with an A-point roof, covered with several inches of snow - a modest house, though better than some.

"Then I shall walk with you across the street," Stefan said calmly as though he had not just engaged in a heated argument.

"I find that highly unnecessary," she replied, turning from him again as she independently negotiated the icy patches in the road.

Once again he was right on her heels as if to stand guard over her every step. "Maria." He called her name tenderly as they reached her front door. "There is something very important that I need to speak with you about upon my return."

She turned to look at him questioningly. "What of importance could you possibly have to speak to me about?"

"Well, if I tell you now, then it won't be something I need to talk with you about when I return," he explained logically.

"If it is so important," she retorted tilting her head to one side and eyeing him with a disbelieving gaze, "then you should tell me now. I may not wish to see you when you come back."

"I would gladly tell you now," he said in a deep undertone, "but I must take care of some business before entertaining thoughts of pleasure."

"Why you insufferable cad!" Maria's eyes flashed anger at him, and she raised a hand as though to slap his face.

Stefan gently caught her by the wrist. "I promise, Maria," he pledged in a very honest and sincere manner, "that you will like what I have to say."

"You seem so sure of yourself. What makes you think I would ever be interested in anything you have to say? You - you're a total stranger, and a foreigner, a fop and a rake, and probably a Catholic as well," she nervously spat out her accusations while trying to suppress the sensation that traversed her body at the warmth of his touch.

For a brief moment while Maria declared all of the reasons why she did not like him, Stefan came very close to revealing his secret and telling her everything, but he held down the flood that was raging within him. With an extraordinary measure of self-control, he turned her hand in his, bowed gallantly, and kissed it in a grand display of chivalry. "Until we meet again, doamna," he said, his eyes fixed on hers as he slowly released her hand.

She was stunned. After all that she had said, he had no reply but to bid her a gentleman's farewell. He looked so cool and sophisticated, so in charge. *No, this man is no weakling,* she determined. But what exactly was he? A spy, perhaps; is that why he was so eager to deceive everyone?

Stefan walked away from her, and only after reaching the shadows did his head fall, his countenance with it. His heart sank heavily in his chest. *She hates me,* he thought to himself morosely. *She hates me!*

Chapter 11

Islands in the Stream

"You can judge for yourselves that when a man or a prince is strong and powerful, he can make peace as he wants to; but when he is weak, a stronger one will come and do what wants to him."

Vlad Dracula, Prince of Walachia, to the officers of Brasov, 1456

"Petru, start packing," Vlad instructed as he briskly paced down the hallway of the Poenari living quarters. "We are taking a journey."

"Yes, my prince. May I ask -"

"And get me Ivan and Sergei at once," he said turning his chin over his shoulder before pushing open the door to his study.

The baffled valet did as he was told and brought Vlad's captain of the guard and chief armas to his study. He opened the door and announced in a formal voice, "My lord high viovode and prince of Walachia; Captain Ivan of Poenari and Domn Sergei as you requested."

"Good, good," Vlad said excitedly as he rose from his chair behind the large oak desk displaying a large, unrolled map. Light streamed in through the open window behind him, encircling the prince with a bright aura. "Come in, gentlemen. As you know, King Matthias has withdrawn his troops, and only yesterday Prince Stephan departed with his army. Although in his generosity he did loan me his personal guard of two hundred, our situation is most precarious at best. Look here." Vlad's full green silk sleeve brushed across the paper as he pointed to a place on the map while the three trusted men moved closer around the desk.

"Sultan Mehmed has troops positioned here, here, and here, south of the Danube. I have on a good source that the sultan himself may be camped at Varna."

"They may try an invasion in the spring, milord," Ivan suspected. "At the first thaw, I'd wager, before you have time to amass an army."

"They wouldn't dare," Sergei sneered. "The Turks are afraid of Prince Dracula. They will wait, send emissaries, and try to talk him into paying tribute."

"I do not believe so, Sergei," Vlad said solemnly. "I think they will attack and maybe even before spring."

"With troops that close to the border it is possible, but still unlikely," Ivan speculated. "Travel is slow and supply lines hard to maintain."

"True," Vlad considered, rubbing his chin with his right hand. "But Basarab is still out there with supporters loyal to him. If they were to aid the Turks, it would be a possibility - one we cannot afford to ignore. That is why I am moving my army to Bucuresti."

"My prince, the fortress at Bucuresti is in no way equal to this one," Ivan declared, opening his arms to gesture to the strong stone walls around them.

"You would be putting yourself in danger," Sergei protectively pointed out.

"The army should be protecting our border," Vlad said with determination, "and I am the head of the army."

"With all due respect, my lord - what army?" inquired Ivan with concern in his voice. "I have two hundred soldiers, there is the guard Prince Stephen left with you, maybe another two hundred Hussar mercenaries, and under two thousand Romanians who just chased off Basarab. The Turks have -"

"I know what the Turks have," Dracula said darkly, raising the glow of his green eyes to meet Ivan's. "You will conscript me an army from these towns and villages I go to defend. You will make known my decree that from each household one male between the ages of seventeen and forty-five shall be henceforth impressed into military service for as long as the threat remains."

"But, Your Majesty," Ivan protested, "how will we feed and provision such a large force in winter?"

The prince's cold stare was unsettling to the captain who was only trying to do his job. Dracula put his hands on the desk, leaned toward the tall, broad-shouldered soldier, and spoke piercingly. "That is not your concern. Just get me the army as you have been commanded."

"Yes, milord," he answered with a salute. "I shall begin today."

"Assemble them here in two weeks. Then we will march to Bucuresti."

"It will be as you say, my prince." With that, Ivan turned on his black heeled boot and strode out of the room, out of the living quarters, and into the snow-covered castle yard, muttering to himself all the while.

"Now, Petru, you, Sergei, and I will be leaving today for Snagov," Vlad said as pleasure recaptured his features.

"Isn't that the monastery you built on that little island in a lake near the Dimbovita River?" Sergei asked, shifting his weight to one leg.

"Rebuilt, to be precise," Vlad corrected him, taking a seat in his desk chair. "I added a few fortress-like features," he gleamed. "Like this refuge, Snagov is virtually attack proof on that island. And if an enemy were to advance across the frozen surface of the lake, one cannon shot would send them all to a frigid, watery grave. Besides," Vlad added with a smile, folding his hands behind his head and leaning back in his chair, "my treasure is hidden there - an all too commonly known fact. But we will store the treasury in a secret place where no one else will ever find it. That way, even if the sultan is successful, he will never see one piece of that gold he so regularly covets."

"Who else do you require I inform of your journey, milord? And who should I secure as an escort?" Petru asked, daring to speak at last.

"Simply inform the staff we are going on a journey and will be back soon. Select two of our most trusted guards, a coachman, and a coach. And don't forget to pack provisions; I do not wish to waste time stopping for meals."

"Certainly, Prince Dracula," Petru concurred as he left to make the preparations.

"Such a small escort - Vlad, do you think that is wise?" Sergei leaned over, resting his elbows on the table as he questioned his master.

"Yes," he replied confidently. "We will draw less attention and move more quickly. We will hire the workers we need to bury the treasure when we arrive. I will then leave to you the pleasure of cleaning up when we are done with them."

A dark smile touched Sergei's lips as he understood the implied directive of the prince.

A warm, crackling fire warmed Kuban's home on that frosty winter night. He and Stefan sat in great, stuffed chairs beside the hearth sipping brandy. "I take it things went well then?" the older gentleman inquired as he relaxed in his wine-colored dinner jacket. The glow of the fire reflected off his balding forehead.

"Well, I am still alive," Stefan chuckled, beaming at the old man who had taught him the fine art of diplomacy. "I just need signatures from the guild members. Naturally, it would not hurt to have a representative of the king sign the agreement as well. Vlad is concerned that Matthias may go back on his word and start charging duties again."

Kuban's eyes beamed proudly at the younger man as he sipped from his snifter. "I have a friend in the ministry department; I'll get you that signature," he promised.

Stefan looked very relaxed, his shirt partially unbuttoned, his boots set wide apart, as he leaned back in his comfortable chair. Kuban eyed him intuitively, noticing a new glow in his deep blue eyes. "Aren't you going to supply me any more details than that you have the prince's signature on the treaty? I've been waiting all this time and am interested in hearing more specifics."

The light in Stefan's eyes dimmed as he thought of the man with whom he had done business. "He has not changed," he uttered sternly. "His atrocities go on. He likes me, though - finds me refreshing," he laughed wryly and took another sip from his glass.

"There is one complication, however," Stefan admitted, lowering his glass and rearranging one foot.

"And that is?" Kuban peered at Stefan intently with his knowing brown eyes.

"I have met a woman," Stefan declared, turning his gaze to Kuban as if to search for approval.

"It's right bloody time, I'd say!" he exclaimed excitedly, sitting up in his chair with a fatherly grin from ear to ear. "I was beginning to worry about you, my boy."

Stefan's cheeks reddened a bit and he cast his eyes bashfully to the floor. When he looked up, his expression was heavy with concern. "I am afraid she may complicate matters immensely."

"Why is that?"

"First of all, she doesn't seem to like me much, nor trust me. On top of that, she hates the prince - enough to try to kill him, and I am afraid that is what she has in mind."

The mirth left Kuban's face as he nodded. "That could be a problem, indeed."

Stefan set down his glass and stretched his arms across his knees, palms facing upward and gazed into the eyes of the older man. "She is different, you know, and..." He searched for words, biting his lower lip nervously. "And I have feelings for her. It is hard to explain." He raised one hand in gesture. "I feel connected to her. Have you ever felt that way?"

"Da." Kuban sat back in his chair wistfully.

Stefan sighed, picked up his glass from the little table and sat back to take another sip. "It will not be easy to complete the business at hand," he confessed. "But if I am successful - and I hope to be - I would truly like to be able to pursue this relationship. Ha," he laughed, trying to calm his own fears at the moment. "She has no money, no title, no land, and is a widow as well. I don't suppose the neighbors would be very complimentary about my choice of a wife."

"Do not be worrying about what the neighbors think, Stefan," Kuban said in defense of the young man. "What matters is that you are satisfied with her. The neighbors don't have to live with your wife - you do."

Stefan looked up to Kuban, his eyes bright again. "You are a good man, Kuban," he declared. "And I am most fortunate to be a part of your household. I only hope that I can be successful and bring honor, not disgrace, upon your house and your name."

Kuban swallowed the last sip from his brandy snifter and set it down on the stone hearth. Then he rose and took a couple of steps, stopping when he stood beside Stefan's chair. He placed a strong hand affectionately on the younger man's shoulder. "I am proud of you, son," he said in earnest, "whatever the outcome of your venture. You must know that."

"I thank you, sir," he replied looking up into Kuban's furrowed face. "It means a great deal to hear you say that. I wonder if...," he began and then shook his head with a sigh. "No, it's better not to think of such things."

But Kuban knew exactly what Stefan was thinking and answered accordingly. "Yes, he would be proud of you, too." The two men's eyes met in a brief exchange of emotion and then Kuban took his leave.

Maria met her friend and neighbor, Nadia, that morning as she usually did to walk into the center of town to the places of their employment. But this time the streets were filled with interesting wagons of many colors. They were ornately decorated, some hitched to painted horses. And standing in the town square, quickly becoming the center of attention, was a band of Gypsies.

A festive atmosphere permeated the air that morning as the residents of Curte de Arges mingled with the strangers, examining the new wares they had for sale, listening to their stories of foreign lands, watching the performers and giving them coins in return, all to the sound of fiddles, finger cymbals, and tambourines. "How exciting!" Nadia bubbled as she looked around with wonder at the strange men and women.

"Have you never seen Gypsies before?" Maria remarked matter-of-factly, as if their presence was of no interest to her.

"Not since I was a little girl," Nadia beamed, looking about with bright eyes. "Come on, Maria, let's have a little fun. You don't have to be at the tavern for hours."

"Fun?" she questioned as though it were a word from a foreign language bearing no meaning for her at all.

"Yes!" Nadia declared taking hold of her friend's arm and staring intently into her face. "Fun. Merriment. Excitement, joy, pleasure - surely you can remember those words."

"Ah, the words I can remember," Maria admitted with a deep sigh. "It is their meaning I have forgotten."

"What troubles you?" Nadia asked sincerely as she stopped walking but still held fast to her comrade's arm. "It has been weeks since Georgi-"

"Six weeks, not long enough for me to have finished mourning. But that is not all that troubles me."

"Tell me," Nadia implored.

Around them swirled the noise, colors, and activity of a festival. A juggler in brilliantly tinted silks passed them tossing small balls into the air in a continual circle. Instruments played a modal tune while men in red cojocs and dark-haired women wearing embroidered lacy skirts danced with tambourines. But at that moment Nadia focused her full attention on only one person - Maria.

"The Hungarian, Stefan, that I mentioned to you."

"Yes, what about him?"

"He perplexes me," Maria said crossly.

"How so?" Nadia asked.

"When I told the story of what had happened to Georgi, he had the most sincere look, and his eyes - they were like he felt my pain, and like he really cared. Then almost immediately he was back to his formal, insufferable self. He even claimed to be a friend of that blood-lusting bastard. He is a paradox - both a dandy and a cad, a fearless protector and an indifferent businessman. I think he is hiding something."

"I think you are fascinated with him," Nadia observed with a grin.

"I am not!" Maria retorted angrily. "I told you, he perplexes me."

"So he does," Nadia said with a smile. "Perhaps he adds excitement, mystery, and intrigue to your life. By doing so, solving this mystery gives you something new to live for."

"I have but one thing to live for," Maria said darkly, her eyes searching the distance with a cold, piercing expression of death.

"Not that again, Maria," Nadia warned gravely. "Don't say it - don't even think it."

"Oh, I don't have to say it or think it," Maria replied looking back into the face of her friend. "I am just going to do it."

At that moment, the scarlet curtain covering the door to the wagon nearest them flew open. A middle-aged Gypsy woman with graying hair covered by a sparkly marama and dangling hoop earrings poked her head out at them. Her eyes were bulging from her tan face and a dozen necklaces hung about her neck. Gold and silver bracelets swayed from the wrist of her ringed hand holding back the curtain. "You," she said pointing a bony finger toward Maria. "Come, my child, and I will tell your fortune."

"I don't need a fortune teller to tell me my future," Maria replied.

"Come on," Nadia prodded, poking her ribs with an elbow. "It will be fun. I will go with you, and we can both have our fortunes told."

"It is a silly thing," Maria protested. "And I don't believe in fortune telling."

"You don't have to believe it." Nadia smiled playfully. "It is all in fun."

"No," the old woman replied in a mysterious voice. "For when I read the cards, I do see what will happen. The cards know."

Nadia and Maria knew that most of their neighbors believed strongly in the predictions of Gypsy fortune tellers and many stories of their unexplained powers had been told. "Go on," Nadia urged, giving Maria a little push toward the wagon. "What could it hurt?"

"A-aren't you needed at the pottery shop?" Maria asked nervously, hoping to find a way out of this absurd predicament.

"No, they can get along without me," Nadia assured Maria as she took another step toward the painted wagon.

Maria was still uncertain about the venture as she settled herself on one of the pillows nestled around a small, round table in the back of the enclosed wagon. Some light peeked through a crack in the drawn curtain; the rest was provided by a dim oil lamp placed in the middle of the table. Nadia sat beside Maria and across from them sat the Gypsy with a large amethyst ring on one of her fingers. The old woman seemed to be staring at Maria in a most peculiar fashion as she shuffled the cards, which completely unnerved the young widow.

"Now," the Gypsy said, "we must have quiet."

Maria gave Nadia a look of dissatisfaction as if to say, *We are already quiet. What does the woman think we are doing?*

"Spirits, guide my hands, speak through the cards," she chanted in a tremulous voice. Maria rolled her eyes, then brought them back to the table where the Gypsy woman uncovered the first several cards and lay them in a row. "Ah," she said. "I see you are a widow who has recently lost a child."

Immediately Maria's attitude changed. Her eyes widened, and her hands slapped down upon the table in disbelief. "Th-that is correct," she answered, completely stunned that the old woman could know such a thing about a total stranger.

She uncovered another card and then spoke. "You are a working woman; you serve people."

"Yes, I work at the tavern," Maria concurred. She still could not believe what she was hearing.

The fortune teller laid face up the next card. "Hmm," she lingered. "You have met a fair-haired man." When she turned over the next card, she added, "But he is not who he appears to be."

Maria turned her stunned expression towards Nadia who herself could not believe what she was hearing. Maria became quite enthralled with the tale. "Can you tell me who he is? Can you tell me anything about him?" she asked urgently.

"I am not certain," the Gypsy replied. "We shall see soon." But when she turned over the next card, a look of terror swept across her face, and she threw her hands into the air, her mouth agape and eyes wide. It was the death card!

Chapter 12

Snagov

"After the death of Prince Mircea, Prince Vlad, whose name was 'the Impaler,' came to rule. The latter built the monastery of Snagov and the castle of Poenari. He inflicted a severe punishment on the citizens of Tirgoviste."

The chronicler Cantacuzino in the 15th century

"The death card!" exclaimed the fortune teller. Maria sat on the edge of her pillow leaning forward with her hands on the table as she peered at the card.

"What does it mean?" she cried, suddenly quite caught up in a practice she had heretofore given no credence.

"The man is dangerous; trouble follows him," she explained. "I cannot be certain if it is he who will die, or if he will kill someone else. But there is most assuredly death on this man, and around him. For whether it is he that will die or he that will kill, either instance would place those near him at risk."

"Maria," Nadia motioned, touching her arm as she tried to gain her friend's attention. "Remember, this is all in fun. We do not know for sure if the things she says -"

"Beware my warning," the Gypsy woman interrupted with a most serious expression. "The cards do not lie. There will be death where this man goes."

"I will heed your warning," Maria replied slowly. "I will be careful of him."

"See that you do," she confirmed one more time with fear in her voice as her wide eyes peered over her crooked nose at the young woman.

Vlad's keen, jade eyes scanned the meadows of the Walachian lowlands as his small party traveled south to visit the Snagov Monastery. Petru, Sergei, and the prince were seated in the crude, black coach with bulky wheels while the two guards rode escort on horseback. For the journey, Vlad had chosen to wear a warm, taupe szur with a broad, astrakhan collar. The three tipped and swayed with the rough ride of the crude coach. "I do enjoy such little outings and communing with nature. Take that hawk, for example," the prince said pointing out the open window. His companions peered out the window at Vlad's request, noticing that the lowland snow had melted in the bright sunlight. They watched the hawk swoop down in a quick, fierce sweep into the brown grass. Then back into the sky it soared with a field mouse in its talons. "You see, it is nature's way," Vlad explained philosophically. "The hawk makes its kill because it is swift, and strong, and decisive, but no one thinks less of it for its bloodshed. Instead, for centuries men have admired the hawk." The prince then turned to his servants who sat across from him as a teacher giving a lesson. "Likewise, the wolf kills a deer - be it a buck, doe, or fawn - and the other wolves do not cast him out. No one says it is only a bad wolf that kills a doe or a fawn. It is simply the nature of the animal. It is his instinct to thin out the numbers of weaker species, lest they over-populate and starve to death. Nature is filled with examples of how the strong survive by preying on the weak, and none says, 'the hawk is evil,' or 'the wolf is demonic.' Why then do their tongues condemn me and their mouths say it is evil when I, their prince, dispose of lesser beings?"

"My lord," Sergei replied, "it is because they are ignorant and do not understand that you are doing our country a great service by ridding it of its most undesirable elements. A proper, moral society should be void of traitors, liars, and adulterers. Your judgment is like the hand of God on Sodom and Gomorrah."

"Perhaps that is it," Vlad mused as he looked out the window once more. "I once had a vision from God; fire rained from Heaven, and I heard a voice say, 'I shall blot out the wicked from among my people.'" Then he turned his gaze to the properly dressed valet. "What do you think, Petru? Why do people say I am evil?"

Petru swallowed hard while his mind and heart raced. He wanted to give a favorable, yet believable reply. "I suspect that there are those who believe men should follow a different order than nature. Yet what do priests and peasants know of the duties, decisions, and responsibilities that fall to those in leadership? You, my prince, cannot just look at the individual, but must consider what is best for the nation."

"You are quite right, Petru. I hold nationalistic ideals. I want to form a united Romania - a homeland for our people, Turks, Saxons, and Hungarians be damned. To do so, we must have three things that we do not have: a strong economy, a strong military, and centralization of power. But I have been trying diligently to rectify those problems."

"Why, of course!" Petru's face lit up as he leaned forward in his seat. "That explains why you dealt so harshly with the foreign merchants."

"Precisely," Vlad answered with a satisfied grin. He gripped the seat as the coach hit a deep rut, and he was flung to one side. "Trade within our borders cannot be dominated by foreign merchants if we ever hope to develop our own merchant class. Romanian merchants would make large sums of money available to spend in our own country, as well as to pay in taxes. And that money is needed to maintain a national army."

"So that is why the conscripting," Sergei acutely observed. "While other kings and princes rely on the service of their nobility's retainers and knights, you have initiated a practice that they criticize and demean, but it all makes sense."

"An army loyal only to the prince who commands it can hardly be used against him, now can it?" Vlad glowed in triumph as his companions began to understand his actions. "Which brings us to the dilemma of the nobility. You won't see the sultan of the Turks bowing and scraping to a class of wealthy landlords to gain their support on an issue. Absolute power - that is what he holds, and what I want. Almost nineteen years ago I eliminated a generation of strong boyars and replaced them with my puppets. Had I been able to remain in power, rather than spend these past years in prison and exile, I would have already succeeded in establishing an independent nation of Romania, at least equal to Hungary and France." Then Dracula's eyes darkened, and his fists clenched as he continued. "But Radu had to spoil all of my plans, that treacherous little brother of mine. Sold out to our enemies, he did. We would be a great nation by now if it were not for him. Now I have to start all over again." Vlad turned his hateful glare out the coach window, and neither Petru nor Sergei spoke a word.

The next day Prince Dracula's party arrived on the banks of an immense fresh-water lake with a partially wooded island surrounded by its waters. "Is that it?" Petru asked excitedly as he leaned to look through the window. He was extremely tired of the uncomfortable ride afforded by the cumbersome coach.

"Snagov Lake," Vlad said with a reminiscent smile. Neither of his aids had ever been there before, but the prince had visited the site on many occasions during his former reign. The lake lay across a tree-speckled field surrounded by forests on its other side, and they could make out the shape of the island from there. As the coach neared the side of the lake nearest the island, Vlad instructed the coachman to turn off the main road and head for a small pier. When the coach came to a halt, Dracula stepped out first, followed by his fascinated assistants. Petru was especially glad to have his feet on solid ground again.

"It is spectacular, Your Majesty," Sergei marveled at the earth-tone brick architectural wonder. With the trees barren of their leaves, the party of six had an almost unobstructed view of the monastery. Several large buildings rose above the wall that surrounded the complex which encompassed the small island.

Petru was surveying the scene with a different eye. "Milord, the ice is very thin, and there is no boat on our side of the lake. How then will we get across?"

Vlad chuckled knowingly as fond memories from his days at Snagov flooded his soul. "Petru," he announced with a grin, slapping a strong hand on his valet's shoulder. "Leave that to me."

Brother Josef was perched high in the bell tower of the Chapel of the Annunciation polishing the big brass bell that hung in the chapel Vladislav II had constructed. The middle-aged monk was happily singing to himself as he worked when he noticed the small party across the lake. They had not received many visitors as of late, so he was curious about the coach and riders. Josef straightened up, his backbone creaking as he did, and raised his burnished left hand to his brow to shade the midday sun as he peered across the lake's frosted surface. They were too far away for him to distinguish faces, but the monk recognized the banner carried by one of the guards. "Order of the Dragon," he muttered, the mirth leaving his worn face. "So the Impaler makes his appearance."

Brother Josef made the sign of the cross and raised his wooden crucifix pendant to his lips while his eyes darkened, and his brows narrowed. He left the bell and began to descend the tower steps, taking care not to trip on the hem of his brown robe.

"My lord, Abbot," Brother Josef addressed his superior upon finding him preparing the altar of the chapel for the evening vespers.

The gray-haired abbot ceased his preparations and turned his full attention to the lean Romanian monk. Having fathered his flock for several years, the Orthodox abbot knew his sheep well. "Brother Josef, why do you look so distraught?"

"Most Holy Abbot, Prince Vlad has arrived and is across the lake at this moment."

"Ah, no doubt checking on his treasure," the abbot consoled Josef placing an old hand on his shoulder. "Nothing you should worry about."

But Brother Josef was not convinced. He restlessly shifted his weight from one foot to the other. "Shouldn't we do something?"

"By all means," the abbot concurred. "Let us go out to greet him."

"But Your Holiness, he has left the church and become a Roman Catholic," Josef protested as he walked beside the more finely attired abbot.

"Political leaders do many things that they believe are in their best interests, but that does not negate the fact that during his former reign he was very generous to this monastery," the abbot reminded him with a gesture of his ring-clad hand.

"Generous?" A stunned expression crossed Josef's face as he recalled Vlad's additions to Snagov in vivid detail.

"Most generous," the older man repeated as they stepped out of the chapel and into the sunlit monastic grounds. The facility was quite large and had grown to the size allowed by the constraints of the island. There were cloisters for the monks and the abbot's residence and several chapels as one might imagine. But also within the brick and stone walls was a small princely palace, dependencies for visiting boyars and their servants, a treasury, and a mint for producing coins. There was also a small grain field, several garden patches, and the wharf, in addition to a few features that one might not expect to find in an Orthodox Christian site.

"He added these fortress walls, a dungeon, and a torture chamber for his own pleasure to our solace of prayer. Is that something for which we owe him gratitude?" Josef was filled with righteous indignation toward this once and once-again prince of Walachia.

"Come now, Brother Josef," the abbot explained as they walked through the grounds. "Do you call that a prison?" The abbot pointed to a lovely three-tiered chapel built by Prince Dracula on the island. A peasant worker raked away a pile of leaves that had collected by the covered well in front of the chapel. It was sturdily constructed of earth-tone brick with three six-sided towers pointing skyward above the entry. The two smaller ones were burnished tan and the larger middle one was ivory. Each cone-shaped roof was topped with an Orthodox cross. It was a large chapel, though not as grand as Vladislav's Chapel of the Annunciation, with arched windows covered in stained glass squares filling the sanctuary with colored light. It occupied a prominent position near one wall with steps leading down to a gate which opened out onto a small wooden planked boat dock. Willow trees marked both sides of the gate, drooping their branches to the water's edge.

"He only built that to compete with his predecessor. That bloody butcher is an abomination to the Church and to God," Josef declared boldly. "Your Eminence, you were not abbot here during his former reign; you did not witness his atrocities. But I was here, a young clergyman having recently dedicated my life to God's work. Yes, he did undertake a building project here and donated huge sums of gold to the monastery, but it was blood money." The two stopped in front of the impressive Chapel Dracula, and the abbot listened intently to Josef's story.

"He turned our island of prayer and meditation into a fortress where he would spend months at a time. During those visits, he would have political enemies brought in, those he distrusted, anyone who had spoken against him, and even those he merely suspected. Very few left alive. The stain of their blood can never be washed from these stones," he motioned to the buildings surrounding them. "Sometimes at night I can still hear their anguished screams as in times past when he would torture them - personally, himself. It was not unheard of to find a body part, lying on the ground, that had fallen from a covered cart meant to haul them to be dumped in the water after dark. Peasant, craftsman, soldier, boyar - even clergymen...rank made no difference to him. But I must add that he was known to have killed many more Catholic priests than Orthodox."

"These things you speak of happened many years ago, did they not?"

"Yes."

"Then perhaps he has changed," the abbot ventured hopefully. "Time may have mellowed the prince. We will greet him as the monetary benefactor to this monastery that he is and pray that his stay will be brief."

Brother Josef sighed and shook his head. "What else can we do without forfeiting our very lives?"

"A secret tunnel - how clever!" Sergei exclaimed as he lit the torch that stood ready in its wall sconce along the dark, descending stairway. "It is like the ground just opened up."

"Yes," Vlad said with a smile. "This is one of my additions. It travels under the lake and is quite deep. Petru, please inform our escort that they may wait with the coach. Then close the hatch behind you." Petru nodded and did as he was told; then the trio continued down and through the tunnel. As the light illuminated their way, rats and spiders scurried out of sight, back into dark corners but never far from the men's feet. The stale odor and closed in walls of the burrow gave Petru a most uncomfortable feeling. Finally, they began ascending the staircase that would bring them out inside the office chamber of Vlad's prison.

"At last," Petru sighed when they exited through a door into the spacious, room laden with tapestries. Sergei carried in the torch and looked around.

"I like it," he said with a contented grin.

"You will really like this," Vlad added excitedly as he quickly led the way into another room. "Look."

Petru and Sergei walked into a small, windowless chamber with a wooden floor. At one end stood a table bearing a three-foot-high statuette of the Virgin Mary with a woven floor mat in front of it. "Is it a chapel?" Petru asked.

"Something like that," Vlad answered in a playful voice, his green eyes glowing in the dim room lit only by light from the torch and the doorway behind them. "Sometimes my dissenters would wish to repent for being disloyal, and I was always eager to allow them to do so. No, step back from the mat," he warned waving a hand at Petru who had walked too close to the altar. He promptly obeyed, but was curious about the warning. Vlad continued. "I would bring them here so they could pray for forgiveness, and then -"

His long fingers grabbed hold of an empty wall sconce, and he gave it a hard, sudden jerk. With a loud noise, a trap door opened up in the floor that had been covered by the rug. Sergei peered over the side and beneath the trap door which still swung back and forth was a pit with sharpened stakes on its floor. Holding the torch over the edge he could make out a few skeletons in the dirt below. Vlad waited eagerly to hear his confidant's approval.

"It is a masterpiece, my prince!" he announced joyously. "The unsuspecting bastards, thinking they will be forgiven, suddenly plummet to their appointed end as they pray. Truly ingenious!"

"Yes, yes," Vlad replied, pleased with Sergei's response. "Well, it was great fun." For a moment the prince paused as he reflected on his time there. He wondered if he would ever be in a position to resume his personal inquisition or not. Then he sighed as he committed his memories to the past. "On now, my friends. We are here to see about the treasure so we must find the abbot," Vlad instructed as he slowly backed out of the room. "And I will show you everything I built here."

"Wasn't your half-brother abbot here at one time?" Petru asked innocently.

Dracula's eyes flashed at him. "You refer to Vlad the Monk, bastard son of my father's misguided liaison, pretender to the throne, and my enemy. Yes, he was, and if he were here now I would have the opportunity to slay him," Vlad spoke as he led them to the prison door. He lay one hand on the latch and then looked back at Petru with an odd, contemplative look. "We were never much of a family. My older brother was murdered while Radu and I were in Adrianople; he turned out to be a Turk-loving traitor who ironically died of syphilis, and of my several half-brothers none supported me - not one. Now only Vlad the Monk lives, and he is my enemy. It shall not be like that with my sons. Milnea, the eldest, will take the throne, and I will teach my two young sons to support him and each other. I will impress upon them how important it is for family to stick together, even if they do have different mothers. As long as they are of my seed, they are royal princes and destined for greatness."

Petru and Sergei nodded in silent approval, and Vlad opened the door into the monastery yard. The abbot and monk spotted them from a few meters away, and the abbot waved a greeting to them. After a cordial exchange and a short tour of the grounds, Vlad brought up the matter of his treasure. The abbot assured him it was safe and sound and brought the prince and his attendants to a locked cell within the treasury. Dracula's eyes brightened at the sight of his store of wealth, and he congratulated the abbot on a job well done. Although some had been lost when Radu's forces had captured the monastery, miraculously most of it had been saved. He then instructed Sergei to go into the neighboring villages and hire about fifty peasants and meet him at a particular spot along the Dimivoti River near there in two days. "I have a plan," he smiled slyly as he sent his trusted man away.

"Maria!" Nadia cried as she rushed frantically into the tavern that afternoon. A veil of desperation covered her young face.

"What is it?" Maria put down her washing towel and immediately left the table she was cleaning to meet her friend.

"This is terrible; I don't understand how it could have happened," she babbled in despair as she clasped arms with Maria.

"What, Nadia? What happened?"

"Jean has been conscripted by the army," she said with a tremor in her voice as frightened eyes searched Maria's face.

"Conscripted?"

"Soldiers came to the shop and said he had to go with them. Dracula is raising an army to fight the Turks, and a man from each family must go!" she wailed. "What will I do? The Turks, Maria, the merciless infidels! My Jean is going to die!"

"Now, Nadia, pull yourself together," Maria said firmly. "He is not going to die, but someone will. This is the final straw." Maria took on a look of resignation as she straightened tall and let her friend loose.

"What do you mean?" Nadia's eyes searched hers as she wiped her nose with a handkerchief.

"Don't you worry about anything," Maria instructed confidently. "Just go back to your shop and take care of things there. Everything will be all right."

"What's going on?" Dimitry asked with concern when he entered the dining hall from the kitchen.

"I need to take tomorrow off," Maria said. "Nadia needs my help."

"Is one of the children ill?" he asked thoughtfully.

"My husband has been conscripted by the soldiers," Nadia answered with a bit less hysteria than before.

"Not Jean, too!" Dimitry remarked and shook his head. "Young men all over town have been taken. Something very big must be happening, and in winter no less!"

Just then two soldiers burst through the door with swords strapped to their waists. They removed their helmets politely and then addressed the bewildered tavern keeper. "Are you Dimitry?" the shorter soldier asked.

"Yes," he replied as his heart rate accelerated.

"The army of Walachia requires one male member of your household in the service of our lord and viovode, Prince Dracula, against the Turks."

"Why…are they attacking now, in winter?"

"I do not know, domnule; these are my orders. Do you have a son-"

"My oldest son is only seventeen, too young for war," Dimitry declared.

"Seventeen is an acceptable age," the taller, bearded soldier replied.

"No," Dimitri said slowly as his fingers brushed across his own salt and pepper bearded chin. "I will not send him. He is a bright boy with plans to attend the university." Maria's face was filled with compassion, and she moved to his side, sliding an arm around his waist and gazed into his perplexed, round face.

Dimitry patted her hand that held onto his upper arm and returned a soft, teary-eyed look. "Show Lucian the business, now, and take care of the tavern for me."

"You aren't -" she started to say.

Dimitry turned toward the soldiers and broke free of Maria's embrace. "I will go with you. Do I have time to make a few preparations, get my son in here to run things while I am away? I need to change my clothes as well."

The soldier who appeared to be in charge answered with a nod. "Report to the town hall at sunrise tomorrow."

Late the next night, when everyone was sleeping, Maria stole quietly through the dark hallway of the prince's quarters at Poenari Castle. Her soft-soled shoes were silent as she moved slowly along the wall of the nearly pitch-black corridor. Moonlight shone through a few small windows in the front room and a candle was lit near the entryway, but even with her eyes adjusted to the darkness, she could barely make out where the doors were.

Her breathing was shallow and shaky, and her heart pounded faster than a bird's wings as she inched her way down the hall, a dagger clenched in her right hand. Death waited for her at every turn. She expected it, welcomed it, but not yet - not until she had sunk her blade into the black heart of the demon prince as he slept in his chamber bed. Her mind raced as fast as her heart beat as she continued to creep down the hallway.

What will I do if he awakens? What if he is not alone in the bed? Oh, God, I hope it is the right room! Sasha said it was the next-to-last door on the left. Next to last - I can't even see the last door! Oh merciful Mother of God, give me strength - give me strength to kill the beast, then I don't care what happens to me.

She tingled all over as she listened for any sound and darted her eyes in all directions with each careful step. There was something, a slight sound back toward the front of the hall. Maria swiftly rolled her back against the cold wall and stood waiting breathlessly. As acutely fearful as she was, she was too determined to faint and too smart to panic. No one stirred. No doors opened. There was no one there. Slowly she loosened her stance against the wall and dared to exhale and take a new breath. It was nothing. Someone rolled over in bed, maybe. Maria collected herself and searched the darkness ahead. *It must not be much farther*, she thought. But even as she took the next step she felt the impulse to check over her shoulder again just to be sure. Glancing back in the direction of the dim, filtering light, she still detected no movement. Maria breathed a quiet sigh of relief just before she bumped smack into something - someone - in the hallway. A man! A slight, startled gasp escaped her lips as she stepped back, raising the dagger above her shoulder to strike. But before she had time to react, a strong hand grabbed her wrist while a second slapped itself across her mouth. The next thing she knew, Maria had been pushed against the hard, stone wall, and the figure moved in front of her, his powerful presence surrounding her. Her mouth opened but could produce no sound, and in her heart she knew she would surely die. Images of Georgi, Nadia, Dimitry, and her old Nanny flashed through her mind in seconds and she went completely numb. "Don't make a sound and follow me if you want to live," whispered a voice in the darkness. It was Stefan!

Chapter 13

Revelation

"You must never believe that a bad man will do any good, his head must be cut off or he be hanged."

A verse from the Ottoman Chronicles concerning Vlad III, by Sultan Mehmed, 1497

Maria quivered beneath Stefan's forceful grasp. She felt his cobalt eyes pierce the dark to study her, his expression remaining grim. "You must not make a sound," he mouthed in a whisper as though her life depended upon her obedience. Wide eyed and with her heart fluttering, Maria nodded and the man dressed all in black released her. "Come," he commanded as he took her by her left hand and proceeded toward the darkest end of the corridor.

Thoughts darted through her mind as her feet trod silently behind the powerful Hungarian. She still gripped her dagger and could use it on him to escape. But no - some one would hear the sound of the struggle, and she would be found out. He knew she held the weapon, and yet he turned his back. He must trust her. Slowly Maria slipped the blade into her apron pocket.

Stefan stopped abruptly, causing Maria to bump into him. Then she knew he had gone crazy, for he had led them straight into a stone wall; there was no escape here. But Stefan's fingers explored the wall to their left until he laid hold of a particular brick and gave it a strong shove. The wall in front of them opened with a gentle scraping sound, and Stefan led her into the secret passage, pushing the door shut behind them. Now they stood in a damp sea of utter darkness.

"How did you -"

"Shh," he cautioned. "Don't move."

Maria stood completely still listening to the sound of striking flint. Soon a spark lit the torch Stefan had left in the wall sconce, illuminating the passage in a soft glow and displaying an iron spiraling staircase that descended into an abyss of black. Relieved to have the light, Maria was glad she had not moved.

Stefan lifted the torch in one hand and caught Maria's hand with the other leading her down, down, down, until their feet finally touched solid ground. A gray mouse scurried away, and the passage was so low that the flame scorched some spider webs draped along the ceiling.

Curiosity had gotten the best of Maria, and she could hold her peace no longer. "How did you know about this secret passage, and what are you doing here anyway?"

Stefan glanced at her over his shoulder, for the tunnel was too narrow for them to walk side by side. "As for the 'what are you doing here' question, I could ask you the same."

Under no circumstances could Maria tell the prince's business associate the true reason for her presence there. "I asked you first," she staunchly replied.

Stefan let out an impatient snort. "I can see that we will have to discuss this matter at length once I have seen you safely home."

"You're taking me home?" Maria felt a load of apprehension lift from her heart at his words.

"Yes," he replied firmly and led her down a narrow staircase of hewn rock that was so small he had to bend down to avoid hitting his head. At the bottom there was a heavy door which Stefan pushed open with his shoulder. He put out the torch and placed it in a sconce as moonlight from the night sky poured through the doorway. "How did you get here?" he asked turning his eyes to the Romanian woman whose hand he still held. "Do you have a horse or wagon?"

"No." Maria hesitated nervously, not sure what to say. She removed her hand from his, replying, "I came over with a work crew to carry supplies into the garrison."

"And conveniently was left behind?" Stefan concluded in a bemused tone.

Maria raised her chin, looking out over the Arges River below and the rise of trees and hills across the valley, then crossed her arms over her chest stubbornly. Just as she was beginning to shiver from the chill of the wintry night air, Stefan draped his black wool cloak around her shoulders and fastened it there. She turned an uncertain gaze up into his face but could find no words to utter.

"My horse is waiting at the end of this path. It is the escape route Vlad used when he fled Radu's forces years ago. It is in disrepair so you must keep hold of my hand and walk carefully; even from this height that would be quite a fall."

Now that they had distanced themselves from the fortress guard, and Stefan spoke at a normal level, Maria noticed at once a difference in his speech. His voice was much deeper, more resonant, more commanding than in the tavern and his Hungarian accent had all but disappeared. "Who are you?" she asked in wonder.

"Right now, I am the best friend you have." His midnight-blue eyes bore their bright gaze straight into her soul, attempting to dispel any fears that might remain. A part of her longed to trust him, but there were still too many unanswered questions.

Stefan pulled the passage door shut and passed her on the ledge, then reached back a hand for her. Having little other choice, Maria placed her hand in his and followed him obediently down the mountain path. Stars peered through the scattered clouds overhead and a cold wind swooped through the valley against the cliffs. Maria pulled the cloak around herself more securely, very glad to have it.

Suddenly Stefan stopped, and she inadvertently bumped into him. "There is a gap in the ledge here," he warned pointing it out to her. "But it is only a few feet wide. I will jump it and then pull you across." Maria glanced anxiously at the gaping hole in their narrow path and the steep drop to their right and then nodded hesitantly.

Stefan easily hopped the rift, laid his back against the stone cliff, and reached his right hand back for Maria. "Take my hand and jump."

If he wanted to kill me, he could have done it at anytime, she thought. *Maybe he wants to present me to Dracula alive so that they can torture me. But maybe...maybe, oh God!* She closed her eyes tightly, clenching her fists as she contemplated her fate.

"Come on; you can do it," the man encouraged. "Trust me."

Well, she thought, opening her eyes and slowly stretching forth her left hand. *I can't stay here all night, and a quick fall would be preferable to torture.* Summoning all her courage, Maria looked him in the eyes, took hold of his hand, and jumped.

As promised, Stefan pulled her across, landing her in his arms. She found his chest to be as firm and solid as the stone cliff that rose behind them. His embrace was warm, comforting, secure, and so very strong. They lingered just a moment as she studied his eyes, his face, the spirit that emanated from him. Surely he was no blood-thirsty sadist like the prince. Neither was he a fanciful fop. But Maria remembered the words of the Gypsy fortune-teller - he was a dangerous man who would kill or be killed in the near future.

Stefan did not want to release the gentle beauty whom he held in his arms. He liked her right where she was - so close he could detect her scent. But why had she been at the castle? Was it to kill Vlad or to meet with him in secret? He knew what his heart told him, but he must be very careful.

Slowly he released his arms from their protective hold and smiled at her. "You did well. It is not far now." He led her the rest of the way.

The mare was tied where he had left her. Stefan mounted then removed his left foot from its stirrup and reached his left arm down for Maria. "Have you ever straddled a horse?"

"No," she answered taking his hand and lifting her left foot to the iron. "But I can learn." Stefan grinned with pleasure at her spirit as she swung her right leg across the horse's rump.

"Hold on; we'll be moving fast." Maria clasped her arms around Stefan's waist, he clicked to his mare, and they were off through the forest paths.

The ride to Curt de Arges was much swifter than Maria's ponderous wagon trip that morning which now seemed to have been days ago. The streets were empty and dark as in the wee hours of the morning all were tucked into their beds asleep. Stefan walked his horse quietly into the stable behind Dimitry's tavern and closed the barn door behind them.

"You wait here while I stable my horse, and then I will walk home with you," he commanded.

"And what if I will not?" Maria replied incredulously. "I will not be ordered about."

"You will do as I say, doamna," Stefan warned gravely while he unbuckled his saddle cinch. "Unless of course you want your actions this evening to be reported."

Maria's face reddened with anger towards this impertinent scoundrel. "For your information, I haven't done anything wrong," she steamed.

"Perhaps not," Stefan answered casually while setting his saddle aside. "But by the look of things, you were at Poenari Castle tonight to murder the prince."

"Preposterous!" she exclaimed as her heart began to pound faster. Maria stepped back, bumping into a stack of hay.

Stefan slipped the bridle over the mare's muzzle and set it with his saddle. "We shall see," he remarked matter-of-factly. "Now." He moved toward her confidently. "I believe I remember the way."

Neither said a word on the way to Maria's cottage. She was furious that he had spoiled her plan to kill the beast and was brazen enough to accuse her of such. But she was also afraid. She didn't mind the idea of dying, so long as she saw Dracula die first. She began to contemplate what story she would devise to explain her presence in the hall that evening.

Once inside the door, Maria lit a lamp, and Stefan busied himself building a fire on the hearth as though he were about to settle down in his own home for the evening. "There," he declared brushing his hands together to clean them. "Much more comfortable. Now, Maria," he turned toward her, "what were you doing at Vlad's Castle?"

"I will be glad to answer you," she said as she removed his black woolen cloak and sashayed behind the kitchen table, putting it between them, "as soon as you tell me why you were there."

"Enough of these games," he said softly taking slow steps in her direction. "That was a dangerous risk you took, and I cannot afford to take such a risk. I must be certain you can be trusted before I can tell you why I was there."

"Me be trusted!" she exclaimed in disbelief. "What about you?"

"I want to believe your story and that we have the same goal, but a pretty face would make a perfect disguise for a spy. If you are working for him -"

"The devil take you, domn, if you think such a thing!" Maria backed away from him against the cracked plaster wall of her great room. The combination kitchen, dining, and living room was meagerly but adequately furnished, displaying some of the finer examples of Nadia's pottery. "That monster murdered my son, and I would die myself before I did his bidding," she insisted angrily. Stefan studied the offended expression on her face as he reached the wooden table. "If anyone in this room is a spy, it is you!" she accused.

"Maria," he began apologetically, holding his palms upward toward her.

But the defensive widow took another step back and continued heatedly. "You are the one pretending to be someone you are not. And you have been the one meeting with Dracula, even if you say you had no part in killing the girl."

"Maria, I didn't -" Stefan interjected stepping closer, clearly agitated by her implications.

"You were at his castle tonight, no doubt plotting with 'your friend' the prince." Her face was flushed, and her back was to the wall, but Maria did not abdicate her position.

"I'm not -"

"And how else would you know about that secret tunnel, eh? Explain that!" she shouted even as her knees trembled and hands shook. "He wouldn't just show off secret escape routes to visiting foreign merchants. It only stands to reason that -"

Stefan determined that it was his turn to interrupt her for a change. He caught her cheeks between his smooth hands and covered her mouth with his own. It was not a punishing kiss, but a passionate, simmering fire. Maria was so shocked by his action that she did not even resist as his thirsty tongue reached into the well of her mouth. In an instant the river that raged through her abruptly changed course, pumping through her veins like something out of a dream. She had never been kissed like this before.

Slowly, Stefan's tongue retreated, and he gently raised his lips from hers, releasing her face. He had even surprised himself. Surely he had wanted to kiss her from the first moment he'd laid eyes on her, but he didn't think he would really do it - not here, not now, not like this. They both stared at each other dumbfounded.

"Why did you do that?" Maria asked softly, the anger drained from her soul.

"Well," Stefan answered cautiously. "At the moment it seemed to be the best way to make you be quiet." They eyed one another curiously, each trying to slow a racing heartbeat. "I will tell you who I am and why I was at Poenari Castle because I believe he truly wounded you and that you did go there tonight to kill him for it. But by doing so I place my life in your hands, for if Vlad ever found out, I would be executed at once. My mission will not allow for that, and it is far too important that I succeed."

Stefan took a deep breath, glanced down at the floor and then back into Maria's waiting brown eyes. "My real name is Nicolae Anton, and my father was the boyar of Cozia. Vlad Dracula killed my family in the purge of '57," he explained in a calm, level voice as if he were telling a tale. "I have come here to kill him before he can begin another reign of terror and to avenge my family."

Maria still trembled, though she did not know why. "But how do I know you are telling the truth now? You obviously lied about who you are once."

Stefan unfastened the top of his shirt and pulled out a gold chain bearing a ring. "This was my father's ring; it bears his seal." He stepped up to her slowly holding out the ring.

Maria touched her fingers to the gold band with an official insignia, brushing Stefan's hand as she did. After inspecting it, she stepped back, still not convinced. "Y-you could have gotten that anywhere," she stammered anxiously, her uncertain gaze cast upon his face. "And how would the Lord of Cozia know about the escape tunnel?"

He let out an irritated sigh and dropped the ring to thud against his chest, visibly disappointed by her lack of trust. He started unfastening his black shirt impatiently. "Because I built the damn tunnel - I and the other boyar youths, all of whom were murdered upon the fortress's completion."

Maria waited breathlessly, wondering what he was doing, wanting to believe him, but afraid to - wanting him in a way that frightened her. He pulled open his shirt and thrust it off his shoulders. She was almost awestruck by the sculptured perfection of his physique. Her late husband had looked nothing like this man. *No wonder he is so strong*, she thought as her eyes swept over him.

"Maybe I could have stolen the ring, but how would I fake these?" He turned away from her, lowering his head. In the warm glow of the lamp and firelight, Maria's eyes were opened to the raised white stripes of scar tissue that crisscrossed his back and shoulders. She reached her left hand tentatively toward him, her mouth agape as she began to realize that he told the truth.

Before she could touch him, the man snapped his shirt back over his shoulders and turned softly toward her. "I was fifteen years old; it was Easter. He killed my parents with all the other boyars even though they were innocent of any crime. The young people were put on a forced march from Tirgoviste to Poenari to rebuild the fortress. My sister and I were with them."

He paused to swallow and leaned back, sitting against the edge of the kitchen table. When he raised his teary eyes to Maria, he saw deep compassion on her face. "She was older than me and very pretty - liked to laugh…but she was more delicate than I." He wiped a hand down his face and tried to blink away the coming tears. His voice was a soft, painful lament. "I carried her as long as I could…I tried to save her - oh, God, I tried! But I wasn't strong enough…I couldn't…" He lowered his head and was overtaken by sobs.

Instinctively, Maria moved to him and wrapped her arms around him, laying her cheek to his. "Oh, Nicolae," she moaned with heartfelt pain while his warm tears moistened her face.

"You must always call me Stefan," he said softly, responding by enveloping her in his embrace. "If you were to call me that where someone else could hear -"

"I know," she whispered. "I won't." Maria slid her right hand across his shoulder and raised it to touch his face. Looking into his eyes she said, "It was not your fault; you did all you could."

"But I never saw her again," he continued, battling to regain his composure. "They were under orders to kill those who fell behind." Still standing in his half embrace, Maria stroked Nicolae's cheek as he spoke. "My father told me to stay alive, so I did. On a moon-less, foggy night I escaped, pretending I had fallen from the cliffs. When I found them, there were hundreds…rotting corpses impaled outside the city. The boyars, their wives, servants." He sighed a long sigh and raised his eyes to gaze into Maria's face. "I found my parents' bodies…and I took the ring."

"What a brave young man you must have been," she praised warmly, trailing her fingertips from his jaw line. Nicolae caught her hand in his and fingered it affectionately.

"I did what I had to; I never thought of it as being brave. My father had a friend - Kuban, merchant from Hungary. I knew I could not stay here without being caught, so I went to him."

"You walked all the way to Szeged!"

A slight grin pulled at the corners of Nicolae's mouth. "I was more dead than alive by the time I arrived. Kuban took me in, adopted me into his family. We decided I should go by Stefan, the name of one of his sons who had died as an infant. And I did become a merchant; so you see, I have not completely lied about my identity."

"So you followed Kuban's profession to honor him?"

"No." Nicolae shook his head and shifted his feet. He repositioned his right arm around Maria's waist as he cupped her in his arm and intertwined his left fingers with hers. "I had a broader goal in mind. I determined on the day I found my parents that someday I would avenge their wrongful murder and rid the world of a great evil. I knew that to be successful in such a plan I would need a great deal of money at my disposal. No longer having the resources of a boyar's lands, the best way to make a fortune is as a merchant. I have been very fortunate during these past years to have accumulated the wealth I needed."

"You were right about why I was at Poenari," she confessed softly as she averted her eyes from him to the floor. Then looking back she added, "But my son's grave is still fresh. You have waited so long. How can you live with that kind of hate?"

"It is not so much hate as the knowledge of what must be done. You were very young during Vlad's first reign and were probably sheltered from many of the horrors. But I have seen up close the face of tyranny. Whole towns burned to the ground with soldiers barring the escape of any. The German historical books count over 100,000 that he has killed. True, those figures include the 20,000 Turks he impaled outside Tirgoviste, but that still leaves 80,000 Christians he has slaughtered. This is not just about my vengeance - it is the vengeance of humanity. It is justice long delayed. I would have killed him sooner, but as long as he remained in Hungary he was under house arrest and constantly surrounded by guards. He still lived, but the blessing was he could do no harm to anyone. But as soon as I learned he had been granted leave to regain his throne, I began to put my plan in action."

"So you were there tonight to kill him yourself, but I got in your way," she deduced in dismay.

"No." He smiled at her and released her hand to raise her chin. "Vlad wasn't even there."

"What?"

"He is off hiding his treasure. I was going through his papers and maps to find out what his next plans are - where he is going and what he is up to." He sighed caressing her soft skin and then slowly dropped his hand to his thigh. "I would have gotten here sooner - I wish to God I had - but I was traveling the principality gathering support among the boyars. Assassinating a prince is not something one can do on his own. But my suspicions were correct. Most of the present boyars either fear or oppose Dracula. They think he may repeat the past and exterminate them like he did my parents' generation."

"So they support you."

"Most do, but Maria," he lamented. "If I had only moved faster, I could have been here before -"

"Stefan, no." She put her fingers to his lips. "What could a Hungarian merchant have done to stop his slaughter?"

Nicolae took in and let out a long breath as he harnessed the anger and frustration that ran through him. "I will help you kill him," Maria vowed. "I can gain entrance to places even a 'friend of the prince' could not go."

"No." It was a final and authoritative word. "You will not place yourself in danger again, do you hear?" He raised his voice and rose from the table bringing Maria to her feet with him. "I have already lost Eveline - I will not lose you."

Maria stepped back and retorted independently, "Domnule, how can you lose that which you do not have? I am my own person."

He gave her a hard look of warning and continued. "I have a plan - one that will work." Maria crossed her arms and gave him an indignant look. Her plan could have worked…if Vlad had been there. "I have in my possession documents signed by the boyars supporting Basarab's reinstatement - a prince who had been backed by the Sultan. I am going to see him to try to enlist his aid in overthrowing Vlad."

"But the infidel Turks, Stefan, they are our enemies!" Maria looked stunned that he had suggested such a thing.

"Vlad Dracula, the damnable impaler, is a far greater enemy to the people of Walachia than the Turks will ever be. They may require us to pay a tribute in gold, but Dracula demands his tribute in blood."

"If you need the help of an outside nation, why not turn to -"

"Hungary?" he interrupted. "Matthias just put him back on the throne. And Moldavia, ruled by Vlad's cousin? Stephen is a just ruler, but he will not go against his own kin this time." He shook his head gravely. "It must be the Turks. I have learned that Vlad is building an army which he plans to move to Bucuresti, near the Turkish border. I think he plans to start something and bringing this information to Sultan Mehmed should win me his trust and support. Then I will meet Dracula in Bucuresti with my sword."

"I know he's been raising an army, an army conscripted from our friends and neighbors. You cannot do this; I implore you! They've taken Nadia's husband and Dimitry."

"The tavern owner?" Nicolae looked surprised.

"Yes, and many others." Maria stepped back to him, grabbing his arms tightly. "They don't stand a chance against the Sultan's trained troops - they'll be cut to ribbons! More of the people you say you defend will die. Isn't there another way?"

Nicolae's face took on a pained expression as he shifted his weight from one foot to the other and raised his hands to caress Maria's upper arms. "It is not as simple as walking in and stabbing him - I wish it were. Many years ago, a group of boyars assassinated Vlad Dracul, his father, and Mircea, his brother. Vlad assumed power years later filled with vengeance and bathed our land in blood. I am not prepared to kill his sons nor all of his kin to protect myself and what offspring I may have from their retaliation. It must look like he was killed in battle. This is what the boyars have agreed to. It will leave them anonymously blameless. But for this to happen there must be a battle, and I will be there. Once I have slain him, the retreat will be sounded, and the battle ended. Mehmed will only want Vlad's head, and he will call off his men."

"And if he does not agree to this?" Maria's countenance was etched with worry and doubt.

"Then we will come up with another plan," he assured her confidently. "I swear I will act as quickly as possible so that few of our soldiers will have time to die." Nicolae drew Maria into his arms and embraced her, kissing her cheek as he did so.

She thoughtfully considered the plan that he had obviously thought out very carefully. "Then we will be partners. I hear things in the tavern, and there is information I can get for you. Even if you take the blade from my hand, I will be a part of his destruction."

Nicolae gave his silent consent as he held her close in his arms, warmed by a sensation that he could never remember feeling, one that filled the emptiness that had long been a part of his soul. Suddenly, he noticed that the room appeared lighter than it had when their discussion began. His senses were heightened to a state of alarm, and he abruptly released Maria and pushed past the table toward the front window. "Damn," he muttered as he turned to pace the length of the room.

"What is wrong?"

"It's getting light out; I've been here all night."

Maria scooped up his cloak from the back of a chair and rushed to him with it. "You must hurry and go before -"

"It's too late," he said stopping to stare out the window. "There are a few people on the streets already. I can't be seen leaving your house. Vlad's law is still in place."

They were both well aware of the strict prince's law regarding the company kept by any man and woman who were not married. Maria's eyes searched his fearfully. "What will we do?"

Chapter 14

Proposals

"And then with great cunning, he had his treasure buried under water. And all of the workers, one after the other, he ordered to be killed, until the last one."

From "Additions to the Strasbourg Printing of 1500," a German account of Vlad III Dracula

Nicolae sighed and ran his fingers up through his hair. Then he turned his face toward hers. "I suppose the safest course of action would be an immediate marriage."

"What?"

"We'll have to get married."

"What for?" Maria protested as her emotions surged up and down, clamoring for prominence. "We haven't done anything."

"You know that, and I know that," he explained logically, "but whoever sees me walk out that door will assume otherwise."

"No," came her shaky response. Maria lowered her head. "I'll not marry you to save my reputation."

"It's not your reputation I'm trying to save." Nicolae took a step toward her and grabbed hold of her arms tightly. His face was etched with concern, and Maria noted the first real signs of fear she had ever seen in his eyes. He raised his voice forcibly to her, saying, "I'll not have you hanging in the public square like that woman, do you hear?"

But she wrenched herself free of his grip and retorted in her own strong voice, "And I'll not have you tied to a penniless, illiterate peasant woman! You have your future to think about, your social position and responsibilities. Besides, I will not marry for simple convenience."

"This is not simple convenience," he insisted as he reached out a hand to her. "You know the penalty under Vlad's law—who would believe that nothing happened here?"

135

"The prince would not harm you," she predicted and turned sadly away.

But Nicolae stepped up behind her, his tone mellowing. "My only concern is for you."

Maria turned slowly and gazed up into his face. "And why are you so concerned for me? Can you answer that?"

Nicolae's mouth hung agape as a whirlwind of thoughts and emotions tumbled through his mind. What could he say? It was one thing to have his offer of marriage rejected and another altogether to have his heart broken. He dared not proclaim his love for her only to be told he was a fool. He did love her with every fiber of his being, but this was such a new revelation, a part of himself he did not know how to control, and that frightened him. Then there was the added omen—everyone he had ever loved had died while he was powerless to save them. Maybe through some twist of fate, she would be safe as long as she was unaware of his feelings.

"Just as I thought." Her words fell from her lips with disappointment. "You are an honorable gentleman, but that sense of honor alone is no reason to marry me."

Nicolae's eyes darkened, angry at himself for his confusion and fears. He clinched his fists and declared with savage determination, "I will not let anyone harm you, Maria. I would die first, I swear it!"

Her melancholy eyes rose to meet his. He meant it, but why? *Please, Nicolae, say that you love me,* her soul pleaded silently. *Tell me it is not a dream, that I am not totally insane. I have never wanted anyone like I want you, God forgive me. But I will not marry a man who does not love me, especially because I love him so. It would break my heart to live with him day after day just to be regarded indifferently. No, no I can't.*

Maria closed her eyes and lowered her head, nearly in tears. Nicolae relaxed his stance, walked slowly to her, and held her tenderly in his embrace. "We'll think of something else," he said optimistically.

Suddenly, Maria sprang to life, and all consuming grin across her face. "I have an idea!"

"This will never work," Nicolae uttered in humiliation.

"Of course it will; just hold still," Maria instructed while she fastened a pin. She had dressed him in a brightly colored long fota and a coordinating peasant blouse.

"Maria," he bemoaned impatiently. "I have a beard and mustache."

"And I have a solution," she declared delightedly. She pulled from the wardrobe a long, darkly colored marama and swept it around his head and face so that only his eyes showed. Its long tails hung down in front and behind his shoulders.

He grunted a bit. "Still, no one would believe a woman is this flat chested."

"Quite right," Maria agreed amiably and searched her bedroom for a small pillow. Then she gripped it in the middle and shook it to send the feathers to opposite ends.

"You're not thinking—" he began.

"Precisely!" Maria answered. She pulled out the top of the blouse and stuffed the pillow in. Then she artistically fluffed the two sides of the pillow, positioning them just so on her subject.

"This is not the idea that comes to my mind when men use the phrase, 'getting into a woman's clothes."

Maria giggled. "I am relieved to hear that, domnule. Now, stoop a bit—you are too tall."

Nicolae snorted in aggravation. "Swear you'll never tell anyone about this," he demanded as he assumed a hunched posture.

"As tempting as it may be, I promise. There, perfect!" she announced. "You can be my visiting Aunt Matilda from Braila if anyone asks."

"Just get me out of here!"

"No, no, a higher pitched voice or say nothing at all."

"Look, doamna, I am a master of disguise. I can manage the voice if I have to."

Maria wrapped Nicolae's cloak around his shoulders and threw on her own cojoc. Then she whisked him out the door and down the street toward Dimitry's stable where his bag with extra clothes was stored. No one seemed to pay them any attention for which they were both relieved.

Prince Dracula, attended by his valet, stepped out of his coach on a small grassy ridge overlooking the Dimbovita River. He held his head erect and took a few steps out to survey the project. At once, Sergei spied his arrival and literally ran up the hill to meet him. He extended one hand to his head to secure the warm, black gluga he had worn on that cloudy, windy day. "Ah, Sergei, tell me of our progress."

"The dam diverted the river's course into that empty ravine as you predicted, milord," he reported proudly pointing toward a thick forest behind the muddy riverbed. "They are burying the iron drums now. Once the river is flowing back in its place, no one but you, my prince, will ever find the treasure."

Vlad's eyes danced with pleasure. "You have done well, Sergei. You are my most trusted man. I know when I give a task to you, it will be done, and done properly. You shall be well rewarded, my friend."

They looked down over the valley as wool-clad peasants lugged heavy iron drums through knee deep mud to the middle of the riverbed. A few others stood watch at the top of the make-shift timber dam in case it should start to break.

"It looks as though they will be finished before nightfall," Vlad speculated. "How shall we locate the exact spot later?"

"I placed a marker," Sergei said pointing to the bank on which they stood. It was a stone carved cross about three feet high not unlike many a shrine scattered throughout the land. "It bears the inscription 'Alpha and Omega' in honor of your first and last reigns in Walachia."

"How thoughtful," the prince commented with a pleased expression.

"You take exactly one hundred paces due west into the riverbed, and there will be the treasure," Sergei concluded.

"You have thought of everything!" Vlad praised his man. Then he continued in a pleasant tone. "This clearing where we stand should be a good spot to pay the men at the end of the day. I have sent for a company of soldiers from Bucuresti who should arrive anytime now to assist you. They must be impaled quickly through the belly or chest so that they will not live long enough to tell what they have done here. Considering the strong prospect of war, I would prefer to place them all on the front lines."

"Yes, Lord Dracula, but you can ill afford to have one opening his mouth about the location of the treasure, else when you return from battle, you find it is all gone," concluded Sergei logically.

"You understand me so well, and why I must do the things I do," Vlad said, his green eyes piercing knowingly into Sergei's.

Petru stood waiting by the coach a few yards away from them. He had picked up bits and pieces of the conversation, but it was not one he had been invited into, so he remained at his post and tried to mind his own business.

Later that afternoon Prince Dracula and his escort returned to the grassy knoll. The Dimbovita River was meandering back through its bed as if it had never been disturbed. Vlad was pleased. Sergei joined his master as he walked through the ranks of corpses impaled there. Abruptly he halted and turned a serious gaze to his armas. "You hired fifty men, did you not?" he snapped harshly.

"Yes, Majesty," he answered innocently.

"Then why are there only forty-nine bodies?" Dracula's cold green eyes shot icy arrows into Sergei.

"Whoever escaped could not have gone far, my lord," he observed. "I will send a detachment of soldiers into the neighboring village, and the others will search the forest. His body will hang here with the others before nightfall!"

Vlad let out an impatient sigh. "See that it does. We must leave for Poenari in the morning. I have a few meetings to attend before we bring the army south for the rest of winter. I will be waiting at Snagov for you to bring me a good report."

"Yes, my prince. I shall not delay."

"Good." Dracula smiled and placed a hand of reassurance on his man's shoulder. "When you arrive, come and have a drink with me."

Sergei bowed his head and took a step back. "It will be my honor, Sire."

The sun glistened brightly on the melting ice crystals the next morning as Petru loaded the luggage onto the coach. The brownish-blue water of Snagov Lake rippled in the breeze while small ice-floats bobbed about like corks in a tub. The coachman secured the harness to the bay and black draft horses, and the two escort soldiers mounted their war steeds. The other troops had been sent back to Bucuresti to prepare for the main army's arrival. Vlad was pleased that Sergei had been able to track down and execute the escaped peasant worker.

"Tis a beautiful morning," Dracula commented pleasantly as he gazed across the lake at the grand monastery he had helped build. "I miss my days here, Sergei. Perhaps when this business with the Turks is concluded, we shall return here and stay a while."

"That would be most agreeable, Sire," he replied.

It was then that they noticed a small clapboard rowboat cutting its way through the frigid water, propelled by two young monks with oars. Standing like an oak at the bow was Brother Josef, a large wooden cross in his outstretched right hand. Vlad focused his attention on the craft, expecting a departure blessing by the holy man of his monastery.

But Josef's red face, bulging veins, and stern expression indicated otherwise. "Damn you, Dracula, you sadistic murderer!" he wrathfully roared. "I saw what you did; God saw what you did! You hired those people to work for you, and then you murdered them all."

Dracula's countenance changed to a brooding, irritated darkness. He narrowed his brow and stroked his mustache contemplatively at the monk's accusation.

"My prince, don't—" Sergei began, but Vlad held up his left hand to silence him.

The rowboat continued to move across the lake, nearing the midway point from the island while Brother Josef continued to shout venomously at Dracula. "This deed will not go unpunished. The Lord Almighty in his great mercy has given you time to repent, but you have not changed your ways. Therefore, you will be cut off from the land of the living, declares the Lord."

Vlad spoke thoughtfully to those around him. "When I was Orthodox, I killed Catholic clergy. Now that I am Catholic, it must be allowable for me to kill Orthodox clergy. Soldier," he said to his nearest mounted guard. "Your crossbow." The prince held out his right hand for the weapon.

"Your time is at hand, wicked Prince Dracula, and within a fortnight your head shall be separated from your body," Josef prophesied boldly. "Your soul will not find rest in death, but shall be cursed to wander the earth a vagabond without a place until the end of this age." The prince raised the loaded crossbow to his shoulder and took a slow and careful aim at the monk. "And then you shall be cast into the lake of fire to burn for all eternity, so help me God!"

Josef's fist and teeth were clenched in righteous anger as the steel bolt struck his chest, plunging him backward into the hands of the young monks who caught him. Their terrified faces were pale with round eyes searching their compatriot's face. "Brother Josef!" one exclaimed.

"Is he dead?" asked the other.

Vlad sighed impatiently, snapped down the crossbow, and handed it back to the soldier. "Have this weapon aligned; it pulls to the left." He snorted and turned his back on the clergymen's vessel. "I haven't time to waste on the likes of him. Let us be off."

Josef clutched the bolt that pierced the right side of his chest and gasped for breath. "My brothers," he uttered. "Back to the infirmary. It is a serious wound, but not to the death, barring a fever. My work here...is accomplished," he eked out and then fainted into their arms.

"Sire, give me a hand cannon, and I will blow the traitor out of the water!" Sergei demanded indignantly, his brown eyes burning with malice toward the monk.

"That one cannot hurt me; I must save my powder for the Turks." As Vlad stepped into the coach, he took one last, long glance over his shoulder at the boat rocking in the icy lake. "He is of no consequence." He snapped back to the entry of his black coach and stepped inside, his fur-collared black cape swirling around him.

The Poenari sentries had reported the prince's approach, and Ivan, dressed in his yellow-gold uniform cape, breast plate, and silver helm, met them at the gate. "Sire, how was your journey?" Ivan removed his helmet and bowed chivalrously before the prince.

"All went well, Captain. And how goes the recruiting?"

Ivan walked briskly to keep pace with the Prince as he struck out across the yard. Petru and Sergei trailed behind them carrying the trunks and bags. "Very well, milord. I have assembled four hundred new infantrymen from the surrounding villages and Curt de Arges. They are all fit and in good health. By my latest report, we are expecting another six hundred from Tirgoviste."

"A thousand—is that all?"

"It has been little more than a week, my prince. I am sure we will be able to add many more to the ranks before the Turks attack," Ivan explained.

"True, true, quite right," Vlad concluded as he pulled to a halt outside of his hall. Most of the old snow had melted from the yard, and patches of white could only be found in shady areas. But the incoming clouds and dropping temperatures threatened to re-blanket the fortress at any time. "At least we have increased our force by one third. Give the recruits three more days of training as to the common commands and use of their weapons, and then we march south. Have the quartermaster stock the supply wagons and see to the powder and shot. Captain, I am counting on you to take care of every detail."

"Yes, Sire. No detail will be forgotten. The army will be ready to move as scheduled." Ivan clicked his heels together and saluted the prince in the Roman tradition and then took his leave to find the quartermaster.

Petru opened the hall door for his prince and stood back allowing him easy access to the warm room. However, Vlad abruptly stopped in the doorway, his eyes fixed on a figure in rough homespun wool. "What are you doing here?" he asked grimly.

The next morning Stefan arrived as expected with a signed copy of the trade agreement securely in the pouch that hung from his ornate baldric. His boots crunched over the crisp layer of new snow that had fallen during the night while a few wandering, fluttering flakes encircled his fur gluga and lit upon his shoulders. He wore again his distinctively Hungarian garb and a most enthusiastic expression. Petru guided his guest to the prince's courtroom and announced him.

Stefan strode forward and in a broad swoop of his arm removed his hat and bowed before the prince. As he regained his posture, he spoke in a light, cheery voice. "Good morning, Your Majesty Dracula viovode. I am pleased to bring you good news." But as his eyes rose to meet Vlad's, found them hollow and expressionless.

Vlad sat casually on his crimson seat of judgment with one leg thrown over the chair arm. He fondled his golden jeweled dagger mindlessly as he turned his eyes from Stefan to the ragged peasant who sat near the front of the chamber. "I believe you have met," he noted gravely.

Stefan took a few cautious steps toward the front and peered at the ordinary looking middle-aged man. "Teo?" he questioned innocently. "He works at the tavern where I have been staying. He sweeps, scatters straw, stables the horses," Stefan enumerated, expressing himself with his hands. "Why, milord? What has he done?"

Dracul motioned toward Sergei who was standing in the side doorway across from the prince's throne. "The question, Domn Stefan Kubana, is what have you done?"

Stefan froze, his face paling as he watched Sergei march across the front of the courtroom with a long, sharp-ended, silver rod in his rough hands. The executioner halted beside Vlad and turned to face the two men. His features were stern and unyielding; firm, tight biceps bulged from under his cap-sleeved tunic.

"This distresses me greatly, gentlemen, but the fact remains that one of you has lied to me." His intuitive green eyes moved from one man to the other. "The one who is true need fear nothing from me; however..." Vlad paused dramatically while swinging his polished black boot back to the floor. "The one who is false will be impaled on this silver pike this very morning." Stefan's stomach caught in his throat as he feared he would never have the chance to put his plan into action.

Chapter 15

The Sacrifice

"We must die one day and we do not mind where, provided we die well."

Pope Pius II, 1464

A knock came at Maria's door earlier than expected that morning while she was still in bed. She sprung up from her pillow with a start and reached for her robe. *Who could it be?* she wondered frantically as she feared the worst. *Someone has found out, and they've come for me.* Her heart jumped as she realized that now she did have something to live for, and she was truly no longer indifferent regarding death. The knock sounded louder.

"Who is it?" she asked with a quiver in her voice as she walked hesitantly across the dull wooden floor toward the door. She pulled her robe around herself as she waited breathlessly before touching her hand to the latch.

"Nadia, who do you think?"

Gratefully, Maria's eyes closed as she put her left hand to her chest, breathed a sigh of relief, and turned the latch. "Nadia, thank God! Why are you so early?"

Nadia entered the cottage, her baby nestled in the crook of her arm, and Maria closed the door. "With Jean gone I have to help out more in the pottery shop," Nadia answered solemnly, her face draped in shadows. The infant lay quietly wrapped in a turquoise, black, and white woven blanket, peering about with round, blue eyes. "Word is they'll be moving out soon, and I don't think I'll get to see him before he leaves."

"Come in and sit down while I get you some tea," Maria offered, ushering her friend to the table.

"Thank you," she replied with a melancholy sigh and plopped into the straight backed chair. Maria swiftly lit the fire and hung the iron kettle on its hook to heat up. "Where have you been the past couple of days?"

Nadia asked. Her baby wiggled and thrust a fist out from under the blanket. He turned his head toward her breast, popping his little lips and reaching up with his free arm.

"I hired out on my day off to take supplies into Poenari, and yesterday I was too exhausted to get up before time for work." Maria put the tea leaves into their small leaf cage, dropped them into the top of the water kettle, and replaced the lid.

The infant began to twist and kick and presented Nadia with a most displeased expression. "Wah!" he blasted once to show his discontent. Nadia responded by pulling down the left side of her peasant blouse and raising his head to reach. The baby instantly latched onto her nipple and began to draw on it, gratified that she finally decided to feed him. "Well, I'm glad you gave up that foolish notion of trying to kill Prince Vlad," she said in relief as she tended her child.

"Actually, I haven't given up the idea," Maria confessed as she took a seat by Nadia at the table. "Things just haven't come together yet." Maria's mind raced as she wondered just how much she could or should tell her best friend.

"I was so worried when I didn't hear from you," Nadia admitted raising her gaze to Maria.

"I am fine," Maria smiled reassuringly at Nadia. "So where is the other little one?"

"At my mother's," she answered and stroked her hand lovingly over the baby's head. "And is the handsome stranger back in town?"

"Stefan?"

"Yes." Nadia looked back to her friend in great anticipation. "Stefan, the wealthy Hungarian merchant you find so fascinating."

"Uh," she stammered nervously. "He's back."

"And? Come on, Maria, tell me—he came to see you, didn't he?"

"He was here." Maria determined it was time to check on the tea.

"And?" Nadia prompted in impatient exasperation.

Maria turned toward her as she reached the hearth. "And he kissed me!" she announced as if she could still hardly believe it.

"Is that all?" her friend interjected hoping to hear of more.

"It was enough," Maria responded as a look of exhilaration swept over her face. "Nadia, it was so intense! I've never felt anything like it—like a fire surging through my veins. He made me light-headed." After only recalling the encounter, Maria was forced to sit on the stone hearth.

Nadia beamed in response. "Maria's in love," she teased and giggled, her bright brown eyes shimmering.

"Now I don't know if I'd go that far," Maria said with some sense of practicality returning to her voice. "There are still things we don't know about him."

"What's there to know? He's single, handsome, rich, and he's in love with you."

"I seriously doubt he's in love with me," Maria replied, dismissing the thought as she lifted the kettle with a thick rag and poured tea into the two clay cups that sat beside her on the hearth.

"He must feel that way, Maria," Nadia reasoned. "He kissed you."

Maria smiled a wise and knowing smile as she brought the two cups of tea to the table and sat down. "There are many reasons why a man may kiss a woman, my dear, most of which have little to do with love."

"Well, if I were you, I'd do as much as I could to encourage him. A catch like that is so rare."

"You may be right," Maria said warmly as she remembered the rest of the story about her mysterious Hungarian. Slowly her glowing visage began to fade. "But I'll not put too much hope into the prospect of marriage. A man like him is beyond me."

Nadia finished sipping her tea and set down the cup. "You never know." She smiled gently at her friend.

Prince Dracula rose to his feet, stepped down from his platform, and paced the front of the courtroom with an even stride. The sound of his boots echoed around the silent hall while Nicolae's heart raced and a myriad of dreadful possibilities played out in his mind. He was aware of his mouth going suddenly dry as Vlad stopped and raised his eyes sullenly.

"Teo has had much to tell me about you, Domn Kubana…or is it Nicolae of Cozia?" The prince studied his reaction very carefully. "Confusing, isn't it?"

"I beg your pardon? My lord, I am not confused about who I am, but I do wonder how the gentleman could have told you such a thing." Nicolae was very careful to conceal the panic that flooded through him. He would be expected to appear nervous at such an inquisition, but certainly not panicked. He was sure that all the color had left his cheeks, and beads of perspiration began to form along his brow, but he held his poise and voice completely in character.

"Ah, yes." Vlad smiled darkly and moved his gaze to his informant. "As you know, Teo cannot speak, but he writes an excellent hand." He looked back at Nicolae, pleased to see the genuine surprise that registered in his eyes. Then he began pacing once more as he continued. "Yes. You see, Teo has not always been a peasant. As a young and energetic supporter of mine, I bestowed upon him the title and lands of the boyar of Cozia. The man he replaced was named Nicolae, and he claims you are that man's son—not a Hungarian at all." Vlad halted once again, lowered his head, and chuckled. He raised his eyes with an amused expression and added, "He seems to think you have returned to kill me."

Nicolae's reaction was authentic shock and bewilderment. *How could he have recognized me after so many years?* He turned his puzzled expression from the prince to Teo. *I can't ever remember seeing this man before,* he thought. *Oh, my God!* He was terror stricken as another scenario crossed his mind. *Did he see me with Maria the other night? Did he overhear us at her house? I must be convincing so that she will not be in danger.*

He raised his hands palms outward as he returned his wide eyes to Vlad. "Honestly, Sire, before last week I had never laid eyes on this man. Perchance he has mistaken me for someone else."

"Maybe," Vlad mused thoughtfully as he smoothed his mustache with his fingers. "Teo has lied to me before; that is how he lost both his title and his tongue," he explained and glanced back at Teo. The frustrated mute made urgent hand motions and pointed at Nicolae. Now he was starting to look anxious and fearful as well.

"Ivan!" Dracula raised his voice to call in the captain of his fortress.

Ivan, who had been waiting outside the chamber for his cue, marched in briskly. "Yes, my prince."

"Ivan," Vlad began speculatively as he looked up to the tall military man. "Do you recall the spring and summer of 1457?"

"Why, certainly, milord. That was when I was assigned to the detail overseeing the re-construction of this castle."

"Did any of the young boyars escape?" Vlad's eyes were dancing like green torches as he awaited a reply.

"Most assuredly not, Prince Dracula!" Ivan swore with certainty. "Escape would have been impossible." For a moment even his heart raced with fear at Dracula's implication. He had not known why he was being called in to testify, but he did know that no one was so highly placed that the prince could not have him executed for any reason he deemed necessary.

"As I thought," Vlad replied casually. "Ivan, do you recognize this man?" He extended his arm in a sweeping motion toward Nicolae.

"Yes, milord," Ivan answered as he tried to calm his consternation and maintain his bold exterior. "He is Stefan Kubana, the Hungarian merchant Your Majesty sent me to bring from Curt de Arges."

"And do you ever recall seeing him before that evening?"

Ivan studied Nicolae's face carefully. He remembered Ivan, the big, black-haired soldier with the pike, the one who had killed his sister. Yes, he remembered Ivan and once had hated him, but now he understood things much more clearly. The soldier had only followed orders and would have been impaled himself had he not obeyed. He didn't want to kill the boyar youths—he knew that now. None of it had been his fault. Dracula alone was to blame.

Nicolae looked at Ivan innocently. He was immaculately attired and perfectly groomed. "No, my lord," Ivan answered after a moment. "Should I have?"

"No. That will be all."

"Yes, Sire." Ivan turned to leave the hall, relieved that he had done nothing wrong. Then he began to wonder what that had all been about.

Teo became frantic as it appeared his accusation was not being corroborated. He jumped up from his seat and made a grunting sound. His features were strained and tense as he made more hand motions and pointed at Nicolae more imperatively.

Prince Dracula strolled leisurely to Nicolae's side of the courtroom and looked at him inquisitively. "Ivan does not remember you, but Teo says he does. Now, I have warned you once, and you know I detest liars. So, what have you to say to the accusation?"

Nicolae did not hesitate long. Above all he had to protect Maria and the boyars who had given him their support. All he could think to do was to continue to remain in character and give the performance of his life. "Most noble prince," Nicolae said as he bowed to honor his judge and then stood tall before him. "If I have in any way, whether in word or deed, offended Your Majesty, or broken your law in any point, then it is your right and duty to have me so impaled, and I humbly submit to your judgment. But, milord, as to this man's claim, I am dumbfounded. As I told you, I am Stefan, Kuban's son, and I am a merchant from the Hungarian city of Szeged. I have brought you my guild member's signatures on our trade agreement," he said as he withdrew the rolled paper from his pouch. "I cannot venture to guess why this man would wish to accuse me, but he must be mistaken. Your Majesty may choose to have me impaled for any number of reasons, but not for lying to you, for that is something I have not done."

Nicolae withdrew his handkerchief and daintily blotted beads of perspiration from his brow as he awaited the prince's decision. If worst came to worst, he could always attempt to kill him then and there. He had a dagger concealed in his boot. Could he throw it from where he stood with sure enough aim to strike Dracula's heart before Sergei's pike ran him through? Maybe a fifty-fifty chance, he thought—not the kind of odds he wanted.

"Yes, I know," Dracula replied as he pulled letters of his own from his cummerbund. "You see, Teo," he began as he paced to the other row of benches, "I suspected treachery from the beginning and requested an inquiry into Stefan Kubana's background. I have received verification of his birth and baptism, a letter from the merchant Kuban giving a physical description of his son, and this just arrived yesterday from the trade ministry department of the Hungarian government advising me that the merchants of Hungary would abide by the agreements set forth between myself and one Stefan Kubana of Szeged. Now," he announced triumphantly as he stopped and turned toward Stefan., "if my delightful Hungarian friend can but tell me the date of his birth, I will be completely satisfied that he is who he claims to be and that all is well." Vlad tilted his head curiously while staring at Stefan with his deep green, enigmatic eyes and awaited a reply.

"Certainly I know my own birth date!" he declared with a relieved smile. Teo's face had become like an ashen veil, and his knees were weakening with dread. Surely Dracula would not impale him. Even if he had been mistaken, he had meant well.

"So you agree it is February 4 of 1442?" the prince asked as he glanced at the church record he held in his hand.

Suddenly the thrill faded from Stefan's expression and was replaced by uncertainty. "Milord, by chance you misread the document. It should say February 14, 1442," Stefan replied in a strained tone.

Vlad smiled, folded the documents, and tossed them into his chair. "You are, of course, correct," he stated. "I should never have doubted you. But, Teo," he turned and stood with boots shoulder width apart, folding his arms across his chest, "I am disappointed in you. What could you have possibly hoped to gain?"

Teo helplessly strove to convince the prince that he was right. He let forth intense groans accompanied by an agonizing grimace as he motioned with his hands, pointing again at Stefan. Exasperated, he grabbed for a crude pencil and scrap of parchment from his pocket and scrawled the words, "He IS Nicolae of Cozia—I swear it!" He rushed forward and put the paper into Dracula's hand.

The prince gave the dirty man a look of disgust as he took the paper. After glancing at it, he replied, "But what proof do you have? There is a host of proof that he is indeed Stefan. Besides, if he was a boyar youth during the cleansing, he would have been here, building this fortress, and we know none of them escaped. Therefore, for your claims to be true, it would follow that I made a mistake—not very damn likely. Sergei, escort Domn Stefan out to the yard and ready a spot for the impaling. There are a few more things I wish to cut off of this man before the execution."

"Dear prince!" Stefan called out as he took a step forward, extending his right hand in earnest plea. "Surely Teo has made an honest mistake. Perhaps I resemble this Nicolae fellow in some way. I am sure his intentions were only to safeguard Your Majesty's well being." Nicolae's conscience tugged at him fiercely. Surely he could not let an innocent man die for simply having told the truth.

"Noble Stefan," Vlad responded lightly. "Always the polite and proper gentleman. I would have expected nothing less of you than a plea for your accuser's life. But I assure you," the prince continued, his timbre darkening, "that this weasel would have no qualms about seeing you skewered with a spear. This time your sympathies are misplaced."

Stefan suddenly thought again of the dagger in his boot. *I could rush him, cut his throat before...but Sergei holds the pike, and he stands closer to Vlad than I. If I am delayed fighting him, Vlad will kill me himself. They will search my bags at the inn and find the list of boyars...no! They've trusted me, and I cannot let them all be slaughtered like swine.* His eyes moved to meet Teo's who had been glaring at him in hatred. *It's not my fault*, Nicolae's eyes returned. But in his heart he felt it was. He could speak out, confess, and save an informant, a spy who intended he be impaled...a man who was still innocent, who had told the truth. But if he did, all was lost: his life, the plan, the rebel boyars, Maria—Maria! Could they trace her to him? Would she fall under suspicion too? And what of Kuban and his family? Could Dracula's arm of power reach even into Hungary? Teo was a sacrifice Nicolae had not intended making, but there was no other choice.

"As you will, milord." The words fell sullenly from his lips.

"Good then. We shall be with you gentlemen momentarily." Dracula turned his glacial judgment toward the trembling Teo as he snatched the dagger in the strong grip of his right hand. He took slow, menacing steps toward his intended victim. "So you thought to lie to me a second time."

"This way, domnule," Sergei instructed as he led the merchant toward the back door. Stefan turned bleakly and followed him with a heavy heart and labored steps. He felt consumed by a dark cloud of guilt as they exited the chamber. *There is nothing I can do*, he told himself.

Once outside the courtroom and in the bright morning light of the castle yard, Sergei inspected the finely clad gentleman somewhat enviously. "My lord Dracula is quite taken with you. He has spoken to me of how you intrigue and amuse him."

Nicolae quickly collected himself knowing that his pretense must go on a while longer. He swallowed and cleared his throat. "I am honored by His Majesty's attention. He is a most intriguing man himself. I have noticed that you appear to be one of his most loyal and trusted aides—his right-hand man, if I may say so."

Sergei beamed proudly. He raised his chin and briefly surveyed the castle yard. People were busily stacking supplies and carrying powder kegs down to the wagons at the foot of the escarpment. Sunlight sparkled on the crisp, new snow. "The prince saved my life," he began in wonder as he reflected on the story, "and there is nothing I would not do for him."

Nicolae turned his eyes to Sergei in feigned interest. "Do tell me the story."

The brawny armas complied with pleasure. "I had been imprisoned in Tirgoviste during Basarab's last weeks of rule and was indeed awaiting execution when Prince Vlad and his troops liberated the city. Being so intent on the abolition of crime, one of the first places His Majesty visited was the prison. He inquired after all of the prisoners before staging his mass impalement to announce his return to power. But when he learned that I had been arrested for killing a prostitute, he proclaimed, 'Release that man at once! He should not be executed, rather rewarded for his deed.' Then he offered me a position in his service. His valet, cook, armor bearer, coachman—even Captain Ivan—are all competent at their work and are loyal servants. But the prince and I have a certain understanding of things," he explained with a knowing wink at the dandy. "We think alike," he added in a whisper.

What a scary thought, he contemplated silently then replied, "How very fortunate for both of you."

About that time the hall door opened, and Teo stumbled out with his hands tied behind his back and fresh blood spots on his trousers and long, white tunic. As he turned an agonized face toward Nicolae, he saw the blood trail down the side of his neck and the bare spot where his ear should have been. Nicolae swallowed hard and diverted his eyes to the ground.

"He's all yours," Vlad said to Sergei as he stepped out and pulled the door shut.

"Thank you, Sire." He brutishly grabbed Teo's arm in one hand and the silver spear in the other and took a few paces out into the snow.

"A lying coward like that does not deserve to die a man," Dracula spoke in disdain as he tossed two human testicles to the ground and then brushed his hands together a few times. A horrifyingly sick feeling arose from the pit of Nicolae's stomach as he comprehended what he saw. He wanted to run, to bolt away and down the 1,400 steps, and keep running until he fell into Maria's compassionate embrace.

Instead, he struggled to push his mental anguish aside and try to act normal—whatever normal in such a situation might be. "Sire, our trade agreement," he started once again, holding out the paper to the prince.

"In due time, my fine fellow. Come." He motioned to a spot on their right. "We will have a better view from over here." Suddenly Teo let out a shriek of terror and a mournful cry of pain.

"My lord—"

"What is wrong, Domn Stefan?" Dracula's green eyes pierced Nicolae's sea of blue with forceful demand. "Don't you want to see the man who falsely accused you be punished for his crime? Remember, it could well have been you dancing from that pole."

He swallowed hard, and his voice squeaked as he replied. "But of course, Prince Dracula. Business can wait." Nicolae's feet followed those of the prince, and he stood by the devil himself at the foot of that silver tree fearing that he had lost his very soul.

Nicolae proceeded straight to his room upon arriving back at the tavern without stopping to speak to anyone, but there was someone he needed to talk to desperately. After a few minutes he opened his door and walked to the top of the stairs. "I hate to be a bother, but there appears to be a spot of dirt on my bed linens. Maria, if you would be so kind as to bring a new set. I do detest dirty linens."

"Certainly, domnule," she replied, filled with anxious anticipation.

"Thank you ever so much," he said with a nod and returned to his room to wait.

Within moments she was at his door with clean linens in hand. "Domn Stefan?" she asked and rapped lightly at his door.

"Come in," he said softly. She could hear the heaviness in his voice and quickly complied locking the latch behind her. As she looked across the room she spied him sitting on the bed, his head in his hands as his elbows rested on his knees.

"Stefan, what's wrong?" Alarm and concern registered on Maria's face as she laid the sheets aside. When he raised his head, she saw that his face was pallid and his eyes red and swollen. His palms slid across his cheeks until they came together in a prayer-like pose resting against his chin. His moment of silence seemed an eternity.

Then he tilted his head inquisitively toward her. "Do you think that I am evil?"

Such an absurd question was like a bolt of lighting from a clear sky to the woman. "Certainly not!" she replied with conviction as she took rapid steps toward him. "Why ever would you say such a thing?"

"While I rush to kill a prince who trusts me, I stood by and allowed an innocent man to die in my place today." Nicolae spoke the words as if he hardly believed them himself.

Maria sat beside him on the bed, tenderly slid her right arm around him, and touched her left hand to his upper arm. "Tell me what happened."

"Teo," he said and swallowed looking at her sadly.

"The Teo who works here at the tavern?"

"Not anymore. He was a spy for Vlad," Nicolae explained.

"Can you be serious? Teo?" Maria could hardly believe her ears. He had overheard her berate Dracula on several occasions, and she wondered what he may have reported about her.

"As it turns out, he was my father's successor as Boyar of Cozia. Obviously he got on Vlad's bad side about something, but he knew who I was. Somehow he remembered me and reported all." Then he paused and lowered his hands, cupping Maria's hand in his. When his eyes returned to hers, they were full of hollow wonder. "But the prince believed me and had Teo impaled on the spot."

"What?"

"Oh, God, Maria, he made me watch!" Nicolae covered his face again as bitter tears stung his eyes. Maria was at a loss for words as she rubbed her right hand soothingly along his back and tried to collect her thoughts. "It was horrible; the pitiful, agonizing way he looked at me will haunt my soul forever. He told the truth and was tortured for lying while I...watched." Nicolae looked up from his hands through lipid pools of midnight blue to search Maria's eyes. "I tried to convince him to spare Teo, that he had made an honest mistake. But he was intent on impaling someone. If it had not been him—"

"Then it would have been you," Maria answered as she raised her left hand to stroke his cheek. As she wiped away his tears, she assured him saying, "No, milord, you are not an evil man. If you were, you would not care what had happened to the very spy who accused you. On the contrary, you are a very good and noble man chosen by God to avenge the deaths of many and bring to an end the tyranny of an immoral despot."

The powerful man trembled at the touch of Maria's hands and at her words. "How can you say that? I just let a man die in my stead."

"Why?" she asked with great insight anticipating his reply. "Why did you then?"

"Because." He swallowed and cast his gaze to the floor. "More would have been in danger of death had I spoken out...the boyars, Kuban, you." He paused for a moment. "And Dracula would continue to rule unhindered once the plot had been foiled."

"You see, Nicolae of Cozia, you are not evil," she said softly. The sound of her speaking his true name so admiringly, so gently in his ear warmed Nicolae's heart. She was the best medicine for what ailed him.

His brightened eyes gazed back at hers and a half-smile tugged at his lips. He reached up and took her hand in his once again, affectionately caressing it with his fingers. "Thank you, Maria," he said warmly from his heart and then brought her hand to his lips and kissed it.

Maria's cheeks blushed. "Milord," she said modestly.

"I am no one's lord," he replied honestly. "Least of all yours, it would appear."

Maria's blood pumped heatedly through her veins at the closeness of this man. He was touching her, caressing her hand, and it set her heart on fire. She was thrilled by the comfort she could give him and by the knowledge that she could be of help to her hero. But she was also intensely aware that she should change the subject soon before she ended up lying in that bed with him. "So, what do we do next? Nadia says the army will be moving out any day now headed for Bucuresti."

"Good. Now 'we' don't do anything. I will leave tomorrow morning for Bulgaria to meet with Sultan Mehmed and present my proposal."

"Then I am coming with you," Maria stated staunchly.

"Oh, no; it is far too dangerous," Nicolae commanded protectively. "As long as I travel through Walachia, I am suspect and could be apprehended as a spy. Then once I cross the Danube into Turkish territory, I am at the mercy of any Muslim warrior who wants to gain glory by killing a Christian. I need to concoct some pretense for my travel, some disguise that would not appear suspicious..." Nicolae's words trailed off as he puzzled about what to do.

Suddenly Maria's eyes lit up. She slid a few inches away from him, turned sideways on the bed, and moved her hands in an animated fashion.

"I have an idea! There is a band of Gypsies in town. Everyone knows that Gypsies move about through both the Christian and Muslim worlds. We could borrow or buy one of their wagons, put on gaudy Gypsy clothing, and travel freely without arousing the slightest bit of suspicion."

"That is a wonderful idea, Maria!" Nicolae agreed. "You are so clever!" He beamed joyously toward her, matching her own triumphant smile. "There's only one thing wrong with your plan," he noted, his countenance becoming more serious.

"What?" Maria's heart sank in bewilderment at his objection.

"You aren't coming," he said softly but firmly.

"Nic—"

"No, and that is final," Nicolae ordered emphatically with a swift movement of his arm toward her. "You don't understand how dangerous this is. First of all, you couldn't possibly be of any help. Secondly, if we are caught together with no marriage license in Walachia—well, Vlad's law is still in place. Plus, if I am caught with these treasonous documents, and you are safe here, there is nothing to link you to the plot. But if you are with me—"

"I don't care!"

"I do!"

The two stared defiantly at each other, each stubbornly determined to have their way in the matter when suddenly a knock sounded at the door.

Chapter 16

Reluctant Warriors

"Had the Turks wished to bring their ships from Constantinople to the Danube they no longer have fording points, because I have burned, destroyed, and laid waste to their towns."

Vlad Dracula in a letter to King Matthias Corvinus, Feb. 11, 1462

Nicolae and Maria were suddenly aware that they had been arguing quite loudly, and someone must have heard them, but who? Had Vlad sent another spy to check up on him? As they stared wide-eyed at the door, another louder knock sounded.

Nicolae swooped his arm around Maria drawing her against his hard chest and lightly pressed two fingers to her lips. Their eyes met with a glint of fear as each played out dreadful possibilities in their minds. As his heart raced beneath his ribs, Nicolae determined that no matter whatever else happened, no one would hurt the woman he loved. He took a breath to steady himself and concentrated on using Stefan's voice. "Who is it?"

"It's me, Carmen. Maria, are you still changing those sheets?" she asked in an exasperated tone. "The tavern is filling up with customers, and I can't do everything by myself!"

Maria closed her eyes, offering a silent prayer of thanksgiving as Nicolae relaxed his hold on her and breathed easy. "Almost done, Carmen," she called. "I'll be right down."

"All right, but please hurry." Maria and Nicolae stripped his bed of its linens in silence as they listened to her footsteps grow faint.

Then Maria's expression returned to one of disappointed ire as she wadded the linens in her arms, raised her chin, and started storming toward the door. But Nicolae was right behind her and caught her arm in his strong left hand. "Don't leave angry," he implored.

She spun around to glare at him. "And how am I supposed to feel? You said we were partners."

"We are," Nicolae replied earnestly as he loosened his grip on her arm. "It's just…you are the partner who stays at home."

Maria laid her left hand on the door latch and cocked her head to one side as she answered him gruffly, "Domn Stefan, you need me, and one of these days you are going to realize that." Before he could respond, she was gone, closing the door in his face as he tried to follow.

Nicolae groaned as he ran his palm down the smooth wood. He turned on his heel and leaned against the closed door, lifting his eyes toward the ceiling. "I do need you," he swore out loud to the empty room. "More than you could possibly know!"

Dimitry and Jean sat on a log warming their hands by the campfire they shared with several other new recruits that night. Each wore his long, white tunic shirt bound by a wide black belt, and a woolen cloak or szur. A round canvas tent with a tournament top stood behind them in an endless row of identical tents along the side of the road in the shadow of Poenari. Activity in the camp was reserved and quiet with a cloak of uncertainty draped around it.

Jean nursed his cup of hot tea conservatively, taking sips now and again to warm his insides. His wavy brunette hair encircled his head and neck, bouncing upon the gray woolen cloak that draped about his shoulders. His usually smooth face showed a day or two's growth because he had found neither the time nor energy to shave. "Do you think any of us will return home alive?" he asked to no one in particular.

"Certainly, Jean," Dimitry was quick to answer. His gray felt cap was snug around his balding head to keep it warm. "Whatever else Vlad Dracula is, he is a brilliant military tactician and a fearless fighter. He always beats the Turks."

"That may be, but what about us?" Jean's worried eyes scanned the men around the crackling fire. "We've been issued old, worn out equipment, scarcely a week's training—he'll use us as fodder."

"Yeah," one of the other young men agreed. "Look at this mail shirt they gave me." He stood so that all could see by the firelight. "There's rust eating through the ends and shoulders and look at this huge hole! How much protection is that?"

"At least you got chain mail; all they gave me was this leather jerkin," Jean replied as he picked up the vest from beside him, showing it to them.

"That's nothing," a fair-haired, bearded man commented as he picked up the weapon that lay on the ground beside him. "Watch this!" He gripped his pole-ax with his right hand and easily pulled off the iron end with his left, then slipped it back on again. "The ax-head comes off, and I'm supposed to fight with this?"

Then a short, black-haired, olive-skinned youth decided to display his army issued helmet. "Gentlemen," he said holding out the conical steel helm. Then with a humorous grin he added, "Let me try to top that." Very deliberately and with much flare he placed the helm on his head, which it covered completely right down to the bridge of his nose. Immediately they all began to laugh at the immensely oversized head piece which hid his eyes entirely. The lad jerked his head from side to side, saying, "Where'd they go; where'd they go?"

The laughter brightened their spirits for a moment. Jean laughed so hard a tear came to his eye. Dimitry was still chuckling as the lad removed the helmet. "Maybe we could trade," he suggested. He pulled off his felt hat and placed a dented helm with its broken nose guard on top of his large, round head, where it perched comically. Once again the small group burst into laughter. Dimitry rose from his log and extended the too small helmet toward the thin, shorter lad. "I'm Dimitry the Brawny, and I am off to kill Turks," he proclaimed humorously, a smile peeping between his salt and pepper beard and mustache.

The black-haired youth exchanged helmets answering, "I am Lucian the Little, and I smite Turks in the knees."

Jean laughed again at Lucian while trying to regain his composure. He was glad to have a comedian in the camp. Despite his fears, he was beginning to feel better. Then the blonde fellow jumped to his feet. "I am Daniel the Daring," he sang out. "I fling my ax-head at the enemy and then battle them with my stick!"

The fifth man did not want to be left out. "I am Hans the Holy," he declared motioning toward his faulty chain mail with a laugh. Dimitry shook his head with a smirk at the joke.

Finally, Jean replied, "I am Jean, and I am pleased to make your acquaintances." Then he hesitated, blank-faced for an instant. "And I can't think of a single clever thing to say." That was enough to send the other men into an extra round of laughter.

Their merriment was interrupted by the appearance of a regular army sergeant's arrival at their campfire. "Soldiers," he addressed them in a business-like manner. Immediately their laughter faded as they looked up into his serious face. His armor was spotless, his helmet fit, his boots were polished, and a sword hung at his side. "You must each wear one of these yellow sashes over your clothes and armor," he instructed as he passed them out. "They are your identifying colors. There is no time to sew uniforms for you all, so you must always wear these. And never kill anyone with a yellow sash, understand?"

"Yes, domnule," they each answered as they tried on their colors.

"We will be moving out at first light," the stern sergeant told them, "so get a good night's sleep."

The men's eyes scanned each other's nervously and when they looked back, the sergeant was gone.

"Tomorrow," Lucian echoed, his voice now void of humor.

Daniel shared his tone of concern. "What if we are all slaughtered? After all, we are being led by a madman."

"What do you mean?" asked Hans urgently, his face lined with anxiety.

"I heard he once killed a man's wife simply because she had sewed his shirt too short," the blonde bearded Daniel explained. "Does that sound like the action of a rational man?" The other young men peered wide-eyed at Daniel, wondering if they were being led to their deaths. Jean looked down at his own long tunic and tugged at the hem just to make sure it did not appear in any way short.

Then the elder of the group determined that they needed reassurance. Dimitry, though having never been a military man, understood the importance of good morale and faith in one's leader to a soldier. The young men would certainly be cut to pieces like cabbage if they entered a battle consumed by fear and doubt.

"He may be eccentric," Dimitry began as he made himself as comfortable as possible on the log. "And he has been known to be cruel," he admitted knowingly. "Gentlemen, we do not have to love him—few do—but to come home alive we must have confidence in his abilities.

From my younger days, I remember Vlad's military exploits against the Turks, and they were all successful, even when he was outnumbered."

"But what about here, at Poenari even, back in sixty-two when he fled?" Hans asked.

"Yes, but that was Radu, with his own army, who had attacked the castle when Vlad fled to Hungary—not the infidels."

"But it's winter," Lucian pointed out as he pulled his forest green cloak closer around his long beige tunic. "Can we win in winter?"

Dimitry leaned his elbows on his knees and held his coarse hands out toward the fire. Wisdom glowed in his hazel eyes as he recalled the events of the past. "One of his biggest victories came in the winter of 1461-1462. Both the Hungarians and the Ottomans demanded our principality pay them tribute. Prince Vlad had held off, diplomatically playing one great power off the other for as long as he could, but things were at a head. He did not wish to subjugate himself at all, but clearly it was better to bow to a Christian king than an infidel. Naturally, Dracula did not tell the Sultan that. Instead he insisted that Mehmed come to the Danube for him to pay tribute, citing the reason of treachery at home should he leave Walachia. There were armed Turkish towns all along the border, for Bulgaria had long been in their hands.

"But Vlad had no intention of paying tribute to Mehmed, and under the cover of darkness, he moved the army across the frozen surface of the Danube and attacked the Turkish forces as they slept. He decimated the army and cut off the head of the Turkish emissary which he sent to King Matthias to prove his loyalty to Hungary. Then Vlad burned all the Turkish towns along the border, killing their inhabitants. Within a few short weeks he had virtually destroyed the Turkish ability to invade Walachia."

"But they did invade," Daniel recalled.

"Yes," Dimitry said raising his index finger. "Mehmed was so angry that he gathered his entire army and set out for revenge against Prince Dracula. But Vlad had not only killed tens of thousands of Turks by that time—he had also taken 20,000 prisoners. Now Mehmed's army outnumbered ours by at least three to one, so Vlad retreated to Tirgoviste, scorching the earth behind him. The Turks had nothing to take but a few remote villages in the south, but Mehmed did not waste time capturing land; he wanted Vlad's head. So he drove his army straight to the capital."

All eyes were fixed on Dimitry as he recounted the tale. The only sound save his voice was the crackle of the fire.

"The whole Walachian army was inside the city gates, and the angry infidels were quickly approaching. Now our forces could easily have been defeated, or laid siege to and starved into submission, but Dracula had a plan. He took those 20,000 Muslim prisoners and impaled them outside the walls of Tirgoviste to greet Mehmed when he arrived. A grisly greeting it was! When the Turks saw an entire forest of their impaled countrymen—more than they could count, more hideously disfigured than they could comprehend—Mehmed could not make them press on. They turned and went all the way back across the Danube, gladly forfeiting the towns they had taken to put more distance between them and the dreaded Impaler."

"I've heard that story before," Jean said, turning his face toward Dimitry. The warm glow of the fire played along his cheek. "But who knows what will happen this time? I have a loving wife and two small children. I am a potter, not a warrior. I've never even killed a chicken, much less a man."

"You must remember," Dimitry told him, "that the Muslim believes if he is killed in a battle to spread his religion, his spirit will go straight to Heaven, so he fights with no fear of death. When you are on the battlefield, every move you make is life or death. You want to live—he doesn't care, and that gives him the advantage. But he may not take proper precautions; you will. Always stay in a group, never alone. Make each strike decisive. Never hesitate or hold a punch. And if it looks like you will be completely surrounded by them, run—as fast as you can, as far as you can."

"That's right," Daniel added. "We are just militia, not professional soldiers. No one expects us to be great fighters. We are padding the army's numbers, that is all. Our main goal is to get out of the fighting alive, and if we kill a few Turks in the bargain, all the better. I have a wife and children myself."

"What about me?" Lucian asked drawing their attention. "I'm only eighteen and have never even been with a woman. I have more reason than any of you to get back alive," he proclaimed with a hint of humor.

Dimitry tried on Lucian's helmet. It was a hair loose, but fit him well enough. He took it off again and rose to his feet. "We foot soldiers will be walking all the way to Bucharesti starting tomorrow. Gentlemen, I don't know about you, but I am going to bed." The others agreed and one by one followed him into the tent until only Jean was left sitting on a log staring blankly into the orange flames of the campfire, his heart enfolded in Nadia's distant embrace, far, far from that mountain.

"Get on!" Nicolae called to the pie-bald Carpathian pony as he slapped the reins across the brown and white gelding's haunches. He had been driving the brightly painted green, gold, and red wagon down the rutted dirt road to Tirgoviste all day, and the small Gypsy horse was beginning to tire. It was not an easy task to persuade a Gypsy to sell his wagon which served as both his transportation and his home, but the Hungarian merchant had gold at his disposal. He found an elderly widower in the band with relations living in Curt de Arges. The old man had decided to settle down for what little time he might have left on earth.

The coat of many colors was a bit snug around Nicolae's shoulders, and the baggy, black woolen trousers were worn out in the seat. An old scabbard hung from the plain, black baldric he wore. Along with the gold chains he sported, he looked every bit the part of a Gypsy traveler.

It had been a long day alone on the bumpy road, his mind haunted by its memory. *Was it here that I fell?* he would ponder. *Is that the spot I lost her?* He could still envision the bodies in the road and hear the scream of a youth being speared. But after so many years, every turn in the road looked like the last. The forest closed in, rocks and boulders stood unwavering, and a frosty blast reminded him that it was not an April day back in '57.

The sun had passed below the trees, its light now filtering through from the west as Nicolae approached the city. He abruptly stopped the wagon to stare blankly across the grassy hill ahead to his left. That was the place. No stakes remained, no bones, no grave markers. The peaceful field lay covered in spotty patches of glistening snow as innocently as if the massacre had never occurred. It was not a place he wanted to camp for the night, but it was hallowed ground that he was drawn to visit once again.

Nicolae tied off the reins, climbed down from the wagon, and took a few steps into the trees at the edge of the road to relieve himself. "Ah." He sighed rolling his neck from side to side. But as he was enjoying his relaxed state of being, his ear detected a sound behind him. First there was a clamor that sounded like it came from the back of his wagon, followed by a thud, some footsteps, and a rustle in the bushes across the road.

Alarmed, he snapped his head around to look but saw nothing. His heart began to race as a host of possibilities flew through his mind. "Who's there?" he called.

Nicolae's senses were suddenly heightened as he heard another crackle in the underbrush. He hurried to fasten his trousers as he took a step onto the dirt highway, reaching a hand to the hilt of his sword. Then a voice answered him from the brush.

"I thought you would never stop! I swear, Stefan, if you had hit one more hole—"

"Maria?"

Chapter 17

Gypsies

"And he told them, 'You must eat each other, the lot of you, or else you must attack the Turks.' And all of the Tartars (Gypsies) were glad to start fighting against the Turks."

From the German pamphlet, "About a mischievous tyrant called Dracula voda," 1460's

Nicolae did not know whether to be relieved or angry to discover who had stowed away for the journey. He walked over behind the wagon and called to her, "Maria, come here this instant!"

"I am sorry to inform you that 'this instant' is not a possibility. Some things are far simpler for a man to accomplish on the side of the road than for a woman," Maria replied impatiently. "There," she said and stood to rise above the bushes where they could see each other. "And if you were any kind of gentleman you would have been facing the other way," she declared as she tramped back through the brush toward him.

"And if you were any kind of lady, you would have done what you were told and stayed home." The two stood at the rear of the wagon, staring at each other defiantly. "I thought I made it clear that this was far too dangerous. Why did you disobey me?"

"Domnule, I am not obliged to obey you," she answered stoically. "You are not my employer nor my husband."

"A fact you must relish reminding me," Nicolae groaned. He placed a fist on his hip and tilted his head toward her inquisitively. "So why did you stow away in my wagon?"

Maria shuffled her feet, averting her eyes from him as she answered in a soft, innocent voice. "I thought you might need me."

A warm smile crossed Nicolae's lips. He relaxed his fist and reached for her hand. "Of course, I need you," he said tenderly as he laced his fingers through hers. "Two under the blanket will be far warmer than one, but it is not worth the risk, my iubita.[25] If we were caught together -"

Maria stepped back from him withdrawing her hand from his as she did so. "Stefan, are you implying that I tagged along to sleep with you?"

A bewildered expression overtook his countenance as he turned his left palm up and motioned toward the vehicle. "Maria, it is a small wagon. Where did you think you would sleep?"

"Oh," she answered shortly. "I hadn't thought about that."

Nicolae let out a long sigh and turned his face from her, running his fingers up through his hair. He felt both embarrassed and offended by having jumped to a conclusion that was obviously not her intent. "Then why did you come?" he asked sharply.

"I want to help," she explained. "I have every right to help kill that soul-less butcher, and I told you I would not be left out."

"Help? What possible help could you be?"

Maria raised her unyielding chin as his cheeks reddened with smoldering turbulence. "I can be quite a bit of help, you arrogant cad. I could support your claims to the sultan by verifying the numbers of soldiers Vlad is conscripting and -"

"You can't tell the sultan anything," he retorted hotly. "He won't listen to a thing you say."

"And why not? I have just as much right -"

"You have no rights," Nicolae explained in frustration. "Not in his country. Don't you know anything? You think women have no voice in our society; to a Muslim you are little more than cattle. Women must remain veiled, walk behind the man, and never speak to one - especially the sultan. If you were even to open your mouth in his presence without him first having asked you a question, it would be considered an offense worth a beating at the very least."

A look of genuine surprise lit on her face. "I didn't know."

"You didn't know," he repeated in annoyance. "Now, what am I supposed to do with you? I can't take you home; that would waste two days of precious time, not to mention that Vlad's troops will be using this road."

"Don't worry about me," Maria answered sullenly, holding back the tears that threatened to spring forth. "I can take care of myself. You

---

[25] iubita - Romanian for darling

needn't be angry. I thought I could help you, and I see now that I cannot, so I will just be on my way."

"Wait a minute," Nicolae demanded abruptly, stopping her from turning away. A chilling, piercing thought had wedged itself into his heart, and he could not shake its possibility. "You wanted to find out if I was going to do what I said I was. You don't trust me, so you hid in the wagon to spy on me, to see what I was really up to. That's it, isn't it?"

"No, that's not -"

"Damn you, woman!" he shouted smacking his fist against the wooden frame of the wagon. "And damn me for believing in you!" Nicolae's blood raced with a fury he had never known, thinking that his love had been betrayed. He breathed heavily as he turned his flushed face toward her, his blue eyes crazed with inner pain. "I poured out my heart to you," he agonized, "told you things that I have never spoken to anyone, and you don't believe me."

"I do - that's not it!" Maria stepped back, a look of terror growing in her eyes.

Nicolae turned from her and punched the back of the wagon once more, shaking it with the force from his blow.

"Stop that," she demanded in a shaky voice. "You are frightening me."

"If I don't hit this wagon, I am going to hit you," he uttered through gritted teeth as he slammed his palm against the wood. "I thought you believed me; I thought -" Nicolae snapped his head up to glare at her. "Who all have you told? Are you along to point me out to them?"

"No one, Nicolae, I swear!" she cried enfolding her arms around herself in a vain attempt at comfort. "I only wanted to help."

"Well, you can't help, and you don't want me, so that leaves no other reason you could have come," he concluded logically. Tears stung the strong man's eyes, and he turned his face from her as he leaned against the wagon. "I opened my heart to you," he said, the anger draining from his voice, "but you thought I just made it up."

Maria trembled but not from the cold night that surrounded them. Slowly she took a step closer to him, realizing the pain he was experiencing. She knew that somehow she must persuade him of the truth, or all of her hopes would be lost. "I do believe you." Her voiced cracked even as she spoke the words. "I made a mistake, and I am sorry. Believe anything you want, but not that I came to spy on you." When he did not answer, she dared to take one more step toward him. "We are partners in this, and that means we both must trust each other. I do believe you," she said seriously. "Will you believe me?"

Nicolae breathed a long sigh and slowly raised his doubtful eyes to hers. As his rage subsided, and he began to regain his composure, he realized how out of control his emotions had been. *How could I have lost my temper so?* he thought to himself. *What is happening to me? No one has ever hurt me this way before...but I don't think she meant to. Maybe she did just want to help.*

"There's food in the wagon; some water and wine also," he said. "Go on and get in." He pulled back the green woolen blanket that served as a rear door.

"What about you?" she asked, her eyes darting about nervously. "Where will you sleep?"

"Anywhere you're not."

"But it is dark, and it's getting very cold out." Maria's concern was genuine. She had anticipated that he would be upset once he discovered she had hidden herself to go with him, but she had never imagined the furious exchange that had just taken place.

"I'll be fine," he replied tersely. "I'll be close by, but I just can't be with you right now. I need a little time."

As their eyes locked, she searched his lipid pools, wishing desperately that she could throw her arms around him and kiss him the way he had kissed her a few days ago. She wanted to tell him that he had stirred her mind, thrilled her heart, and revived her soul. But this was not the right moment. He would not believe her and would dismiss her declaration of love as a vain attempt to quiet his anger and convince him she should stay.

Maria trembled as her hand came to rest on his shoulder. "Be careful, and come in if you get too cold." Then her voice hushed to a whisper. "Nicolae, I..." What could she say? She lowered her head in sorrow for having caused him unnecessary grief. Slowly, she placed a foot on the back step to the wagon, and Nicolae helped her inside. Once in, she looked back over her shoulder to find he had already gone.

Nicolae led the paint pony forward to park the wagon in a level area just off the road, unhitched him, and secured his tie to let him graze on what little brown grass remained. *If only she had come to sleep with me,* he thought. *But no - I'm glad she is not that easy. I want to believe there has been no one since her husband died.*

The long shadows were fading into total night, but the stars and moon illuminated the open field ahead. Memories of that fateful day flashed on his consciousness as the fair-haired man took grave steps up the slight incline and across the level ground. He had not strayed too far from the wagon when he dropped to his knees on the cold, moist earth. "Mother, Father," he spoke in a still, reverent voice. "I came back, like I said I would. I know it's been a long time, but soon justice will be done." He paused for a moment, his eyes peering up toward the heavens. "I really could use your counsel now...your experience, your words of wisdom. I need to know that I am doing the right thing. Innocent people will die - one already has. But the soldiers." He stopped to swallow and then continued as he raised his palms from his sides in a plea toward the silent sky. "Vlad will engage the Turks whether I speak with the sultan or not, but by ending the battle with his death, many will be saved." He breathed a puff of steam into the air and lowered his head. "Life is so much harder than I thought it would be when I was a child. I wish you could tell me what to do about Maria...but you can't. And I don't even have a God that will listen or speak to me. I feel so utterly alone!" he agonized. His knees grew weak, and he sat back on his heels, burying his face in his hands.

Early the next morning, before the rooster welcomed the dawn, Maria was awakened when she rolled against something hard and warm in her bed. It took her only a moment to realize that sometime during the night Nicolae had come in. She readjusted her pillow and lay still with her back toward him, not wanting to wake him so early. Her heart began to pound just knowing that he was so near. *He must be over his anger,* she thought in relief. *Today will go much better. I will be good and do whatever he tells me to,* she determined. She closed her eyes in hopeful anticipation and tried to no avail to fall back asleep.

The Walachian army made quite a parade as it marched briskly down the southern highway. Prince Dracula, surrounded by the Moldavian guard clad in purple waist capes, rode near the front of the procession, taking personal command of the troops as was his custom. Mounted on a jet black war horse, he donned his silver breast plate, mail skirt, and reinforced steel boots. He was easily identifiable by the fur collared black cape and favorite crimson head piece he wore as well as the banner his flag bearer carried. The symbol of the red dragon on the black square cloth was unmistakable, as was the presence of Sergei at his side.

Next in the procession pranced the Hussars, mounted Hungarian mercenaries who rounded out the cavalry units. These mustached horsemen had already gained a reputation as an invaluable addition to any fighting force. They provided their own chain mail armor, royal blue tunics, lances, and side weapons such as broadswords, axes, and Saracen swords. The bulk of the army marched behind on foot: the pikemen, some with breast plates and yellow waist capes; the swordsmen, attired in mail and yellow tunics; archers, with their steel kettle hats, leather armor, short swords, longbows, and crossbows; and the poorly outfitted militia bearing whatever weapons and armor could be dredged up for them, some being left with nothing but a pitchfork. Trailing the ranks were the supply wagons and the artillery. Each wagon and cannon was pulled by a quartet of horses or pair of oxen led or driven by a cannoneer. The Walachian army relied mainly on light cannons with wooden-spoked wheels and copper barrels that fired a lead ball, but they also had acquired a few hand cannons, crude hand-held, black powder fire arms. The army was roughly three thousand strong when they entered the first city on their route, Curt de Arges.

Prince Dracula noticed that the columns ahead of him had slowed to a near stand still and inquired as to the problem.

"Milord," answered one of the Moldavians ahead of him. "The square is blocked by Gypsy wagons. We can only get past two at a time."

"The hell with the Gypsy wagons!" he shouted. "Move them, smash them, burn them - just get them out of my way!" Vlad kicked his horse and pressed his way to the front with Sergei riding his chestnut Arabian right behind him. Some of the purple-clad guards had already begun moving the painted wagons as civilians scurried out of the way.

"Gypsies," Dracula muttered in disgust to Sergei. "Nothing but a bunch of tramps and thieves! Dirty, vulgar foreigners. Why, if I weren't in such a hurry, I'd -"

"Sire," Sergei injected brightly, "perhaps we can make use of them. You did want those more expendable for the front lines, correct?"

Vlad's eyes lit up with the inspiration. "Marvelous! Make the announcement. All of their men are conscripted as of this moment."

It was a difficult task to be heard above the noise of the army, the clamor of the wagons, and the verbal exchanges of soldiers and civilians. "Make way for the prince!" The stern commander struck one of the horses hitched to a wagon with his whip, and it took off with a startled whinny.

"Silence!" Sergei yelled as he pulled to the front. "Conscript these Gypsies in the name of Prince Dracula," he ordered to the troops. "Put them with the militia."

"What?" questioned a befuddled Gypsy, his long black hair stringing down his face as he tried to move his cart. The travelers turned to one another in alarm, questioning among themselves what they should do.

"You are all going to be soldiers in the army of Walachia. All men fifteen and older fall into ranks, now!" Sergei's harsh voice and glaring eyes indicated that he meant business. Some of the guard in purple capes who had dismounted to move the wagons began to push Gypsy men into the midst of the sea of mounted warriors.

"Wait! You can't do this," protested one of the men.

"Don't take our men!" cried one of the women in dismay. "What will we do."

By that time Vlad had ridden into the center of the Gypsy gathering. The Moldavian guard parted to give the prince ample room. Sergei tried to quiet his high-spirited Arabian as he pranced in place, wide-eyed and nervous about the commotion. "Your pitiful little lives are of no consequence," spoke the prince in disdain. "You will at last make a contribution to our society and serve a useful purpose defending our principality from the Turks."

"I beg you, Sire, do not take them all," cried one of the women as she fell to her knees raising her clasped hands toward him as if in prayer. Her haggard face was carved with dark lines, and tears welled in her brown eyes.

"My lord," called one of the brightly clothed migrants. "I cannot go with the army," he explained in distress. "My wife is ill, and I must stay with her." He protectively wrapped his arm around a frail woman in a gray shawl and pulled her close to his side. She peered up at the prince with sunken eyes.

"Is that your wife?" Vlad asked.

"Yes, great viovode. She is a good wife, and I love her. She has born me four healthy children, but after the last baby she took ill. We are traveling west to find a warmer climate for her. But you may take my horse and cart if they will be of any use to you," the husband offered.

Vlad's index finger slowly slid down his nose, across his lips, and off the edge of his smooth chin. He locked eyes with Sergei and nodded to him. The armas dismounted while Vlad spoke. "You may each have your own excuses as to why you cannot join my army," he said coolly. A hush fell over the crowd and all eyes were on the prince. "But nevertheless, you will do as I say. Sergei, eliminate this man's excuse."

The Gypsy's heart leapt to his throat when he saw the brawny executioner draw his sword. "No!" he cried as he cradled his wife in his arms and tried to lead her away. But they were encircled by purple-caped knights, and there was nowhere to go. "For Christ's sake, I'll go!"

Sergei seized the woman, ripped her from her husband's arms, and plunged his sword into her belly. The crowd was terrified. As he withdrew the blade dripping red, the Gypsy men could not comply with Vlad's directive fast enough. "Take me; I'll go," they all said making their way into the line.

"You killed her," the shocked husband uttered as he caught his wife's body and lowered her to the street.

She reached for him and gazed up into his face, for the light had not yet fully faded from her eyes. "I love you," she vocalized faintly. "Now go." She fell limp in his arms.

"No!" he roared as in a moment his world was changed forever.

"Now," Dracula said darkly as he leaned forward in his saddle. "You have no excuse. Get in line."

Sergei grabbed the man by the arm and tore him from his wife's body without hesitation. "You heard the prince. This is your own doing. You should have obeyed at first."

"Nina," he agonized, tears of grief streaking his cheeks as he looked back at her over his shoulder.

"Mama, Tata!" cried out several small voices. Two of the women caught the children, holding them back as they reached desperately toward their parents.

"We will take care of them, Aurel. It will be all right," called one of the women. "Go, before there is more bloodshed," added the other.

As if in a daze, Aurel's feet carried him to where the others stood in the ranks. One of the Moldavian soldiers dragged the body from the road, and then some Gypsy women went to her.

"Forward," Vlad commanded. "We are wasting time here." In an instant the guards had remounted, and the procession continued through the town and southward toward Tirgoviste.

Nicolae was awakened by the bright sunlight pouring in through the open flap in back of the Gypsy cart. He rubbed his eyes and reached over to feel an empty blanket and pillow. "Maria!" he called groggily.

"Out here," she replied in a pleasant tone of voice. Nicolae ran his fingers through his hair and pulled on his boots. After taking his morning trip to the bush, he traipsed to the front of the wagon to look for Maria. She had freshened up already, having changed into a clean blouse and brushed her hair. She greeted him with a hopeful smile just as she buckled the last strap on the horse's harness. "There," she announced triumphantly. "All set to go."

His eyes quickly scanned the rigging as he leaned against the wagon, exhausted "Where'd you learn to do that?"

"I told you I was not totally useless. You may be quite surprised by the things I can do," she quipped.

"Indeed." Nicolae smiled raising a brow.

"Did you sleep well?" she asked politely.

Nicolae snorted shaking his head as he pushed himself upright and took a few steps toward her. "Hardly at all. Maria, I wish to apologize about last night. I should not have lost my temper so; it is quite unlike me." His sleepy blue eyes glowed softly and sweetly warming Maria's heart.

"I know I am to blame, and I also beg your forgiveness," she responded turning toward him. They stood by the pie-bald pony just out of each other's reach.

"I may well forgive you," he said, "but that will not in any way solve our dilemma. I have given this much thought." Maria trained her eyes on his face anxiously as he explained. "I cannot take you back, and I don't want to leave you in a strange city. But there is one solution if you'll agree to it. You can travel with me on the condition that you pretend to be

173

my wife. Likely no one will ask to see a marriage license, especially of a Gypsy couple. It is the only way for us to safely travel together."

Maria hesitated only a moment to bite her lower lip before agreeing with a nod. "I could pose as your wife," she submitted quietly, "in public."

A chuckle escaped Nicolae's radiant face as he took another step closer to her. "And I promise to stay on my side of the blanket until you request otherwise."

"Until?" she glittered provocatively. "A bit presumptuous, aren't you?"

Nicolae extended his hand gallantly to his lady with a seductive gleam in his eyes. "Come, my dear. We need to do something with your wardrobe."

Maria sat on the driver's seat beside the man who was thoroughly enjoying playing his new role. "Your dresses and skirts are a bit conservative for a Gypsy, but I think they'll do provided you wear lots of jewelry and lip color. And as difficult as this will be for you, a Gypsy wife is very submissive to her husband." Nicolae smiled at her exasperated expression. "Now, turn this way for a moment," he instructed as he gently turned her shoulder so her back was toward him.

"What are you doing?" she asked as he began running his fingers through her hair.

"A married Gypsy woman never wears her hair down," he replied. He reveled in the feel of her silky black strands as his hands passed masterfully through them.

"Where did you learn to do that?" she marveled.

"I had a sister, remember?" Dividing her hair into three sections, he easily braided it. "Do you have a clip?"

"Yes." She drew a simple hair clip from her apron pocket, and he fastened it at the end of her braid.

"You have very nice hair," Nicolae was surprised to hear himself say out loud. Maria's cheeks flushed at his compliment. He turned his attention back to the pony who had slowed to a crawl. He clicked to him and wiggled the reins as he moved through the city gate. "Now you are the most beautiful Gypsy woman in Walachia, but when we present you to the sultan as the wife of a wealthy Hungarian merchant - a former and possibly future boyar at that - you will need the most expensive Italian import we can find."

"Nicolae!" Maria was taken back by his offer to buy her only the best. "We will take it back after meeting the sultan, won't we? I don't want to cost you -"

"I won't hear of it," he insisted. "There is a lovely boutique here in Tirgoviste that sells the very finest ready-made gowns. It is the only one of its kind in Walachia, and I am sure they don't take returns. Saints above, it's been a long time," he declared as he peered up and down the busy city streets trying to get his bearings. The little horse's hooves clip-clopped over the hard streets of the capital. "I used to hate going shopping with my mother and Eveline...now which street?"

"We could always stop and ask directions," Maria suggested.

"That won't be necessary," he answered in typical male fashion. "I'm sure I can find the shop." Maria rolled her eyes at him but dared not complain. He was taking her to the vital meeting and buying her expensive new clothes in the bargain.

Nicolae turned the painted horse down the next street to the left and studied the arrangement of buildings. "Ah-ha! There it is," he announced pulling the wagon to the side. "I told you I could find it. Now, Maria," he said taking her hand to get her full attention. He looked her in the eyes tenderly. "Remember, we are a married Gypsy couple, and I just came into an inheritance and am buying you a new dress."

"Don't worry," she assured him. "I can do this."

They walked into the exclusive shop, Maria's hand resting in the crook of Nicolae's arm. The regal looking matron eyed them with contempt. "Dandar, I think you are in the wrong establishment," she proclaimed in a haughty voice as she looked down her long nose on the shabbily attired pair.

"This is Doamna Camelia's boutique, is it not?" Nicolae inquired politely.

"Yes, but -" She gave him a curious look as he drew a pouch of gold coins from his cummerbund and set it on the counter. The shop was immaculate with fine lace curtains and artistic tapestries on the walls. The furnishings looked like those Nicolae remembered from his parent's sitting room. "If that is stolen -"

Then Maria smiled and spoke understandingly to the woman. "Doamna Camelia, my husband was not always a Gypsy. He joined our clan when he married me. His mother's brother was a wealthy merchant who recently entered into his rest, leaving my Stefan as his only heir. Now we are traveling so I can meet his father for the first time and he wants to present me properly in a fine lady's dress. I assure you that his gold is as good as anyone's."

Nicolae flashed her a well-pleased smile. "Very well then, doamna. This way," the owner motioned with only a minor hint of hesitation.

"Make yourself comfortable, Drag[26]," Maria smiled batting her eyes at him. "I should like to try on everything she has in my size." Nicolae sighed, shaking his head at her, and quietly retired to a velveteen hardwood chair.

Maria was trying on her third ensemble when a ruffled, gray-haired man with a round belly and a full snowy beard pushed open the door. He looked completely lost in the aristocratic ladies' clothing salon. His wide eyes darted about until they came to rest on Nicolae. "Domn, is that your wagon out front?" he asked briskly in an anxious tone.

"Da," Nicolae replied standing politely to greet the stranger.

"I know most folks don't care much for your kind, but my daughter married a Gypsy, and he turned out to be a right honest fellow, so I thought I'd warn you," the stranger said in a scratchy voice that was loud enough for his own failing ears to hear. "The prince and his army are marching down the main highway toward the city and they're conscripting every Gypsy they see."

---

[26] drag - masculine form of the Romanian word for darling

Chapter 18

Mehmed

"I am young and rich and favored by fortune, so I intend to surpass Caesar, Alexander, and Hannibal by far."

Mehmed the Conqueror

A rush swept over Nicolae. "Thank you, kind domnule," he replied. The man nodded and quickly exited the shop. Nicolae turned toward the curtain separating him from the women. "Maria," he called in a concerned tone.

She stepped through the curtain to model the ornately decorated ciupag and poale ensemble with a dazzling smile. The thick wool ciupag had wide, raglan sleeves and was richly embroidered in silk threads. The poale skirt bore three inch wide vertical stripes and a wide meticulously embroidered waist and hem band in the exact style and colors as the matching ciupag. "It's the latest from Milan," she beamed, but her enthusiasm faded when she detected his troubled expression.

"Good, we'll take it. How much will -"

"Sweeting, there are many others to try. Must we choose now?"

"It's time to go, Maria," he stated gravely as he stepped to the counter. "Get your things; we're leaving now."

"But she'll need petticoats and matching shoes," Doamna Camelia commented helpfully while Maria dutifully moved behind the curtain to change back into her traveling clothes.

"Then we will get them later. I have just been reminded of a very pressing matter that my wife and I must attend to immediately."

"Very well, then," the matron said with a disappointed sigh. "That will be twenty-five ducats, and a bargain at that. Are you sure I can't interest you in -"

"Not today," Nicolae broke in as he handed her the money.

Observing Nicolae's urgency, Maria rushed to change and re-entered the front of the shop a bit ruffled with the lady's suit draped over her arm.

"Let me put that in a box for you," Doamna Camelia offered as she reached for the garment.

"No thank you," Nicolae replied as he took Maria by the arm and led her out of the shop. "Good day, doamna; it has been a pleasure," he offered before dragging Maria through the door.

"What is the matter with you?" she demanded while he continued to pull her over to the cart. "That was so rude!"

"We don't have time to argue," he replied bluntly. Then he easily lifted Maria and set her up on the wagon seat. She gasped unexpectedly at his action and once settled, glared down at him. She was just opening her mouth to demand an explanation when Nicolae gave it to her. "He's on his way with the army conscripting Gypsies." He climbed up onto the seat beside her and took the reins. "We've got to put some distance between us and that army, Maria, and fast. If he sees me like this -"

"I know," she interjected realizing the predicament they were in. "It's all right; let's go." Nicolae clicked to the paint horse and slapped the leather on his rump. "By the way," Maria added as she tucked her new clothes through the flap behind them into the wagon. "Thank you for taking me shopping. I have never had such a beautiful dress, and I am sure the Sultan will be impressed."

He smiled softly at her and then turned the rig down the next street to head south out of town. He wanted to buy her a dozen such dresses and a fine carriage with a team of horses. He wished to adorn her with jewels and perfumes and take her to live in a grand manor house. As his blue eyes melted into the warmth of hers, Nicolae desired to make all of her wishes come true. "You're welcome," he replied simply, and reluctantly focused his attention on getting them quickly out of the city.

Three days later the couple took a ferry across the Danube River into Turkish controlled Bulgaria. They had alternated telling stories along the way to pass the time. When they would stop to camp, Maria would cut potatoes, carrots, and onions into a big pot of water over the campfire while Nicolae would snare a rabbit or squirrel to go in it. The nights were not quite as cold there in the low country as in the mountains, but cold enough that Nicolae was grateful to have Maria's body heat next to him. There were times he was content with their arrangement, and there were times he longed to throw caution to the wind, gather her into his arms, and make passionate love to her. Often he worried that his desire was all too obvious.

It apparently was not. Maria was determined to guard her heart and her dignity. She was a Christian woman who had always been taught to flee the evil of lust and the sins of the flesh. It was even forbidden for a woman to display signs of pleasure when with her own husband. "Humans are not animals and should not enjoy sexual intercourse; it is for procreation only and should be avoided unless trying to have a child, lest one's mind be turned over to her carnal nature." Women were always being portrayed as villainesses - Eve tempting Adam with the apple, the evil queen Jezebel, Delilah ruining Samson, Salome demanding the head of John the Baptist, and so on. If it appeared for even a moment that she wanted Nicolae, Maria feared she might be thought of as a sinful hussy. But she did want him, so much so that she was sure she would have to offer much penitence upon returning home.

And so they traveled in the guise of husband and wife, but in their actions toward each other as brother and sister. It was safe, uncomplicated, and oh, so difficult.

Once they were out of sight of the ferry, Nicolae suggested that they change their clothes in case they met any of the Sultan's men. Their story would be more convincing than if they looked like poor Gypsies. As they continued down the road that took them deeper into the Ottoman Empire, Maria began to get nervous. "How will we know how to find the Sultan? What if he doesn't believe us and finds it amusing to hack us to pieces?"

Nicolae winked at her with a half grin. "I told you it was too dangerous...but hardly more dangerous than sneaking through the corridors of Poenari, dagger in hand, to murder Prince Vlad."

Maria turned away from him with a pout. "You are supposed to reassure me, not ridicule me."

"I'm sorry." Nicolae slipped his arm around her waist and gave her a little squeeze. "Everything will be fine. He should have received word to expect me, and I have the boyar's letters. The only possible trouble we could run into...is them."

He pointed to a dozen horsemen racing toward them in a cloud of dust. Maria held tight to Nicolae who absently felt for his sword; it was there, but he did not draw it. "What do they want?" she asked, her voice shaking.

179

"We will soon find out," he replied as he steered the pony off the road and pulled him to a halt.

The party of black-bearded Turks soon surrounded their little cart laughing and jabbering in Aramaic as several them waved curved Saracen swords in the air. Each wore a white caftan[27] over his shirt and chalvar[28] and a tarboosh[29] bound by a white turban on his head. Sheathes and pouches hung from the kusaks[30] tied around their waists. The boisterous Muslim warriors were mounted on sleek Arabian horses of black, bay, chestnut, or gray.

Nicolae held up his hands to show he was unarmed and first greeted them in Romanian and then in Latin. One of them on a beautiful dapple-gray stallion recognized the language of the learned. "Now how many Gypsies are there who speak Latin?" he asked playfully. Maria shrunk away from one of the Turks who had brushed his hand across her.

"I'm no Gypsy," Nicolae answered in Latin, glad he could communicate with at least one of them. "I am Lord Nicolae from Hungary with a very important message for Sultan Mehmed. I would be very grateful if you could lead us to him."

The Turk laughed and spoke to his men. A collective hoot went up from the bunch and then one of them who had his eye on Maria said something. Nicolae narrowed his brow at the dirty man and readjusted his arm around her.

"Suppose we simply have a good time with your woman, take your valuables, and send you on your way," the Turk on the gray stallion proposed.

"Suppose I slice off the hand of any man who dares to touch her," Nicolae replied with steely eyes. He remained seated, cool, seemingly fearless. Maria was frustrated because she didn't know what was being said, but she noticed when the mirth vanished from the man's face.

"I wouldn't make a threat I couldn't back up, my friend. There are twelve of us and one of you. I could kill you where you sit."

---

[27] caftan - winter over garment of the Turks, usually made of wool, similar to a long robe
[28] chalvar - baggy trousers that fit close around the lower leg and ankle wore by the Turks
[29] tarboosh - traditional hat similar to a Fez that sat atop the crown of the head bound by a turban
[30] kusak - wide waist sash worn as a belt

"And suffer your Sultan's wrath? I don't think so. I have knowledge that he can be...shall we say, merciless to those who cross him. If you think us spies, then take us to your military commander, and I will speak with him. Sultan Mehmed is expecting me, and I bring him important news. Any delay could cost the lives of hundreds of Muslim soldiers. Would Allah consider that an equitable trade for a mere two Christians?"

The Turk took a deep breath and placed a fist on his hip while his steed pawed the ground restlessly. His eyes studied Nicolae as he repeated what had been said in Aramaic.

"What is happening?" Maria whispered. Nicolae inclined his head toward her but did not speak as he kept his eyes fixed on the Turk. They talked among themselves for a few minutes. In his mind, Nicolae played out his moves should he need to fight them.

"Very well. Abdul will search your wagon first. Then when I am satisfied, I will take you to our captain. If I suspect treachery for an instant, you will both be killed."

"Fair enough. Come, search," Nicolae invited as he relaxed his stance. "I have nothing to hide."

"Great Voivode." Octavian, captain of the Bucuresti fortress, bowed as he opened the door ushering the prince and his entourage into the great hall. Octavian was a professional military man in his middle years. Stout and stocky, he wore his hair cropped short and his lined face clean shaven. His yellow-gold waist cape swished around his glistening breastplate as he saluted his commander-in-chief.

Vlad strode in, his chin held high and hands clasped behind his back as his eyes scanned the hall in inspection. As it was a Sunday, he was attired in his crimson Order of the Dragon suit and black cape. Sergei and Ivan followed, and they were joined by two other officers. A servant scurried to bring a tray with wine goblets to the huge oak table in the midst of the hall. It was furnished similarly to the hall at Poenari with a few coats of arms, hanging racks of oil lamps, and windows boarded against the cold.

"This will be an acceptable base of operations," Vlad announced and then turned toward Octavian who was closing the door. "How many are garrisoned here?"

"Two hundred regulars, milord, but we have raised another two hundred militia camping in tents around the castle," he reported as his eyes nervously twitched at the Impaler. "We haven't provisions or weapons for any more."

"I see," responded Dracula speculatively. "I want six hundred more to round out my army within a week."

"But my lord," began Octavian as he held out a hand and took a step toward the others.

"Butts are for sitting on," Vlad rebuked him. "So let us have a seat so that I can lay out my plan to you all."

The men took seats on the benches around the heavy table, and Dracula sat in the chair to one end. The skinny servant boy distributed the chalices, careful not to spill any on the prince, though he trembled in his legendary presence.

"Can the city support my men with extra provisions?" Ivan asked Octavian as they settled on the bench beside each other. Distinguished by his salt and pepper hair and sideburns, Ivan displayed a staunchly commanding presence in his armor and helm, sable wool cape, and broadsword at his side. Even seated, he towered above the other officers.

"Bucuresti is a young city of mostly poor peasants," he explained in an off-handed manner. "To collect more rations from them would be -"

"Difficult, but possible," interrupted Dracula with a stern look towards the captains. "Better for the peasants to be a little short of bread this winter than to be decorating pikes in the spring."

"What makes you think they will attack?" inquired one of the other officers with wavy auburn hair and beard.

Vlad's savage, verdant eyes penetrated the younger officer's doubt. "Because Mehmed knows I am back."

"You make it sound personal," Ivan observed.

"It is." The prince paused to sip his red wine.

"My Lord Dracula, I have seen to some added defenses around the fortress," Octavian began to explain, "and we could -"

"There will be no defenses," Vlad declared cutting him short with a raised hand. Then he rolled his slender fingers into a fist. "We attack!"

Ivan and Sergei already knew of the plan, but the others were astounded. They stared at one another with gaping mouths. "Surely, my prince," began the last officer to speak.

Anger flashed from Vlad's eyes like arrows at the gray-haired man in chain mail and yellow tunic. His lips went dumb under the prince's icy glare.

Octavian meekly offered another suggestion. "If we work through the winter, we could construct a proper defense that would certainly halt the Turks."

Dracula grit his teeth and vaulted up from his chair, toppling it in the process. "You fools!" he raged as he swatted his wine chalice across the length of the hardwood table. "That is how easily Mehmed will spill your blood. Do you not think Constantinople had defenses?" he bellowed with grand gestures toward the stunned captains. "And yet he captured that great city of Christendom, slaughtered its inhabitants, looted the cathedrals and monasteries, then turned them into houses of Islam. Do not underestimate Mehmed - a man I know well," he warned as his tone eased a bit. "They do not call him 'the Conqueror' because no other titles were available. During his reign, he has doubled the size of the Ottoman Empire, an empire more vast than that of Hapsburg. He likens himself to Julius Caesar, Hannibal, and Alexander the Great; his ambition has no end. He sees Walachia as a weak, impoverished principality, easy prey, and territory to be added to his possessions."

The auburn-haired officer dared to speak. "But under Basarab -"

Bitter indignation once more raged from Dracula's eyes. "Basarab was his puppet! What use would a military invasion be when he already had us?"

"I pray, Sire, if the Sultan is so powerful and his army so unstoppable, why not pay the tribute and save ourselves?" asked Octavian in exasperation.

Dracula took a deep breath making a conscious decision not to execute all of his officers as his impulses would have him do. "Cowards never learn, and they are always defeated." The philosophical words hissed softly from behind his clenched teeth. The prince retook his seat in the chair which the trembling servant boy had righted and commenced to explain. "Appeasement is never the solution. This year it is twenty bags of gold, next year thirty, and so on. Walachia *is* a poor country and can ill afford to send tax money to a foreign power which provides no service in return, save refraining from pouring annihilation on us. You must always stand up to a bully or prepare to make yourself his doormat. I, gentlemen, will be no man's doormat."

Vlad paused to receive the new cup of wine the lanky lad brought him. All were quietly reflecting on his words while he took a sip and then set down the goblet. "It is true the Turkish army outnumbers us greatly, but they are not all gathered in one place. If we attack now - before they can organize an offensive - we can catch them completely off guard. We will defeat their regiments one by one and lay waste to their border cities as we did in '62." The men began to nod positively as his fiery, charismatic speech had won them over. A smile tugged at Vlad's mouth as he saw confidence build in their faces. "I want to send Mehmed a message loudly and clearly: leave Walachia alone, or gravely suffer the consequences."

The sun hung low on the horizon by the time they reached the Ottomans' camp. In the several hours since meeting the Turkish patrol, Nicolae and Maria had traversed several different roads. The round, tournament topped tents were pitched in a secluded forest clearing seemingly not near any town. "Stop here," instructed the Saracen in Latin. Nicolae halted the wagon and waited for instruction. "Come with me," he called gruffly as he dismounted his gray Arab.

Nicolae climbed down from the seat and extended a hand up to Maria. "No!" The Turk scowled at him. "My men will look after your woman for now. If it turns out you have lied, they will have her."

Nicolae nodded to the bearded Turk then looked back to Maria. "You must wait here for now," he said reassuringly.

She nodded. "God go with you," she bid him as his finger tips trailed from hers. Nicolae straightened his coat and followed the Turk through the camp past several rows of tents. Many of the bored warriors stopped what they were doing to study Nicolae, the wagon, and Maria. Nicolae almost bumped into his guide when he stopped in front of a large cream and purple tent.

"Wait here." A small, curious crowd began to gather around the stranger dressed in Hungarian clothes. They whispered, pointed, and laughed out loud. One called to him in Aramaic, but Nicolae could only shrug at the soldier, not understanding his words. As the gathering slowly pressed in closer, he began to feel uneasy. He cast a glance back toward the wagon and Maria. Turks were gathering around her as well.

Nicolae was relieved when the Turk re-emerged from his captain's tent. "He will see you," he said, trying to stand taller than the Christian. "And I'll take that sword for now."

Nicolae pulled the baldric off over his head and handed the sheathed sword to him as required. The Turk opened the tent flap and ushered him inside. The interior of the tent looked luxurious for a field camp. Large candles on gold and silver stands illuminated the fragrant, silk-draped residence. Nicolae's eyes scanned the abode to spy several men-at-arms, a fat man in a gray cloak warming his hands over a brazier, and several women who appeared to be preparing food. An important looking individual clothed in silks sat on a crimson and gold silk pillow at a low table straight in front of him.

"Nicolae, I presume?" The well-dressed man was handsome with dark features and a well-groomed beard. He wore a ruby pin in his turban and extended a ringed hand in welcome to his guest.

"Yes." He took a few steps, holding his fur gluga in his hands. His eyes continued to scan his surroundings for any sign of an assault.

"Welcome," the Turkish captain spoke to him in Latin with a warm smile. "Have a seat with me. I am Hazim, the vizier of Bulgaria, commander of this fine army." His boisterous, good-natured greeting both set Nicolae at ease and put him on guard. He quietly stooped to sit on a pile of pillows across the table from the vizier. The amiable Turk grinned at him, displaying a gold tooth which undoubtedly replaced one he had lost in battle. His white silk robe was trimmed in gold and drawn with a gold sash around his red linen tunic. "I have nine camels, three stallions, fifteen mares, ten servants, three wives, and four concubines," he boasted in good humor. "Tell me, Hungarian merchant, boyar of Cozia, what do you have?"

Nicolae thought of his dwindling pouch of gold, his rickety Gypsy wagon, and a woman not even his. Then he smiled wryly. "Names, Your Greatness; I have names."

"Names?" His dark brows scrunched together. "What is this...names?"

It was time. Either his plan would succeed or it would all soon draw to an end. He reached his hand into his cummerbund and withdrew his closely guarded secret - the folded papers bearing the signatures and pledges of the boyars. "More than fifty names, signatures with seals, written pledges by Walachian boyars to support Sultan Mehmed's choice of Basarab over Vlad Dracula. Your master's nemesis is the scourge of our country. The nobles would prefer to pay tribute to a just Muslim than live in constant fear under the tyranny of a madman. I also bring news of Vlad's military plans, his army's whereabouts and make-up, and much more which is for the sultan's ears. I fear it would be far too easy for a powerful vizier to find me unnecessary if he could himself present all of the information to his emperor."

Hazim, who had already glanced through the papers, brought his smiling dark eyes to meet Nicolae's and laughed out loud, slapping the table. "A shrewd negotiator...I like that. But do not presume that I need stoop to thievery and murder to gain favor with my lord; Allah would not have it to be so. You have been very helpful. Now, take your little cart and pony and your one wife and go home. The mighty Mehmed will soon dispense with Dracula, and your boyars will have Basarab back on the throne."

"No!" Nicolae insisted with bold urgency. "I must be allowed to speak with the sultan."

"It is not permissible," said Hazim with a shrug.

"You don't understand - he'll step right into Vlad's trap. Your men will die needlessly."

"The great conqueror knows how to fight," Hazim replied with a hint of irritation.

"Yes, he does," Nicolae agreed as he leaned across the table, his face tense as he spoke quietly. "And Vlad Dracula knows how to defeat him. If you will but let me, I will give you the bastard's head on a platter. I implore you - take me to your sultan."

The vizier hesitated a moment as he studied the daring Hungarian. Then the heavy-set man by the brazier turned to face them and shed the gray woolen cloak that had concealed his royal garb. "There is no need," he spoke in fluent Romanian. "Mehmed is already here."

Chapter 19

Transylvanian Terror

"And then he invaded Transylvania and Tara Barsei which he burned...he had people shredded like cabbages and took others away to his country where he had them impaled."

From the German pamphlet "About a mischievous tyrant called Dracula voda," 1460's

It was dusk when Nadia pushed through the tavern door and rushed over to the bar, her wan face etched with worry. "Lucian, Carmen," she called to them. "Have you seen Maria? Has she been in today?"

The beardless youth and the voluptuous tavern maid shrugged nonchalantly. "No," Dimitry's son replied as he set aside an empty flask. "She has probably not yet returned."

"Returned from where?" Nadia was at her wits end. Maria had been missing for days and had said nothing to her at all about leaving. This was totally unlike her, and Nadia feared the worst.

Then Carmen replied, "She told us she needed a few days off to go visit her aunt in Tirgoviste who has taken quite ill. She was not sure exactly what day she would be back."

"That's just it!" Nadia lamented. "She doesn't have an aunt in Tirgoviste or anyplace else." She began to pace, wringing her hands, her troubled eyes moving to the floor and back to the tavern workers. For the first time she now noted a hint of concern on their faces. "Have either of you seen Stefan, the merchant?" They shook their heads and shrugged.

"Maybe he went back to Hungary," Carmen guessed.

"But his horse is still in our stable," Lucian noted as he, too, began to puzzle over the mystery.

"It's all my fault," Nadia moaned as she turned on her heel and paced in the opposite direction. "I encouraged her with him after the fortuneteller said he was dangerous."

"Domn Stefan, dangerous?" Carmen laughed and batted her hand in the air with a limp wrist. "Why the dandy is as gentle as a daisy. He couldn't hurt a fly."

"Or that's what he wanted us to think," Nadia suggested.

"Why would a man like that want to hurt Maria?" Lucian asked, brushing a hand through his long, wavy brown hair as he smoothed it back out of his eyes. "It would not profit him. And why leave behind such a fine Sckweiken? Wealthy or not, that mare would be hard to replace."

"I don't know," Nadia pondered as she at last came to light on a stool in front of him. "Unless it was something else. Maybe I am looking at this from the wrong angle; perhaps she has gotten them both injured, and he is innocent as you think."

"Maria?" Carmen questioned as she leaned her elbows on the bar. Her drooping breasts brought the white linen of her peasant blouse to brush atop the wood as well. Her reddish locks swooped over her shoulder and bounced against her round cheek. "Surely she has more sense than to invite him to stay the night and then be caught in fornication!"

"I agree with you in that," Nadia said tapping her finger tips across the bar, "but there was something else - a plan she was cooking up. I can't talk about it now." Immediately Nadia bolted off the stool and looked Maria's coworkers in the eyes. "If she or the Hungarian return, please let me know at once. I am very worried for her safety. I can't believe she would strike out without letting me know!" Nadia sighed and brushed her hand across the bar. "I only pray she is safe…that he has not harmed her." Nadia's brown eyes trailed off as she shuddered at the possibilities.

"I am sure Stefan has not hurt her," Carmen spoke in conviction. "It was obvious to us all how much he admired her, how he protected her from that drunken rake, and called for her to attend him. I cannot believe he would do her harm."

Nadia nodded absently. "I'm sure you are right," she said as she turned to slowly negotiate her way around the tables and chairs that were beginning to fill with customers. "Get over here, Carmen!" a loud one yelled. But it was not Stefan she had referred to in her prayer.

"Your Highness!" Nicolae quickly scrambled to his feet, a stunned expression on his face. He bowed deeply, circling his right hand in the

Muslim custom to denote honor and homage. He did not raise his eyes from the floor until the sultan gave him leave to do so.

"Nicolae, disinherited boyar of Cozia, I received your letter. Come," he said motioning to him. "Sit with us and tell me why you would wish to aide an enemy in his quest."

Slowly Nicolae raised his eyes to the Conqueror. He was a large man, though no taller than Nicolae, with a regal air and commanding presence. From the front, one could see the emerald pin in his turban which was wrapped around his purple tarboosh. Narrow brows arched above a long, slender nose and slate-gray eyes which were busy scrutinizing his visitor. His fuzzy brown beard was tinged with rust color and his hair was either short or gathered up inside his turban. His silk, purple-trimmed cream robe hung loosely over his green silk shirt so as not to bind his great belly. His baggy cream chalvar trousers were drawn about his waist with a cord. He wore soft-soled indoor slippers with pointed, curled up toes upon his stout feet.

"Vlad Dracula, the man who murdered my family, is my enemy, and all who oppose him I see as allies," Nicolae spoke with conviction. Then he ventured to voice a request in his native language in which they were conversing. "Great sultan, my nevasta[31] is alone in my wagon surrounded by your soldiers. They may find her very attractive and be inclined to sample her sweetness. I pray thee that she be brought to me safely, and I will tell you all."

Mehmed laughed a huge belly laugh. "I pity you, Christian. Mohammed saw the wisdom in permitting more than one wife. If ill were to happen to one, a man has others to comfort him. But you, my friend, have only the one." He shook his head and stepped toward the table where Hazim sat. "Khalaf," he called to one of the men-at-arms who stood watch within the tent. In Aramaic he ordered him bring the woman in. "It shall be done," he said pleasantly and Nicolae's tension eased.

"You have remarkable timing," Mehmed commented as he and Nicolae took their seats on the pillows that surrounded the table. "Basarab Loiata is in my camp as well." He motioned toward a man on the far side of the shelter whom Nicolae had not even seen when he entered.

Basarab strode toward them in the embroidered attire of a Romanian noble. His graying brown hair was cut short at his neck, and his full beard

---

[31] nevasta - Romanian for a man's woman or wife

and mustache were almost snowy. The nephew of Vladislav II, known as Basarab the old, did indeed look older than Nicolae expected. Although both he and the sultan numbered a few years more than Vlad, the former prince was nimble enough to take his seat unaided.

"My Lord Basarab, 'tis an added honor to meet you also this day," Nicolae offered in humble greeting.

"And 'tis an honor for me to learn I still have so many strong loyalties in my homeland," he replied pleasantly.

Suddenly the tent flap opened, and Khalaf announced, "The Hungarian's woman." All eyes were immediately set upon Maria who was as nervous as a bride on her wedding day. She was still not convinced she could pass herself off as a noble lady. Though relieved to no longer be the object of coarse jokes she did not understand, she felt suddenly weak in the knees as she realized she was in the presence of royalty.

"You were right to be concerned, Christian," Mehmed said in a suave tone, his heated eyes soaking in her frame. "She is beautiful indeed and had you not already wed, I would ask for her hand myself."

Maria felt the blood rush out of her cheeks as she stood by the opening. But Nicolae offered her a confident smile and extended his hand toward her. "Come, my lady," he said gallantly. "I wish you to meet His Excellency Sultan Mehmed the Conqueror, Sire Hazim, the vizier of Bulgaria, and Prince Basarab Loiata of Walachia. Gentleman, my wife - Maria of Curt de Arges."

Fearing she would clumsily stumble or maybe even faint at any moment, Maria played her part. She curtsied as she had seen noble women do and nodded to each with a pleasant smile. Having glided the few steps toward them, Khalaf offered her a pillow behind Nicolae, and she managed to light on it with all the grace of a princess. Remembering his instructions, she refrained from speaking since no one had as yet asked her a direct question.

"And I boasted of my wives," Hazim said with an envious laugh, his eyes sweeping over Maria desirously. "I see why you would not wish to leave her behind."

"I do recognize the touch of Doamna Camelia, do I not?" Basarab inquired. Nicolae nodded, a proud gleam in his blue eyes. "My wife buys all her gowns at that exclusive boutique."

Maria kept up her meek, pleasant, demure facade, but inside her mind thoughts were flying. *Why do they look at me so and call me beautiful? And they talk about me like I was nothing but his possession. The next thing I know, they'll be bargaining for me!* But her thoughts were interrupted when the sultan spoke.

"You say these boyars support Basarab and agree to pay me tribute," he said as he looked over the papers.

"Yes, Your Greatness. Others I spoke with agreed verbally, but were too afraid of Dracula to sign. They fear since many of them were instated under Radu or Lord Basarab that Vlad will soon initiate another cleansing, as he did when he assumed the throne in 1456," Nicolae explained.

"That was when he killed your parents," the sultan assumed.

"Yes, Sire."

"Then we share a common bond, young man," noted Basarab. Nicolae turned his attention to his elder who sat crossed legged on the colorful silk pillows. Shadows of sadness hung in his eyes as he reached his arms to lean on the table. "For you see, Vlad Tepes killed my father as well." All eyes fell on the Romanian as he told his story. "For generations there has been a feud between my family, the Danesti, and Vlad's family, the Draculesti. Both families had an early reigning prince, and both claim the right of succession to the throne. When the impostor prince usurped power in 1456, he killed my uncle, Vladislav II, who was the reigning prince. But that was not enough for him. Knowing that the prince's brother and my father, Dan III, might lay claim to what was rightfully his, Vlad set out to kill him as well."

Nicolae rested his elbow on the table and his chin on his fist as he pictured the events in his mind's eye. He had been young, but he remembered hearing his father discuss these events with his retainers. "My father fled to Transylvania to escape persecution. He sent my mother and me away to safety in the north where I started gathering together my own army. But I was without renown among the Saxons, and it took time. Meanwhile, Dracula's hatred and irrational fear of Dan grew. In the winter of '59, he launched a devastating raid through Transylvania. Were it not for this merciless and meaningless campaign, the sentiment of the Germans and Hungarians might never have turned against him."

Maria was completely enthralled in the prince's story, for she had been too young to remember these events. She was glad that with the men finally speaking the only language she knew, she could learn more about her enemy's wicked deeds, but she was not content to be sitting behind Nicolae instead of at his side. She felt left out, spoken around, not to, as though she was of no more consequence than a fly on the wall. Then she recalled what Nicolae had told her about the position Muslim women held in their society.

"He slaughtered whole villages in his quest for my father - men, women, children who fled helplessly in terror - he struck them down. He ordered his army to burn their homes and shops, trapping them inside. Any who escaped he had impaled. It is said he would take his meals at table in front of the impaled while butchers hacked off their limbs. He would drink their blood and make sport of their suffering, amused by how they twitched on the pikes." Maria felt a sick knot forming in her stomach, and she longed to hold fast to Nicolae's hand in comfort. She knew he was thinking of his parents...and of Teo. Her heart went out to him but she dared not touch him in the sultan's presence.

"But he did not stop there. He marched his army from town to town, including Tara Barsei, demanding they give up Dan, then impaling and burning, boiling, hacking to pieces their inhabitants. He even attacked the sacred Church of St. Bartholomew, the oldest Romanesque church in Transylvania, burning it along with its treasures and priestly vestments. His bloodlust still not sated he turned his army against Brasov. There he captured and impaled thousands, but my father was not among them. He had been forewarned and had gone into hiding on a country estate. Dracula's expedition had been a failure, and he returned to Walachia angry and bitter.

"When my father saw the destruction and bloodshed the bastard had wreaked in seeking him out, he was filled with remorse. He felt the weight of the blood of innocent villagers who had no knowledge of his whereabouts and swore vengeance upon Vlad. It is doubtful he would ever have attempted to usurp the throne had Dracula not slaughtered the Transylvanians, but at that time Dan had no trouble raising an army. Fueled by the terror that had been inflicted on them, the men of Transylvania flocked to his side, and the surviving merchants of Brasov backed him financially. I implored him to await my arrival and the small army I was bringing, but he was impatient and hot with vengeance. In March, at the first spring thaw, he invaded Walachia.

"I fear he did not plan so carefully as you have, Domn Nicolae," Basarab motioned toward him. "He failed to alert my family's supporters of his plan, or no doubt they would have come to his aid. His battle was lost, and my father was taken prisoner. In a grand spectacle before his court and officers, the damned Impaler forced the rightful prince to dig his own grave and had a priest perform a liturgical mass for the dead in his presence. Then with his own sword, Dracula severed his head from his body which fell into the grave, and he had all of his captured followers impaled."

"Perhaps it was fate that you were not among them, Prince Basarab," observed Hazim. "Your small army would not have turned the tide, and you, too, would have perished."

"You may be right in saying so," he agreed, "but I have always regretted not being there."

"I am grieved for your loss, Prince Basarab," Nicolae said moving both hands to the table and folding his fingers together, "as I grieve for tens of thousands of our own people he has slaughtered - as well as your people, Great Sultan," he quickly added with a deferent nod to Mehmed. "But you are correct in the thoroughness of my plan, and if we can all agree on the course of action, I will destroy the monster before he can take root."

Basarab nodded to him, and the sultan spoke. "You have mentioned your intent, and your reason, but why seek me out? And what news of his plans have you to bring?"

"Your Majesty," he began humbly, spreading his palms face up on the table. "I am just a common man. I have the education of an aristocrat and the training of a warrior, but no rank, no title, no power...just a pouch full of gold earned in good investments. There is no reason for you to receive me, to sit at table with me, save that I speak the truth, and that I will fulfill that which I promise. I have knowledge that the Impaler is amassing an army which he has moved to Bucuresti and plans to attack you across the Danube while it is yet winter - perhaps within the week."

"What?" Mehmed exclaimed, with obvious disbelief. "Hazim, what information did you get from the prisoner you told me about?"

The vizier hung his head in embarrassment. "None, milord. He...he feared Tepes more than he fears you. I tried torture -"

Mehmed held up his hand. "Does he live?"

193

"Yes, Sire. I thought to persuade him to talk after a while."

"Don't you see," Nicolae explained. "All you can do is kill him, but if Vlad learned of his betrayal, his entire family would be tortured to death. The animal we speak of slices open pregnant women and roasts babies on a spit. Your prisoner will not talk."

Mehmed eyed Nicolae intuitively and nodded. "Release the prisoner on the morrow."

"But, Sultan -"

"Do as I say," he ordered. "Nicolae is right, and the soldier is no fool. You forget - I grew up with Vlad, and I know him well...his cruelty, his envy, his paranoia. He was never meant to rule. His older brother, Mircea, held the right to succession. It was he Dracul groomed for the throne. And Radu the Handsome, everyone's favorite," Mehmed said in a softer tone, a misty touch to his eye. "He was charming and witty and displayed gratitude for the kindness my father afforded to both him and his brother while living in our household." He scratched his beard, then let his arm fall to the table. "Then there was Vlad." He shook his head and stared blankly ahead as if he wondered what had gone wrong.

"My father used impalement as a punishment for the worst of crimes; I have used it myself. But Vlad was even then morbidly fascinated by watching the prisoners die. He once commented, 'this is far better than watching my father's hangings.' He scowled at beheadings, saying they were over with too quickly, and soon my father would no longer allow him to be present at executions. He has a sick mind, but he is not stupid. As ill prepared as he is, you think he would dare attack the strongest military in the world?"

"That is exactly what he plans to do, to catch you off guard, to strike when you do not expect him. He has already doubled the size of his army and is conscripting more militia each day."

Maria could contain herself no longer. She saw the doubt in the Sultan's eyes and felt if she did not speak out on Nicolae's behalf she would burst. "It's true, Your Majesty!" she blurted out. "I w-, I was in a tavern and saw soldiers taking men and boys from every home in Curt de Arges to place them in the ranks. There is no food to sustain an army that size through the winter. He must plan -" Maria stopped short, suddenly aware that all eyes were on her and that she had broken protocol.

"You are strange, Christian," Mehmed said in a tone more amused than offended, "to let your woman speak."

"I beg your forgiveness, Merciful Sultan," Nicolae cried out as he bowed his head and averted his eyes. "The fault is mine, not the lady's. I obviously did not instruct her well enough at home; but Sire, she is only a woman and not knowledgeable in your customs."

Only a woman! Maria fumed inwardly. *Doesn't he know I am merely trying to help?* But by that time her cheeks were flushed, seemingly from embarrassment. She lowered her chin, folded her hands in her lap, and tried to appear meek.

"Have no fear, Nicolae," the sultan reassured him with a smile. "I am sure you will ride her hard this evening to let her know her place. Now," he leaned over the table in earnest. "Does he truly plan to attack?"

Maria was infuriated. *If Nicolae dares touch me*, she swore to herself. But even as she did, she knew she had disobeyed, had stepped out of line. And the thought of this courageous man - who had the ear of an emperor - touching her sent tingles down her spine. *I will play the part*, she repeated to herself, *to a point.*

"Yes, quite sure. He knows the positions of your troops, how they are spread among the border towns. He plans to pick them off one by one before you have a chance to amass them together. And he does not care how many of his own men are killed in the process. He knows he cannot wait for you to attack him in the spring - which he believes you will do - for he knows your strength exceeds his own. And he will not pay tribute," Nicolae explained.

"It is good you have brought this to my attention," Mehmed said contemplatively as he stroked his reddish beard. "It proves you are an ally who can be trusted. You spoke also of a plan."

"Yes, Highness." Nicolae was encouraged and boldly set forth his design. "No one knows that I have come; no one even knows that Nicolae of Cozia lives. He died building the fortress Poenari. But Stefan, the Hungarian merchant, has entered the circle of the Walachian prince and will not be suspect. If in one week's time your army were to attack him at Bucuresti, I could get close to him in the battle and slay him. You would then withdraw your troops, carrying the Impaler's head home in victory, and place Basarab back on the throne. This is what the boyars have agreed to - that it appear Dracula has fallen in battle to the Turks, and no suspicion of a conspiracy would fall upon them or Basarab. But I implore you to withdraw your troops as soon as you have word of Vlad's death so that no more of your men, nor mine, may die on his account."

A look of wonder danced on Mehmed's face. "You are strange for a Christian," he noted. "You have reverence for the lives of Muslims as well as your people, yet your society persecutes Jews and Muslims alike. Here in my empire, we practice tolerance. I do not force the Bulgarians, Gypsies, or Jews to convert lest they perish, for Allah teaches that all law-abiding people have the right to live, regardless of their faith. You have the heart of a Muslim, Nicolae," he commented proudly. "Can I not persuade you to follow the true religion?"

"I am deeply honored by your words, Great One," he replied in sincere humility. "But I must decline. Despite my own lack of faith and the fact that I despise the schism within our church, I have always been and must always remain a Christian."

Mehmed nodded in understanding. "You are true to your fathers as I am to mine, and I must admire you for that, but I believe for one to be as bold as you, he must assuredly possess a measure of faith."

"I am bold because I believe that my course is right and just and for the greater good. Maria believes that I am the chosen instrument of God to smite a demon from our land," Nicolae explained. He sighed a deep sigh as he considered the spiritual realm. "I have no certainty of that on my own, but I do vow before you this day that I will complete what I have set forth to accomplish. And if there is breath left in me when I come upon him, I will take the head of the Impaler and bring it to you. It is what I have lived for these nineteen years, and I will not fail you."

"Nineteen years," Mehmed repeated nodding his head, "is a long time to hold a grudge."

"'Tis more that that," Nicolae confessed openly. "If it were only for my parents' blood, I would have let it lie long ago; but for the blood of a hundred thousand souls, Dracula must die."

Then Basarab spoke with the authority that was almost his. "If you succeed, my man, and return with your life, then when I return to power, your father's title and lands shall be restored to you as surely as I live. I will have great need of a worthy boyar such as yourself."

"Thank you, milord."

"Sultan Mehmed," Basarab said, turning his face toward him. "My troops and I shall join you on the battlefield to lessen your burden, and when I am again prince, you shall receive the tribute payment as was our arrangement in the past."

"Very well," the sultan proclaimed, "let it be done. I tire of battles and war. I now desire to foster learning, trade, and the arts in my land. With this last enemy out of the way, I can see my way clear to an era of peace and financial prosperity. In one week's time we march and we shall all meet again on the plains of the Danube at Bucuresti. And may Allah bless our righteous cause, and His will be done."

They all nodded in agreement, and Nicolae felt an overwhelming wave of emotion sweep over him. He had met with success in the sultan's tent. All had come together as if it had been divinely orchestrated, even without his believing it. Maybe Maria was right after all.

Mehmed clapped his hands, and at once servants brought trays of steaming shish-ka-bobs resting atop round pita breads and set them before the men. Bowls of flavorful sauces were placed on the table along with beverages and bowls of dried fruits and nuts. Nicolae's eyes lit up at the aroma of the roasted lamb cubes skewered between chunks of onion and peppers, and his mouth began to salivate. The sultan praised Allah, and all began to eat - all except Maria who had not been served a portion. She nudged Nicolae with her toe, and he looked over his shoulder at her. "Don't worry," he whispered. "The women will be fed after the men are finished; that is their custom." Then he turned back to the distinguished table.

Maria folded her arms in an impatient and irritated gesture. Her stomach growled as she smelled the delicious foods and watched them heartily having their fill. *He's probably loving this, chanting, "I told you so," to himself. Well, we'll see if he gets any congratulatory kiss from me tonight,* she told herself; but all the while she hungered for his kiss much more than she hungered for the lamb.

After the meal, Mehmed sent Maria in the company of his servant women to eat in his harem's tent and there to be bathed and prepared for the evening, while the men enjoyed the entertainment of musicians and dancers. When the hour drew late, Nicolae was shown to a small guest tent where he was soon joined by Maria, fragrant from her bath oils. She took a quick look around the intimate, candlelit surroundings and said, "I can easily gather the sultan's intent; there is only one bed."

Nicolae smiled from his reclining position across the expanse of pillows in the center of the abode. He gazed at her with dazzling blue eyes filled with the thrill of victory he had won...or would soon win. "I wonder if they'll be listening," she muttered in disgust.

"I don't know," he mused in a deep, romantic voice, "but let's not disappoint them."

Chapter 20

Intimacy

"I feel compelled to condemn Dracula for preferring the pleasures of this world, thereby deserving of the punishment of hellfire."

From "The Story of Prince Dracula," by Russian diplomat Fedor Kuritsyn and the monk Eufrosin, 1486

Nicolae sat up in the bed and beckoned to her with a wave of his hand. He had shed his coat and boots but was still clothed in his shirt and trousers as he had been every night of their journey. "Do not worry, my Dear," he spoke sweetly. "I have not forgotten our arrangement. But they believe us to be husband and wife and wish this evening spent in their camp to be a memorable one."

She relaxed somewhat at his assurance and sat on the edge of the bed opposite him to unfasten her shoes. "It has been memorable, all right," she admitted. "I have never felt so humiliated in all my life!"

"Maria, they were highly impressed with you," Nicolae explained, surprised at her outrage. "They thought you were magnificent."

"They thought I was a thing," she said dejectedly, plopping a shoe to the ground. "They see me as your trophy or prize mare."

"Iubita, I warned you -"

"Oh, I knew that was coming!" She spun around on the bed to face him. His response was only a warm, gentle smile, and she could not remain angry when he looked at her that way. "But I guess," she said slowly while unpinning her hair, "that you did tell me at that. I should be glad we got what we came for, and I am." She shook her long, black hair loose, and it swirled around her shoulders with an aroma of lilac. Nicolae's ardent gaze continued to penetrate her as he lay back on the pillows, his hands behind his head.

Maria's cheeks reddened at his seductive scrutiny. "You were quite amazing this evening, milord," she admitted, her eyes dancing at his in a way she had not willed them to do. "Such persuasive speaking, what bold passion - you were marvelous, and you succeeded as I knew you would." She tentatively lay down upon the pillows, well on her side of the bed, while a tingling sensation began to crawl down her spine, her breath coming short. She felt him touching her with his eyes though he had not moved.

"The plan made sense, but it is only the first step," he said and turned to blow out the candles nearest his side of the bed. "I still must meet him with my sword and prevail, and I know he is an able warrior."

"And I know your heart, your courage, your strength." She heard the words pour from her mouth with conviction. Was it all too obvious the fool she was to fall for one she could never have? Then she added the words, "your destiny."

Nicolae raised himself on his right elbow and gazed over at Maria lying on the silk pillow beside him. Her dark eyes shone in the amber glow of the few candles that remained lit. He tenderly stroked her cheek with his left hand then began to slide his fingers between the silky, black strands of her hair. "You are so beautiful," he murmured as he looked on her with a touch of awe.

Maria's cheeks flushed again. "I am getting old."

"So am I," he replied with a smile.

"You?" she questioned in disbelief. "You are the fittest man I've ever seen. There is very little old about you."

"That's just because of my training," Nicolae explained in humility.

"What training is that?"

"Many kinds." He shrugged. "Fencing, fighting, doing manual labor. I push my body so that there will never again come a time that I am not strong enough to do what I must."

Compassion instantly flooded Maria's eyes. "My lord, you are strong in so many ways. Do not think about that now."

"You're right," he replied sweetly, a slight mist to his countenance. "I have other things to think about tonight." Nicolae moved toward her and closed his mouth around hers. The searing passion of his kiss shot through her like a lightning bolt. His tongue parted her lips as he pulled her head closer with his left hand. Maria could scarcely believe what was happening to her as she felt an electric energy rushing through her veins. She found herself eagerly accepting his tongue and caressing it with her own. He thrilled her beyond her imagination. It was as if she were caught up in a whirlwind, not sure when or if she would land.

Gingerly, Nicolae pulled back from the kiss, his azure eyes studying her face. Maria tried to compose her voice. "What was that for, if I may ask?" She had been left practically breathless and hoped he hadn't noticed.

"Well," Nicolae began with a sudden uncertainty in his voice. "You are attracted to me, aren't you - at least a little?"

Her dazzled eyes widened as she observed the boyish questioning in his expression. "I suppose…at least a little. But Lord Nicolae -"

"Maria," he interrupted her softly, cradling her chin. "There is no need for such formalities. My title and lands are long forfeited. I'm merely a merchant now."

"But when this is over and they are returned to you -"

"If," he corrected her, placing his finger across her lips. "There are no guarantees - I may not even live through the final meeting with Vlad. But if my property and title are returned, I will not be changed, nor will the way I look at you."

Maria was breathless, his fingers so close she could taste them. She wanted to kiss his gentle hand, to feel his flesh next to hers, but she was afraid. "I'm frightened, Nicolae," she admitted shyly, her heart pounding faster in her chest.

"It's all right," he comforted, gliding his hand along her cheek. "We are safe here. The sultan believes us to be married, and even if he did not, it would be allowed in this country."

She hesitated, her eyes searching the depths of his. "That's not why I'm afraid."

"Do you trust me?" he asked.

"Yes." She swallowed. "I wouldn't be here if I didn't."

"Then trust me now," he said in a most compelling voice. "I will not hurt you." Then Nicolae lowered his lips to hers once more for a brief, tender kiss. When he raised his head, she nodded at him. An aura of joy radiated from his face as he gazed down at her.

Nicolae raised up on his knees in the bed beside her and began to unbutton his shirt. Then he stopped, haunted by a sudden thought. "If the scars bother you, I can leave my shirt on," he offered, fearful of offending her.

All uncertainties melted away from Maria as her eyes warmed to him. "No, Nicolae, it's all right," she uttered dreamily. *How considerate he is,* she thought in amazement. *If I had ever known there would be a man who could care for me so much...* Then the words poured out from her heart. "I want to touch you." She sat up, reached her hands to his loose shirt tail, and began to help him unfasten the buttons.

"You already have," he answered with a deep, permeating sound, "more than you know." He let the shirt fall off his shoulders while Maria tugged one sleeve over his hand. She could not take her eyes from his sculptured chest, broad and muscular, with a little trail of hair trickling from a star over his heart down to his tight, toned stomach. "Are the scars disturbing you?" Nicolae asked with concern when he observed how she stared at him.

"No, not at all. They're hardly noticeable. My lord, you are magnificent," she sighed in wonder at him.

Nicolae smiled, his cheeks reddening. "None of this lord talk, now."

"My husband was so thin and bony - not at all like you. And it has been years." Maria raised her dark, glazed eyes to his, which blazed at her with controlled passion.

Nicolae lowered her to the bed and spread himself over her womanly form. This time when he caught her lips in his, Maria wrapped her arms around his shoulders, pulling him in closer. She plunged her own tongue into his mouth thirstily, sending a wave of euphoric excitement through his being.

While supporting his weight on his right elbow, Nicolae trailed his left fingertips down Maria's satiny neck and over the fabric covering her breast to cup it in his hand. His fingers jostled her a bit, and she could feel various muscles tighten and relax spontaneously throughout her body. When her right leg moved, drawing up slightly, Nicolae slid his left knee between her limbs. Maria broke off the kiss desperately needing to draw in some air. Once inhaled, the breath escaped her lips with a quiet but audible sigh of desire. The two exchanged a dark and provocative gaze expressing a deep yearning for more.

Heated blood pumped wildly through his veins as Nicolae fought to control his own pent-up passions. He lowered his lips to her neck, placing moist, warm kisses along her vulnerable throat. Maria tangled the fingers of her left hand into his sandy hair, holding on tightly, while her other

1and tenderly traced the whip scars on his back. To her they were like a victor's crown, proclaiming Nicolae to be a surviving martyr, and a beautiful reminder of the inner pain that had drawn them together.

Nicolae rubbed his thumb across the peak of her breast as he gently sucked against the base of her neck. A hushed gasp escaped her mouth as Maria leaned her head back exposing more of her throat. *Too many clothes*, he thought as he pondered how to proceed. Slowly his tongue wet a path down her upper chest to the edge of her blouse where he planted a heated kiss. He raised his midnight blue eyes to spy her impassioned visage. The pleasure he observed there encouraged him to venture a suggestion. "Maybe you would be more comfortable sleeping in less restrictive clothing." Nicolae waited breathless for her response.

Maria's eyes darted to his in surprise at his request. She responded meekly and with a slight hint of hesitation. "I suppose I could sleep in my shift," she began as she glanced down at the costly, tight fitting, winter ciupag he had bought for her. Then her eyes locked onto his. "But somehow I don't think that is what you have in mind."

Nicolae pushed himself up a few inches above her warm, inviting length. "Maria," he addressed her sincerely, "whatever is most comfortable for you."

The soothing tone of his voice, the earnest truth in his eyes, and selfless nature of his words were both a comfort and enticement to Maria's soul. *Whatever I want*, she thought to herself in wonder. A part of her wanted to remain safely behind the protective wall she had built around her heart. The other part wanted to melt into his strong embrace and give herself to him completely.

As she began to stir, he rolled back to his side of the bed in satisfaction brimmed with anticipation. Maria slowly stood beside the bed with her back toward him while she unfastened her clothing. "It is quite a lovely dress you bought me, and it would be a shame to wrinkle it in bed." Nicolae smiled humorously but refrained from laughing at her excuse. Then she leaned her head over her left shoulder toward him with a question. "Nicolae, if you don't mind me asking, how is it that you have not married?"

"It's an honest enough question," he replied, then strove to give her a thoughtful answer. "I was fifteen when I left Walachia - a youth, just recently aware of his own manhood, having never touched a girl. I came into maturity in a land that had not been my home. Naturally, I had the same desires and needs as other young men. But when I became established in my career and was of marrying age, I found there to be certain complications," Nicolae explained while Maria removed the ornate ciupag blouse and coordinating poale skirt. He watched her warmly as he reflected on his past.

"Complications?" she asked, noticing that he had become quiet.

"Yes," Nicolae continued. "It is not that Hungary cannot give birth to an attractive woman, although I find I am drawn to tan, raven-haired beauties," he mused causing Maria to smile and blush. "But no one there could possibly understand the forces that shaped my life. They have never known the senseless savagery of a sadistic, evil ruler. But I was considered a very eligible man, and many a father tried to arrange a match for his daughter with the wealthy, handsome merchant from the house of Kuban. I finally agreed to court one of them," he continued as Maria swiftly slipped between the silk sheets beside him. He smiled at her affectionately.

"What went wrong?"

"She saw my scars, was horrified, and asked what had happened. It is difficult to explain that before becoming Kuban's son, the merchant, I was a Walachian boyar's son and then a slave. After that I informed the social circles of the city that I preferred to remain a bachelor." Nicolae turned on his side toward Maria and took her hand in his, intertwining fingers with her.

"Then why did you not move back to Walachia?" she asked in curiosity.

"For what reason? Vlad was still in Hungary. As long as he remained under guard, I could not get to him, but then neither could he do any harm. I did think about returning, but the thought of coming home brought back so many memories. It was too painful. Then when I heard that Dracula had been officially named prince once more, I knew it was time to act, before he could start another slaughter." He gave Maria's hand a squeeze and nuzzled his face next to hers. "I am sorry, my sweet Maria, that I was not able to take action sooner." He brushed a kiss to her cheek. "I had to collect letters of support from the boyars and get the documents in order from the merchant's guild bearing Stefan Kubana's name. I wish now that I had come to Curt de Arges first."

Maria turned toward him, kissing his mustached lips lightly. She took her hand from his to cradle his face. Oh, how she loved touching him! "No, Nicolae, you cannot blame yourself. You had a good plan and have followed it through. You didn't know what he would do or when. You take too much on yourself. It is important that you have come now, and that you let me be your partner." They moved together as one, joining in a searing kiss of passion.

The two encircled each other in an embrace once more while Nicolae rolled over onto Maria. When he pulled his mouth away to breathe, he found himself confessing more than he had intended. "I've wanted to kiss these lips since the first time I laid eyes on you in the tavern," he said airily, his breath coming fast and hard. "But when you told your story and my heart went out to you, I was sure everyone in the room could see straight through my disguise and into my soul. And in case you haven't noticed, Maria, I have become quite enthralled with you. I feel we are somehow connected, though I cannot explain it."

"You don't have to," she responded with a loving gaze. Nicolae impulsively covered her lips with his in a deep kiss. He slid his left hand erotically up her side over the thin white cloth of her undergarment until it rested on her right breast. While he caught her tongue and pulled eagerly on it, his hand slid nimbly beneath her shift from its loose, low cut neckline. His index finger caught the narrow strap, pulling it down off her shoulder. After giving the heated kiss a slow, smoldering finish, Nicolae raised his head, casting his gaze down as he lifted her breast out from under her garment. Unconsciously, his mouth dropped open, and he almost began to salivate.

"I'm too big, aren't I?" Maria voiced nervously. "It comes from having nursed a child."

Nicolae returned his darkened eyes to hers as they danced with delight. "On the contrary, my dear; everything about you is just right." With that his eyes snapped back down, and he covered her summit with his mouth.

Maria began to move beneath him, writhing in passion as his tongue circled her nipple, causing it to rise even harder. Then as he began to draw it into his mouth with rhythmic urgency, she inhaled a gasp and bore her fingernails into his shoulders with a strong grip. "Oh, Nicolae," she moaned feverishly. Her eyes closed tightly as an even stronger surge of desire flooded her being. She could feel the dampening between her thighs.

Nicolae, who was himself spurred on by a heated rush, brushed his hand across her torso to touch the bare skin of her thigh. The electric touch of his fingertips on her inner thigh sent strengthening vibrations through her that made her head spin. As he shifted himself to rest tight on her hip, she was ignited by his hard heat that pressed against her from within his trousers. Her heartbeat accelerated even more when his hand traveled up under the edge of her shift. Nicolae was thrilled by the warm moisture that penetrated her bloomers. As he reveled in her response, one of his fingers inadvertently stroked a particularly sensitive spot.

"Nicolae, what are you doing?" Maria cried out in desperation.

Quickly his hand retreated to the outside of her hip, and he raised his head from her breast. "I'm sorry, Maria; I am losing myself in you. I didn't mean to -"

"No, don't be sorry," she corrected him as she drifted blissfully toward the canopy above them. "What I mean is, I have never felt these things, and I don't know how or why." Maria tried to catch her breath. "Something that drowns my body in such pleasure must be sinful."

A slight smile crossed his lips as he answered, "I do not believe it to be so when experienced this way."

"I hope you are right," she replied as her eyes searched for his.

Nicolae pushed himself up higher in the bed and brought his left hand to her right shoulder, slowly lowering that strap as well. "I want to see you," he said dreamily. He sat up beside her, took her hand in his, and glided her to an upright position. With only a little help, her shift fell revealing her rounded shoulders and ample breasts in the flickering candlelight. "My God, you are beautiful!" he declared taking in the sight before him.

Maria felt embarrassed. She had never had a man just sit and look at her before. Nicolae immediately sensed her tension and raised the straps of her shift back up her arms and over her shoulders. "Here. I did not mean to make you feel uncomfortable." It was then that he noticed a unique birthmark on the back of her left shoulder. "What is this mark on you that looks like a white heart?" he asked with an intense curiosity. He rubbed his finger across the image as he studied it.

Maria adjusted the front of her undergarment and replied casually, "It is my birthmark - I have always had it."

Then old thoughts long forgotten began to click away in Nicolae's brain. He lay back down onto the soft down silk pillows and requested, "Maria, tell me what you can about your family and where you are from."

"I don't know much," she admitted as she settled beneath the blanket beside him. "My parents and brother and sister all died of the plague when I was about three years old. I don't know where we were living then. I remember my nanny moving with me to Curt de Arges where I have lived ever since."

"Your brother and sister, did they have the same birth mark?"

Maria answered with a bewildered expression. "I really can't remember. Nicolae, it's been so long and I was so young…why? What are you thinking?" she asked searching his eyes apprehensively.

"I seem to recall my parents talking about friends of theirs, and all the children had this distinguishing birthmark like their father. They were neighbors - I know because my mother went to visit when their baby was born, and it wasn't far. They had an estate near Cozia."

"You're talking about a boyar family, aren't you?"

"Yes," Nicolae said, turning his soft blue eyes to her. "I must have been around nine years old when they all died of plague."

"A lot of families were devastated by plague, Nicolae," she reminded him.

"I know." He slipped his hand under the blanket and sheets and searched for hers until he found it and intertwined his fingers with hers. "My mother must have been friends with the lady because she cried a lot when she heard the news. Father was worried that we might get sick, too. I wish I could remember their names, but…"

"But don't you think if that was my family, Nanny would have told me? And wouldn't I have some inheritance?"

"No," he said thoughtfully. "With the black death, they would have burned the house and everything in it. You would have been too young to inherit anything, and lordship of the lands would have been awarded to another family. It would have served no purpose for your nanny to have told you these things while you were very young and could not understand. Then it was only a short time until Vlad came to power, and you were much safer as a peasant than if he discovered you were the child of an old boyar family, especially if they had opposed his father's rule. A wise nanny would have kept her master's child well hidden in anonymity."

"I can remember a recurring nightmare from my childhood of a burning house, but this is too much to fathom..."

Nicolae turned on his side toward her and propped his head up to look down upon her face. "Maria, I'm not saying this *was* your family, but I think it might have been. It all fits. Is your nanny still living? We could ask her."

"No," Maria answered with a disappointed sigh. "She died last year, so I suppose there's no way we'll ever know for sure. In all likelihood I am nothing more than a plain peasent."

Nicolae smiled warmly at her, his bright eyes sparkling as he gave her hand a squeeze. "My dear, there is nothing plain about you." He lowered his lips to hers and kissed her mouth lovingly. It was a slow, affectionate kiss, one Maria would give anything to feel again and again.

With his plans set, Vlad rode out on horseback the next day to the nearby Snagov monastery, accompanied by a small escort. Once across the lake, he strode into his chapel and waited for the abbot. He languidly traversed the tiles, soaking in the splendor he had constructed. Colored light danced across the sanctuary from the stained glass with statues of St. Joseph and the Blessed Virgin looking on. He felt as though the figure of Christ carved on the large crucifix that hung above the altar was staring down at him, mayhap in disapproval.

He spun around abruptly at the sound of the chapel door behind him. "Father Abbot," he called in a concerned voice. "How fares the impetuous monk whom I shot? 'Twas quite regrettable, but he cursed me," Vlad explained innocently. "His own prince and he was spouting venomous curses at me."

"He is recovering, Sire," the abbot informed the prince as he deliberately tread down the long aisle. "And we have received word from the great monastery in Cozia that your oldest son is excelling in his studies."

"Good, good," Vlad replied contentedly. "But there is another matter I have come to see you about. Soon I will enter the field of battle against the infidels, carrying with me the cross of Christ. I have come for your blessing to undo the curse pronounced by your misguided novice. My army holds up the crusade for all Christendom, Catholic and Orthodox alike. Therefore, regardless of my new affiliation with the Roman Church, I fight for your cause as well."

"Then I will come to Bucuresti and say mass for all your army, sending them off with the blessing of the Holy Mother Church," the Abbot agreed.

"Yes, Your Holiness, that is good," Vlad spoke hesitantly then took a few more strides toward the man of the cloth. "But I also wish you to say a blessing over me - my person - the one ordained by God as your prince."

"By all means, Prince Dracula," the abbot replied compliantly. "The Apostle Paul instructs us to always pray for the leaders who govern us."

The prince appeared nervous and distracted in a way the abbot had never witnessed before. Some unnamed, unseen fear seemed to haunt his eyes. "If any are redeemed, then surely those ordained by God would number among them. Is that not correct?" he asked fervently.

The abbot breathed a contemplative breath and chose his words carefully. "Our Lord taught that if any man were to confess his sins, no matter how grievous they be, and repent, calling on the forgiveness and grace of God through Jesus Christ his son, he would indeed be saved."

"I would gladly confess my sins," Vlad said with a gesture of humility, "if I could think of any I had committed. And if I have at any time sinned, it could only be in the excess of my zealous war against sin itself. I have dedicated my life to stamping out that vile entity where-ever I saw it, in whatever form it takes. I have persecuted the non-righteous with a holy fire like that which rained down on Sodom to make my principality into an ideal paradise for the Godly. Surely the Almighty will be pleased with me." Vlad continued to pace in circles in the aisle, speaking to the air. "I have built monasteries and cathedrals and donated much wealth to the Church. I have protected Europe from the onslaughts of the infidel hordes and brought low their mighty leader. Surely God will reward me for such."

"Does my lord fear death?"

"Fear?" Vlad's eyes shot up, revealing more than he intended. Then his expression hardened to one of anger. "I fear nothing or no one!" The veins on his reddening neck bulged, and his penetrating eyes darkened menacingly at the abbot.

"No, Your Majesty, you misunderstand. Do you feel...a premonition of sorts that your own death is near?" The abbot had an unsettling calm about him. He did not cower or shudder at the prince's wrath which upset Vlad even more. But he straightened his plum coat and stood tall to face his spiritual advisor.

"Some great men have died choking on a chicken bone; 'twill not be so with me. A man knows that every time he goes into battle there is a chance he will be slain." Dracula's temper subsided to a degree as he answered the abbot. "It is not that I fear the wild monk's curse," he explained lifting a hand in gesture, "but nonetheless, it would be prudent to see it undone. That is your job, Lord Abbot, to attend to the welfare of your prince. It is what God would have you do."

"Sire, if you would come with me and kneel at the altar in humility, I will bring forth the holy water and anointing oil to give you a proper blessing," the abbot offered and began to walk past Vlad toward the altar.

Dracula frowned. "Why can you not say the words here and now?" he demanded forcefully. "You are putting me off with rituals. Could it be that you do not wish to bless your prince?"

"Milord." The gentle abbot turned to Vlad with deep concern in his expression. In a pure voice he honestly replied, "I wish very much to bless my prince, but he is unwilling to humble himself before God. How much would my blessing mean if his own heart is not right?"

Vlad swore under his breath and struck the abbot's face with the back of his hand. "You religious leaders always speak in double-talk! You purposely evade questions and give answers no on can understand. You want to keep yourselves aloof, above mere mortals, as it were," he spouted brazenly. The abbot returned his eyes to Dracula without raising a hand nor taking a step in retreat. "You are not, you know. I am God's chosen prince," he declared, pushing his own thumb to his chest. "I rank higher than you, you who would tell me to kneel." Still the abbot's intuitive eyes stared back at him unyielding. "Do you not fear me?" Dracula thundered as he leaned to within a hair's whisper of the holy man.

"I fear God," he replied simply.

"Give me a blessing *now*, or I will give you cause to fear me more than God!"

"I have long wished to bless you, that you may in turn bless our people." The abbot lifted the small wooden cross that hung on a row of beads around his neck and raised his right hand above the prince's head. "In the name of the Father, Son, and Holy Ghost: the Lord bless you and keep you; the Lord make his face to shine upon you; the Lord be gracious unto you, and give you peace. May the Lord protect you and guard and guide your footsteps; and may the perfect will of the Almighty be accomplished in and through our prince, Vlad Dracula. Amen."

Satisfied, Vlad expelled a little huff. "There. That wasn't so difficult, was it? I liked the 'perfect will of the Almighty being accomplished through me' part."

"So did I," the Abbot said with a wry smile. Vlad wrinkled his brow. It was as though the abbot knew something he did not. "The monastery here at Snagov has been grateful for your patronage through the years, and we look forward to your return after your campaign has been completed."

Vlad's countenance relaxed at the abbot's gracious words, and he nodded with a pleasant smile. "Then I shall most assuredly return."

Chapter 21

Ready or Not

"We do not want to leave unfinished that which we began, but to follow it through to the end."

Matthias Corvinus, 1462

Maria and Nicolae sat together on the driver's seat of the Gypsy wagon the next morning as they traversed the bumpy road back into Romanian territory. The sky was dark and cloudy with a genuine cold biting the air, but the couple was partially comforted by a big lap blanket spread across their legs. Because the front seat was not very wide, they were obliged to sit quite snugly pressed together, welcoming the body heat.

They rode along in silence for what seemed a very long time. Maria felt certain that Nicolae had been disappointed in her the night before. She had never considered herself to be very beautiful, and now she was certain he had come to the same conclusion. *'Twas an experiment,* she thought. *He was testing the waters to see if there could be anything between us. Obviously,* she assumed, *there was not. I must not be the woman of the world that he is looking for - totally inept at romantic ventures.* But he had brought up that interesting question about her family. She wondered, pondered, and considered the possibilities, then shut her eyes dismissing them. *No,* she told herself. *I cannot seriously consider such things. Even if I had been from a noble family, what difference would it make now? It makes me no less an ignorant tavern maid.*

Nicolae's thoughts had been of a far different nature as he contemplated the younger woman who sat beside him and his own inexperience, having been a bachelor all his life. He wondered if he could live up to the memory of her husband. Curiosity finally got the better of him and after what seemed like endless hours of silence, he struck up a conversation. "Maria, tell me about your husband."

She was surprised by the question but more than eager to say something, anything. At least he was finally speaking to her. "Let me see," she began, thinking, *what is there to say?* "He was a good man. He treated me well, was a good provider. However, I must honestly say he was quite a bit older. He had two grown daughters from a previous marriage, and though I'm not certain, I think one was older than I."

Nicolae grinned to himself. *At least I haven't one foot in the grave.*

Maria continued. "He was kind and did his duty by me; he was able to give me a son."

"But did you love him?" Nicolae asked.

"Love? Well, I..." she stammered honestly not knowing how to answer the question. "I cooked for him, cared for him - did everything that was required of me."

"That isn't what I asked," he corrected.

"The marriage was arranged between him and my Nanny," Maria explained. "She said 'twas the best I would get having no dowry. She said he was an honest man and had a good position as a carpenter. I barely knew him before our wedding night." She hesitated uncertain of how much of her story she should tell him, how she was somewhat relieved when after a mere ten minutes he had rolled over and fallen asleep. It had not quite been what she dreamt of in a honeymoon. Then she began to think about how Nicolae broke off in what seemed to be the middle of his advances toward her. Perhaps she had that effect on men. Maybe she was not simply unattractive, but completely repulsive to men.

"So you did your duty by him; it was a marriage not of your choice," Nicolae pieced together. "But were you close? I mean -"

"Close?" she repeated, rousing herself from thoughts of her own inadequacies. "He did not confide in me, if that is what you mean. Small talk, a bit about the weather, but never anything important. I presumed that he, like most men, reserved important conversation for other men. No, we never talked of plans or dreams or hopes...he never told me his inner feelings or thoughts, nor did he inquire about mine. He did say he loved me once, but I think he more loved having someone there and not being alone." She looked up at Nicolae and could see that his eyes were trained on her.

"I see," he responded sympathetically. Then he turned his eyes back to the road which meandered through the lowland farm country and began to relate his own story. "I don't know if my parents married for love, but I can attest to the fact that it did come by the time I was old enough to know." The pony clip-clopped along, kicking up an occasional rock from the dirt. A cold wind blew the few remaining dry leaves across their path. "Father always had a gift to bring mother when he returned from traveling - jewels, flowers, chocolates, a new gown." His eyes began to grow soft and misty. "He would compliment her with words of her beauty and praise for how she managed us children. Time and again she declared he was the most handsome and elegant man in all of Cozia. He was dashing, I must admit."

"If you are anything like him," Maria interjected, "then I can readily see why your mother would think so." Her eyes sparkled at him as she considered his appearance and manner.

Nicolae lowered his head to conceal the blush rising in his cheeks. "Ah," he replied modestly. "I suppose I've finally filled out to his stature. But if I were ever to marry," he mused, raising his chin once again, "I would want a marriage like theirs. I would want it to be a home and family filled with love. I suppose that is the real reason I have not yet married - I was waiting to find that one special woman who would warm not only my bed, but also my heart."

She was not sure what to make of his declaration. Perhaps he meant to let her down easy, that she was not the one. But she dismissed the thought, not wanting it to dampen her spirit that day. She returned his gaze with wonderment. "How fortunate you are, Nicolae," she said passionately, "to have known your parents, to have lived in such a home filled with love."

He started at her words, his brows arching up and his mouth dropping. "Fortunate?" he balked. "They were taken from me without a moment's notice, and I was left alone in the world."

"Yes," she replied softly, "but you were fifteen. You had grown up in such a wonderful home, being raised by them, your sister, the love you shared as a family. You knew what your father was like; you knew your mother's songs as she sang to you. Yet I do not even remember my parents. They, too, were taken from me."

"That's different," Nicolae insisted.

"Maybe under different circumstances," Maria admitted, "but nevertheless, I was just a tot when they died, and I have been an orphan all these years without even so much as a memory to hold on to."

Maria's words struck at Nicolae like a flaming arrow into his heart. Instantly images long forgotten were aroused within his consciousness, joyful memories long buried. He saw himself playing with Evie in front of a warm hearth; he heard his mother's voice singing to him as she rocked him to sleep. He recalled the hunting trip with his father, how they shot the buck and carried it out of the forest together...laughter around a full table, affectionate hugs and kisses...Tears began to stream from his eyes as Nicolae scanned the countryside and rubbed the leather reins between his fingers. In that moment his eyes were opened to his life in a different light and a powerful wave of emotion rushed, foaming, to splash upon his heart. "You're right," he uttered at last and swallowed the lump rising in his throat. His right hand searched for hers beneath the blanket and clasped it tightly. He turned his face toward her, his eyes misty in wonder. "Maria, I want to thank you for what you have done for me."

"Me?" she questioned in astonishment. "What have I done?"

"You have opened my heart and my mind to so many things. All these years I've focused on what I lost, but you have reminded me of the irreplaceable years of joy that I did have. Thank you," he repeated earnestly.

"It is I who should thank you," Maria said in a most compelling tone. Her warm, brown eyes danced at his, and her face was aglow as she spoke. "You have treated me with respect in a way no one else has ever done. "You have talked to me about deep and important things as though I really matter. You have actually asked how I feel about things, and you have shown me such consideration that you make me feel as though my life really has some value after all."

He smiled at the joy and amazement that radiated from her face toward him. "That is because you do have great worth as a person, and you are so valuable to me." Nicolae shifted the reins to his right hand, tucking them between his fingers without releasing her hand. Then he lifted his left hand to gently cup her cheek, gliding her face towards his. He brushed his lips across hers ever so softly. He wanted to carry her to the back of that wagon and make love to her with wild abandonment. For an instant he wondered if he even could after so many years of strict discipline and self-constraint. But Nicolae believed that if anyone could unlock that door, i was the courageous, head-strong beauty whom he was touching at tha very moment. He felt a tremor go through his body at the warmth of her lips and knew he must release her now, or he would not at all.

As he pulled away, their eyes met, and he wondered if she saw the longing there, the desire that burned within him. But he feared he had come on too strongly the previous evening and the last thing he wanted to do was to scare her away. *I must be patient,* he told himself, *and take things slowly.*

Maria's eyes searched his hopefully but with reservation. She could sense the honest caring he demonstrated toward her, but was it only as a friend, or could it ever be more? As she recalled the night before, she wondered if his retreat had been prompted by her own mention of the morality of their actions, or because he actually did not want to pursue her. If she could have seen how tight his pants had become beneath the lap blanket, then her question would have been promptly put to rest.

Reluctantly, Nicolae slid his fingers from her cheek, snatched up the reins in his left hand, and swatted them across the rump of the plodding pony. Instantly he picked up his pace once more over the rutted highway that led back to Curt de Arges.

As they stopped to sleep those several nights on the return trip, Nicolae would hold Maria in his arms, her head resting on his shoulder only to awaken with his head lying on her breast. He regarded her tenderly but was ever mindful not to make improper advances, though the restraint only served to fuel his desire. Each night Maria would pray for guidance and right thoughts, for strength and for their safety. Although she thought her feelings might fade with his mastery of temperance, Maria discovered that with each day spent in Nicolae's company her feelings for him deepened.

Ivan strode through the camp near dusk, his head bowed with responsibility weighing heavy on his broad shoulders. He was brooding darkly about the imminent battle hoping that his new recruits would be up to the task when Dimitry stepped out waving for his attention. "Uh, Captain, Sir?" he inquired with concern as he removed his felt hat to address the officer.

"Yes, soldier, what is it?" he replied absently as he shuffled to a halt.

"I don't mean to be a bother, Captain, but the men in our unit have not received their rations yet," Dimitry reported and then took a moment to scratch. Living in the camp was akin to rolling out the welcome mat for every itchy little parasite in town.

Ivan issued a disgruntled sound. "They may be running behind this evening; I'll speak with the quartermaster." Turning his eyes back to his path, Ivan started to walk away.

"But Sir," Dimitry called. "We haven't been fed all day."

"What!" Ivan spun around, his black cloak swirling around his armor-clad torso. "That's preposterous! You mean your entire unit has not received any rations today?" His voice boomed as his muscles grew tense.

"No, Sir, none." Dimitry presented himself meekly to his superior who seemed just as upset over the matter as the hungry men. Several of the others from Dimitry's group ambled up beside him, looking hopefully to Ivan.

The big captain swore under his breath then raised his chin authoritatively. "I will see the quartermaster immediately, and whatever the mix up was, it will be straightened out."

Dimitry nodded to him, satisfied that his commander would resolve the problem, his empty, gnawing belly hoping it would be soon. Ivan spun on his heel, his jaw set, and hastened his steps toward the quartermaster's wagon. "Janos," he called sharply to the man in charge. "Why were the militia under my command not provided with their proper rations today?"

"Captain," he answered with a startled glance at the looming figure who glared down at him. He wiped his wet hands on a coarse apron that was tied around his long natural peasant shirt and brown trousers. "There is not enough food; our supplies are running low, and the prince ordered the Hussars and Moldavian guard be fed from our stocks."

Ivan was seething with fury at having his men's supplies being diverted to other troops. Puffs of steam trailed from his open lips while his brown eyes darkened. "Why do they not provide their own? I had plenty of supplies for all of the Poenari soldiers to last for weeks - what has become of it all?"

"Sir," Jonas stammered, fearful of what Ivan might do to him. "We have picked up so many men since packing the supplies; the food has all been used up. It is not my fault, really it's not," he swore, taking a step back.

"Bleeding Christ," Ivan hissed and snapped around and stomped toward the fortress, muttering to himself all the way through the castle gate. His temper was almost under control when he requested an audience with the prince. "My Great Prince Viovode," he began with a bow as he removed his silver helm. "There must have been some mistake or miscommunication made."

Vlad raised his chin in a vain effort to look down upon the mountainous captain. "Oh? And what might that be, Ivan?"

"I gathered, packed, and brought with me ample provisions for my troops from Poenari and the militia we gathered from Curt de Arges, but someone has been distributing it to other regiments, and now my stores are empty. There is no food left to feed my soldiers."

"Yes, that is quite unfortunate, but it will not be a problem for long," the prince explained. "Once the fighting begins, we will suffer casualties and not have as many mouths to feed. You must understand the necessity of seeing to the professional soldiers first."

"Yes, milord," Ivan replied, his eyes desperately searching for satisfaction. "But two hundred of those men *are* professional soldiers - my guard from Poenari. I will not see them go without. Besides, Sire, what good will the men be to us if, when we enter the battle, they are too weak from hunger to fight?"

"I recognize your concern," Vlad said, placing a hand on Ivan's broad shoulder and steering him toward the gate. "Might I suggest that you take a detachment into the city and conscript supplies for your troops. If anyone resists, first tell them it is Prince Vlad's order to relinquish the food. If they still give you trouble, kill them." Their eyes met, and a cold chill ran down Ivan's spine. He despised directives that involved the killing of civilians, considering it both cowardly and self-defeating. After all, wasn't the army supposed to protect and defend the citizenry of Walachia?

"I will see to it immediately," he answered in a steady, steely tone. For a split second, Ivan contemplated the powerful physical advantage he held over the prince. He could crush the smaller, older man with one blow, but he was not one to commit treason. He just liked knowing that it could be done. He took a step toward the gate as Vlad returned his hand to his own hip, then he looked back at the prince. "What guarantee do I have that the supplies confiscated for my men will not disappear like the last ones did?"

Dracula narrowed his eyes and clinched his jaw toward the big captain. He did not like the accusation filled timbre of the question nor the idea of being challenged by one of his officers. "You can be guaranteed, Captain, that your men will soon see battle - we march day after tomorrow. Once the Turks are defeated, we can feast on their stores. Give that promise to your soldiers as an incentive for victory."

Ivan nodded, bowing subserviently toward Dracula, then snapped around, replaced his helmet, and strode through the gate.

Octavian meandered over to the prince in the midst of the castle yard as his long shadow fell before him. "What was that all about, Your Majesty?" he asked.

Vlad snorted a puff of steam then turned to Octavian. "Ivan was informing me that we are short on supplies, and I sent him to the city to collect more."

Octavian astutely detected an irritated tone in the prince's voice and saw an opportunity to score a political point. "Does Ivan displease you, milord? I have heard that his mother was a Transylvanian slut and his father deserted his post when the Turks invaded back in '62 - shot in the back by an arrow as he fled."

But Vlad's keen understanding of politics saw straight through the ploy, and he shot his officer a most disdainful glare. Immediately Octavian lowered his eyes and fudged on his accusation. "Naturally I have no personal knowledge of these things...it is only what I have heard said."

"Ivan is undefeated in combat, a valiant warrior, and he inspires confidence in his men. He is a most capable leader, and he cares for those under his command." Vlad paused to find humor in the humble expression and posture Octavian now displayed in his presence. "However, that could be a detriment if he were ordered into a position where high casualties were expected. He may be tempted to retreat, thinking only of the lives of his regiment rather than the overall victory."

Octavian's eyes brightened. "I am ready to fully obey any orders you issue, Majesty, regardless of personal danger."

Vlad raised his brow in suspicion. "Is this the same Octavian who only a few days ago wanted to submit and pay tribute to Mehmed?"

"Forgive me, my lord," he said bowing, "but now I understand your plan."

"Then you may lead the attack, Captain, and I expect you to make good on your promise." Dracula dismissed Octavian with a wave knowing full well the subterfuge he had just made. Yet someone must lead the attack, someone who would not spare the lives of his men, someone who was himself expendable.

Gossip began to spread down the streets the moment the little Gypsy wagon passed through the city gate of Curt de Arges. Maria sat beside Nicolae on the front seat wearing a blue pleated valnic covered by a white apron and a black fur-lined cojoc over her embroidered white blouse. At her side, Nicolae wore the same cream Hungarian suit he had first arrived in. Though glad to be home, Maria was nervous about what to tell people. "Leave it to me," Nicolae had said. *That* was what worried her most.

Since the day was well spent and most shops had closed, the villagers had nothing else to do but speculate over the mismatched couple in the Gypsy wagon returning a week after they had disappeared. By the time they reached Maria's house, a little crowd had gathered outside her door. Before the pony had even come to a halt, Nadia rushed to Maria's side of the wagon.

"Where have you been? My God, Maria, I have been so worried! How could you run off like that without saying anything to me about it?" Maria hesitated, hoping Nadia would continue bombarding her with questions so she would not have an opportunity to answer.

Then Nicolae stood, a broad smile beaming across his face. "Friends, neighbors," he announced proudly. "May I present to you my new wife."

Chapter 22

A Time to Love, A Time to Hate

"To everything there is a season, and a time to every purpose under Heaven:…a time to love, and a time to hate; a time of war, and a time of peace."

Ecclesiates 3:1, 8

Maria's head snapped up in disbelief, and she sent him a seething glare. "Maria!" Nadia exclaimed in relief. "Why didn't you tell me?"

"It was all so sudden, Nadia," she answered between gritted teeth, holding her eyes on that idiot beside her. "I was surprised myself."

"Ladies and gentlemen," Nicolae spoke apologetically as he climbed down from the seat. "I am dreadfully sorry that we could not make a formal announcement and hold the wedding ceremony here so that you could all be invited." He looked up holding out a hand for Maria, but he noticed she was already exiting the other side of the wagon. "You see, friends," he continued in his impeccable Hungarian accent, "that I have been a bachelor all these thirty-four years and upon finding the woman of my dreams I deigned not to wait a moment longer. Now that we have returned from our honeymoon holiday, I am certain that Maria is quite exhausted and ready to retire for the evening."

"Domnule, may I see to your pony for you?" asked an eager young lad in the crowd.

Nicolae smiled at him and handed the boy a coin. "Certainly, son; you do me a service."

"But Maria," Lucian asked in bewilderment as his brown strands fell limply over an eye, "where is your ring? Shouldn't you have a ring?"

Before Maria had a chance to contrive a response, Nicolae spoke up, walking around the pony to Maria's side. "Not just any ring will do for my lady," he boasted. "I ordered one especially made by the jeweler. It should be ready in about a week." He took Maria by the elbow to usher her to her door.

"Maria," Nadia called softly, keeping close to her. "I want to hear all the details," she said brimming with excitement. But upon noticing the disturbed look on her friend's face, she questioned, "What is wrong?"

Maria forced a smiled and drew closer to Nadia, embracing her in a friendly hug. "I'll explain tomorrow," she whispered. "I've a lot to tell you."

"Very well," she consented, relieved that Maria was alive and well.

Maria unlocked the door with a key from her apron pocket. She let out a startled gasp when Nicolae scooped her up into his arms, kicked the door wide, then turned toward the townspeople. "Ladies, gentlemen, thank you for your gracious welcome home and all of your well wishes. We now bid you all a good night." Maria caught her arms around his neck to keep her balance as he whirled her around again, proceeding to carry her over the threshold and then kick the door shut behind them.

"Put me down!" she demanded with a fierce scowl. "Have you completely lost your mind?"

Nicolae laughed as he dropped one arm allowing her feet to fall to the floor. "Maybe…maybe not," he replied with lively dancing eyes.

She immediately pulled away from him and stalked to the far side of the room. His mirth began to fade as he noticed her mood. "You had no right to do that - to lie to everyone! Now what will I do?" She spun to face him only to find he had busied himself building a fire on the hearth. "Oh, no you don't, Nicolae!" she scolded. "Don't go making yourself at home like you are planning to spend the night!"

"It's cold," he answered calmly. "Lord knows this room could stand to be warmed." He shot her an irritated, uncertain glance and then struck his flint to the straw beneath the logs.

"I suppose I will have to move away once this is finished," she thought aloud as she strolled back across the length of the room trying to put as much distance between Nicolae and herself as she could. "I could not possibly think of staying here and trying to explain any of this. Did you think, Nic? Did you think for one minute what a deception like this would do to me?" Distraught, she turned toward him. He stood beside the crackling infant fire with his arms folded over his chest, his szur tossed over a chair. "It is one thing to make a pretense in front of strangers, but another altogether to announce a fraudulent marriage before my friends and neighbors." He looked even taller and more broad-shouldered than usual silhouetted by the small light forming in the fireplace, the rest of the room in shadows.

"It doesn't have to be a lie, Maria; simply agree to marry me."

"I told you, I will not marry for convenience, or even to make true a lie. Thank you for your noble gesture," she quipped cynically, "but I know it is naught more than that. I could just imagine being introduced in your circles - 'meet my illiterate peasant wife; she isn't up on the social graces, but she sets a fine table." Maria was so distressed she was almost in tears. She finally stood still, her arms crossed and her eyes to the floor in desolate failure.

Nicolae ran a hand through his fair hair, his voice filled with compassion. "Maria, I am not asking you to marry me because it is convenient, or to save your reputation, or even to turn a lie into truth." He took a small step toward her and reached out a hand. "I'm asking you to marry me because I love you."

Immediately Maria's chin rose, her mouth falling open as her eyes searched his. Her heart began to pound, and she felt as though she was trembling all over at the words she thought she heard him speak.

Nicolae felt a lump form in his own throat as he tried to present his case as convincingly as possible, hopeful to win her heart, not knowing he already had. "For many years I believed that I could never love again, that I had been wounded too deeply. Then I met you, and all kinds of feelings long buried stirred to life. You have opened my eyes and my heart to so many things that I can't imagine going back to the life I had before." He sighed and shifted his weight to one foot. "I know the timing is dreadfully bad to ask you this, since tomorrow I rush to face my destiny and cannot promise that I'll return. I would never want to cause you the pain and heartache of leaving you a widow for the second time, but neither could I abide the thought of dying without having told you how I feel."

On trembling legs Maria took a few tentative steps in his direction, almost stunned speechless. "Nicolae, I..."

He reached forward and caught her by the arm. "But Maria, this much I can promise you: as long as there is springtime and harvest, as long as the ocean meets the shore, as long as stars shine in the heavens, I'll be in love with you."

"Oh, Nicolae!" Maria rushed to embrace him, to feel the comfort of being wrapped in his strong arms. Tears fell on his shoulder as they held each other tightly. Wave upon wave of emotion crashed over her as she clung to him. "Yes, oh yes!" she cried in release. "No one has ever said such things to me, and I thought no one ever would." She swallowed and tried to collect her thoughts. "The first night we met and the captain came and took you away, I prayed for you, for your safety. As I grew to know you, I loved you in secret, afraid to even hope you might feel the same." She lifted her head from his shoulder and looked up into his face with damp, dazzled eyes. "And here you are...and..."

Nicolae claimed her mouth with his, her warm, moist lips calling to him with urgency. She responded by plunging deep into the kiss, rejoicing, reveling, celebrating in the touch and taste of a man who truly loved her, whom she truly loved. She crushed her fully blossomed breasts against his firm, hard chest, pulling herself to his body with all her might. His hands moved slowly along her back, drawing her to him, touching her, igniting an unquenchable fire deep within her being.

At last the kiss subsided but only for their need of breath. Nicolae opened his eyes to her and was unable to hold back any words that formed in his mind. "Oh, my love, I so much want to become one with you."

Her deep brown eyes fixed on his as her breath came fast and shallow. "Milord, I am afraid."

"I'm not asking -"

"I know." She quieted him with a brush of her lips to his. "But don't you think I want it too?" She loosened her grip on his shoulders and ran her fingers through his hair. "If you were not to return -"

"Shh," he uttered, lowering one hand to her rounded hip and raising the other to cup her cheek.

"This is a good time for me, when my womb is ripe. When you go to meet him, the knowledge that I may carry your child could give you courage. Let the hope that your father's line may not end with you and that your seed will go on for many generations provide you with the extra will to win. And if, God forbid, you lie dying, you may find comfort knowing that ultimately you have still won - that he has failed yet again to destroy your family line."

"Maria." An awestruck look of wonder washed over his face at her selfless offer. Being unable to form words, he took her lips with his and easily parted them, their tongues dancing to the beat of their hearts. Then he lifted her in his arms as his eyes glowed into her face. "Are you certain?"

"I want forever; we may only have tonight."

He nodded and carried her to the warm spot before the fire. He took his great coat and spread it on the wooden floor while she slipped off her cojoc. Then Nicolae cradled her face in his hands and brought his lips to hers. "It has been a long time since I..." Her words trailed off, and her eyes glowed at him sensually.

"It's been longer for me." He lowered Maria to the floor and followed her there, never letting go of her. Clothing fell to the side as they moved in concert to consummate their love. Nicolae found himself lost in a sea of flowing black hair, not caring if he drowned there. He was on her, beneath her, within her; he was both lost and found in her embrace. She had unleashed a passion that sent him reeling out of control, yet he did not fight it; he let it come and possess him even as he gave her possession of his heart.

Thrilled beyond her imagination, Maria discovered that there was indeed an art to love-making and her fiancée was a master artist. He brought her to the brink of ecstasy, retreated, then came again. Every touch sang of his love; every kiss testified that it was true. She moaned and cried out in a symphony of pleasure at the sweet torture she endured at his hands. And just when she thought she had reached the pinnacle and could soar no higher, he came again, alternating a soft, gentle touch with driving urgency, touching her in a new way, kissing where she had never dreamed, until at last, exhausted and spent, they fell limp in each other's arms before the hearth's flames and embers.

Nicolae felt as weak as a kitten, unable to do anything save breathe and experience the electric tingle of the subsiding tide. "So this is how it feels to be alive," he voiced in wonder, his eyes transfixed on the dancing lights and shadows playing on the ceiling.

"I never knew," Maria marveled as she felt a floating, whirling sensation. "You are so -"

"Incredible," he finished. "I never felt so -"

"Complete." They turned their eyes to each other's, gazing past the flesh and into the soul. In that moment the two realized the magic and fulfillment of true unity. After a long moment of realization and awe at what they had encountered together, they engulfed one another again in a joint embrace.

Sounds from the street and a ray of sunlight slowly awakened Maria the next morning. As she found herself in that twilight between fantasy and reality, she rolled over in her bed to find she was alone. Immediately her eyes snapped open and her heart was seized with panic. *Had it been a dream? No, it was too real. Did he leave without saying good-bye?* Clutching the sheet to her bare breast, she sprung up in bed, scanning the room with anxious eyes. She sighed in relief as she spotted Nicolae sitting in front of her mirror wearing only his trousers. His attention was focused on the mirror as he carefully shaved away the whiskers from his chin and upper lip with a straight razor.

"Good morning," she uttered dreamily as she pulled her knees up and clasped her hands around them.

"How does it look?" he asked turning towards her.

"You shaved off your chin beard!"

He smiled and rubbed his hand over his face to check for smoothness. He needed to go over a few spots again. "Yes," he replied then ran the blade across his jawbone one more time. "This time, I want Dracula to recognize me. I want him to know exactly who it is that smites him down." Nicolae splashed water on his face from the basin then blotted it with a towel.

"I know you'll be leaving soon," Maria said in resignation. "I'll get you some food to take along."

She began to rise, but by that time Nicolae had stepped across the room and stood before her. Flashbacks from the night before lit through her, and she could feel a pulsating between her thighs as she beheld his bare, muscled chest. He smiled and sat beside her, taking her hand in his. His deep, blue eyes gazed into hers fondly for a few moments and then he shook his head. "There are no words."

Maria lowered her head with a bashful smile. When she raised it again her expression had changed. "Do you think he has ever known this - to have loved someone?"

The warm glow left his eyes, and he sighed, casting his gaze out the window. "Once, when he was married to his first wife, Vlad had a mistress. She adored him, doted on him, worshipped him. No matter what he did, she lovingly took his side. Then one day he fell into a state of melancholy, and she was worried for him. Each day his depression seemed to deepen. So, wanting to cheer him up, she told him she was with child. At first it did cheer him, but in a short time he became suspicious. He called his physicians to examine her, and when it was discovered she was not pregnant, he flew into a rage." Nicolae stopped to swallow and turned his eyes back to Maria. "In the presence of his court and many witnesses, he took his dagger and split her down the front. He thrust his hand into her womb shouting, 'Show us the child I have created! Let the world see where my seed has been'."

A sickening feeling rose from the pit of Maria's stomach as he recounted the tale, and though no danger was near, she felt genuine terror. "Then he left her there," he continued bleakly, "to lie on the floor in a pool of her own blood, her entrails falling out of the slit. He neither finished her off nor would allow the physicians to tend her, but left her to suffer, writhing in pain, until she bled to death. When she pleaded with him and reached out to him in anguish, he looked on her with indifference, as though she were nothing more than an insect."

Maria buried her face in her knees, wishing she hadn't asked. Then Nicolae slid his arm in comfort around her shoulder. "Anyone who could sleep with a woman night after night, accepting all the love she could give him and then do that to her without a second thought, is a monster totally incapable of love and deserving of utter destruction. I will destroy him, Maria, and then return to you to make you my wife in truth." She lowered her knees and moved her arms to embrace him without a word.

Only a few minutes had passed until they stood at the door to say their good-byes. Maria had thrown on a robe and filled a bag with bread, cheese, and salt pork and a goatskin with water for his journey. She recalled the black clothes he wore from that fateful night in the corridor of Poenari. At his side hung a silver sword, and he wore his black woolen cape to keep him warm.

As they gazed into each other's eyes, Nicolae thought to remove his chain that bore his father's signet ring. "Here," he said draping it around her neck. "Wear this as a sign of my pledge until I replace it with a wedding band." Her eyes bore into his with longing, but no words would come. "If for any reason I am not successful -"

"Nicolae -"

"Shh." He placed a finger to her lips and a hand on her shoulder "Listen to me. If you do not hear that Vlad is dead, or if you receive word of his return, it means I have failed, and you are in grave danger. You must leave Curt de Arges immediately for Szeged to the house of Kuban Show him this ring, and he will know I sent you."

"But Nicolae," she protested.

"Think, Maria; give me hope. You may now carry our child whose life cannot be risked by your stubbornness. Promise me," he demanded, taking hold of her face in both hands. "Promise me you'll go."

"I promise!" she cried out in desperation, not wanting even to consider the possibility. She faltered leaning toward him, but Nicolae caught her in his arms and pulled her close, claiming her lips with his own. The kiss aroused a fearful, frantic passion in them both, searing them with an eternal fire as if it must last them for a lifetime.

Slowly Nicolae pulled back, knowing he could not waste time, knowing it was already too difficult to leave her. Their eyes met, relaying all they could not say. "I will pray for you, my love, that God will grant you victory and bring you safely home."

Nicolae smiled softly. "I thank you, Iubita, for what good your prayers will do."

Maria stepped back and looked into his eyes with bewilderment. "Do you not believe in prayer?"

"I have seen nothing in my life to convince me God hears or answers prayers."

"Nicolae, surely..."

"Oh, as a child I prayed, as did my father, mother, and sister. I will never forget my last prayer." He leaned against the door frame and slid his hands down her arms to clasp her fingers. "With all that was in me, I earnestly pleaded with God to spare Eveline. I even offered Him my life in return for hers, but He didn't listen. I suppose there are many matters of much greater importance to occupy His time than the request of one Romanian boy. After that I decided that either God was no longer interested in the affairs of men, or in His sovereignty, He will do as He pleases, so why bother to pray?"

"But Darling, don't you see? You have been chosen, raised up for a holy, divine mission. If your sister had been restored to you, if you had taken her to Hungary and spent all these years with her there, you might have become content and given up your plan to kill Prince Dracula. The tragedies of your life helped to make you strong; they made you who you are."

Nicolae withdrew his hands to his hips and snorted, a hurt, disgruntled expression on his face. "I would rather believe that God did not hear my meager prayer than to think He manipulated me into His plan by killing my parents and sister. Who could serve a God like that? What about you? You've lost more than I; do you not blame Him?"

"No," Maria tried to explain, her eyes softly and compassionately searching his. "God makes the rain to fall on the just and the unjust alike. He no more killed my son than He killed your sister; Vlad Tepes, that son of the devil, is the harbinger of evil. What I am trying to say is that I know God answers prayers because he answered mine…insignificant as I am. I prayed for Him to send a hero to rescue us from tyranny, to destroy the beast." She slid her hands up the fabric of his black shirt over his firm chest as she stepped into him. "And I prayed that He would send me someone to love, a man who would truly love me. Both of these prayers have been answered in you, and I know you cannot fail."

Nicolae wrapped his arms around her one more time, pulling her head to rest on his shoulder. "Maybe it is because of your depth of faith that your prayers were answered. Maybe I was somehow lacking, and it is my own fault they were not."

"Or maybe your prayer was answered, just not in the way you thought it should be." They held each other tightly for a long moment and then feeling Nicolae's urgency, Maria let him go. They looked into each other's eyes with a knowing intensity. "I love you," Maria voiced.

"As I love you," Nicolae replied, then spun out through the door, taking long hasty strides toward the tavern where his horse was stabled. He clutched the bags of vittles in his left hand and did not look back. She leaned on the open door frame, wrapped her arms around herself against the cold, and followed him with her eyes.

Just as he rounded the corner and Maria was about to retreat inside, she heard a voice call her name. As though awakened from a dream, she turned toward the sound. "Nadia."

"Where is he going?" she asked with interest as she waltzed up to her friend's door.

"He has work to do," she answered solemnly, gazing back at the empty corner where last she saw him.

Nadia noticed the serious look of concern etched on Maria's face but wanted to be encouraging in her speech. "I was right, wasn't I?" She said hopefully. "He is a terrific lover, is he not?"

Maria turned to Nadia with a soft glow in her eyes. "Yes, you were right...we all were: you, me, the Gypsy fortune teller." Maria's eyes alertly darted up and down the street, and then she took hold of Nadia's arm. "Come in." The words were more an order than an invitation. Maria bolted the door behind them. "There is so much I want to tell you."

As the day wore on, the wind picked up, and heavy clouds covered the sky. Nicolae was still fifteen miles from Tirgoviste when the blizzard hit. Unable to stop lest he freeze to death, he pushed his steed forward through the swirling snow, at times losing sight of the road entirely. It was dark when he dragged himself into a local inn to rest before pursuing another fifty mile trek on the morrow.

The next day was clear but bitterly cold. Two feet of snow covered the ground all the way to the Danube which was itself crusted by a thin layer of ice. Vlad was sitting at table with Sergei and his officers, breaking their fast, when an urgent knock pounded at the great hall door. Ivan looked up from his porridge to see a servant open the door.

"A messenger for Prince Dracula," he announced without admitting the man. "He says it is most urgent."

Without looking up from his meal, Vlad signaled with his left hand to show him in. The dirty soldier's hair was frazzled and wet and snowflakes still rested on the cloak that bound his shoulders. He rushed to the table, knees trembling and face pale. "Milord, the Turks..." Vlad's spoon rested still, and he raised his narrow gaze to the soldier. "They have crossed the Danube; they have invaded."

Chapter 23

Destiny

"You are appointed by God to punish the evil doers."

From an old German narrative;
a placid, Catholic monk referring to Prince Dracula

Prince Dracula gritted his teeth and bolted to his feet. "When? How many?" he asked deliberately, his eyes piercing the messenger. The other officers stopped eating and turned their stunned expressions toward the shivering soldier.

"Early this morning," he reported frantically. "They are many - a large army…and Basarab rides with them."

"Basarab!" Vlad smashed his fist into his palm, seething with fury. "Mobilize the troops at once; I will not be trapped in this city. We will meet them in the field!" He tramped toward the hall door then abruptly spun back to face his officers who were still trying to process the information. "Where is Octavian?"

"He is sick, Your Majesty," the red-bearded captain answered tentatively.

"Sick! Bloody hell, he is not allowed to be sick. I demand an audience with him at once. You captains see to your men. Strike camp, line up the troops, we leave in an hour. Where is that insubordinate coward!" he thundered.

In moments Octavian was ushered into the hall wearing his robe and supported by an aide. Two physicians escorted him. "Prince Dracula, my lord," the bearded physician addressed him. "Octavian is not shirking his duty. He has a stone."

"A stone?" Vlad frowned.

Octavian groaned, a severe grimace lining his face. "My prince, if I were not in such constant excruciating pain," he offered, looking up into the prince's dark countenance.

"Will he die?"

231

"Probably not, milord," the older, thin physician explained. "They usually pass in a few days, but if not he will be in constant pain until the end. I have ordered leeches for him and a regimen of extra water every hour to flush out the stone."

"It also makes it almost impossible for him to relieve himself, Majesty. It is truly a serious condition," concluded the brown-bearded practitioner.

"But you were perfectly healthy yesterday," Vlad puzzled aloud.

"I am sorry, my prince," Octavian uttered then grabbed a hand to his side, contorting his torso to try vainly to relieve the pain. "It came on suddenly."

"It always does," the old doctor confirmed. "Let us tend him, and he can join you in a week with God's speed."

Dracula grunted. "Damn, they're attacking today! But I may yet have use for you, Octavian. Obey the physicians and me, and be thankful I believe their report, or I would have you dangling from a spike this very hour for cowardly treason!" The prince spun about in frustration and stomped out of the hall. "Ivan!" he shouted as he halted to pull on his gloves.

"Da, my prince," he called as he trotted back across the snow-covered yard.

"You will lead the attack; Octavian is ill." Vlad's jade eyes met Ivan's gravely. "I know you are without fear and without equal in combat. We may suffer many casualties, Ivan, but you must not shrink from the battle, even if it is to the last man, do you understand? We are all that stands between the infidels and all of Christendom." He placed a confident hand on the big captain's shoulder. "I know I can count on you to do your duty."

"Yes, sire; I will not fail you nor my people. We will hold."

"Good."

The army of Walachia marched to the southwest. By late afternoon, advance scouts reported back to the prince who rode beside Sergei, surrounded by the Moldavian guard.

"Sire." The scout saluted from his seat atop a bay destrier. Vlad pulled his black steed to a halt and held up his hand, stopping the caravan behind him. He focused his gaze on the plain-clothed scout. "The infidels are making camp in the forest two miles ahead across that field," he indicated, pointing behind him. "They are presently just out of range of our cannon."

Vlad did not immediately reply, and all waited quietly as his intrepid eyes scanned the trees that protected them. "He plans for the battle to occur in that meadow where his greater numbers will give him the advantage." The prince reined his horse around to face his officers and troops. "Backtrack half a mile and make camp. Officers, stay with me for a few minutes, and I will give you the plan."

Without question or hesitation, the army retreated and began to set camp along the road and between the trees. His officers maneuvered their horses into a circle around the prince awaiting his instructions.

"Mehmed thinks he will slaughter us on that field, but I have a plan." Dracula's eyes caught those of his officers as they focused their attention on him. "We will meet him on the field at dawn with our militia."

"The militia?" Sergei questioned.

Vlad smiled darkly. "Yes. He considers his army superior, and we will let him continue to think so. Once we are losing badly enough, Ivan will sound the retreat and lead the remainder through these trees into the forest where we now stand. They will pursue, and that is when we shall have them. The archers and artillery will be waiting hidden in the trees on the flanks." He motioned toward the stands of timber as he spoke. "Once our soldiers are in full retreat, they will rain fire and lead on the Turks. The pikemen and Moldavian guard will be waiting here as the enemy advances, and instead of catching up to the battered militia, they will run headlong into our best troops. Then the Hussar cavalry will be unleashed on their rear. As we tighten the trap around the infidels, we will crush them in our grasp." Vlad demonstrated by rolling the fingers of his right hand into a fist and raising it in triumph. The officers nodded, agreeing it was a good plan. "I want everyone in position by dawn, and strict silence must be observed by those in the forest to conceal our numbers." Vlad turned his horse and began to trot toward the campsite, followed by the others.

Later that evening four thousand Walachian men knelt in rows before their prince. Vlad, dressed in full military array, sat upon his big, black horse so that all could see him by the light of dozens of fires. He addressed them with a strong voice of authority. "Men of Walachia, soldiers of Christ, you are our only hope."

Kneeling side by side on the long fourth row of militia were Dimitry, Jean, and their new friends with the ill-fitting, broken equipment designated for the expendable militia units. Dimitry's eyes were raised to the prince in grave concern as he prayed that God would preserve them on the morrow. Jean shivered as the frosty snow melted beneath the warmth of his knee and soaked into the woolen cloth. The young man was open to any hope and encouragement his leader could offer.

"Your wives, your children sit at home this night at their family altars praying for you, praying that you will save them. You are all that stands between the Turkish infidels and your loved ones. Tomorrow morning you will face one of the greatest armies in the modern world, and you can do one of two things." His eyes scanned the ranks who remained silent in his presence. "You may flee in fear and cowardice like rats before a rising tide, letting your mothers, sisters, and wives be taken by their ravenous savagery before they are slaughtered like sheep. If you are lucky, you may escape with your lives, but your country will be lost, and afterward Hungary, Moldavia, and even the Empire will fall until darkness covers all the earth. Or -" He paused dramatically, raising his chin and his voice before the army. "Fight!" Dracula cried, drawing his black sword with twisted serpentine handle and thrusting it upward into the December night air.

As with one voice, a cheer went up from the ranks while their prince cantered across the front, first to their left and then back to their right. He pulled his steed to a halt and raised his left palm to them quieting their enthusiasm. "Good. Men, the facts are simple: you alone defend the Christian world against the leader and the army that toppled Constantinople." Vlad lowered his eyes as if in sorrow and then looked back to the men soberly. "Some of you will not return home alive, but together we can stand against them, turn them back, and drive the infidels from our land as we have done in the past. Your officers have been informed of my plan to crush the enemy beneath our heels; obey them as you would me. Stand," he commanded in a loud voice over the hushed multitude. "Stand together, and you will be victorious!"

The army leapt to its feet with exuberant cheers, applauding their leader. "You're right, Dimitry," Jean said to the older barrel-chested man beside him. "He can lead us to victory."

Dimitry hid his own misgivings and smiled at Jean. "Yes. Now remember what I said - we stick together and when the time comes, run like hell."

"Da," he replied with a glint of good humor in his eyes. "That I will."

An eerie, early morning mist rose from the meadow as it was touched by the first rays of light. Each Romanian warrior stood in his appointed spot with muscles tight, ears alert, prayers said. Dimitry's squad was pressed close together in the center of the militia unit. Daniel had tied the iron head onto his pole-ax with a little leather cord. Lucian, clothed in a leather jerkin and conical helm, was dwarfed by the taller, heavier Dimitry who held a firm grip on his sword hilt. Jean adjusted the straps on his round, wooden shield to secure it better.

Without warning the signal was given, and Ivan ordered the charge. Waving the banner of Walachia, the big knight led his soldiers into battle from horseback with an array of weapons at his disposal. With a mighty battle cry, the citizen soldiers burst out behind their commander across the open field. They had barely cleared the woods when Turkish artillery started to pummel them with hot lead. But with the fog for cover, the cannon fire was not accurate, felling few of the Romanians. Soon they could make out the image of advancing Turks through the evaporating moisture.

"This is it, men!" Ivan shouted back at them at the top of his lungs. "For Christ and country!"

"For Christ and country!" they echoed and then plunged into the enemy ranks.

The fighting was intense as the armies met in bloody, personal hand-to-hand combat. Soon the fog cleared in the morning sun, and Vlad watched from the edge of the timber. The bodies of the dead and wounded littered the field to the extent that soldiers from both sides could not move without treading upon a fallen friend or foe. Slowly the Romanians were pushed back, their numbers dwindling before the superior strength of the Turkish forces. Basarab led the fighting in the field while Mehmed commanded from the rear.

Ivan, ever cautious to edge back and prevent his army from being surrounded, kept up the battle as long as he could, despite heavy casualties. When the point came that more than half of his command lay still in the crimson snow, he called for the retreat. Vlad readied the others but commanded them to wait patiently for his signal. Cannon were loaded, archers set. The Hussars were mounted, holding their steeds back from the sounds of battle that beckoned them.

Amid the din and confusion of the ensuing melee, Dimitry spotted the signal flag and was passed by a fleeing Romanian. He clashed swords with the Saracen before him and called to Jean who was fighting close by. "Retreat! Run, Jean!"

Jean's shield sprung up as with a mind of its own to block his opponent's blow. He plunged his sword beneath the lower edge of the shield into the Turk's groin and then swiftly withdrew it as the Muslim warrior doubled over in pain. "Let's get out of here!" he shouted in reply and hastily spun toward the forest and their waiting reinforcements.

Dimitry laid both hands upon his sword hilt and putting his weight behind the blow, knocked his adversary's sword from his vibrating hand. He did not waste time striking a fatal blow to his unarmed foe, but used those precious seconds to catch up with his younger friend.

As they sprinted across the field, side-stepping bodies, Dimitry was only aware of a blur of noise behind him and the safety of the forest ahead. Suddenly he heard a muffled cry and a thud. Turning to his right, he spotted Jean lying on the ground with an arrow shaft protruding from the back side of his shoulder. The steel-tipped bolt had penetrated the old leather armor which offered the young man little protection. In an instant Jean was on his hands and knees groping forward through the littered snow. "Jean!" Dimitry yelled as he spun back to his comrade.

A strong hand laid hold of Jean beneath his good arm and hoisted him to his feet. Although his head was light and spinning, Jean began planting one foot in front of the other as the big tavern keeper led him away. But the Turks were rapidly chasing them, closing the distance with every step.

"Steady," Vlad cautioned as he held his reserves in place. "Just a few more moments." He waited until most of the militia was out of the way and the Saracens were in full pursuit. The prince raised his right hand while all of the officers focused on him intently. "Now!" he shouted striking his hand downward in a swift motion. Immediately the artillery opened fire on the Turks, and the archers fired their arrows onto the field. A wave of the tan, bearded Muslims fell beneath the shower of death that Vlad had given them.

Dimitry and Jean were almost to the tree line when a heavy-set Turkish warrior whacked Dimitry in the side of the head with his spear handle, sending his helmet skipping across the frozen ground. As all went black, Dimitry tumbled to the crisp, white earth. Jean felt him fall and spun around to spy the Turk raising his spear point above his friend. Jean instinctively reached for his sword only to discover his scabbard was empty. He must have dropped it when he fell. But in an instant the Romanian pikemen emerged from the trees, rushing into the unsuspecting Turks. Their yellow capes flapped in the breeze, and their silver armor glistened in the sun. Dimitry was saved.

Jean grimaced as he grabbed Dimitry's arm and dragged him the few remaining yards from the field. Then he stumbled to the ground beside him with a cry of pain. The pikemen and swordsmen were slowly gaining ground on the Turks while fire and arrows still poured down from the sky.

"Milord, the tide is turning!" Ivan reported breathlessly as he trotted up to the prince poised on his black stallion. Sweat poured down his face despite the cold, and his wet, dark hair hung limply out from under the rim of his Spanish cut helm. Vlad's verdant eyes gleamed as Ivan made his report. "The fighting is intense, but thanks to your plan, I believe we can take the day."

"Excellent, Ivan!" he rejoiced. "I wish to have a better view of the battle," he said, scanning the area around them. "There," he pointed, "that little bald hill. Ivan, take command of the fighting and inform me if there is any change. I may need to alter our strategy if Mehmed reinforces his troops as well. Sergei," he said, turning to his trusted aide, "accompany me."

The two turned their horses and cantered toward the small, raised mound. Ivan reigned his war horse back toward the field but paused for a moment to catch his breath. He removed his helmet and wiped the sweat from his face with the hem of his cape. Then he lifted his eyes to the meadow. His heart was pricked by the scene of hundreds of ill-prepared militia whose bodies sprawled twisted and lifeless across the field. *It was necessary,* he told himself. *There are casualties in war. What matters is the final victory.* He replaced his helmet with a deliberate motion and drew his sword to the ready. "Yah!" he yelled and kicked his destrier in the flanks, rejoining the struggle.

For some time Nicolae had been watching from a safe distance, waiting for the Moldavians to join the fighting and leave Dracula unguarded. At last he had his chance. Stealthily he slipped through the woods toward the little hill where Sergei and Vlad were dismounting their horses. "I love this!" Vlad reveled as his black boot crunched into the undisturbed snow. He swirled away taking quick strides up the summit while stretching out his spy glass. Setting both feet, he raised the instrument to his eye and surveyed the battle. "Look how beautiful, Sergei," he said in wonder. "Look at the colors, how the crimson paints upon the white canvas of snow, how the bodies create a random geometric pattern that represents the essence of life's toil upon this earth. Can you smell it, Sergei?" he asked lowering the cylinder and gazing at Sergei with morbid excitement dancing in his eyes. "Do you hear the sweet music of war?"

"Yes, sire," he replied, pleased that his prince was enjoying himself. "It is much more exhilarating than a hunt or even an execution."

"Yes, yes," Vlad gleamed excitedly. "You can feel the power in the air - the strength, the desperation, the struggle for life and death. We shall kill every Turk and traitorous follower of Basarab. The pretender to the throne will be beheaded, but Mehmed," he pondered, glowing with anticipation, "he is a prize to be flaunted before all of Europe. Mayhaps if I present him in chains to Pope Pius VI, he will see fit to bestow on me the title of king. Think of it, Sergei - the Kingdom of Walachia."

"My lord is most deserving of such an honor. I wager the pope will even bestow on you the coveted title of Athlete of Christ."

Vlad grinned from ear to ear at the prospect. Then he raised the spy glass to his eye again to watch the battle. "Prince Vlad, I need to excuse myself for just a moment," Sergei said humbly. "I will return in a heartbeat." Vlad did not reply, too engrossed in watching the combat.

Nicolae quickly crouched behind some defoliated undergrowth as Sergei stepped into the woods to relieve himself. His heart raced as he prepared to put his plan into action. *Should I sneak past Sergei and slay Vlad first, to avoid any unfortunate event of being defeated by the armas? Or do I strike him first so he cannot interfere with my assassination?*

The decision was made for him when Nicolae shifted his weight and a twig crunched beneath his boot. Sergei was alerted. Quickly Nicolae

hrank a few steps deeper into the woods and stood still behind a thick
ree.

"Who's there?" Sergei voiced warily. He fastened his trouser flap and
ook a few steps in the direction of the sound, drawing his sword as he did
o. But Nicolae wanted to lure him farther away so that Vlad would not
ear their duel. He carefully picked up a cone and threw it deeper into the
orest.

"Come out!" Sergei demanded as he moved more quickly down the
ill. "If you be friend, you may live, but if you persist in this game, I will
urely slay you."

Nicolae dashed a few more yards and hid again. By this time Sergei
was both angry and afraid. He could hear the shuffle sounds but had yet to
catch a glimpse of a man. "I am Dracula's chief armas, and you will die a
slow and tortuous death if you do not show yourself immediately!"

Just then Nicolae stepped out from behind a conifer and faced his
adversary. "Stefan?" At first Sergei blinked, not certain if he could
believe his eyes. "What are you doing on the battlefield, and where are
your Hungarian clothes and beard?" Then as though a bolt of lightning
fell from the sky, Sergei put it all together. "Bloody hell, you are a spy for
Basarab!"

Nicolae met the accusation with a steely, confident posture. "If
anything, Basarab is serving my purposes," he said in a powerful, deep
voice. He drew his sword, his midnight blue eyes piercing his foe. "Are
you prepared to die for your lord, the devil?"

Sergei grit his teeth and raised his sword. "I am willing to give my life
for Vlad, but you are the one who will die this day!" He rushed toward
Nicolae, and their swords clashed together. Sparks flew from the striking
steel as they dueled back and forth among the stands of timber. Red hot
with ire, Sergei slashed with his blade as he stepped forward aggressively,
but Nicolae jumped back avoiding the blow. Immediately he raised his
broadsword and brought it down with force aimed at his opponent's
shoulder, but Sergei agilely blocked the impact.

Nicolae eyed Sergei intently as they circled one another in deadly
combat. He drew near to a tall conifer with drooping icy branches
intending to use it to his advantage. Then he bounded to the right just as
Sergei lunged forward with a forceful jab, his sword lodging into the soft

pine. Without hesitation, Nicolae struck his chest with his blade, piercing the chain mail with the power of his sharp steel.

Sergei released his sword hilt as he sank toward the snowy forest floor. "Who are you?" he asked, his eyes searching Nicolae's as he held onto his last breath.

"A ghost," he answered gravely, "of one of the thousands of innocents your master murdered. Do not worry, Sergei; he will join you in a few moments."

A veil covered Sergei's face, and then he breathed his last. With resolve Nicolae turned up the hill and with swift strides rushed to embrace his destiny.

On the forest's edge adjacent to the combat ground, Dimitry was regaining consciousness. "What the he—?" He opened his eyes to Jean's anguished face while raising a hand to touch the blood that was drying on the side of his head.

"Thank God!" he cried out in relief as he swiftly spun to meet Dimitry's gaze. The arrow shaft was still sticking out of Jean's back so that he was unable even to reach it. "Can you see? Are you all right?"

Dimitry felt a hammer pounding inside his skull, but he answered affirmatively. "I'll live. Let me see about you." Gingerly he pushed himself to a sitting position from which he could examine his comrade's wound. "Praise Mary, a wooden shaft! This will hurt, Jean, but it must come out."

"I agree with you." Jean braced himself against a tree and wrapped his arms tightly around its trunk. "I'm ready...I think." He bit his lower lip in nervous anticipation.

Dimitry took hold of the shaft with both hands and abruptly broke the fletching from the wood. Jean cried out in pain and began to shake. "Now, I need you to move your chest away from the tree, Jean; I have to push the tip through."

"You're going to push the arrow the rest of the way through my chest!" he gasped in horror. His eyebrows raised with his widening eyes. "Won't that kill me?"

Dimitry smiled sadly. "No, but yanking it out the back might. There could be a barbed tip on that arrow. Besides, it is too high on your shoulder to cause serious damage. I vow it won't even touch your lung. Now hold very still."

Jean repositioned himself, quivering in dread of the pain he knew would follow. In a strong, swift motion Dimitry shoved the shaft through as once again Jean emitted an unintelligible wailing sound. Dimitry lowered Jean's bleeding back to the ground, gripped the shaft of the arrow, and wrenched it the rest of the way out. He tore a strip from his tunic, wadded it into a ball, and pressed it against the exit hole. "You'll be fit as ever soon; just rest now." Jean's eyes had already closed.

"Sergei," Vlad called as he heard the footsteps crunching through the snow behind him. Hearing no response, he lowered the spy glass and glanced over his shoulder. Surprise registered on the prince's face as he whirled about in disbelief. "Stefan, what are you doing here? This is a battle, man - you may be hurt." Nicolae stopped a few yards from the prince and crossed his arms over his chest as he sized up the older man before him. "Stefan?" Vlad questioned as he took a tentative step. "You look...different."

Nicolae unfolded his arms, lowering clenched fists to his sides. "I am Nicolae Anton of Cozia, and you murdered my family. I have come to rid the world of a horrible plague. Namely, you."

Alarm and anger consumed the prince as he shot back his reply. "Teo was right! You who would take the high moral ground are a liar and a murderer as well, for you allowed an innocent man to die."

But Nicolae was ready for this and was not shaken. "You ordered Teo's death while I plead for his life, as I recall. And as to lies?" His eyes twinkled at the prince playfully. "I never lied to you. I am a merchant from Hungary. Kuban adopted me after I escaped and gave me the name of his son who died. So actually, we both told you the truth."

"It makes no difference," Vlad spat as he drew his sword. "You are a fool if you think you can best me in combat."

Nicolae drew his sword and challenged Dracula with a strength of body and will that surprised the prince. Yet the seasoned leader held his ground for blow after blow. Nicolae had not anticipated the power the prince wielded behind his sword nor the skill he displayed. Killing him would not prove an easy task even now that they were alone. They countered each other's blows while circling one another with menacing glares. "You will burn in hell for your crimes, Tepes!" Nicolae swore between gritted teeth as he struck a blow. "The blood of thousands of innocents has cried out from the ground to God Almighty with a thunderous roar that he cannot ignore. This is your judgment day!"

Vlad blocked the blow with his blade and followed it with a jab and parry of his own. "What greater crime is there than treason?" he blasted with avarice. "You will join Basarab in death!"

"As you will join Sergei," Nicolae taunted.

"You bastard!" Dracula roared and swung a mighty overhand blow toward Nicolae. But his reflexes were quick, and he blocked the prince's black sword stepping to the side. Nearby the battle waged on, but it was becoming increasingly difficult to determine who held the advantage.

"God hates those who shed innocent blood, Dracula, and so do I." Nicolae advanced swinging his broadsword with a grunt.

Dracula's sword struck his with a fury. "You are a blasphemer who sides with the infidels against Christendom - it is you who will burn in hell!"

Nicolae's mind raced as he realized they had been engaged in this duel for several minutes. Someone was bound to take notice of them soon, and he must devise a way to finish Vlad quickly before he became the target of an archer. He rushed his adversary, clashing weapons and then used his left fist to throw a punch. But Vlad's breast plate covered his chest, shoulders, and the middle of his back. The ribs along his sides where the fastening straps were located were the only vulnerable spots. Vlad pushed him off with his sword and then drew his dagger from his belt with a wicked gleam in his jade eyes. "I shall enjoy slicing you to bits - slowly!"

Remembering his training, Nicolae's mind grabbed hold of a strategy that was sure to take his opponent down. Victory glinted in his eyes as he maneuvered to his right. Suddenly he felt his boot slip in the slush the two had created in the snow. Awkwardly he hit the ground with a thud. Exhaling a puff of steam, his frantic blue eyes shot up to see Dracula standing over him, his sword raised high and a twisted grin shimmering from beneath his broad, black mustache. "Now, Nicolae, you finally die!"

Chapter 24

Death and Resurrection

"But he was finally killed in the war with the Turks, and his head was brought to Mehmed II as a gift."

Extract from the Chronicle of Antonius Bonfinius

A very faint whoosh sounded through the still mid-morning air. With all the noise from the raging battle below their vantage point, Nicolae could not be completely certain that he had heard it at all, but he saw the bolt strike Dracula in the gap between his armored plates beneath his upraised arm. Without a moment's hesitation he sprung to his feet, swung his sword up to shoulder level and spun his whole body, severing the prince's neck. His head hit the snow and rolled over one time, a stunned expression still on his face. Blood trailed across the white powder, and his lifeless body fell still. Nicolae raised his eyes to see where the shot had come from and who it was that had aided him. He did not expect to see a dark-haired woman wrapped in a blue cloak holding a crossbow by the edge of the trees.

"Maria!" he called in disbelief. He held his sword at his side as he staggered toward her, panting for breath. She lowered the weapon and met his gaze with a serious expression. "Maria, what are you doing here? It's dangerous," he explained in an exasperated tone. "I told you -"

"I know what you told me, Darling, but did you honestly believe I would stay behind?" she replied. Her body tingled all over as she was swept by the realization that at last Vlad Tepes was dead, and she had a hand in his death as she had vowed she would. A surreal vapor encompassed her, and her soul grew numb. She felt neither remorse nor joy at his death, just the sense that at last her nightmare was finally over.

Nicolae's mouth dropped as he was left speechless. He honestly had not ever imagined to see her there. "And where would you be now if I had not come?" she asked as relief began to filter through to her heart.

He swallowed, his eyes still fixed on hers incredulously. "I would have thought of something."

"My prince!" They both started at the sound of a booming voice and footsteps rapidly approaching. "The Turks have reinforcements, and the battle is -" Ivan stopped short as he reached the top of the little bare hill "Prince Dracula?" he questioned as he looked around. Then his eyes fell upon the body with blood staining the snow and scanned the short distance to where Nicolae stood a few feet in front of the woman wrapped in blue "Stefan?" he questioned in bewilderment. "What happened here?"

Nicolae set his jaw and gripped his sword tightly as he advanced through the snow with grave determination. "I am Nicolae Anton disinherited boyar of Cozia. Your Prince Vlad murdered my mother, my father, my sister, and would have killed me had I not escaped. Now his debt is paid; must I kill you, too?"

Nicolae stopped suddenly and searched the big captain's eyes earnestly. Ivan looked down in amazement at Nicolae. "I remember you," he said as recognition registered in his features. "You're the boy who carried his sister."

Nicolae nodded. "I have no quarrel with you, Ivan, but I will not allow you to call for help and risk Maria's capture." Ivan's gaze went past Nicolae to the woman who stood by the edge of the clearing. He recognized her as a waitress from Dimitry's tavern. His confident eyes flashed back to the man who faced him. He knew from experience that Nicolae was strong, but he also knew he could easily take him in single combat. Loyalties battled within the mighty warrior but only for a moment, and he relaxed the tension in his arms.

"I had no great love for the prince," he answered gruffly. "My only concern is for my men."

"Then fall back, sound the retreat," Nicolae instructed carefully. "They will not pursue you."

Ivan stared pointedly at Nicolae. "How can you know that unless -"

"Don't ask." Nicolae's stern expression said enough.

Ivan nodded and began to turn away. Then he looked back to Nicolae with a troubled countenance. "There is something I must tell you," he said hesitantly. "That day, on the road to Poenari, I was the soldier who stayed behind with your sister."

"I know," Nicolae answered simply without emotion.

Surprise lit Ivan's eyes. "You know? And still you saved my life that night?"

Nicolae shrugged. "I realize it was not your fault. I feel sure you took no pleasure in it, but were merely following orders."

"That's just it," Ivan said sincerely taking two steps toward Nicolae. "I did not follow my orders that day. The last time I saw your sister, she was very much alive."

"What?" Astonishment, disbelief, and hope jostled about in Nicolae's heart. His eyes widened, and his pulse raced as he took quick, short steps up to Ivan. "Where? How?" he stammered.

"I am a warrior, Nicolae, not a murderer of sleeping girls. I knew what my orders were and the penalty for disobedience, but even as a young man I had some sense of honor," Ivan explained, opening his palms. "I could not bring myself to perform so lowly an act. I remembered passing a woodcutter's cabin just a short way back down the road, so when the column was out of sight, I picked her up and carried her there. I told the woodcutter and his wife that she had fallen ill and asked if she could stay with them until she was well. They took pity on her and agreed. Then I killed a small animal, smeared its blood on my spear tip, and ran to catch up. No one wondered what took me so long; they all assumed I had taken her first - which I did not," he added hastily.

Ivan's eyes swept to Maria as she tenderly wrapped her fingers around Nicolae's arm. She had overheard bits and pieces and gathered they would not be fighting, so she laid the crossbow aside and came to join him. Her eyes displayed hope tempered with apprehension at the possibility of finding Eveline. Exhaling a breath, Ivan looked back at Nicolae and confessed, "I do not know if she is still alive or not, or where you might find her now, but what I have told you is true."

"Can you take us to the cabin?" he inquired anxiously. "The woodcutter may know what has become of her...if he is still there."

Ivan nodded. "Yes, yes, but I must return to the battlefield now. I will meet you at the north gate of Tirgoviste two days hence and take you there."

Nicolae reached out his hand in friendship to Ivan, and they clasped forearms. "Ivan, I will recommend you to Lord Basarab. If you are willing, I can ensure that you keep your command." Their eyes met in an exchange of understanding, and Ivan nodded to him. Then he turned and made haste to the battleground.

Nicolae patted Maria's hand where it rested around his upper arm, but both were speechless at the moment. Then he reached into his pocket and withdrew a small black powder rocket on a stick. He knelt, pushed the end easily into the snow, and struck his flint to the fuse. "It has colored powder," he explained. "It will signal Mehmed that Vlad is dead, and the battle will end."

Once the fuse was lit, he stood and ushered Maria a few feet away, watching to ensure its success. The little rocket flew into the sky and burst with a pop showering red and gold sparks. "We must be away," he instructed taking her arm. "How did you get here anyway?"

"In the wagon you bought," she replied logically.

"And you drove that thing through the snowstorm?" he asked incredulously.

"I did not say it was easy," she replied, lifting the edges of her skirts to maneuver through the fallen branches that littered the forest floor.

"Maria, that was the most reckless, idiotic thing that you could possibly have done," he scolded in a raised, harsh voice. "Did you think of the danger to your own life or to that of the child - *my* child - that you may now carry? Good God, Maria," he ranted. "Did you think at all?"

"Yes," she snapped back. "I thought of you - of how you would be facing a very uncertain situation alone with no one to watch your back. I was thinking that I could not bear to live without you. I was never in great danger," she explained as her half-boot crunched down on a twig. "It would be easy enough to blend in with the camp women."

Nicolae muttered something and shook his head, his gaze falling to the ground in front of them. "Which of the saints has chosen you as his favorite, that he watches over you so closely? Or is it Mary herself who time after time has delivered you from the jaws of death?" Then he stopped in his tracks and took a firm hold on Maria's shoulders, squaring them toward him. "I mean it, Maria, you must swear to me that you will never again take such a foolish chance with your life." His gaze bore down on her with an intensity such as she had never seen in him before. Mixed with his demanding tone and power of grip, it was enough to shoot fear through her being. "Swear it!"

"Very well, then," she retorted in an offended manner and struggled to wriggle free of his hold. Realizing that he might have been using excessive force, Nicolae lifted his hands, setting her free. An apologetic look swept over his face as Maria turned and continued to tramp through the forest toward her waiting vehicle. He sighed and took a few long strides to catch up with her.

"By the way, thank you...for saving my life." His simple words melted her anger and brought a smile to her lips.

Nicolae was exceedingly anxious when Ivan halted his horse in front of a short path leading to a log house nestled into the side of a mountain. He pulled on his reins, and Maria stopped the wagon. "Are you sure this is the one?" he asked as his heart leapt into his throat.

"This is it," Ivan confirmed. Slowly they rode up to the cabin allowing Maria to park the Gypsy cart and pony off the main road.

"What if -" he began, his eyes darting from the big captain to his fiancée.

"Do not fret so," Maria comforted as she tied off the reins. "We will have to ask and see."

Ivan dismounted his destrier, and Nicolae followed his lead. "As I told you, I do not know where she is now, but we can ask and perhaps -"

"Who goes there?" asked a cracked voice from the cabin porch. A wiry old man with short gray hair and deep lines across his face stood in front of his door, bearing a woodsman's ax. Nicolae gave Maria a hand down and then turned wide-eyed to spy the elderly peasant.

"I am Captain Ivan of Poenari, and this is my associate Lord Nicolae of Cozia," he said sweeping a hand toward Nicolae as he and Maria joined him.

"How do you do?" Nicolae greeted politely as he nervously shifted his weight from one foot to the other.

"Look, I don't want any trouble, captain," the old man grumbled, narrowing his bushy brows. "None of your runaway Gypsies have been seen in these parts, so you may as well keep moving on."

"We aren't interested in Gypsies," Nicolae began taking a step closer, but Ivan held out a hand and stopped him. Removing his helmet, the tall captain strode up to the edge of the porch. From his stance on the ground he stood eye level with the hunched old woodcutter, studying him with inquisitive eyes.

"Did you and your wife live in this cabin nineteen springs ago?" he asked earnestly.

The old man hesitated, re-gripping his ax handle. "Who is it, Andrei?" The door closed as a hunched old woman tottered out onto the porch with a curious yet pleasant expression. Curls of white hair peeped out from under her cap, encircling her round cheeks.

"Just some gentlemen who have the wrong house," Andrei replied warily. "Nothing to concern you, Ana Marie."

"But it can't be the wrong house," Nicolae declared in desperation as he stepped up beside Ivan with Maria close behind.

"Oh, now, husband, mayhaps we can help them find who they are looking for."

"Nineteen years ago I brought a red-haired girl to this cabin and left her with a kind woodcutter and his wife," Ivan explained.

"She was my sister," Nicolae blurted out, opening his palms before them as he peered up with frantic eyes. "All this time I had thought she was dead, and then I met Ivan. Do you know where I can find her?"

Maria stood nestled beside him sharing his concern, ready to steady him if need be.

"As I told you," the old man began gruffly.

"Now, wait a minute, Andrei." His wife stepped out and gave him a patient nod. "We might have heard something. Young man, what did you say your name is?"

"Nicolae," he answered hastily. "Her name was Eveline, and she had long, red hair and caramel brown eyes. She was about Maria's height," he motioned, "only she was light complexioned like me."

Andrei and his wife exchanged glances. Then he sighed and nodded to her. "Come in, won't you?" she invited with a bittersweet expression.

They all sat around a small, cracked kitchen table sipping the tea Ana Marie had set before them. "Of course, we took her in," Andrei explained calmly. "The soldier said she would be left to die if we did not," he said glancing at Ivan who sat quietly studying his tea cup. "She was sick for a couple of weeks."

"Completely exhausted, the poor domnisoara.[32]" Ana Marie clasped her hands together on the table, shaking her head.

"When she was well, all she wanted to do was to find her brother," Andrei continued. "By that time we all knew about the naked boyars building Prince Vlad's castle and that he must be with them. I told her we must wait until the fortress was finished and the workers were released; then we could search for him."

"But the workers never were released," Nicolae added soberly. Ivan felt very uncomfortable, shadowed by guilt and remorse. He placed his elbows on the table and lowered his head into his hands. Maria, who sat between him and Nicolae on the bench, placed a soothing hand on his arm to reassure him that the past no longer mattered.

"No." Andrei sat up straight and set down the cup he had just sipped from.

"The poor girl was completely devastated," the old woman said with a sigh. "She hasn't been quite the same since. She lives in a world of fantasy...took to calling Andrei and myself Tata and Mama. She called the dog Nicolae."

A glint of hopeful humor lit his blue eyes as he was swept with anticipation. "Where is she now?"

"In the bedroom," the woodcutter answered, "but, son, she may not know who you are. My wife and I are childless, and when we saw that she could not survive on her own, we adopted her. She is very innocent and childlike, and I don't want anything upsetting her."

"I understand." Nicolae swallowed and slowly rose from the table. "I must see her," he said meekly.

"Of course," Ana Marie agreed and rose to walk with him to the bedroom door. Maria and Andrei followed behind, waiting outside the door so the room would not be too crowded. "Eveline, my sweet, you have a visitor," the woodcutter's wife said cheerfully as she opened the door.

Eveline looked up from her seat on the side of the bed. Her auburn hair was neatly braided and pinned to the sides of her head. Her soft hands lay neatly folded on the apron that covered her lap. The green wool peasant dress she wore complimented her natural coloring. Nicolae

---

[32] domnisoara - Romanian for "Miss"; title of respect for a young, unmarried woman

looked on her with awe. He remembered a girl, but she was a woman, thin yet well rounded with the face of an angel.

His heart racing, he slowly crossed the floor as she raised her eyes to him inquisitively. "Do I know you?" The sweet sound of her almost forgotten voice lifted his soul.

"Yes," he said breathlessly as he stopped in front of her. "Evie, I'm your brother, Nic. Do you remember me?"

"No," she smiled sadly, shaking her head, then looked away at a blank, brown wall. "My brother is dead."

"Eveline, I'm not dead," he said urgently. "Look at me." Gently he reached his hands down to hers, guiding her to stand before him. Raising her chin with two fingers, he brought her gaze to his. "Look at me, Evie." His eyes searched hers with longing. "All this time I thought you were dead...but here you are...like a dream or a miracle."

Eveline studied his face and curiously reached a hand to stroke it. "You are so tall and old looking."

He smiled enchantingly at her. "I have grown up; so have you. Oh, Evie, don't you know me?"

The anguish in his voice and the yearning gaze from his cobalt eyes hit a chord somewhere deep within the troubled woman, and she drew back her hand suddenly with a gasp. "Nicolae? Is it really you?"

"Yes, Eveline, it is!" he declared excitedly as he brought his hands to her waist.

"Nic, you are alive!" She threw her arms around his neck as he embraced her tightly. Tears began to stream from both their eyes.

"Oh, God, thank you! Thank you," he cried into her hair as he held her close. "Maria, you were right!" He closed his eyes blissfully repeating, "You were right."

Overcome with joy, she hurried to his side. Nicolae reached one arm around Maria, holding them both to his chest and kissing both their cheeks. Ana Marie's face resembled that of the mother of a bride as she wiped a joyous tear from her own eye. Andrei was not sure whether to be happy or sad about the discovery. Ivan stood alone, looming darkly in the doorway like a distant shadow. *She is beautiful,* he thought to himself, *just like the day I brought her here.* His soul was pricked by her resurrection. Though a triumphant occasion, he could not forget the others...so many others. Quietly satisfied that Nicolae and Eveline were together again, he lowered his head and stepped out of the doorway.

"Evie, I want you to meet Maria, my fiancée," he said as he lifted his head. Maria and Eveline gazed at each other warmly.

"We want you to come and live with us in your old house in Cozia," Maria took the liberty of offering the invitation. Nicolae's eyes twinkled at her, a broad smile across his face.

"Our old house?" Eveline asked in amazement. "The one we grew up in?"

"Yes, the very one," he replied with delight. Then he loosened his embrace on his women and looked back to the kind old couple who stood near the doorway looking on. "And I would like to invite both of you into my household, if you would do me the honor." The three turned toward Andrei and his wife, and Nicolae stepped out from between the women. "Your kindness toward my sister will not go without reward. If you will come and join us at my manor, you will never need toil nor work again - only enjoy your retirement for the rest of your days. Because of your generosity, my sister is alive and well, and I wish to return to you now the hospitality that you extended to her."

They looked at each other in amazement, and Ana Marie burst out in joy. "Andrei, we aren't losing a daughter - we are gaining a son!"

"It is really you," Evie uttered in awe as they walked together out of the bedroom.

"Yes," he smiled.

"But what about -" A horrified expression flashed upon Eveline's face as she stopped in her tracks.

"It's all right," he assured her. "Vlad is dead, and my friend, Basarab, is prince now. Everything will be as it was before; you will see."

Melodie Romeo

Epilogue

Cozia, December 25, 1476

"Care to dance, my Dear?" Lord Nicolae extended his hand to his elegantly attired bride with a debonair smile while the musicians played a lively tune on the fiddles, lutes, and reeds.

"I would love to," Maria replied merrily as she placed her hand atop his. "This was a wonderful idea of yours to invite all of our friends to a Christmas wedding celebration," she commented as she swayed beside him toward the center courtyard where various guests were enjoying a dance. "And I am so very glad to finally meet your adopted father, Kuban. It is so very special that he could come."

"Yes," he smiled, his warm gaze melting into her eyes. "I am most glad he could finally meet you."

Mehmed had returned to Constantinople bearing Vlad's head on a spike, indicating to all the world that the Impaler was dead at last. The monks of Snagov Monastery came and took Dracula's body, burying it in a tomb beneath the floor of his chapel. Basarab had made good on his promise to reinstate Nicolae to his father's manor in Cozia. The elderly widower who had been residing there, an appointee of Basarab from his previous reign, was given a smaller estate to manage. Although the returning prince was busy re-establishing his affairs of state and could not attend, he did send a letter congratulating Nicolae on his marriage and thanking him once again for his assistance. Earlier that day, a small, private ceremony had been held for the couple's closest friends and family, making their marriage official, but all who wished to attend, boyar and commoner alike, had been invited to the gala Christmas event.

Across the crowded Mediterranean styled courtyard, Eveline spied Ivan standing alone by a table of refreshments. She slowly wandered over to where he stood. "Ivan, I haven't seen you dancing all afternoon," she commented coyly.

A note of surprise registered on his face. "Milady, do you know who I am?" he asked in wonder.

"Yes." She smiled at the tall, dumbfounded captain. "Nicolae told me. You are the man who saved me. I admit there have been times when I wished I had not been saved, but now I find myself eternally indebted to you."

Ivan was struck speechless and fumbled with his wine glass as he tried to think of something to say. "Uh," he uttered meekly. "Well, really, domnisoara -"

"Come," she invited, extending her dainty, gloved hand to him. "Aren't you going to ask me to dance?"

With a quick, clumsy motion Ivan set down his half-empty wine glass and took her hand in his. His heart fluttered with anxiety for he was not fluent in the social graces. He inclined his head to her and swallowed the lump from his throat. "It would be my honor, domnisoara."

"Call me Evie," she said casually and walked with him into the sea of dancers.

Her fingers felt light and delicate to his broad hand, and the captain could have sworn he was walking on air. His mind began to replay the events of his life in rapid succession as though his heart was about to stop and end his existence at any moment. Then a truth burst onto his consciousness more real than any he had ever known. *In all my forty years,* he concluded, *all the battles, all the conquests, all the victories I have ever won, pale into meaningless dust beside the best thing I ever did - the day I disobeyed my orders.* "As I think of it, Milady Eveline, I believe you are the one who has saved me."

From the midst of the dance, Maria smiled at Nadia who stood along the sand colored courtyard wall with Dimitry, Jean, and the children. Dimitry's head was wrapped in a clean cloth bandage, and Jean's arm was in a sling, but both were heartily glad to be there, for many of their comrades had been lost in the battle.

"This is the happiest day of my life," Nicolae declared as he beamed at the new wife he led in the choreographed dance. He had remained clean shaven giving him a slightly younger look. A sparkling diamond ring pressed against a solid gold band adorning her finger. Crowning her raven-black tresses was a verdant wreath of holly to celebrate the season.

"Mine, too," she added radiantly and then winked at him with passionate promise. "Until tomorrow."

Epilogue 2

After the successful popularity of Bram Stoker's *Dracula*, people in the west became interested once again in learning more about the Vlad Dracula on whom the vampire count was based. In 1931 and 1932, a team of archeologists and historical researchers traveled to the Snagov monastery in Romania to try and locate Vlad's final resting place. They were told by the monks that the traditional resting place of the Impaler was below a tombstone in the floor of the chapel just in front of the altar. They were told he had been buried there so the monks could more frequently read scriptures and say prayers above his body, possibly bringing rest to his troubled spirit. But when the archaeologists excavated the site, they did not find even a coffin - only a deep hole in the ground with the bones of various animals and some small, wooden stakes.

They did, however, find a headless corpse in another location, wearing silk brocade clothing and a faded crimson cape. Could that have been Vlad's actual remains, or, as the vampirologists would have us believe, could he still be out there, taking his coffin with him, as he seeks to drink the blood of new victims? That, my friends, is for you to decide!

Melodie Romeo

Author's Notes

Mankind has always been fascinated by both the most pure and holy manifestations of our realm and the most grotesque and evil. With the invention of the printing press in the mid 1400s, the Bible and other religious writings immediately became the best-selling books in the western world; tales of Vlad III Dracula sold the second most copies. Even in his own lifetime, readers throughout the Holy Roman Empire (Germany), France, Russia, and the rest of Europe were drawn to stories of Vlad's cruel tortures and insatiable lust for blood. Other versions were more pro-Dracula in their sentiments, casting him as the conqueror of the Turks and the hero of Christendom. These publications often had a good deal of influence on those who read them. Machiavelli's *Prince* could easily have been patterned after Prince Dracula. Czar Ivan the Terrible of Russia heard the tales as a boy and made a conscious decision to immolate the Impaler's model of tyrannical leadership and he succeeded. But just how much of the story you have just read is fact, and how much is fiction?

In *Vlad, a Novel,* I have mixed carefully researched historical facts with the fictional characters of Nicolae, Maria, and the townspeople. All of the information pertaining to Vlad Dracula, King Matthias, Stephen the Great of Moldavia, Basarab, and Mehmed II is historically accurate. The dates and place names given along with accounts of battles and their outcomes are all recorded in various chronicles. But there is much more information than what I included; some was omitted for brevity's sake and some because the tales were too shocking and gruesome to include for the general reader.

Vlad Dracula was born in 1431, the son of Vlad Dracul who was a prince of Walachia. He was a middle child. In 1442 his older brother, Mircea, was murdered along with his father while Vlad and his younger brother, Radu the Handsome, were being held under house arrest in Turkey as security for tribute money. Dracula was allowed to leave in 1448 when he was seventeen years old, but Radu decided to stay with the Sultan's family for 14 more years. He also had a half-brother known as Vlad the Monk.

Left out of my novel was Vlad's very brief first reign as Prince of Walachia. Supported by a Turkish cavalry force, young Vlad seized the throne, only to be ousted two months later by Vladislav II (who built the grand chapel at Snagov). When Vlad was older and had recruited a larger army, he orchestrated a coup in 1456, killing Vladislav and those responsible for his father and brother's assassination. This began his longest reign of six years.

All of the Vlad stories told in the novel come from original documents dating back to the 15th century, and though in some instances exaggeration may have been applied, they are generally considered accurate because a number of different chroniclers from different countries repeated the same tales. It was during this six years that Vlad's most notorious acts of cruelty were perpetrated: the impaling of the boyars, the naked children rebuilding the fortress, the St. Bartholomew's massacre, the utter destruction of Transylvania in search of Dan, and his strict enforcement of the death penalty for any and all offenses. In the words of a German chronicler: "he invented frightening, terrible, unheard of tortures. He ordered that women be impaled together with their suckling babies on the same stake. The babies fought for their lives until they finally died. Then he had the women's breasts cut off and put the babies inside head first; thus he had them impaled together."

Even the Freudian analysis of his personality has been suggested by various Vlad historians. It seems evident from the writings and his behavior that Dracula hated women. And it has been professionally suggested that his fascination with impaling could stem from his own feelings of masculine inadequacy. Whatever the reasons, he seemed to place harsher penalties on female offenders than on males. (The story of murdering his mistress is also quite well documented.)

Vlad Dracula was a very capable and successful military leader. In 1462 he successfully ended a Turkish invasion of Walachia, defeating Mehmed the Conqueror with the horrific forest of the impaled. Estimates of the number of Turks he impaled around the capital city vary, but most seem to settle on the figure of twenty thousand. But it was Radu and his army that finally chased Vlad from his fortress of Poenari late in 1462. This was when his first wife (or mistress, as accounts vary) leapt to her death. Expecting to receive help from King Matthias of Hungary, Vlad was surprised to find himself once again a prisoner - albeit, one with many privileges. He did marry a female relative of the king, but accounts differ as to whether it was his sister or his cousin. When a new Turkish threat seemed to present itself in 1476, Matthias supported putting Vlad back in power to hold the infidels at bay. With Matthias's help and that of his cousin, Prince Stephen of Moldavia, Vlad entered Walachia with an army, and he chased out Prince Basarab the Old (a member of a rival family who paid tribute to the sultan) but failed to kill him.

Vlad's final reign was not a long one. He probably seized power between September and early October, 1476, and was killed in a battle with the Turks somewhere near Bucharest in mid to late December. Accounts differ on exactly how he was killed. One version tells that he went up a small hill to watch the battle and was shot with arrows by his own men. Another tells of a Turkish spy who masqueraded as one of his aides and then stabbed him while the battle was in full force. All that history records for certain is that he was killed by an unknown assailant during the battle, but not in the battle itself, and that Mehmed carried his head back to Constantinople on a pike. So although my novel's version of his assassination is fictional, it fits very neatly into the available historical information surrounding his death.

The reader should remember that Vlad Dracula was not a simple one-dimensional villain, but a very complex character. We should also not forget that his type of tyranny has been repeated again and again from leaders throughout history - from Ivan the Terrible to Adolph Hitler. Even in more modern times Romania has suffered under a cruel dictator, Ceausescu, who was recently executed by the new Romanian government for his crimes. Although I sought to bring you an exciting tale, I would never want any of us to forget the lesson from history that Dracula has taught us - we must never give an evil man the power to rule.

The major historical resources I used in researching the life of Prince Vlad Dracula III were *Vlad III Dracula; The Life and Times of the Historical Dracula*, by Kurt W. Treptow and *Dracula, Prince of Many Faces*, by Radu R. Florescu and Raymond T. McNally. I would recommend these to anyone seeking more detailed information on Vlad Tepes and Romanian history.

About the Author

Melodie Romeo is a high school history teacher and music minister who loves to write. She lives in Mississippi with her two children and numerous cats, dogs, and horses. Melodie received her master's degree in history from the University of West Florida in 1996. She is currently working on a historical romance set during the Viking Age. *Vlad* is her first novel.

Printed in the United States
94661LV00001B/276/A